A CLEAR PATH

THE SENSES PART ONE

DEIRDRE LYONS

CONTENTS

AUTHORS NOTE

Dear Reader,

Welcome to The Auctus. See, touch, smell, taste, and hear—only a rare few are born as Enhanced Sense Adepts. Immerse yourself in a world that awakens all your senses.

This story ends on a cliffhanger. *If you're seeking a Happily Ever After, <u>too bad</u>. Patience is a virtue.*

Content warnings are listed on the following page and contain spoilers.

I'd be truly grateful if you could leave a review on Amazon, Goodreads, or wherever you like to share your thoughts. Reviews make a huge difference for indie authors like me, helping more readers discover my books. Thank you for reading, and I hope you enjoy this journey.

-Deirdre

CONTENT WARNING
THE SENSES PART ONE ENDS ON A CLIFFHANGER

- *Death of a parent*
- *Open-door intimacy*
- *Human trafficking and collars*
- *Attempted kidnapping*
- *Deception involving the loss of a pregnancy*
- *Violence and murder*
- *Depictions of panic attacks*
- *Substance abuse (alcohol)*

This is an Adult Fantasy intended for 18+ mature audiences. Blood, violence, slow burn, steam, angst, betrayal, and adult language exist.

Mental health is essential and should never be minimized or ignored. If you, as a reader, feel others would benefit from any additional trigger warnings, please email me at LyonsWritesLove@gmail.com.

To my anxiety—proof that I, too, have the gift of foresight. Thanks for creating worst-case scenarios in my dreams and running every possible (and impossible) scenario so I'm always prepared for whatever the future holds... probably.

And to my husband—thank you for supporting me through every anxiety-filled vision. I love you, even when my subconscious doesn't.

THE APERION SEA

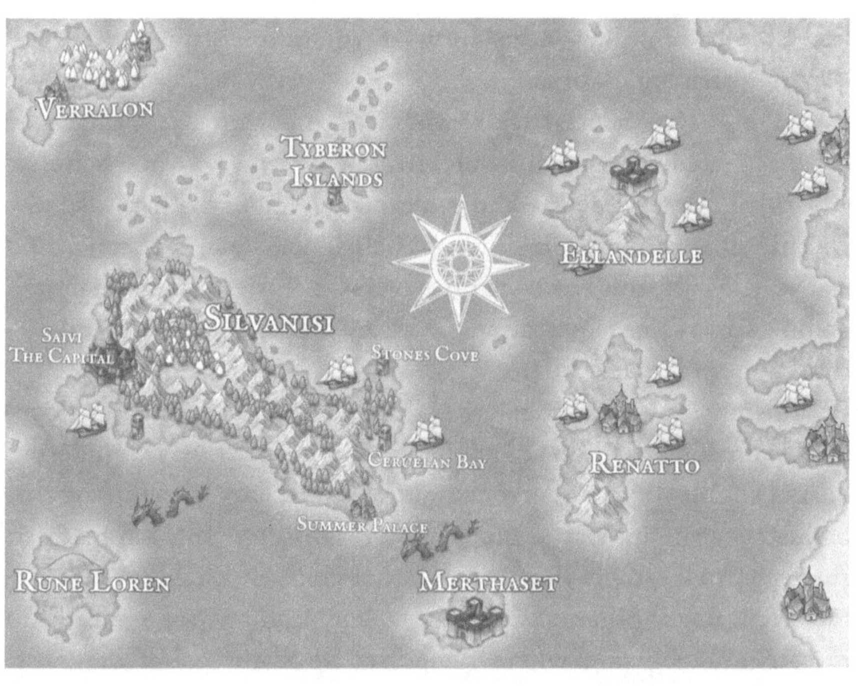

CHAPTER 1
LYDIA

Y ou can't have a Vision when you're too drunk to see. Yes, that logic works.

My boots stick to the tacky floorboards, soaked and dried repeatedly with spilled ale, wine, and who knows what else. The thick scent of sweat and stale beer mingles with the smoky warmth of a wood-burning fire and hangs heavily in the air. For the last seven years, this has been my haven—a reprieve from the never-ending stresses of expectations, authority, presentation, and decorum. None of it matters here.

The music pulses through the cramped space, vibrating the floorboards, making the iron chandeliers tremble with every thundering beat. Laughter and shouts rise above the chaos, a symphony of bodies pressing in, lost in the fevered revelry. Tonight, I'm ready to surrender to it—to let the burn of liquor cloud my Sight, even if just for a few fleeting hours. One night. One night where I can drink myself into oblivion, where sleep will be nothing but darkness, untouched by the relentless, merciless Visions that haunt me the moment my head hits the pillow.

You can't have a Vision if you don't sleep. Yes, that logic works, too. I'm so logical. Go me!

Why is the room spinning?

I love this song!

Tall, dark, and handsome at three o'clock. Hello.

Ryo bumps my shoulder, pulling my gaze away from what might have been a pleasant diversion. Grabbing the prince's shoulder, I steady myself. Mixing in a water between drink's isn't the worst idea.

Breathless from dancing, he grabs a refill and finishes it in three gulps—our awe-inspiring future monarch.

"We have a problem." He elbows my ribs, leaning close to whisper conspiratorially, but it's too loud, so he shouts in my ear.

"Is that a royal 'we'?"

"No, my dearest Lydia. It's a we-we." He snickers, too amused by himself. Potty humor from the prince. His perfect smile brightens his angular face. Such a handsome visage if it weren't for the bloodshot eyes and the crimson lipstick on his cheek.

"Colleen just walked in with Tobias. They haven't spotted you yet."

Well, this is a problem. My mind is light and fuzzy, a delicious balance I don't want to ruin by confronting my caretaker with my mentor. The lectures on the proper decorum of an Auctus representative would descend.

A peek into the future isn't needed to know how Tobias would respond.

"Lydia, you are the future hope of Seers and Adepts worldwide. It's your duty to be the best and brightest the Auctus has. This gift of your Sight should not be taken for granted or diminished with something as base as alcohol."

Hypocrites. They're both here, and I doubt it's to hunt me down and drag me back to the castle.

My eye roll makes me lose my balance, knocking me into the shoulder behind me. Tall, dark, and handsome catches my elbow, steadying me. He peers down, smiling. This night might be looking up.

"I've got you, little lady."

The man's seductive smile quickly turns into a scowl as our eyes connect. He rips his hand away as though a lingering touch is venomous. He wipes his palm on his thigh.

"Uh...look where you're going next time." His eyes dart around the bar as he steps toward me. "Go home, abomination. No one wants your curse in here."

I step back. Damn. There goes my post-bar plan, although his reaction is a bit extreme. This isn't unfamiliar territory, but I can't say I'm used to outright vitriol.

"Well. Well. Well." Hand on her jutted hip, Colleen is ready for one of her trademark scoldings. This time, I'm thankful for her interruption.

The man's gaze bounces between us, and he thankfully chooses to leave me alone, letting the rowdy crowd swallow him. I get Brandon's attention, since he's my assigned guard tonight, and mime to him to handle the bigot. He nods and takes off in the same direction. I refuse to let some small-minded asshole ruin my night.

"I thought we agreed you'd keep your head down until this drama dies?" Colleen slaps her other hand on the table but grimaces when she has to peel her palm off the sticky surface. She tries to wipe it off on a napkin, fails, and throws the already-soiled cloth back on the table in a disgusted huff.

"Stress isn't healthy for my Sight. I need to be able to let loose once in a while."

"Neither is brown liquor, but I don't see that stopping you." Okay, she may have a point "Lydia, people like that man. You need to be more careful. Where is your guard?"

The opposite side of the packed space is cast in shadows, but it doesn't stop me from keeping an eye on Brandon. He has the guy cornered, squeezing the man's shoulder as he leans in, probably whispering something threatening into his ear. The man winces.

Brandon lets go and steps back, and the guy cannot find the exit fast enough.

"Brandon has it covered. Thanks for the save there. You can pick out my dresses for a week if you get Tobias away before he spots me," I plead.

Her eyes brighten at the prospect. She brings her fingers together, tapping the pads against each other.

"Please. I need tonight. I can feel it. Two weeks?" My best pleading pout, perfected in childhood, makes an appearance. My big, round eyes don't hurt either. The ability to not blink has its benefits.

"That shouldn't work at your age. One month," Colleen teases, patting my flushed cheek. "Be home well before sunrise. You know how a hangover affects your Sight. Lest we forget your attitude when you've imbibed too much the night before. It's unpleasant and unladylike."

"You are a goddess among mortals. Fine, one month," I squeal while planting kisses on both of her cheeks. She smiles and pats my head like I'm a puppy. It's condescending, but I'll tolerate it if she can get Tobias away.

"Oh, and Lydia," she calls over her shoulder, flashing me a knowing grin. "Stay out of trouble, even if trouble comes looking for you. Keep your head down."

Her gaze flicks to the man she interrupted, now being half-dragged toward the door by Brandon. She doesn't explain, doesn't need to. Instead, with a flick of her hips, she's already weaving her way back through the pulsing crowd, her body swaying effortlessly with the beat.

She reaches Tobias, the ever-stoic man lounging at his usual table. She leans in close, her dress dipping dangerously low, practically spilling her intentions into his lap. Her fingers slide through his stark white hair as she whispers something against his ear.

Tobias roars with laughter, the sound booming across the bar like a clap of thunder. The deep creases around his eyes carve shadows in the dim light, making him look almost... happy. He slaps a few bills onto the wobbly table and rises with an ease that belies his years, and together, they slip out the door.

They think I don't notice. That I haven't put the pieces together. It's cute, really. They both deserve a little happiness, and I won't stand in the way of it. But knowing the details? Getting dragged into the mess between my mentor and my caretaker?

No, thank you.

Slowly, my lungs fill, and then I push all the air out when the heavy door slams back in place. Shaking it all off, I let the man's hostility roll away and rejoin my friends.

"Luck is on your side tonight. Cards?" Ryo settles into his seat and starts to deal out the cards. A pretty blonde makes herself at home on the prince's lap. Ryo whispers something in her ear, swaying a bit in his seat before regaining his balance. He misses a pile, and the card goes flying. The blonde's fake giggles grate on my ears. She'd find anything said or done by the heir to the throne hysterical.

"Sure, I can take some money from the royal coffers. Are you playing... Sarah, was it?" I ask the blonde, dropping a beer onto the table. Foam sloshes onto the filthy surface. Can't make it any dirtier. Ryo glares at the mess, but there's no sincerity behind it. Little distresses him, or so he'd have the world believe.

Blondie shoots me a glare. "It's Seraphina. Surely the prince has mentioned me?"

Nope. He has not, and she won't be around long enough for me to bother learning her name. They never last, so what's the point? If it makes him happy, it makes me happy.

He knocks over a few empty glasses scattered across our table, his deep laugh resonating over the music in a failed attempt to appear sober.

"Where are my sisters? Or do I not want to know?" Ryo asks. He picks up his cards, fanning them out, and I do the same.

"Why do you come out with them if it bothers you? Seems like a waste of time. Iris is dancing and Kira is probably in a dark corner with Amos," I tease, winning the first hand. We each toss in a coin. I win the second hand and the third.

"They're my sisters. Of course, I worry." Ryo's voice is softer now, the usual teasing lilt fading. Then his gaze flicks to me, and something shifts. "I worry about you, too, you know?"

For a second, his jovial mask cracks, and I catch a glimpse of the man he's becoming—the one he isn't quite ready to face. He rakes a hand through his jet-black hair, still messy from dancing and, no doubt, Serena's wandering fingers. Then, just as quickly, he pastes on a grin, but it doesn't quite reach his almond eyes.

"Alright, I'm out," he declares, slapping his cards down with exaggerated defeat. "Playing against a Seer—what was I thinking? Shit cards."

Before anyone can respond, he pushes to his feet, wobbles slightly, and turns to the nearest blonde. "Sophia, may I have this dance?"

She giggles, easily charmed, even as he bows gallantly—if a little off-kilter—and whisks her toward the crowded dance floor. Not that she corrects him. Probably because her name isn't Sophia. No, wait —was it Stella? No, Stella was the one who threw a drink in his face last week. Sasha? No, Sasha was the one who cut his hair while he was sleeping.

Whoever she is, she doesn't seem to mind.

Fiddling with my golden star pendant, I steal his seat and survey the crowd. It only takes a minute before my eyes lock with soft gray ones, and a delicious, nervous tingle spreads through my belly.

It's just a crush. He's made it clear I'm bad for his career.

Our eyes connect for less than a second, but it's enough to pull up the corner of his mouth. If he ever decides to make a move, I'd be an open and enthusiastic recipient.

There's just something about Tiernan that draws my attention. Sure, he's attractive, and I'm the opposite of blind. But it's more than that. He's quiet and observant, watching us from the sidelines. Most of Ryo's guards, Brandon included, let loose a little when we go out.

They remain vigilant, but they dance, tease, and gamble. Not Tiernan. He stands with an uncanny stillness, surveying the crowded space, ready to pounce.

His light honey-brown hair is cropped short in a soldier's cut, with intricate lines and a star shaved into the side, marking his rank. It's a similar sandy color to a mountain lion's coat. Probably soft to the touch, but like any wild animal, I might be wise to keep some distance. I don't want to, though.

With the way my body responds, I'd be inclined to think he's an Adept, too, if I didn't know better. Adepts are drawn to other Adepts. It's a biological impulse, but it's not everything. Brandon is the only Adept I ever had a relationship with, and look at how well that ended. Thank the gods there's no awkwardness between us and we can be friends. But Tiernan? He draws my attention no matter where we are.

It's just a crush. I'm too old for crushes.

"You two have been trading gazes for weeks now. It's getting pathetic. I'm almost embarrassed for you," Iris says, falling onto the seat beside me and hiccuping.

"Did you see Tobias earlier?" I ask, trying to change the subject.

"Deflect all you want. He tracks you when you aren't looking, you know?" Kira pipes in as she breezes by not even bothering to stop. Iris's twin and the devil on my shoulder, she doesn't wait for a response. She drops her opinion and saunters back to her corner.

"I don't want to talk about Tiernan. If anything was going to happen, it would have happened already." A glass shatters. Laughter and a few boos ripple over the music.

"He's too serious anyway," Iris says.

"Seriously hot." Kira laughs, crossing back to join us. Another glass shatters as wood scrapes across the floor and the music slowly comes to a pause. A door slams open. The air is thick with tension. Amos joins us, grabbing Kira's elbow. Iris shoots up from her seat, scanning the crowd for our guards.

"Let's go," he says. He glances at me and Iris and nods toward the back door.

"Where's Ryo?" I ask. I won't leave without him.

A horrifying thud of fist meeting flesh breaks the dam, and mayhem is let loose. Bodies, dating and laughing a few minutes ago, are shoving each other to find an exit or dive into the brawl. Our table is shoved into my stomach, pinning me to the wall. That's going to leave a bruise. Shouts ring out as the table presses back farther.

"Fucking Adept scum. Think you're better than us!" someone shouts. More fists are flying, and wood splinters as someone groans. "Yeah, you fucking stay down. I'll show you where you belong. At the bottom."

"See how you like it down here with the rest of us," another voice says. I don't need to see what's going on to get a grasp on the situation. I do need to get some air before I pass out in a bar full of Anti-Adept idiots.

An all-out bar brawl takes over. A fully grown man flies over a table and slams through a window. All the movement, however, gives me a chance to shove the table back. Iris grabs my hand and pulls me out just as her guard, Marcus, tosses her over his shoulder and takes off at a run.

Broad shoulders block my view. I need to find Ryo and make sure he's okay, but two strong hands grab my shoulders. I look up into gray eyes, wide and dilated.

"The exit is blocked. I can't get you out safely. You need to hide until this dies down." Tiernan steers me into a back storage closet down a dark hall. He shoves me into the tight space as he squeezes in behind me. The door clicks closed, trapping us both in darkness.

His chest is pressed against my back, radiating heat. His warm breath is a caress across my neck. I'd be excited about this development if I wasn't worried about discovery.

"I've got you." Tiernan leans down and whispers into my ear, sending shivers across my sweaty skin. "Brandon is dealing with the brawlers, but they're going after Adepts. They're either too drunk or too dumb to realize the prince is here and there's about a half-dozen guards. We'll be free in no time."

With each inhale, he presses into me, and I feel the loss on every exhale. "Thank you," I murmur. "For getting me out of there."

"Just doing my job." He steps back. As much as he can in the tight space.

The door flies open. The light from the hall momentarily blinds me.

"This is cozy. Let's get the hell out of here before the commander comes and gives us a lecture. I'm too old for this shit," Ryo grumbles, holding out a hand.

Tiernan's eyes shift from me to the prince as he steps aside. Ryo wraps his hand in mine and pulls me into the hall.

Brandon has the space in order. Four burly men and Mr. Tall, Dark, and Handsome lie unconscious on the floor. If Brandon used his Enhanced Touch, they'll be out for a few hours.

"I'll take it from here, Captain Whitlock. Thank you for reacting so quickly." Ryo pats Tiernan on the shoulder while not letting go of my hand.

"Just doing my job," he says again, barely sparing me a glance.

It's just a crush. If anything was going to happen, it would have happened already.

"One more drink?" I ask, knowing Ryo won't say no. We link arms and head into the night. One more drink should be enough to keep the future out of my head for one blissful night.

CHAPTER 2
LYDIA

The buttery-soft blankets beckon like mythical sirens, dragging me back into their blue depths from the edges of semi-consciousness. I chased the sunrise, crashed, and now I'm already running late.

A few hasty notes get scribbled down in my journal after a restless night. So much for my brilliant plan to drown my gift in indulgence. Now, I'm left with sandpaper on my tongue and a pounding headache. My handwriting is nearly illegible, but I'll figure it out later. I roll off the bed, slipping my feet into the warmth of the slippers resting on the thick, cream-colored carpet. In my groggy state, I kick over a trash can—thoughtfully placed beside my bed by Colleen—but thankfully, it's empty.

The carpet and slippers help ward off the chill in this old, drafty castle, though they're no substitute for the warmth of my blankets. I want nothing more than to dive back under them. It's too damn early, and I'm too damn hungover. Such is the balance of enjoying my life and fulfilling my duty.

My bedroom is a study in serenity and faded elegance, all shades of blue. The color quiets my thoughts, cooling the anxious fire that so often simmers just behind my ribs.

Three tall windows stretch from the faded floorboards to the dark wood ceiling, their square grid panes forming perfect frames of the garden beyond. In spring, the view is a riot of cherry blossoms and jade leaves; in winter, a sculpture of frost and stillness. The windows let in a glorious wash of sunlight during the day, casting shifting patterns across the tatami-inspired woven rugs. But they also welcome icy drafts at night, the wind whistling through cracks in the old glass like some wandering spirit come to whisper secrets.

In spring and summer, the view is a riot of color, calling me outside to stroll along tidy, winding paths. A maze of scents, the softness of grass beneath my bare feet—I never wear shoes between May and September unless decorum or Colleen demand it.

Winter, though, is a different kind of beautiful—brown on brown, a coating of ice atop a smooth, untouched blanket of snow, glittering in the morning light. I love this season just as much. It's peaceful and patient, a reminder that spring will come again, and with it, the feeling of grass underfoot.

One never needs a calendar in Silvanisi. Winter shifts to spring on the same day each year, then spring to summer with a warm western wind. The cycle is unchanging, reliable.

Low, lacquered shelves line the far wall, filled with books and stitched-bound journals, tiny relics from my training. A screen of painted rice paper—a swirling mountain-and-moon motif—shields my sleeping space from the entrance. The bed itself is a platform of dark wood with a high, carved headboard and piles of deep blue cushions. It is sparse but not uncomfortable. Familiar. Mine.

"Get your robe on." Colleen barges in and tosses a heavy bundle of white fabric at my distracted face. "A bath is being prepared that will warm and wake you. It won't sober you, though. That's what this is for." She thrusts a tall glass of pale-green sludge into my hands. It doesn't smell terrible, so if I close my eyes, I might manage to drink it. My brain feels slow and foggy.

"The bath will be ready in a few minutes." She grabs my empty glass then twirls open the last curtain, blasting morning sunlight into my bloodshot eyes. "If you don't move, that water will be cold. And don't think I'll empty and refill your bath just because you overindulged."

Dust motes float lazily in each golden beam of light. I pull the soft robe over my shoulders, silently thanking the gods that Colleen loves me—even if she never says it outright. She hung my robe in front of the fire before throwing it at me, after all. I tie the belt tightly, trying to trap any lingering warmth around me, and wince. The table to the ribs certainly left a bruise.

"Is Ryo up yet?" I curl into a chair before the carved gray fireplace, pressing my fingers into my temples. Two graceful but chipped female figures flank the hearth, goddesses carved in stone, their hands supporting the mantle. One of them is missing an arm.

Kira thought she could take Ryo down once—but she was only five, and he was already a developing twelve-year-old warrior in training. Iris had tried to stop them, hurling a small statue from the bookcase at her brother. She barely missed his head. Thank the gods she did—otherwise, it would have caused severe harm, not to mention a succession crisis.

"Get up." Colleen snaps me out of my thoughts, tugging me from my little cocoon and shoving me toward the bathroom. "I don't need your fancy Enhanced Sight to know Prince Ryo won't be up for hours. She snuck into his room again last night—later than you snuck in here," she adds with a teasing glance and a raised eyebrow.

Her knowing smile and little chuckle warm her soft cheeks. "Into the bath with you. You can hunt him down later. Tobias wants to talk to you. It sounded important, but you know how he is—everything is dire. I've already laid out your ensemble for the day. No deviations. I can't wait to dress you for a whole month!" She claps twice before disappearing with a maniacal laugh.

A groan escapes me. The outfit she'll have picked is obvious—something too fussy, too fitted, and certainly not warm enough. If I dare wear a knit sweater over it, an earful will follow. Colleen is fiercely protective of my precarious position—say that three times fast—and has strong opinions on nearly everything. Fashion is her battleground; warmth, mine. I should never have given her a full month of control over my wardrobe.

Presenting me like a perfect doll won't somehow secure an advantageous marriage or alliance that elevates my prominence and increases my security—along with hers.

Steam clings to the smaller bathroom window. Outside, the latest snowfall dusts the dense forests of dark evergreens that stretch out toward the Interior from the back side of the castle, covering every hill and peak in white, as if powdered sugar were sprinkled over them. It's a shame it's too cold to enjoy fresh snow. I bet I can convince Ryo to sneak away later. We're not too old for a good snow-ball fight.

I sink into the steaming bath, reveling in the borderline painful tingle. My sigh is so deep it borders on a moan. On the other side of the door, Colleen grumbles about "naughty, ungrateful children running amok."

I'm twenty-four, hardly a child. Very soon to ring in twenty-five with fanfare and drama.

Sliding under the surface, I attempt to make sense of my latest Vision before discussing it with Tobias. Colleen is right—the hang-over isn't helping. I'll never admit that, though.

Tobias will want every detail. I need to be prepared for his relent-less interrogation, his obsession with nuance and meaning. Visions are not a place for subtlety. The more room for interpretation, the more people will doubt the message.

A dream is nothing more than my subconscious at play. But a Vision? A Vision can bring down a kingdom—or raise one. A Vision can end a life. My own is always at risk. Seers are rare, valuable, and often the first to be hunted in battle. No one wants their enemy to hold the power to see the past or the future.

Eyes closed, I slow my heartbeat, focusing on the blood coursing through my veins. My eyes twitch beneath my lids as I survey every detail methodically, cataloging them in an order I don't fully understand, but my Sight recognizes instinctively.

My lungs burn, and I gasp as I break the surface. Pieces of the puzzle, scattered for weeks, begin to slot into place, forming a clearer path forward.

Dragging my hands down my freckled face, I sigh. It's all so unfashionable. I know I shouldn't envy Iris and Kira for their porcelain-perfect skin, but... no one's perfect. Least of all me.

Pushing the thought aside, I scrub away the night—vigorously enough to turn my skin pink. Once my hair is finally clean, I step out of the bath—only to be greeted by an icy rush of air. A shiver racks through me.

The towel is on the far side of the room. Of course it is.

A mad dash, nearly wiping out on the slick stone floor, arms flailing wildly—somehow, I manage to grab it, wrapping it around myself in a victorious, if undignified, flourish.

My reflection stares back at me. My green and blue eyes look tired. The shadows beneath them make the green one look darker today, but my blue eye remains the same—cobalt, like the cloudless sky outside.

I need a decent night's sleep. Maybe I'll take one of Colleen's sleep aids. Or maybe just a drink or two with Ryo and the twins—no, bad idea. I can't keep up with them.

Colleen's chosen outfit is as expected—pretty, impractical, and cold. The thin lilac silk itches where the inner robe clings too close, its layered seams pressing, and will leave a mark where the dove gray sash is cinched too tight. Wide sleeves drape past my hands, and brush the floor, useless against the chill depsite the swaths of fabric. A fur-lined wrap rests stiffly across my shoulders—more ornament than comfort—but at least the soft gray fur against the purple fabric creates a striking contrast. It's a pretty effect. I'd never tell Colleen that.

Maybe Tiernan likes purple.

Ugh. I'm pathetic.

CHAPTER 3
RYO

A warm sensation skitters across my overheated back in the darkness, a welcome distraction from the relentless pounding in my skull. It takes a moment to catch my bearings. My head throbs. My mouth is dry as cotton. I have no one to blame but myself. My sisters and Lydia? Yes, this headache is their fault.

My bare legs are tangled in cool sheets, and soft kisses trail down my spine. The familiar perfume stirs my senses, and my body stirs with it. Blood flows lower. Dizzy for a moment, I recover quickly.

Veronica has been a regular fixture in my bedroom for the past year. I don't remember her at the bar last night, though, so I must have sought her out on my way home—or she was already here when I returned. Giving her full access to my apartment has led to many indulgent mornings like this one.

Veronica and her transparent motivations. I'd care more if I wasn't so aware, and if she wasn't so much fun. My tongue is sandpaper, and my mouth tastes like chalk. I groan and roll over, swinging my legs onto the frozen floor.

"Leaving me so soon, my love?" She pouts, her plump lip jutted out. Her lush body is artfully tangled in my sheets, long blonde hair cascading over one shoulder in a golden waterfall. It's a performance —every movement choreographed for maximum effect—but she's such an artist, it's hard not to appreciate her talent.

It's been made clear to me—and everyone else at court—what she wants. It's something I can't give her, even if I wanted to, which I don't. My intentions are known, but she refuses to be deterred.

"Just getting some water. What time is it?" I grumble, rubbing my eyes. Morning light stabs through the gaps in the curtains.

"It's time for you to come back to bed. You know I'm the best at making you feel better," she purrs, dipping the sheet a fraction to showcase her glorious breasts.

As crown prince and heir to Silvanisi, with an aging and ill king, men are starting to look to me for leadership. Women are beginning to look to me for marriage. At twenty-eight, I should already be wed, but lenient parents and a lack of personal interest allowed me to continue my fun. It can't last forever, I suppose.

She wants to be queen. My sisters despise her with a passion, and the feeling is mutual. My mother would drop dead of a heart attack if I ever entertained the idea, but gossip continues. Trapped inside during our long winters, there isn't much else to do but drink, fuck, and gossip—all of which are Veronica's prime hobbies.

"While I'd love to lounge with you all day, darling, I have meetings. Dull meetings with dull people about dull things." I roll my eyes while my stomach growls, the sound echoing off the walls. I need water and breakfast—something to soak up the remaining alcohol in my system.

As though the gods hear my silent plea, a soft knock lands on my door. My valet slides in with a tray laden with food, enough for two. He doesn't acknowledge either of us, simply sets the tray on the table, tosses more logs onto the fire, and slips into my bathroom to run a bath. His quiet way of nudging me to get moving.

I make a quick sandwich of biscuits, eggs, and bacon and devour it in three bites. "I'm taking a bath. Feel free to have some breakfast."

"Would you like some company?" she asks, sliding across the silky sheets to join me.

"No, darling. I'll return to your arms in a few minutes. Have some breakfast and wait for me, would you?" I need a moment alone to recover from this pounding hangover—or to vomit in peace.

Veronica has been extra clingy lately, irritated that all the attention is on Lydia. The one thing she hates more than being ignored is my friendship with Lydia. With Lydia's upcoming celebration, marking her transition from Novice to Master Seer, the court is abuzz. What will everyone wear? What food will be served? Will Lydia pick a husband? Veronica huffs every time someone mentions it.

Traditionally, someone in Lydia's position would choose a spouse or be assigned a post at another court, as we already have a contract with Master Tobias. Everyone in her life is jockeying to point her in their direction—just as they are with me.

Kira and Iris are too young, but that hasn't stopped my mother from making marriage suggestions to push her political agenda. Eventually, we will all be expected to do our duty and marry for the benefit of our homeland. I'll enjoy my freedom while I have it.

The door clicks shut behind me, and the steam curling off the water wraps around me. Sliding under, I reemerge and scrub my short, ink-black hair. Stubble is creeping along my jawline—almost a beard now. My mother would have plenty to say about my unkempt appearance. She'd insist no beard should ever obscure my face, scold me for drinking too much, and lecture me about my penchant for gambling and partying.

She's big on scolding.

I enjoy the benefits of my position. She's not wrong. Perhaps I indulge too much, but I also do my duty. The branding spiral on my forearm is testament to that commitment.

I scrub harder, but I can't wash away the weight on my shoulders.

Why do our most intrusive thoughts surface in the bath?

After leaving the warm water, I take a few moments to collect myself then shave—choosing my battles with my mother wisely.

Wrapping a towel around my waist, I return to my dark room and find Veronica waiting patiently in my bed. I wonder how many poses she tried before settling on this one. The pleated sheet drapes over her hip, leaving just the right amount of suggestion—a perfect tableau of lust and manipulation.

She pouts when I head to the breakfast tray instead of returning to her. There's something satisfying about keeping her on her toes. She doesn't realize how transparent her act is, but she's beautiful, and I'm a weak, foolish man who thinks with his dick too much.

I've never lied to her, but she'll still be furious when this ends. There will be fallout. I should address it before she becomes a real problem. I should do my duty. I should end this.

Later.

A full glass of water disappears down my throat, followed by a handful of berries. She wiggles her eyebrows, a slow smile spreading across her bronzed face as she leans back onto the pillows, her smooth legs spreading lazily.

Later.

CHAPTER 4

LYDIA

The heavy door squeaks and scrapes against the stone floor of Tobias's study. The sound vibrates through my teeth, setting my ears ringing. It takes all my strength just to shove it open a fraction. I lean in and give it my most ladylike grunt, and finally, it budges enough for me to slip through.

Oppressive heat from the roaring fireplace smothers the air. Master Tobias sits in his favorite worn leather chair, wrapped in multiple blankets, pouring a hot cup of tea. He gingerly blows on the steam curling from the mug.

"I heard you stomping down the hallway. A little more grace, Lydia, dear. Perhaps a little more stealth wouldn't be remiss? How do you expect to bar-hop with the twins until dawn if someone with weak human hearing can hear you from miles away—much less an Enhanced Listener?" A hint of a smile hides behind his stark white beard, softening the chastisement.

Busted.

Not a single strand of hair on his head or beard is anything but pure white. He keeps it neatly trimmed, always. His nearly black eyes are a stark contrast to his pale, gentle face. When the light hits just right, the difference between his dark-brown left eye and jet-black right eye becomes more pronounced—the mark of a Visionary Seer. All Enhanced Seers possess sharper eyesight, whether in daylight, darkness, or across vast distances. But Visionary Seers, like us, bear the distinct sign of two different eye colors.

I don't know how old Tobias is, but he's attractive for an older man. He keeps his body in peak condition and insists he could take on a much younger soldier and hold his own. Enhanced Sense Adepts have longer lifespans than Laymen. We're prone to fewer illnesses and heal faster from minor injuries. Our leading cause of death before old age? Violence.

"I don't need to sneak around in my own home, Tobias. If I want to enjoy my life, I have every right to do so," I grumble, sliding into the chair beside him in front of the enormous fireplace.

Pouring myself a cup of tea, I snatch the plate of pastries before Tobias can intercept it. He reaches for it at the same time, but finds only empty air. Grinning, I settle the plate on my lap and begin munching, a fine layer of crumbs and powdered sugar quickly coating my purple dress.

"You can't afford to be reckless, even in your own home. I trained you better than that. The enemies you face won't always be obvious. *Clear mind, clear path.* That's how you stay alive."

Tobias possesses a remarkable ability to balance warmth and authority, a contrast to the fact that he is still a cutthroat politician. No one reaches or holds an elevated position within the Auctus without getting their hands dirty. Anticipating when to seize an opportunity—or avoid one—is a trained and necessary skill. One I have yet to master.

"Master your Sight. Hone it like a weapon only you can wield, and it will keep you safe."

That lesson was drilled into me from the moment I had my first Vision. But whoever came up with that wisdom never mentioned how flawed the plan is. My Sight isn't a neat, orderly roadmap—it's a chaotic storm, jumping from one moment to the next. Some glimpses are of tomorrow, some of the past, and some are nothing more than my overactive imagination running wild.

True mastery isn't just about having the Visions—it's about shaping them into something useful, carving out a clear path from the mess of images and whispers. It takes precision. Artistry.

Through exhausting study, Tobias and I sift through the chaos, piecing events together like a puzzle, forcing them into a logical sequence. If that fails, there's always the second option—stepping back into a Vision while awake, chasing clarity like a drowning man gasping for air. But that method is draining, leaving me raw and spent.

So instead, I keep a journal by my bedside, filling its pages with fragments of the future, hoping that when the time comes, the right piece will be waiting.

Tobias continues munching on his pastry, unhurried, waiting for me to kick off our morning routine. A brief meditation follows. I struggle to sit still long enough to focus my mind and narrow the path before me. *Clear mind, clear path* is the goal, but getting there is a battle on a good day.

After my failed meditation, we move on to the day's reports—news, gossip from the court and city, and updates from the coastal towns. Tobias's private Auctus network of Sense Adepts fills in details the Saivi captains miss. He always knows more than he lets on, but he keeps me well-informed. I think.

The divide between what Tobias knows, what the king knows, and what the captains know is like weak mortar between the bricks of reality—riddled with unseen gaps. How much overlap is there? How wide are the cracks? Could a trickle of dissent find a crevice and slowly wear the wall down?

The rising violence and propaganda spreading from the cities into the larger towns are becoming too significant for the king to ignore. Rebellions against the crown, direct attacks on the Auctus, and growing hostility toward Sense Adepts are dominating discussions.

"You need to be careful," Tobias warns, wagging a finger. "All your gallivanting, even with an armed guard... Well, you know how valuable you are."

His duty is to keep me safe and see me complete my training as a Master Seer. But rules were made to be broken.

I never go out without guards—not because of orders, but because I never go anywhere without one or both of the princesses or Ryo. Saivi is safe for any city, but I know it's streets and alleys be heart. It's the safest place I could be outside of Auctus headquarters on Merthaset.

"We will always be a target while the Auctus continues to require registration and mandatory training for Adepts," I say, voicing the most obvious solution to the most common accusation. "They should be given a choice. Change the law. Maybe that would soften the anger toward the Auctus."

Compulsory training starts young—typically eight or nine, sometimes earlier depending on the abilities and the Enhanced Sense.

"The system isn't perfect, but it ensures the safety of both Adept and Laymen children. An untrained Enhanced Handler could permanently injure someone with a single touch. The consequences of a child's tantrum could last a lifetime. You and I were both born on Merthaset. It's different for us."

"Born there but never permitted to return. What if there's answers? Surly Morgan knows something about my birth? My parents?" I've asked for years and been denied repeatedly to visit Merthaset.

"Your place is here. Merthaset is no place for you. Morgan entrusted you into my care when you were a baby. It's a responsibility I take seriously," Tobias says, refilling my cup and his own.

Sipping the piping hot tea, I can't let it go like I normally do. "I find it hard to believe Morgan, or the Star Table has no knowledge of a baby being born."

He sighs. "We've gone over this before. I wish I could give you answers on your parents but what would it truly change? Morgan isn't all-knowing despite what she may believe. Nor are the rest of the Grandmasters. They are fallible."

"If they are fallible then they should be open to change."

"I do not sit at the Star Table, therefore I do not have a vote in any changes to our education structure," Tobias snaps. "The walls have ears. Change takes time, and impatience is a gift of youth."

My eyes practically roll into the back of my head, but he does have a point. Whether it be enemies within Silvanisi—of which we have many—or a faction from another house in the Auctus, someone is always watching, waiting for us to make a mistake.

"Now, back to the rebels. This information is from our private network, so let's keep it that way until we know more," Tobias says with a side-eye. "Three missing Adepts—two low-grade Seers and one teenage Listener. The boy was untrained and unregistered, a foolish decision, but still, it's being investigated. We've confirmed the rebels are targeting Adepts, particularly Seers. There aren't many of us to begin with. The Auctus has tasked my team here to investigate. That makes twenty-two missing since the summer festival. I don't begrudge your fun with the twins for propriety's sake. I warn you, because I genuinely fear the rebels are focused on anyone with Enhanced Senses."

The Auctus expects a certain level of loyalty from all trained Adepts—especially those committed to becoming Masters. We are their arm in the world, and in exchange, they protect us from those who would target us. If the training registry has been compromised, the rebels have a detailed list of every registered Adept on the island —their Enhanced Sense, their level of training.

"I need you to be careful. It's only a matter of time before they send a troop of Handler soldiers to put an end to this. Then the gloves will come off, literally and metaphorically." Tobias walks a delicate line—disdain for the lifelong politicians at the Star Table, but unwavering dedication to the Auctus's original mission.

"I wish the Grand Masters could explain their disdain for those who choose not to be trained. One shouldn't require training to be a protected Adept. How do they justify it?" I ask.

Leaning back in his chair, Tobias presses his lips together. A lecture is coming—I can feel it. He sets his cup down, palms outstretched, and raises his right hand.

"One side believes that regardless of training, a person born Adept is part of our greater community. Even those without an Enhanced Sense deserve protection from those who can offer it. A person's worth lies in their humanity, not in how useful they are to the Auctus." He lets the words settle before raising his left hand. "On the other hand, there's a counterargument. Not studying your Senses is like wielding a dangerous weapon without knowing how to use it. It can be deadly."

"That's all fine on paper, but we live in the real world. These are real people and families. Not everything is black and white, nor should it be."

He takes another sip of tea, allowing me my indignation. "Let's discuss some real-world scenarios for educational purposes."

I groan, but he ignores me.

"What are the two most dangerous Senses?"

"Any Enhanced Sense can be dangerous under the right circumstances."

"Don't be pedantic." Tobias rolls his eyes. "An untrained Handler touches someone in anger and causes irreparable damage. A Seer child fails to adjust their eyes in the sun and is blinded. A Complex child throws a tantrum and unleashes all five Senses without understanding the consequences. The list goes on, but training prevents these things."

"If the path of my Visions remains unchanged, we'll need every soldier we can muster—including the Auctus Army. The brewing storm of rebellion is spreading to the other islands. Division within our ranks is a crack in the wall that will widen if left unchecked."

"I don't hold a seat, Lydia, nor do you. If you ever do, you can use your vote to change things. Until then, let's do what we can to protect the people of this island—both Adept and Layman." Tobias places a reassuring hand over mine, squeezing gently.

With my twenty-fifth birthday approaching and my final Master's evaluation on the horizon, these quiet, reliable mornings will soon end. This transition is a time-honored dance where anyone with power pursues a little more. Few Adepts attempt the path to Mastery, so this spectacle only happens once or twice a decade.

Marriage proposals flood in alongside new opportunities to forge alliances or climb the endless ladder of power—a controlled, regulated, and deeply corrupt game within the Auctus and its political web.

I hope Tobias stays by my side forever, naïve as that may be. He is my rock. But Silvanisi doesn't need two Visionary Seers, and there are so few of us. I expect to be sent to another island's court, a treasure to be protected and manipulated on foreign shores. Alone to question motivations. Alone to be constantly doubted.

"Your Sight will keep you here for now—I've seen that much. When you go, it'll be by choice, with conviction that you're on a clear path. In fact, you'll help row the boat on your way out," Tobias says. "Your birthday is still months away, and the queen and council haven't received a proposal they find worth presenting for your consideration."

"What about Grandmaster Morgan? Won't she have an opinion?"

Tobias's eye twitches at the mention of our houses leadership. "Morgan believes in letting Master's choose. She won't interfere."

"I find it hard to believe a member of the Star Table won't push *someone*."

"Morgan will keep her word. I cannot speak for the others. In the meantime, you can keep galavanting with those wild twins and your charming prince. But please, Lydia—be smart. Be vigilant. Keep your head down. Don't draw attention."

"Ryo is my best friend, practically a brother. And Kira and Iris are not feral. They're testing the boundaries of freedom before they're shackled into political marriages they have no say in."

"True." Tobias exhales, his tone heavy with something unspoken. "They'll marry whomever their mother commands. I almost pity the poor men tasked with controlling either princess." He scoffs, the sound bitter.

"You're a target, Lydia. Your Visionary Sight makes you a threat, your connections to powerful figures put a target on your back, and let's not forget—being a woman in this world doesn't exactly earn you sympathy. Associating with the lynx cubs won't protect you. If anything, it might make things worse. The rebels grow louder every day, their resentment festering, their numbers swelling," Tobias warns.

I sigh. "Yes, they whisper that Adepts slither too close to the throne, spinning our webs of control, pulling strings they refuse to believe the crown holds itself. To them, we are puppet-masters, and the monarchy is weak for allowing us to linger in its shadow."

Tobias shakes his head. "This is serious. They need someone to blame, and we're an easy target. The Auctus has always been seen as the power behind the throne, the ones pulling the strings. It doesn't take much for the Laymen to turn their fear and anger on us when things go wrong."

Frustration bubbles up within me. "And now my relationship with the heir is just more kindling for their fire—another so-called 'proof' that Adepts are sinking their claws into the next generation."

"Many among them are calling for an end to our long-standing alliance with the crown." Tobias watches me over the rim of his cup. "The council has tasked Asher Montcliff with looking into it, though I suspect the slippery bastard already has his own agenda. No doubt, he'll find a way to corner me about it soon."

"Well, that's terrible news. And what am I supposed to do with that?"

"Avoid him if you can. But if you can't, don't draw attention to yourself. We can't afford a war within the cabinet, not when tensions are already so high. And Asher's dangerous in his own way—popular with the Laymen, a master of feeding their worst fears and turning them into weapons." Tobias exhales sharply, his piercing gaze locking onto mine as he delivers his final warning. "Keep. Your. Head. Down."

My skin crawls. Asher Montcliff, my most persistent thorn, fancies himself a ladies' man, convinced he is magically entitled to whatever—or whomever—he desires. To him, birth and status grant superiority over everyone, and he makes sure they know it. I wish he'd take the hint that I'm not interested and move on, but his persistence is unwavering as we approach my Master promotion.

"That isn't what I need today." I wave off his warnings despite the weight they settle in my stomach. Time for a change of subject. "That recurring Vision is clearer now. Finally. The rainbow fog came at the beginning and the end this time, hanging in the air without catching a breeze. If your Vision aligns more precisely, we'll need to tell the council. But I'm confident I have it sorted. Mostly. Yes. Probably." I shrug, lacking the confidence I'll need when the time comes to present this to the king.

"Well, that sounds...*ominous*. No room for judgment or interpretation, or they'll eat you alive. Try again."

"I have it sorted. It's in order. Will you let me get on with it?"

"By all means, my dear, walk me through what you saw. I trust your Sight implicitly, as much as any of us can trust an ever-changing timeline." Tobias leans back in his chair, his left leg crossing over his right as he settles in.

Visions aren't fixed. They shift before, during, and after. Decisions ripple outward, like a stone thrown into a still pond—one small disturbance that can reshape everything. Most people refuse to throw the stone, believing a Vision is infallible or unalterable. They don't see the multitude of paths that can lead to different outcomes.

I clear my mind and slow my heartbeat, focusing on the gift in my blood. I follow the path to open my Sight.

Breathe in.

Five, four, three, two, one.

Breathe out.

Five, four, three, two, one.

Five things I can see, four I can touch, three I can hear, two I can smell, one I can taste. Then I let the Vision unfold.

Clear mind. Clear path. It's one of the first techniques taught to Adepts to connect with their Enhanced Sense and center themselves.

Unburdened by distractions, my Senses fully surrender to my Sight, leaving me vulnerable. I detest making myself this defenseless before others, so I do this only in Tobias's company. He understands the trust issues drilled into us.

The muggy embrace of the multi-colored fog tugs at my mind, pulling me inward, propelling me forward. My eyelids flutter. Familiar trees spread out before me. Twigs roll aside, leaves scatter, stones shift, and branches bend as the most likely path reveals itself. I've walked this particular path many times over the past few weeks; the soil is now compacted beneath my steps. The misty rainbow undulates, wraps, and pulls me deeper. My muscles clench. Sweat beads along my brow.

The colorful fog is thick and warm, weaving through the bare trees. I peel off the stupid wrap Colleen made me wear. The forest isn't as dense here, and the path is clear. The moon—bright and nearly full—casts deep shadows through the branches in my mind, though it's morning where my body remains. I step beyond the forest and onto the main street that runs down the center of downtown Saivi, clearing the haze, ready to be the messenger.

THE WIDE MAIN avenue from the castle down the steep and winding road to the harbor is deserted. Where confection shops once spilled sweetness into the air, even the memory of sugar curdles on my tongue.

Something is wrong—wrong in my marrow, in the bones of the street itself.

The air hangs, warm and wet, clotted with the scent of flowers blooming out of season. Their petals, soft as skin, nestle in ornately carved boxes on windowsills—too bright against the gray. Beautiful. False. Out of place.

There are no voices. No footsteps. No trace of the city's heart. Silence, but for my boot heels clacking on the cobblestones. Lanterns sway faintly on their hooks, casting long shadows through the barren branches like reaching hands. And above it all, the moon. Watching. Waiting. Waning.

The outer gate yawns open with a groan—wide, expectant—a predator's jaw ready to swallow me whole. The inner gate, by contrast, remains closed. Towering. Impenetrable. Absolute.

A crack in the outer wall shines with a light—no, a flame—glowing thin and sharp as a blade smoldering on the forge. A crevice in the stone that spreads. Dragging my fingers along it, the crack opens, shifting under my presence, as though it recognizes me. Grants me entrance. Or passage. Or sacrifice. We shall see.

Inside, the king's tower burns hot, rippling the air around it. Flames climb in silence—too steady, too deliberate. A signal, but no one comes.

Alone in the once-bustling courtyard, I watch and hold my breath.

The crash of stone, wood, and glass shattering—cracking and collapsing—splits the air for one aching moment. But even that echoes wrong.

The tower falls.

The silence returns. So quiet it scratches the insides of my ears.

I call out. Nothing answers. Not wind. Not people. Nothing.

A horse, dark as dried blood, emerges from the smoke. Its eyes burn—not red, but gold, like the caramel in the confection shop windows. It sees me as though it has been waiting. And I know: this is not a rescue. This is compulsion. This is the path.

It does not wait for my command. Its nose nudges. Its impatient neigh is the only sound.

We flee, not toward safety, but into the darkness of the Interior. Into the mountains, where even the trees recoil as we pass. Nothing stops this determined steed.

When we break through the forest at last, the eastern coast emerges. Cerulean Bay.

But the still water does not shimmer beneath the waning moon. Nothing moves.

Nothing ripples or shifts.

And there floats an armada. Ships without sigils. Without banners. Without soul. Their black sails hang like limp shrouds. Death dressed in linen. They do not drift. They do not breathe.

Men line the railings, row upon row, still as statues carved from ash. Covered faces with dead eyes. Not watching me—but waiting.

The sea beneath them is still. Not calm. Not peaceful. Dead. A mirror so flawless it reflects stars not yet born.

The air pulses—thick with a certainty I cannot name, but feel in my blood. Something ancient. Something final. A dam straining at its seams, ready to burst beneath the weight of power long contained.

Then the horse moves, and I understand: There is no choice. It steps onto the water as if it were frozen.

Ripples rise—reluctant—as though even the sea fears to disturb the stillness. Waves build, slow and immense, answering a call older than sound. I pull at its mane, but the horse does not yield. It knows. It acknowledges but it ignores all, cresting each growing wave like fences to be cleared.

We reach a strip of sand, barely wide enough for a breath. An island only in name. Fleeting. An illusion. A stage. A stain to be washed away by the incoming tide.

The ships remain. Distant, yet present. Unmoving. Unyielding specks of black blocking out the starry sky, one sail at a time.

I dismount when the beast at last comes to rest. I walk toward wreckage scattered across the dark shore—splinters of a battered ship like ribs exposed to the sky.

A door, broken and half-buried in the sand, beckons. I reach for it, but the horse rears back and screams—wild and fierce—kicking me to the sand.

I blink—the earth shakes. Silvanisi's mountains rise from the beach like a phantom surfacing.

They groan as they climb, dragging moss and trees and wet soil and rot into the air.

But the silence returns. Only silence. Only the ships below, waiting.

From my perch atop the peak now overlooking Saivi Harbor, the eyes along the railings tilt up. Unblinking. Unwavering. And they lock on me.

One by one, they leave the ships—slow at first, then swelling. A surge of bodies undulating across the ground in a silent scream, breaching the walls with no sound, only dread.

I LEAN BACK in my chair, letting the Vision fade. Calling my Senses back.

Five, four, three, two, one...

"The rainbow fog returned, pulling me back to sleep. I'm sorry it wasn't more, but I thought it best to discuss before I got lost in the mist. I mean—I rode a horse across the sea. What does that mean? It's so irritating when the mist decides to be symbolic."

Tobias passes me a flask. I take a sip. The sharp liquid burns, grounding me before exhaustion claims me.

"Your mist shows so much more than mine but certainly takes some... poetic license. To see the future the way your Sight sees it would haunt a lesser mans sleep. Trying to interpret it would break his mind." His eyes flex wide and he shakes his head. "I'll meet with the king this afternoon. Do not repeat this Vision to anyone. And if Asher comes sniffing, avoid him. We can't afford his attention." Tobias jabs a finger at me.

I arch a brow. "Is that your way of saying your Vision confirmed something? Should I prepare? Sharpen my sailing or riding skills? Learn how to talk to animals?"

"You know, this one time I tried to negotiate peace with a goose."

Here we go. "I'm sorry—what now? A *goose*?"

He nods solemnly. "A white one. Pure white. Flawless, but angry as sin. Guarding a sacred garden in Ellandelle. I was trying to sneak through to escape the guards, obviously—"

"Obviously."

"—and it honked at me in what I *swore* was an accent. I'd been drinking fennel tea, so my Sight was heightened. I thought I heard it yell at me."

I stare at him. "You thought you had Interpreter abilities?"

"I'm not saying I *don't*," he says with a shrug. "Sometimes, things come to me. Words. Feelings. Urges. We all lean toward a second Sense more than the others. Anyway. That's not the point."

I roll my eyes. "Do go on..."

"The goose and I locked eyes, and I felt something pass between us. So I bowed, made a gesture of goodwill, and said—very respectfully, mind you—what I *thought* was a goose greeting."

"You what? Honked at it?" I blink. "And?"

He nods, grim. "Bit me right on the thigh. Latched on and wouldn't let go. My friend Rafi—he *is* an Interpreter—was doubled over laughing. Said I basically challenged the goose to a duel."

"You tried to parley with a goose, Tobias."

"I was diplomatic!" he protests. "I made eye contact. I used a respectful tone. I even bowed!"

"And got bit trying to speak *goose*."

"Right here." He pats his leg dramatically. "Still twitches when I pass farms."

I'm laughing now, wheezing. "So what did you do?"

"I fled, obviously. Lost a boot in the process, but retrieved a very valuable plant hidden in the center of a cursed maze. Not important."

"Tobias—"

He cuts me off with a smirk, already walking again. "But that's a story for another time."

"You're the only man I know who could start a turf war with poultry."

"I've done worse," he says cheerfully. "Once got cursed by a raccoon."

"Stop talking."

Tobias smirks. "My dear, never change."

CHAPTER 5
LYDIA

I don't share everything with Tobias, especially not my latest Vision. Not yet, anyway. There are paths I've glimpsed that I'm not ready to follow—or explain. A knot of guilt tightens in my stomach, but I shove it down. It's personal, something I need to work through on my own before I'm ready to talk about it. Tobias has enough to carry, and besides, he doesn't tell me everything, either.

Tiernan stands rigid as ever outside Ryo's door, sliding into my path with that same smug smirk he's been wearing like a badge of honor. The twelfth time this week, not that I'm counting. Arrogant as always. Still, I can't deny the rest—broad shoulders, honed muscle, a face practically designed to tempt disaster. And yes, fine, he's objectively attractive—annoyingly so. I notice. Not that it matters, since my crush on him is as pointless as it is infuriating. I'm not blind, just acutely aware—and I hate how much it bothers me.

Those attributes have caught my attention from a respectable distance. We've been circling each other for weeks—an exchanged glance here, a teasing joke there—until he politely shuts down, and the captain's mask slips back into place. We all wear masks. If he won't reveal what lies beneath his, neither will I.

"Captain, I'm not in the mood today. I need to see the prince, and if I'm the one to wake him, so be it." I wave him off and attempt to duck under his arm, which rests against the doorframe. His other hand hovers over the hilt of his sword, a silent warning that he's on duty. The smirk doesn't waver—he doesn't take me seriously.

He shifts suddenly, forcing me to step back to avoid colliding with his chest. His soft gray eyes, framed by unfairly long lashes, narrow, daring me to try again. I am to be humored but managed. He's patronizing me. Underestimating me. Any appreciation for his handsomeness vanishes under the weight of my irritation.

"He's not alone in there, and I don't need to start my day with a jealous woman's tears." Tiernan leans lazily against the doorframe, his stance relaxed under the black armored vest emblazoned with the Silvanisi crest.

I step closer, watching the way his muscles tighten and shift. I wish I were an Enhanced Listener so I could track his heartbeat.

"Don't you worry your pretty little head about that. They won't be my tears." I pat his rock-hard chest right where the crest is centered. His subtle shudder makes me grin. So, he's not as indifferent as he pretends to be. He wants to push me? Fine. I can play.

"I understand you're new to this post, but trust me, blocking my path isn't in your best interest. Step aside." I hold his gaze, drawn into the stormy depths of his eyes.

"Sorry, stopped listening after you called me pretty," he says, that damn smirk still in place.

"That's your takeaway? Of course, it is. Now, please, let me pass."

My hand not-so-accidentally trails down his chest. He bristles, shifts toward me for a heartbeat—then pulls back. His stare remains unwavering, intimidating, overwhelming. But I refuse to be the first to break eye contact. One of the benefits of Enhanced Sight? I don't have to blink. It comes in handy.

A slow smile spreads across my face as I lean in. I know I've won. I do make him uncomfortable. I dart my tongue out to wet my bottom lip, watching his eyes follow the motion.

Tiernan may be a seasoned soldier, but he hasn't been in Ryo's guard long enough to understand the intricacies of my relationship with the crown prince. While there have been many, many, *many* women in Ryo's life, I have never been jealous of a single one. Nor would I ever be. Sex isn't a part of our connection. It should be simple, yet somehow, it's impossible for others to understand.

Tiernan sighs, defeated. "Very well. This is about to be uncomfortable for you. You were warned." He steps aside.

Sliding past, I move closer than necessary, his body heat pulling me in. The sharp intake of breath we both fail to suppress rings in the air. Keeping my chin high, I ignore the awkward shift between us and press forward into the prince's suite.

Down the dark hallway lit by scattered lamps, I throw open a few curtains. Late-morning sunlight spills into the room. These should have been opened hours ago.

As I reach the ornate red door, an obnoxious, tittering giggle drifts from the other side. Why do they all have the same giggle? If she thinks that sounds sincere, her acting needs work.

It's likely Veronica. She already loathes me, and I have no intention of giving her more reason. I can't damage that relationship any further. I strike the door with four precise knocks, then push it open without pause. It's enough of a warning—and a coded signal to Ryo about exactly who's stepping inside.

"Lydia, for fuck's sake!" Ryo groans, lifting his head from between Veronica's thighs.

She screeches like a banshee and dives under the discarded blankets. Now she chooses modesty? There's a first time for everything.

"Sorry to interrupt breakfast, but we need to talk. Privately. This is far more important than the tableau now burned into my brain." I drop into one of the chairs by the fireplace, draping my legs over the armrest. I make myself at home.

"My sweet," Ryo purrs in Veronica's ear, "please give us a few minutes. Why don't you take a bath? I'll join you once I'm done dealing with this."

With a profane gesture in my direction and a lingering kiss on Veronica's shoulder, Ryo shoos her into the bathroom.

She wraps the thin sheet around her voluptuous body and glares at me the moment his back is turned. I may not be able to see Auras, but a nasty soul lurks beneath her beautiful face.

She clenches her jaw, growls, and tosses her silky blonde hair over her shoulder before turning away. Then, with an exaggerated pout, she lowers the sheet just enough to expose one golden shoulder. It's a blatant attempt at manipulation, but it won't work the way she hopes.

"Don't take too long, my love. I don't want to get cold without you and have to find other ways to stay warm."

It might sound like a threat if all of Silvanisi didn't know how desperate Veronica was to hold Ryo's attention.

Men like Ryo have an endless supply of beautiful women. No one has figured out how to keep him interested for long. Veronica has been warming his bed for months—far longer than expected. Kira lost ten coins on that bet.

It's not that he doesn't enjoy other women, but his continued return to Veronica has given her an unearned confidence. She thinks herself untouchable, destined to be Silvanisi's next queen. It's a joke. He would never marry her. Her time is already running out.

That doesn't stop her from whispering cruel things about me or sniping at Ryo's sisters behind his back. I know it stems from her misplaced jealousy.

Rumors about me have ranged from being an old flame desperate to regain his attention, to his bastard sister—gross, when paired with the old flame theory—to a sad orphan he befriended out of pity. The most recent? That I'm a political pawn, a move to appease the Auctus and his parents.

None of those theories encompass what we are.

Ryo is the most important person in my world. More than anything, I want to remain by his side—his Seer, his advisor—when his time to rule comes.

The latch clicks shut.

Ryo exhales and wraps a bedsheet loosely around his trim waist before sinking into the chair beside me. He leans forward, elbows on his knees, dragging both hands through his pitch-black hair. The motion exposes the shaved sides—reminiscent of the soldiers—but unlike them, he refuses to carve his rank into the buzzed edges. Instead, he keeps the top longer, letting a few inky strands fall over his eyes.

He is, without question, the most handsome prince in the Seven Islands. Possibly even the entire continent. Strong yet elegant, his high cheekbones and sharp features could have been sculpted by the gods themselves. But this morning? He looks wrecked. Shadows smudge beneath his almond-shaped eyes—the same dark, piercing eyes his mother and sisters share. Too much fun, too little sleep. And judging by the sluggish way he blinks at me, he's probably dehydrated, too.

He studies me, silent for a beat, then groans, scrubbing a hand down his face.

"Go ahead," he mutters, voice rough from the night before. "Lecture me. Get it over with."

I arch a brow, arms crossed. "Oh no, Your Highness. I wouldn't dare."

His glare is unimpressed. "Liar."

I smirk. "Drink some water first. Then I'll start."

"No need to stall. Let's get this finished so I can return to my breakfast." He chuckles, his full lips pitching into a smile. "When did you become so vulgar? Spending too much time with my sisters or ogling my new captain?"

"Can't it be both? Tiernan is a pain in the ass, by the way. A pretty pain in the ass, but a pain nonetheless. I was hoping you could explain how you and I work to him. It would make life much easier if it weren't a battle to talk to you." I wave it off and sit upright in the chair, ready to move on. Ryo's captain isn't why I came this morning. Sparring with Tiernan is just a bonus.

"So, what's the problem?"

"My Vision wasn't complete, but what I did see was horrifying enough. Asher and I stood together at the altar in the Rainbow Temple. You were beside me, holding my elbow, moving me toward him." I gag a little and can't keep my voice from shaking.

Whenever Asher contrives a reason to corner me alone, he professes his undying love. His body language contradicts his words. All I see when I look into his beady, dark eyes is a promise of possession, lust, and pain. He's pushing the queen to recommend him. No, thank you.

"Lydia, Vision or dream? You know the difference. This sounds like a nightmare. You know Mother can't force you to marry that snake, though she might lean heavily on guilt. Are you sure your dream told you that you were marrying Asher, or just that you were getting married and he happened to be there?"

Ryo drops his head, a shiver running through him at the thought of Asher. The reaction comforts me for a moment, a shared revulsion that feels like solidarity, but it doesn't change the truth. Asher still holds power. And influence.

Ryo shakes off a chill, his lean muscles rippling in the firelight. His oath brand shimmers between darkness and light, wrapping around his elbow and up to his shoulder. Each ancient letter burned into his flesh rises and falls with the tensing and relaxing of his muscles, twisting to form the face of a lynx.

The weight of the promise behind the brand has always intrigued me—the one he received at the tender age of thirteen. A promise so enormous it left its mark on him—literally. But I've never had the courage to ask, not even of my closest friend. It's too personal. Too raw.

I remember the ceremony. It was a grand affair, quiet yet heavy with significance. Afterward, he disappeared for a month. When he finally returned, the brand was there, etched into his skin—massive and unmistakable.

Binding oaths are different from regular tattoos. Small, rough things—almost like scars or burns—but with intricate designs, raised from the flesh. They're not just marks of duty or allegiance; they're lifetime promises. To break one is to risk madness or death.

Ryo's oath, though, was different. The long, winding black script stretched across his arm, unlike anything I'd ever seen. The words weren't just symbols—they were warnings. Warnings of what would happen if the oath was broken. The consequences were serious, irreversible. A life-altering weight for a thirteen-year-old to bear.

"This is a life oath," I murmur, my voice barely above a whisper as I watch Ryo run his fingers across his forearm, where the script twists beneath his skin.

Ryo glances up at me, his expression unreadable. "You've never asked, have you?"

"No. I wasn't sure I wanted to know."

Ryo snorts softly, though it's not entirely amused. "You think I'd answer, even if you did?" He shrugs, a gesture that only partially masks the tension in his shoulders. "It's a burden, Lydia. One I'm not sure anyone should ever carry."

I lean forward, my curiosity tugging at me despite my discomfort. "What's it like, Ryo? To carry something that heavy at such a young age?"

His gaze hardens, and he falls silent for a long moment. Finally, he speaks, voice low, almost like a confession.

"It's like living with a shadow. Always there, always watching. A promise you can never break, not without losing everything." He glances at the brand on his arm, a flicker of something—regret, perhaps—crossing his features. "And I don't know if I'll ever be able to keep it."

"I need your help," I press. I unsheathe the little silver knife under my purple skirt, always strapped to my thigh. I prick my index finger, a tiny bead of blood rising to the surface. "I need your oath that when you become king, you won't push me into marriage for political purposes or punish me if I choose otherwise. You'll protect me from the Auctus if they try. Your father is ill, and I will miss him when he's gone. We all will. But you'll be king sooner than you care to admit, and that transition impacts more than just you."

Ryo doesn't meet my eyes, his sharp jaw flexing. "A binding oath? You cannot be serious. I won't make that kind of promise. I'll be king —I can't put my health on the line if you don't like my suggestions or if it would help our country. I love you. I'll do everything possible to see you happy, but my duty comes first."

I beg him to meet my gaze. Guilt? Puppy eyes? Anything? But when he looks up, those hauntingly beautiful onyx eyes are filled with sorrow. He wants to say yes.

But he won't.

A cold pit forms in my stomach, its heaviness settling deep in my chest. It was foolish to think one promise from Ryo could solve all my problems.

Every day, the weight of his father's illness piles higher on his shoulders. He's not the same carefree young man he once was. The playboy prince is starting to look like a ruler-in-the-making—one who never asked for the job but was born to do it. If he can find the strength and maturity to rise to the occasion. And I know he will.

"Maybe a nap would help your foul mood," I tease, tossing a pillow at him. "Or a few days at the Summer Palace?"

He shoots me a half-hearted glare. "I wish," he mutters. "But that will have to wait. I can't wait to sign a million more treaties and listen to politicians argue for hours." He pauses. "I'm living the dream."

"Maybe you should take up a hobby. Something relaxing. Knitting, maybe. Or, I don't know—burn the paperwork." I chuckle.

Ryo smirks, his tired eyes flickering with amusement. "I've considered it. But I think I'd burn the entire castle down before I got to the good parts. Then where would I nap?"

I laugh, but concern lingers. The weight of the world presses down on him, and I refuse to add to that burden.

Ryo already carries the kingdom on his back. I won't be the weight that tips him over the edge. He deserves more than that.

"I understand. It was foolish to ask," I mumble, grabbing my handkerchief to wipe away the drop of blood bubbling on the tip of my finger. "Is it because of the binding oath on your arm? Would it conflict somehow? Is that why?" I ask, defensive and embarrassed for bringing it up in the first place. He rarely says no to me. I'm not used to it.

Ryo sighs, slumping back into his seat as if the weight of the world has decided to rest on his shoulders. His voice drops low, almost too quiet to hear. "When I turned thirteen, I was bound to Silvanisi forever. We traveled to Rune Loren, where I swore to my father and the High Witch herself that I would put my people's survival—and, with a bit of luck, their prosperity—before everything else. My wants, my needs, even my life. That oath... it comes first. Always."

His hand moves to rub over the thick black script coiling across his arm, twisting in intricate swirls and arcs to form the face of a lynx. The brand is distinct and unmistakable—the mark of a future monarch, a binding promise that carries weight beyond words. I watch as his fingers brush over the ancient symbols with a quiet reverence, as if it's both a blessing and a curse. The witches wouldn't have bestowed it upon him if they didn't deem him worthy. I know that much.

"I suppose the High Witch saw something in me," he adds, his voice softening as the barest hint of a smile curves his lips—just enough to catch my attention. It's the only trace of pride in his tone, pride for his role, for the path he's been forced to walk since he was just a boy.

The tension in his shoulders and the furrow in his brow speak volumes as he talks about his responsibilities. Struggling, he tries to step into the shoes of the king he never expected to become so soon. A king burdened by his father's legacy and the generations before him. It's a weight too heavy for anyone to carry alone.

"So," I tease lightly, breaking the silence between us, "you're basically married to Silvanisi. I hope she treats you well."

Ryo raises an eyebrow at me, and for a moment, there's a flicker of that familiar playful smirk. "I didn't exactly ask for this 'marriage' to my country."

He tugs at the slipping sheet around his waist, adjusting it. It's a small, almost imperceptible shift, but even in that, there's something vulnerable about it—something that strips away the bravado.

I could point it out. I could tease him for the slip-up, but something in the way he looks at me stops me. Instead, I offer a small, knowing smile.

"You're doing all right, Ryo. Even if you don't believe it yourself, I believe in you."

His eyes flick toward me, a mix of exhaustion and gratitude in them. "And if I don't? What then?"

I shrug, my gaze steady. "Then we just keep pretending. Together."

Ryo chuckles, his laugh low and dark, the tension in his shoulders easing for a moment. "A perfect plan," he mutters, shaking his head, as if trying to dismiss the weight of everything closing in on us. "For now, I'll pretend the world's not falling apart at my feet." His eyes flicker with something darker, something I don't fully understand, and a knot tightens in my chest.

"You're not fooling anyone with that act," I say, my voice steady, though an edge of concern slips through.

He meets my gaze, and for a brief second, I see something raw, unguarded in his eyes. "You have no idea how much this brand hurts," he murmurs, barely above a whisper. "Not just the mark on my skin, but the one it burns into my soul. Once the oath is blessed, it's not just a tattoo you can get at any parlor. It's a contract forged in fire."

My brow furrows, concern mixing with confusion. "So, you didn't have a choice?"

"I did and I didn't," he says, his voice thick with an emotion I can't place. "The brand burns the promise into you. If I break it, the price is severe: sickness, madness... or even death. There are no loopholes, unless someone is willing to bind their life to mine. And who, in their right mind, would risk that?"

I swallow hard, my voice steady but laced with something sharper. "So, what does that mean for us? For me?"

Ryo runs a hand through his hair, exhaling a frustrated sigh. "I can't promise you anything, Lydia. Not if it conflicts with my oath to Silvanisi. And you're smarter than this—you know that." He looks at me, a challenge in his eyes, as if expecting me to grasp something deeper. "I can't promise that asking you to sacrifice your hand won't be the key to our survival."

I freeze. "Sacrifice my hand?" I echo, my voice tight with disbelief. "What are you asking me to do?"

His gaze softens, but pain lingers in his eyes. "Nothing. But never is a long time. You still have the freedom to choose your partner—or none at all. But would you change your choice if you knew another path could save countless lives? I'm not saying it's fair. I'm not saying it won't hurt. But you and I both know... life isn't fair. We know that better than most." His voice drops to a near whisper. "Choice is an illusion."

"So, you're asking me to sacrifice everything for the greater good? Just like that?"

"I'm not asking you to sacrifice everything. Just... think about it. The world is burning, and what if we were the only ones who could stop it? But to do that, we might have to play a game we're not ready for."

"That's a bit melodramatic, don't you think?" I say, my breath shallow, my mind racing. "I didn't ask for this. None of us did."

Ryo's voice softens. "None of us did. But we have no choice but to fight. And sometimes, to win a war, we have to make sacrifices we never imagined."

"Wow, that got depressing fast. Perhaps you're right. Who knows what the future holds..."

Laughter bursts from Ryo before he can stop it, loud and unexpected. He wipes at his eyes, grinning. "If anyone knows what the future holds, it's you."

A thunk from the bathroom draws our attention to the door. Veronica is eavesdropping. Moisture wavers under the door's crack, shadowed feet impeding the steam. She must have dropped in some oils; the air is thick with vanilla. I hate vanilla. I hate her.

"Why are you with her?" I ask. "She's horrid."

"She does this thing with her tongue." He winks and tightens the sheet around his waist as he stands.

"Is it really that simple for you?"

"It's simple until it's not. And I'm going to enjoy simple for as long as I can." He kisses my forehead and heads toward the bath. Her shadow still lurks in the gap beneath the door.

He has every right to enjoy the pleasures of his position now—before those choices are no longer his to make. As do I.

He must marry someone fit to sit beside him on the throne. Love and passion are luxuries, not requirements. Ryo will sacrifice his happiness to uphold his oath to Silvanisi. In many ways, Ryo, Iris, and Kira have far fewer freedoms than I do.

Then again, would I sacrifice my freedom of choice if it would help those I love? Probably.

"We're surrounded by enemies. The pirates keep raiding, the Auctus are demanding more, and the old threat of Verralon looms again. Not to mention the rebels—who always seem to be upset about something." He exhales. "And those are just the threats I can openly discuss."

Curiosity sparks in me. What is he not saying? He knows Tobias and I have our own network of information.

"Us lynx cubs may be the best bet for keeping the kingdom safe." He pauses. "But all that aside, I can promise you this—Asher has nothing to offer but lies and deceit. He's the last man in the Aperion Sea I'd ever consider as a husband for my worst enemy—let alone my most cherished person."

Ryo doesn't blink. He's never given me a reason to distrust him.

He knows my soul. I choose to trust him, though trust can be a fragile thing.

He disappears into the bathroom, and I remain in front of the fire. Could my dream have been a nightmare? It wasn't a clear Vision in the traditional sense. No warm, hugging, multi-colored fog, no mist surrounding it, and no darkness at the end for me to slide out from.

A squeak in the floorboard behind me breaks the silence. Veronica stands there, naked, every inch of her flawless curves on display—no awkward attempt to cover herself in the false modesty she presented earlier.

"I know what you're trying to do, you little monster. Do you think you can take him from me? Do you have what he needs to stay satisfied? I don't care if he loves you. You'll never have him. And the first thing I'll do when I'm queen is marry you off to the first offer from any other island but this one," Veronica hisses, spewing her venom. It warps her beautiful features into a bitter scowl. She won't age well, and her venom will someday be the death of her.

"You don't know what you're talking about, Veronica. My love for the prince is nothing like that, nor his for me. Also, just so you're aware, no queen or king can require me to marry anyone against my will, though they may make any recommendation they wish." Master's designation grants this luxury—a reward for service to the Auctus, though few have the mettle to take advantage of it.

"I'm not talking about your love. I'm talking about his. The entire court knows what he desires, what he asked of his parents years ago."

Veronica's bright kaleidoscope eyes slide over me from head to toe with disgust. She flips her blonde hair over her shoulder and returns to the bathroom where her prince awaits. She'll do anything to maintain her position—or whatever position Ryo wants to see her in.

The slamming door jerks me from my thoughts, the sharp sound reverberating through the silence like a thunderclap. Her words—

thoughtless, reckless—linger in the air, unsettling me in a way I can't shake. Still, a nagging doubt settles in the pit of my stomach. Were they really as careless as they seemed? Or is there something more beneath them, something I'm not seeing?

Ryo would have told me if he approached his parents about proposing to me. He's been my constant friend. He would have told me, right?

Slamming Ryo's door for good measure, I spin on my heels and barrel down the corridor. My cheeks are hot as I blink back tears. I can't decide what I'm upset about: Veronica's words, the implication of Ryo going behind my back, or whether there might be any truth to his supposed feelings.

Tiernan shifts uncomfortably, quietly observing my emotional upheaval. He, fortunately, respects my need for a moment—a brief respite before the inevitable "I told you so" hangs in the air.

A shaky breath catches in my chest, impossible to contain. I sniffle, quickly blinking away the tears threatening to spill. My reflection in the massive mirror feels like a stranger—disheveled, fragile.

Fingers tug at the itchy fabric of my dress, trying to ease the tension in my shoulders, but it only tightens the knots. My skin, pale and blotchy, parades every freckle—a map of imperfections I can't escape.

My hand dives into my hair, attempting to tame the unruly mess, but it's a losing battle. Curls, once neatly styled by Colleen's careful hands, now rebel, slipping free from their prison.

I meet my reflection in the mirror. Mismatched, bloodshot eyes stare back—larger and more haunting than before. I can't decide whether to hate them or love them. They are both a gift and a curse, forever reminding me of the weight I carry, the responsibility that will shadow me for the rest of my life.

My eyes are my only inherent value, the only reason Ryo would approach his parents, if he did so in the first place.

A tear sneaks past and slowly ambles down my flushed cheek.

A hand appears before my face, offering a handkerchief. Tiernan holds it out to me like a peace offering.

"If there's anything else that might lift your spirits, I'm game to be of service," Tiernan teases, trying to lighten the mood with a wink. My heart flips. He could have teased me. He could have delivered the 'I told you so,' but instead, he's offering me a handkerchief and a distraction with a side of dimple.

Ready to play the game and forget about everything else, I grin. "Is that an offer, Captain?" I hold his gaze, letting the question hang in the thick air between us. I take one slow, deliberate step closer and relish the butterflies in my stomach when I catch the corner of his mouth twitch.

CHAPTER 6
TIERNAN

That little hurricane of a woman comes barreling out like a gust of wind pushing through a window someone forgot to lock. Her cheeks are flushed pink, her eyes blinking back tears. I knew I'd regret letting her pass, but the prince had always given the order to allow his inner circle to enter, no matter the hour. Everyone in Silvanisi knows the lovely Seer falls at the center of that circle.

I try not to turn my head and draw her attention. Out of the corner of my eye, I watch as she takes a few deep breaths outside his door, twirling her star necklace. A nervous tick I've witnessed frequently enough.

Her pale skin glows in the torchlight of the hallway. Freckles run across her cheeks and her perfect nose. How many freckles are under that dress? I want to unwind the sash and open the robe to count them. It would take me ages, and I'd enjoy every minute, even knowing it would end in inevitable ruin.

Stop!

Shaking those thoughts away becomes a necessity. An Adept she is, the king's treasure, and the prince's beloved—whatever that means in their tangled relationship. Trouble follows her, a distraction from the goals I must focus on. That necklace alone stands as a clear warning to stay far, far away.

I can't see her most striking feature, though. With her eyes shut tight, forcing an image out of her mind, I can't see her one green eye and one blue eye, but I know what they reveal. They are the mark of danger and power—the mark of a powerful Seer, a Visionary.

While I appreciate her curves underneath that purple dress, I know those eyes are just the beginning of what makes her a distraction and a threat. Lydia should be avoided, lest she turn her gaze on me and look too closely. What would she see? All my appreciation for the way the gods fashioned her? It's best to avoid her.

The whispers of the prince using others to console his unrequited love for Lydia have avoided her attention. How she isn't aware baffles me. She can't be that blind—pun intended. That, or she ignores what's right in front of her.

A fake cough escapes, clearing my throat to remind her of my presence at the end of the hall. She looks up, and those eyes fix on me—unblinking and evaluating.

A tear slides down her cheek, and her attempt and failure at sniffling it back is more than my cold heart can bear. I hold out a handkerchief like it's a peace offering. Maybe it is.

"If anything else that might lift your spirits, I'm game to be of service." I wink, hoping it will lighten the mood. I could have teased her. The "*I told you so*," is right there, but I bite it back and attempt a friendly grin that usually works with women.

She gives me a wide smile. Her eyes no longer shine with glassy tears but with mirth. "Is that an offer, captain?" She holds my gaze, letting the question dangle between us. She steps closer, and it takes all my willpower to suppress the corner of my mouth from twitching. *Shit, this backfired.* I should have known she'd push back. She doesn't strike me as a woman who would curl up and retreat to lick her wounds.

Unwritten rule number 35: Steer clear of the prince's Seer.

But the problem with that is I like her. She's *likable*, charming even, and it's all too easy to forget who she is and what she is. It doesn't stop me from leaning down to reach out for a strand of hair. I hold the curl in my hand, tugging on it. Lydia holds my gaze. She's not one to blink first, and I like that about her.

Gaze fixed on those all-seeing eyes, I watch as she moves with precision—deliberate, predatory, the Auctus operative hiding beneath her innocent façade. Her head tilts slowly, sharply, like a hawk poised for the kill. Confidence radiates from her now, or maybe it's just the mask slipping back into place. Likely both.

She smells of cherry blossoms and an early morning mist. Like springtime when the world hasn't woken up yet and the sun hasn't burned away the fog. I tuck the hair behind her ear. Her smooth, pale skin shivers. She takes a long step back and breaks eye contact. The moment has ended. My victory in this round is bittersweet.

"Enjoy the day. Try to stay warm." I cease the teasing. I need to stay on task. Divided focus is the death of a soldier, though I follow each step of her swaying hips. She meanders down the gallery in no rush. I don't take my eyes off her until she turns the corner. This is such a dull post, but her presence makes it a bit more interesting.

Veronica strolls out of the prince's room a bit later. We must let her pass anytime she comes by until the prince says otherwise. My men follow orders, but there are a few side-bets to how long she'll be permitted such access. She must be tired from the sounds throughout the night, but she's flawless, refreshed, and ready with sharp claws.

She doesn't even bother to look in my direction, straightening the vee in her low-cut dress and centering the jeweled necklace that had to have been a gift from the prince. A gift she will spend the day showing off to all the other gossiping, conniving ladies that flock around her. They'll all turn their backs on her the moment she's replaced.

Hips swaying, less subtly than Lydia and far less enticing. Attention gathers as she glides down the long gallery, the floor-to-ceiling windows reflecting light off the long blonde hair worn loose to catch every ray. She walks down the center of the sage green carpet, forcing everyone to stop and sidestep or risk bumping into her. A smile greets every man she passes, provided they rank correctly.

"Tiernan, I need to speak with you. Please come in," Ryo commands from my side. I'd been so focused on the gallery that I didn't notice the prince leave his chamber. I'm slacking on the job.

"How can I assist you today?" I nod to one of my lieutenants across the hall, Brandon, to assume my post momentarily. Most of my men are cooperative and efficient units, handpicked by me and loyal to me first, but this one is an Adept and has been with the prince for years. He's decent enough, but everyone knows Adepts have conflicting loyalties.

The prince leads me into his room and gestures to a seat in front of a lit fireplace. The open but warm space is decidedly masculine, with sunlight pouring in through the cracks in the curtains. I take the offered seat but avoid reclining. This isn't a social call.

"I need you to keep a distant but constant eye on Lydia until her birthday celebration," Prince Ryo orders. He sits back and evaluates my reaction. I lock down my expression and keep my emotions off my face, but I did not anticipate this turn of events. What the hell happened when I let her in here?

"I understand." *I don't understand.*

I have no clue how this will play out or how it will affect my standing with the Commander, but I pretend like I do. Whether the prince is jealous, questioning her loyalty, or worried about a kidnapping—none of it matters. What matters is that he wants me to spy on her. It's not my place to ask questions; I'm here to follow orders. Still, a timeline would be helpful.

I hesitate before speaking. "And once she's settled?" The question hangs in the air, a quiet uncertainty in my voice. The only way that might happen is if she gets married or leaves the island—and neither of those things will happen without endless negotiations between the countless people trying to exploit her Sight. This assignment could stretch on for far longer than I'd hoped.

"It should only be a few months. With her birthday and Master promotion, the Auctus will most likely send her an Adept personal guard. Tobias had mentioned they were finalizing the list."

A Master of the Auctus will never be bound by anyone other than a person of their choosing. It's their promise to any Master Adept who devotes their life to their service. Fuck those bastards and their desire to manipulate everyone and everything. They preach about freedoms and the gifts of choice granted by those who swear the oath to the dark star. The reality is that they will tell Lydia where to go, and she will abide like a good soldier.

They wonder why fewer and fewer parents register their child's Enhanced Sense yearly. The "gifts" of the Auctus come at too steep a price.

"Brandon will cover my door and take over your responsibilities here. Your focus needs to be on Lydia. She needs to be watched, and I expect you to keep me apprised of any issues needing my attention." Interesting choice of words from the prince, but who am I to question? The Royals are getting wise. Silvanisi has been bending to the Auctus for too long. They may call it a partnership, cooperation, or an alliance, but everyone knows they can't be trusted.

"Yes, my prince, right away. Am I to notify the lady about my new responsibility? She will ask questions. Lord Tobias may also have questions," I pry as delicately and diplomatically as possible. I'm no politician.

Lord Tobias is her guardian and the ambassador for the Auctus, but he's also a trusted advisor to the crown. He dances a delicate line between the two loyalties, as does Lydia. Perhaps the prince suspects that line might be more fragile than he thought.

"No, keep this between us for the time being. Discuss it with no one," Prince Ryo snaps, rubbing his hands across his face and through his inky-black hair often styled with effortless precision that softly sweeps across his forehead.

Unless the higher powers within that shady organization choose to put their foot down about who ultimately controls the little Seer, Lydia will remain under royal protection. I don't want to be between anything with the dark star on one side. When the Auctus decides to put its foot down, the world shakes.

CHAPTER 7
RYO

This day is already slipping out of control, and it's not about to get any easier. What was Lydia thinking, asking that of me? An oath, of all things? Those are no small matter—next to impossible to break.

I'd do anything for her. Well, almost anything. I've been half in love with her my entire adolescence—more in awe, if I'm being honest. I've never doubted her Sight, even when so many others have, and still do. But this... this is the first time I've ever second-guessed her. And it doesn't sit right, like sour milk curdling in the pit of my stomach.

I want to support her—I will, always—but an oath? That's too much. Too constricting. The consequences are too dire. My mother keeps telling me to grow up, to step up, to stop thinking small. But an oath? That's the farthest thing from small.

It wouldn't surprise me if Asher has already made his move on the crown. His sense of entitlement is so thick that he probably believes he's owed Lydia, as if she's some treasure to claim. I'd never agree to their marriage, but in the end, it's not my choice. It's hers. She has to decide if she's strong enough to stand up for herself and say no. She'll face the consequences, but it's her right to refuse. She's earned that right.

She's not asking for my oath—she's asking for someone to be in her corner, to remind her that she still holds power. To remind her that the decision is hers, even when everyone around her is pushing her in different directions. She needs someone to be on her side with no hidden agenda, no personal stake. The question is, can I be that person for her? I hope so.

Dressing in front of the mirror, I wrap the coat around myself and tie the wide fabric belt. The dark-green wool fits well, but only highlights the dark crescents under my eyes. Stress, a hangover, and lack of sleep have caught up with me, the consequences of my nocturnal activities now unmistakable.

A final check in the mirror, then I drag myself toward the first of many meetings. It's time to step up, take my father's seat, and pray for his speedy recovery. More time is needed.

Outside the council chamber doors, the carved cedar panels loom like a judgment already passed. My jaw aches from clenching too long.

You've been here before. You know how this works.

A breath in. Count to five like Lydia always says.

They want to see you falter. Don't let them.

The wool coat is soft beneath my hands, cuffs straightened even though they're already perfect. Every line is sharp, pressed with precision. Not because of concern for their opinions—but because they'll seize any excuse to call me careless, immature, or unworthy. Not a chance I'll give them that satisfaction.

You were born for this. Raised for this. You've survived worse rooms than this one. Just walk. Just breathe. Just don't let it show.

I roll my shoulders once, feel the tension crack like ice at the base of my neck. My mother says posture speaks louder than words in a room like this.

The guards slide the doors open with a soft *shhhk,* and I step forward into the silence, into the weight, into the eyes waiting to see me fail.

Let them wait. I'm not here to fall.

The chamber is colder than the corridors outside. Not in temperature—though the floorboards beneath my boots creak with winter's bite—but in something deeper. A silence that settles into the bones.

Dark cedar beams loom high above. Every angle of the room is precise, intentional. Unforgiving. The tatami-style floor, woven in shades of ash and charcoal, muffles each step so I can't even hear myself approach—like the room is swallowing my presence whole. Maybe that's the point.

I keep my spine straight as I enter, head high, though every part of me wants to vanish into the woodwork.

The council chamber is full, and the meeting has already begun.

A hush falls as I enter. Chairs scrape. Robes shift. One by one, they rise and bow with measured deference.

All but one.

Asher waits a beat too long before he stands—just enough to make a point without speaking a word. His smirk is polite. His eyes are not. I catch the possessiveness in the way he watches Lydia, like she's something he owns. It coils in my gut, sharp and hot. I loathe that man.

Behind the council, the lacquered paper screens cast the chamber in perpetual twilight. Dyed in storm shades, ink-brushed with mountains and cranes and the arching silhouettes of bare trees, they sway gently when the wind finds the cracks in the woodwork. When they move, the room feels like it breathes.

My boots strike stone, a deliberate rhythm, as I follow the winding path that cuts through the chamber. Trees grow from iron pots along the walkway—bent into beauty over decades, their twisted limbs a quiet lesson in patience or cruelty. Willing or not, they bend. An unsubtle metaphor, but a true one.

Every eye follows me.

They're all waiting for me to slip. I feel it in the silence, in the too-long pause between greetings, in the way no one speaks first. As if I must earn the right to sit. To speak. To exist in this room.

I was raised in these walls, taught to bow just so, to weigh every word like a blade. And still—still—I feel like an imposter. Like no matter how well I perform, they're only biding their time, waiting for me to fail.

Maybe they're right to.

But my mother taught me how to wear stillness like armor. My father taught me how to hold a room without needing to raise my voice.

So I walk forward—unhurried, unbending—until I reach the head of the table.

My father's seat.

I don't fidget. I don't lower my eyes. I let the silence stretch out like a challenge and wait for them to break it.

If they want to see me stumble, they'll have to wait.

"Your Grace, thank you for joining us. We were beginning to wonder if we should start without you." Asher smirks. The other men exchange glances at his sarcastic tone. "Was it Lady Veronica who delayed you? Or Lady Lydia? I saw them both exit your chambers this morning. Busy man." His tone may be friendly teasing, but it grates that he's not only watching me but feels secure enough in his position to point it out.

"Lydia is of no concern to you, Asher. Know your place. Let's start this meeting and keep your nose out of places you don't belong," I snap, suppressing the anger simmering beneath my skin. When I'm king, he'll be the first to go. But until then, it's politics as usual.

He has the decency to shut his mouth and sit. His thin lips press tightly into a line, his face scrunching to suppress the agitation he would never publicly vocalize to his prince.

I move to the head of the table, normally reserved for my father, the king, and take my seat. This is happening more often. Speculation, and I'm sure wagers, are rampant about when the crown will pass. I don't want to know if the odds favor my success or failure. I have enough doubts swirling in my own head to add to the perceptions of others.

"Lords and lady," I begin, addressing Lady Isobel, my mother's closest friend, a force in the operation of the crown, and the lone female in the chamber. When I'm king, that will change. Lydia and my sisters will also be here. "What is the latest from the soldiers along the northern coast about these raids? Pirates? Verralon? What are we dealing with?"

"They've been striking all along the coast—abducting Adepts, killing some Laymen, but stealing little. Not that there's much to steal from most of the targets. Whoever's behind this is clearly hunting Enhanced Sense wielders. With more Adepts disappearing, anyone showing signs of an Enhanced Sense is going into hiding. The unregistered don't trust my men, and they certainly don't trust the Auctus. Hostility toward both the crown and the Auctus is rising," Commander Cormac says, his voice a clipped summary of the growing unrest threatening our long-standing alliance.

"Do we have confirmation that these raids are the work of rebels, pirates, Verralon, slavers? Any or all of the above?" Isobel asks, glancing at Tobias, the Auctus emissary. But he remains tight-lipped as always.

We have no shortage of enemies. I doubt it's Verralon to the north, an ally of the Auctus when it benefits both sides. Our longtime animosity, however, keeps them at the top of any list of suspects. They take goods, not people.

"Verralon has brought this to our attention, but we never know where their loyalties lie. I'm guessing it's the rebels attacking Adepts to provoke the Auctus and draw them out. Or it's slavers hoping to capture more Adepts for quick profit," my ancient Master of Laws, Lord Mori interjects. He's older than dirt and has seen a thing or two.

"Tobias, what is the word from the Auctus?" I ask their emissary and spymaster.

"It appears to be focused on Silvanisi, Your Grace, making us believe it's the work of rebels against the crown and not a wider issue. The threat to Adepts, particularly Seers, cannot be ignored. If it grows, they will send... support," Tobias replies, leaving the implication of a foreign army on our shores hanging in the air.

"And then we'll be overrun by Auctus soldiers, making a bad situation worse. It's better the dark star stays in Merthaset and minds its own business," Commander Cormac says with a sharp edge.

"What is their business if not to protect Sense Adepts worldwide?" Tobias counters, goading Cormac into a response he might regret. They bicker like sisters.

"Our citizens are going missing, and they don't trust their crown or its representatives to protect them," I say, bringing the conversation back to the most basic facts of the problem before the bickering escalates further.

Our relationship with the Auctus has been unbalanced for years. We work together and support each other, but not everyone approves of the methods. Untrained Sense Adepts are becoming a growing problem, leading to people rejecting education or using dangerous, makeshift methods.

A few weeks ago, an unregistered drunk Handler killed two men in a bar fight. Last month, an unregistered Complex child accidentally burned his little sister while they were bickering. He was so distraught and overwhelmed by his five Enhanced Senses that he strained his gift and injured himself. It was horrible for the family, made worse when it turned out all their children had Enhanced Senses to varying degrees. The Auctus had to step in, and the children were taken to Merthaset to begin training.

Enhanced Senses were once considered a divine gift. However, this gift comes with responsibilities: education, registration, and, for those who choose to pursue advanced Mastery, loyalty to the Auctus through a branded oath—binding them to Merthaset to a lesser degree than my binding to Silvanisi.

"We need a stronger presence along the coast, and we must tread carefully. Even if these raids aren't the work of anti-Adept rebels, they still need to be stopped, no matter their motivations," Lady Isobel says, always observing and thinking three steps ahead.

"It makes us look pathetic and lacking control of our shores," Commander Cormac interrupts, pounding his fist on the table to emphasize his point. He's a gruff bully of a man, but his years of service and steady leadership are undeniable.

"Pull some men and redistribute them across the forts along the coast. Take five ships from the fleet here and have them run patrols in overlapping rotations. Let's see if we can't catch these raiders on the water," I order, my instructions clear and my voice steady.

Respect for my decision fills the room, except from Asher and Cormac, whose reasons for dissent differ. Cormac's disregard for my authority is no secret—he's known me since I was a snot-nosed kid and probably still sees me that way. Or maybe he just rejects any order that isn't his idea. This room is full of egos, and he's no exception.

"That would leave the castle and the city vulnerable. Pulling ships would also expose our waters to Verralon," Asher interjects. "We can't afford that while the rebels are growing bolder and our king is weak."

"Your king isn't weak!" I shout, defending my father and everything he has done for the kingdom. "Your king is indisposed. This does not warrant disrespect, Asher. You should remember who placed you in your lofty position."

Asher would not hesitate to use my father's illness to his advantage. "I meant no disrespect, but we've all noticed your increased involvement in cabinet meetings recently. We're all here to support the crown, no matter who is at its helm or how young and inexperienced they may be," he replies, always with a backhanded compliment.

"We must all support the crown in any way we can until the king is well enough to return to his rightful seat," Isobel says, attempting to smoothe things over.

"In the theme of supporting the crown, now and in the future, has there been any development on the prospects for Lydia's hand?" Montcliff asks. Every person at this table knows he's set his cap for her, and she has shown no interest in him or any of the men who have proposed thus far.

Tobias steps in before I have a chance to shut Montcliff down. "Everyone is eager to know what decision Lydia will make, but remember, this is her decision, and she can take all the time she needs. While it may be tradition to announce a decision on her birthday, she's not bound by that and can decide whenever she's ready. The Auctus and the king have received all the proposals and are considering them carefully. However, the decision lies with Lydia. As her guardian, I support her and will stand by her, no matter what."

"Should such an important decision be left to a twenty-four-year-old woman? Should her king not have the final say? She should marry someone from here if she is truly loyal to Silvanisi," Asher presses, hunting for allies. To question Lydia's loyalty to my father and my family is ludicrous.

Isobel leans forward, her eyes scanning the faces around the table. "If Lydia stays in Silvanisi, it's most likely Master Tobias will return to Merthaset or be sold to whoever can offer the Auctus enough resources to claim a Visionary Master Seer. No offense, Master Tobias," she adds with a hint of humor to soften the insult. "It's equally possible that Lydia will be assigned to a post elsewhere, or maybe she'll choose a foreign match. Everyone is watching her decision, and the gossip—the betting pools—they're ravenous. They'll devour any scrap of news."

I run a hand through my hair, frustration tightening my chest. Lydia's decision to stay unmarried? That's not truly a choice. The Auctus, Tobias, her king—they all have political stakes in her marriage. No wonder she's asking for a binding oath when everyone around her is pushing her in their direction. She's caught in a web, and she knows it.

"Again, should such a decision be left in the hands of an easily influenced girl?" Asher smirks, tossing the question into the air, his gaze sweeping the room. But no one takes the bait. Not a single response. He's alone in this—his words hang there, weightless. He has no true allies here. All he can hope for is unwilling cooperation for mutual benefit.

Asher believes that having Lydia on his arm, or better yet, under his thumb, would elevate his status in court, cementing his place. But he's wrong. The Auctus won't back him—not if Tobias is telling the truth. So what does Asher really have to offer?

The fact that he thinks Lydia is easily influenced shows just how blind he is. She's not some pawn to be played. She's destined to be a Master Seer—maybe even a Grandmaster someday—and she'll wield more power across Aperion than Asher could ever imagine. He's clueless if he thinks he's the one calling the shots.

I add a mental note to my never-ending list: learn more about the other proposals. The more I know, the more I can protect her. I owe her that much, at least. These vultures would tear her apart if they had the chance. I am her most potent ally.

CHAPTER 8
LYDIA

Those gray eyes follow my every move. I fidget on a wooden bench with the princesses in the open central hall as they update me on last night's shenanigans. Of course, I'm also watching him out of the corner of my Sight. Tiernan is hard to ignore.

The bench is one of many lining the side of the hall. The wood is carved to resemble a tree, with winding branches that form a cozy canopy for the occupant. The opposite wall has large windows, with glass panes arranged to look like clear leaves. With sage green rugs and flowers scattered everywhere from the queen's greenhouse, the effect is a harmonious blend of practicality and nature.

Above me, exposed wooden beams arch like the ribs of some great, slumbering creature—each one notched with ornamental joinery, a subtle nod to Silvanisi craftsmanship and the delicate precision of old-world builders. Filigree adorns the corners where walls meet ceiling: silver-leafed branches and curling ivy motifs, as though the forest itself has crept inside and chosen to stay.

"Oh, Tiernan, there you are! We were just discussing you," Kira calls out, a little too loudly to be princess-like. No, that sounds wrong. Ladylike. The entire hall falls silent, the chatter ceasing abruptly as everyone turns. Tiernan has been shadowing me since I left Ryo's two days ago, and I made the mistake of telling them. He thinks he's being subtle, but Tobias has trained me since birth to keep my eyes open.

My cheeks heat. My neck, too. Damn, pale skin reveals everything. Controlling that natural reaction is still a work in progress. I asked the twins to be discreet, but it's not in their blood. They might have tried harder if they weren't bored. It seems they've chosen mischief today.

Iris, tall and willowy, moves with the effortless grace her mother drilled into her from an early age. She glides through the room like a goddess, every step a study in refinement. But beneath that polished surface lies a mind constantly at work, an insatiable intellectual curiosity with no proper outlet. She's the true mastermind behind every bit of trouble that stirs in the palace.

Dance became her necessary distraction, a way to channel her restless energy—but it's never been enough. Her heart longs to study ballet at the University on Renatto, to follow her passion before she's expected to settle down. But as a princess? The idea is scandalous. It seems criminal to waste such raw talent, such potential, simply to keep her tethered to tradition. She's slowly bringing her parents around, inch by painstaking inch, but with the king, duty will always come first. I don't see him ever bending on this.

That won't stop her, though. She'll continue to subtly make her case, methodically chipping away at her father's objections, one carefully crafted argument at a time.

While she closely resembles her sister, Kira is a bit shorter and more muscular, though still tall and slender compared to me. Like Ryo, they both share their mother's full lips and sharp, angular cheekbones. Quick, fierce, and never one to sugarcoat her thoughts, Kira often lacks the diplomacy her sister wields like a weapon.

Tiernan bows. He takes Kira's hand and kisses it a moment longer than is polite. She pulls her hand away. "I hope you were singing my praises, Princess. I did see you paying close attention to my skills in the training ring yesterday," Tiernan says with a wink, glancing at me to see if I react. I'm trained to play these games, but it doesn't mean I like them. A fleeting chill rolls over me, but I shake it off quickly, hopefully before Tiernan notices.

"There's nothing wrong with appreciating someone skilled. I'm sure you have many talents, Captain, both in and out of training," Kira says. Oh, she's setting him up for trouble. Or me. Which one will entertain her more today? I wonder if he even senses the trap being laid around him. I recognize all her signs. Well, I'll play along. I'm bored, too.

"Your presence comes at precisely the right time," Kira continues. "We've been summoned to the greenhouse and require a guard, for some ridiculous reason. We aren't even leaving the inner walls." She rolls her eyes and smirks, as though letting Tiernan in on some secret.

"The guard dog routine won't last, but let's humor the elders for now. Are you available, or will lurking occupy the rest of your day?" Iris asks, her polite mask barely hiding the playful challenge behind it.

He squirms then quickly pulls himself together, sliding his mask back into place. One might have missed the brief moment of discomfort.

"I am here to serve the crown, my princess, in any way the crown sees fit. Should we depart now, or should you change before meeting with Her Majesty?" Tiernan asks.

The princesses glance down in unison, taking in their tight leggings, dirty sweaters, and muddy riding boots.

The twins have cultivated a reputation for mischief, though nothing too serious has ever been directly traced back to them. Their innocent beauty is their greatest ally, letting them slip past even their parents' watchful eyes. Long, silky ebony hair cascades down their backs like a still pond at midnight. They share their mother's onyx eyes, framed by thick lashes, and her flawless porcelain skin—but that is where the similarities end.

The king can't look into their faces without seeing his beloved wife, and Naomi can't help but see the echo of her husband's eyes, making it impossible for either of them to discipline their daughters. If the queen weren't also a bit of an eccentric herself, she might try to assert more control over them. But instead, she looks the other way, almost as if she admires their antics. She knows, though, that the time for such carefree mischief is fleeting. Duty will always be the shadow that follows every sunset.

Kira stands, brushing dirt and dust off her sleeve. "Very well. We'll go change. Lydia, keep Tiernan company since you already look flawless. Doesn't she look lovely, Iris?"

"Lovely indeed, sister. Tiernan, doesn't she look lovely?" Iris asks with a broad smile. She doesn't wait for an answer. She links arms with her sister, and they leave us alone.

Uncomfortable on the bench, I fidget with the intricate arm. Tiernan looms, casting his shadow over me. The silence stretches on, but it's unbearably loud in my head.

"No longer on Ryo's door, Tiernan?" I ask. I've been testing my theory since last evening, taking ridiculous loops around hallways I hadn't walked in months, but he remains a safe and discreet distance away. Always.

"No. Today, I get to accompany you to the greenhouse. Where is your coat? You'll need it with the wind picking up." He pauses. "We may get some snow this evening with the clouds starting to build." He pauses again, shifting from one foot to the other. "The sunshine this morning was a nice change."

Are we talking about the weather? What happened to flirting and banter? Bring it back! If Ryo said or did something before I even got the chance to get to know Tiernan, I'm going to shave the prince's head in his sleep.

"I'll grab it now from my room, and we can meet back here before we head out. I'd rather not walk back in a blizzard." The dull gray clouds roll overhead, and the trees sway and groan in the winter breeze. Damn, more weather talk.

"I'll walk with you, my lady." He takes my elbow and pulls me up from the bench. Before I can retreat, he tucks my hand into the crook of his arm. "May I ask you a question, Princess?"

"You can ask me anything, but stop it with the 'princess' and the 'my lady.' It's Lydia." I'm not a princess and hold no official position or title beyond Auctus Novice. The formality of the court can quickly become grating, especially when it lacks respect or sincerity. But I don't think that was his intent. I'm just jaded now, accustomed to the reminder of my lack of blood relation or proper position in the castle. I realize it's not always the intent, but it happens often enough to be annoying.

"How does your Sight work? Or is it rude to ask? Is it true other Seers have different gifts and can use the other Senses?" he asks, his eyes bright with genuine curiosity. I'm taken aback. Most Laymen jump straight to asking if I can see specific things for them in their futures. No one has ever asked about my own experience.

"Well, there are some things that are secrets held by the Auctus." I wink. The rumors about the mysterious Auctus are rampant—often hysterical, seldom dangerous, and rarely accurate. But we do keep our trade secrets close.

"My Sight is considered strong among Visionary Seers, so Tobias diligently works with me to hone my skills for greater service. I'm not born to master all the Senses, but we all learn the basics in child-hood, just in case we need to assist a fellow Adept. My Enhanced Hearing isn't terrible, but it's nowhere close to that of a born Listener. It's pretty watered-down. That's about it, though."

"That sounded rehearsed. How old were you when you were taken and forced to work?" he asks, his voice dropping.

My body tenses, and I force it to relax. I'm sure he can see the shift.

"I don't work for them, and I was never taken. I was born on Merthaset. I represent their mission by using my Sight to help others to the best of my abilities. I'm grateful they've chosen to educate me so I can make the most of these gifts. What's the point of having such a gift if I don't use it to its fullest?"

I yank my arm free, leaving him standing outside my door. The door shuts behind me with a snap, a little harder than necessary. His questions are finished. It sounds rehearsed, but the truth is, I'm grateful to Tobias—and by extension, the Auctus. I recognize the gifts I've been given, but I remain acutely aware of how others perceive me, fair or not.

I could have handled that better instead of lashing out at what was likely just a poorly worded question. I shouldn't assume the worst of everyone. It's exhausting.

CHAPTER 9
RYO

As the day drags on, my patience begins to wane. My headache worsens, shifting from a dull throb into an eye-pulsing pain. How has my father done this for thirty years without losing his mind? He has my mother, who helps, I'm sure. Mother would likely make some comment about how this might be easier for me if I had a partner.

She'd also make remarks about Veronica leaving my room this morning. I'm not married—who do I have to hide from? Hopefully, I won't want a mistress when I find a wife and future queen. I'd like to find something akin to what my parents have—a partner to share both the burdens and joys of life. Mother would also remind me that Veronica is not that someone.

Veronica isn't what people think. She's been kind to me, giving me space when I need it and always showing up when I least expect it. Yes, she's vain, but honestly, she's one of the most beautiful women at court, and she has every right to be. Maybe she's a little shallow, but that doesn't change the fact that she's been nothing but decent to me.

My sisters may have their reasons to dislike her, but I've never had any intention of marrying her. She knows this—I've made it clear. If she chooses to live in denial, that's on her, not me. I'm not stringing her along. She understands where I stand.

Lydia's right, though. I've been making excuses, and I've been thinking with my dick.

As I rise to leave the council chamber, my father's brother and closest advisor, Prince Oscar, stops me with an affectionate pat on my shoulder. While my father is battling his lingering illness, Oscar is full of life and loves little more than reminding the young soldiers that he can still kick anyone's ass.

"Ryo, my boy. Your mother asked me to speak with you. Better sit back down." Oscar pulls me aside, away from the other council members, who look over, trying to overhear our conversation. My heart reaches for the open door, but my feet stop before my uncle. I was so close to being done for the day.

Oscar gives the remaining council members a look with coal-black eyes that could turn a man to stone, and they all bow before continuing to exit. I need to work on mimicking that look.

"Dearest uncle and glorious prince," I say gallantly, giving him an exaggerated bow. "How can I be but your humble servant?" I slide into the closest chair, rejecting the formality of the large council table.

"Smart mouth, little snot," he replies with a small smile he can't hide. He sits beside me and pulls out a folded piece of paper from his pocket. "Your mother has given me a list of suitable brides. She wants you to narrow it down. Be settled while your father still reigns, so stability and an heir—or two—will be established when the crown falls onto your dense head. You'd be wise to heed her advice. She's always been the smartest among us."

"We're all in the business of keeping my mother appeased. Who's on this list of hers? I assume no one fun?" I reach out for the paper and unfold it. I glance at the names of various princesses from across the Aperion I don't know. As well as a few acceptable women from Silvanisi whom I know all too well and would never consider. However, one name has my heart stuttering at the bottom.

"Why would Lydia be on here? We've talked about this." My breath catches in my throat. My eyes water as I swallow. I cough and sputter. Thank the gods we're alone in this room. I look ridiculous.

"It's a suggestion, my boy—nothing more. Something to consider. You already trust and care deeply about each other. It would keep her close to the crown and to Silvanisi. Half the court already thinks you're in love with her. It makes a great deal of sense. Plus, it would bring powerful Adept blood into the bloodline." He lists each logical, clinical reason on his fingers. Reasons that have clearly been discussed in conversations that I wasn't privy to. He was prepared with this list of women—and why Lydia should be on it. Maybe even at the top.

When I was younger, consumed by raging hormones, I used to entertain fantasies about Lydia. I wondered what it would be like to have those blue-and-green eyes gazing up at me, what her mouth might taste like, or what she might look like, flushed with passion beneath me. But those thoughts passed. What Lydia and I share now is something far deeper—something unique. She is my best friend, my closest advisor, my most trusted ally.

I would kill for her. I would move mountains for her. But I don't want to have children with her. I don't want that kind of love from her. Once, maybe. But not anymore. I let go of that idea long ago, yet no one believes me.

"She can be crossed off. It will never happen." Firm in my resolve, I grab a pen and cross her off myself with an exaggerated slash, tearing the page.

"Never is a long time. Seems simple enough to me. You trust her, and she's grown into a beautiful young woman inside and out. What's there to object to? Tobias approves, the Auctus approves, and your parents both approve. We just need to get the two of you on board," Oscar declares. They've all been discussing this behind both of our backs. There's no doubt in my mind that Lydia has no clue what's being plotted around the two of us, especially after her request for the binding oath.

"My answer is no, and I'm confident hers would be to laugh in your face. Who else is on this list?"

"The princess in Renatto is the next best choice. She's the heir and has no siblings. She's a bit young—nineteen or twenty—but her parents have made a compelling case in her favor. You'd stand to unite two of the seven islands under your rule. If Kira and Iris could each marry one of the princes of Ellandelle or secure the Verralon warlord, we'd secure a much-needed web of peace across the sea. We could stop bickering with each other and present a unified front against the continent."

He and my mother have been working tirelessly, scheming to unite the entire Aperion Sea. It makes strategic sense, but it feels wrong—bartering your own children. Can't we be the generation to break this cycle?

Who am I kidding?

One day, I'll no doubt hypocritically find myself part of these conversations about my own children. The thought twists something deep inside me—a painful acknowledgment of the reality. Alliances are what keep us alive, prosperous, and safe. What better way to forge them than through marriage and children? Logically, I get that. But a small, naive part of me never imagined I'd end up here, on this side of the table. Or maybe that's just childish denial.

"And what do we know about this Renatto princess, other than she's young?" Renatto is too close to the continent and cares more about wealth and building their merchant empire than protecting or cooperating with the people across the Aperion. If I have to eventually pick, I'd like to know where her loyalties lie.

"She's said to be quite smart and clever. Well-educated and rumored to be pretty—but that could be a matter of opinion. You know how these things get embellished."

"Invite her if it will keep Mother off my back, but I make no promises. Lydia isn't on the table. I won't be the one to take away her choice, no matter that you all are working behind her back." I roll up the paper and shove it into my pocket, ready to end this conversation, but Oscar sets his beefy hand on my shoulder before I can rise.

"Just talk to Lydia about the idea. It makes sense." He shakes his head and sighs. "Deal with Veronica before we invite prospective brides to court."

I cannot invite prospective brides and have my mistress making their lives miserable with her claws out. It's rude and would leave a poor impression on any future queen. Image is everything; ours is weakened among the islands with all these little rebellions. A visiting court cannot see us as weak or unable to control our people. Veronica cannot embarrass me or my family.

"Deal with it quietly. We need allies right now. Distraction should be avoided at all costs." Oscar follows me out of the council chamber, off to report to my mother immediately.

"Invite the princess, and I will deal with Veronica," I reiterate. Today has gone from bad to worse, and my headache renews its torment with vigor.

Whispers float around me as faceless bodies step aside in the hall. A few hesitate, wanting to ask for something, but then avert their eyes. I glare and plow forward, heading toward a large drink.

An hour's walk fails to clear my head. I wander into the billiard room of my favorite elite club in downtown Saivi. Low tables scatter the jewel-toned rugs strewn across the cavernous, circular room, dominated by a massive round fireplace at its center.

Asher blocks my path to the bar, a drink already in each hand. He reaches out, offering me one.

"Asher, I'm not in the mood." I reject his outstretched offering, preferring to pour my own. It's an insult, to be sure. A few other men milling about the room watch us from a safe distance.

"My prince, you seem a bit on edge. I'm simply trying to help. I understand congratulations are in order. Rumor has it you'll be a father soon," he teases, taking a long sip of his drink and slurping through his teeth. A smirk spreads across his face.

The bottle slips from my hand and shatters. The scent of the rich amber liquid permeates the air and soaks into the rug beneath me.

"Where did you hear that? Who is spreading these false rumors?" I grab him by the collar and pull him close. The crunch of broken glass fills the silence for a few heartbeats. Even those observing hold their breaths.

"Why, the mother—the coveted Veronica herself. The timing is somewhat suspect, or perhaps convenient is a better word. We could have a joint wedding ceremony when Lydia comes around to accepting my offer," Asher retorts, his tone wavering slightly, clearly feeling the weight of my open hostility at the mention of Lydia. He pulls back and straightens his coat, brushing off invisible lint to regain his composure.

"What are you going on about? Veronica isn't pregnant, and Lydia has already responded to your offer loud and clear. Spreading gossip is beneath even you, Asher, especially at your age." I grab another bottle and pour myself a drink, ignoring him completely as I turn my back and settle into one of the chairs lining the opposite side of the room, as far away from him as possible.

"I trust that if I were to assist you with your Veronica problem, you might grace me with a favor of my own?" He joins me uninvited in the opposite chair. He can't take a hint. I assigned my personal captain to keep Asher away from Lydia. I loathe his obsession with her. I have an inkling of what favor he might ask.

"And I'm sure you won't hesitate to tell me what this will cost me?" I hiss, not bothering to hide my disdain. This is how he's grown in power. He's only a few years older than me, yet he uses blackmail and leverage to exploit everyone around him.

"Your word with the king and queen on my proposal for Lydia's hand. We cannot risk losing a treasure like her to another kingdom. She should stay here, where she will be appreciated—and appropriately managed," he replies. I bet he'd love to be the one to "manage" her. Good luck. Lydia would never agree. He must be desperate to ask me for assistance, and a desperate man will do dangerous things to get what he wants.

"Never." I walk out without a second look. I have enough to worry about.

"Never is a very long time," Asher muses, his words trailing me long after I've left.

Sparring sounds promising. Punching someone might distract me for a bit from the barely suppressed rage that simmers through me every time I'm forced to interact with this man. I'll imagine his face is on the receiving end.

CHAPTER 10
LYDIA

A pile of clothes grows on my closet floor. I root through it like a hog in mud, searching for my favorite sweater, the warmest coat I own, and my fur-lined hat for good measure. I toss the silly little shoulder wrap across the small bench in the center. Tossing them over one arm, I lock the door behind me and pop back into the hall.

Tiernan is waiting down the hall. My body hums while I take the time to appreciate his muscular body leaning against a column. His pensive eyes track the impending snowstorm beyond. I wish I knew how to paint. Perfectly framed in the window, light shafts pour around his casual strength from what little sun remains through the clouds. I walk toward him, lost in the thought of my imaginary painting, but slam into an unwelcome figure blocking my path.

"I require a moment of your time, my Vision." Asher has planted his feet in my way, his hand squeezing my elbow to pull me down the hall. I note it's not a request of my time. He requires and demands it, leaving no room for a challenge.

Gossip can be cruel and is often unfair to the lady. I can't pull away without causing a scene. Not to mention Tobias's warning to keep my head down. The castle is busy at this time of day, and everyone is bustling about.

"Now isn't the right time, my lord. Lady Lydia is scheduled to meet the queen," Tiernan says, stepping in front of Asher. Their shared contempt is apparent. Tiernan towers over the smaller man. He takes hold of my other arm to separate me from the threat of being pulled away, but Asher does not let go. It would be mortifying for this to turn into a tug-of-war.

"Know your place, Captain, and your betters," Asher growls. He grabs my coat and hat and shoves it into Tiernan's arm. He has no choice but to let go or everything will fall to the ground. Asher squeezes my elbow, almost painfully now—a punishment for Tiernan's perceived lack of deference.

"I'll be a moment. Wait here," I instruct Tiernan. My eyes widen, a silent plea to not cause a scene or draw attention. I can manage Asher myself and have been doing so for years. Asher thinks I'm dancing to his tune, but I'm no wilting flower. Tiernan hesitates, adjusting my heavy coat in his arms, then moves to the side, letting Asher drag me around the corner into a small side hall.

Asher releases me and steps back, his hand pressing against the wall next to my head. He looms over me, but his attempts at intimidation have long lost their sting—they're a familiar, worn-out tactic by now. Whether he's too egotistical to notice my hatred, or if he simply doesn't care, it doesn't matter.

The nook is small, forcing his face to hover just inches from mine. His hot breath brushes my skin, suffocating me, and I fight the urge to flinch. I'll never give this man the satisfaction of seeing weakness. I haven't yet, and I don't plan on starting today.

"Lydia, my treasure, my Vision," he says. His hot breath makes my skin crawl, like his pet names make his motivations less obvious. My value is solely in my Sight. I'm not a person, I'm a currency. "I understand an announcement will be made soon—in a matter of days, if the rumors are true. Is there anything you would like to say to your future husband?"

I stifle a laugh. "I haven't announced any future husband. Can you see the future too? If so, you've been keeping secrets, Asher." I shouldn't provoke him, but I tap my chin thoughtfully. "Husband... hmmm. So many options. Ellandelle, perhaps? Though their king is rather old and already has plenty of heirs. Or maybe the continent for me? I've always wanted to travel, even if it's to an uncivilized, barren wasteland that despises my kind. As a council member and Master of Trade, you'd know the benefits of a foreign match far better than little ol' me," I taunt, my words dripping with sarcastic venom as I never break eye contact. My mismatched green and blue eyes unsettle most, and I can go an awfully long time without blinking.

A niggling shiver skitters down the back of my neck. I may have pushed too far. I don't think this is what Tobias had in mind when he told me to keep my head down.

He removes one hand beside my head and places it on my neck, right where the shiver has settled. What would be a caress from anyone else slowly increases in pressure. He squeezes, and I flinch. A small, sadistic smile crosses his lips at my recoil and his desired reaction. He releases my neck, satisfied, and slides his hand down to my waist.

"Don't be stupid. I'm to be rewarded for my years of service with something worthwhile, finally. It'll be a pleasure to bring you to heel." He leans back to gauge my reaction, basking in his perceived victory.

"The sprawling seaside estate of Stones Cove and Master of Trade hasn't been enough of a reward for you? Bit greedy if you ask me," I taunt, sliding away from his grasp. "But, sadly, none of the choices for a husband presented to me have looked terribly appealing." I sigh and shrug my shoulders, feigning disappointment in the lackluster marriage game. I attempt a look that will convey, *What's a girl to do?*

"My lady, it's time to go meet the queen." Tiernan turns around the corner and halts, holding my thick burgundy velvet coat out for me. I wonder if he's been listening in.

Asher grabs my wrist, not bothering with subtlety. I know exactly what he wants: to dominate my Sight, exert control, bring me down and confine me to a place he thinks I belong. I've heard how much he relishes total control—often in a painfully obsessive way. I shudder. Asher's beady eyes drill into mine.

Tiernan's warm fingers envelop my elbow, thankfully, pulling me away from snapping and saying or doing something I might regret or would get me in trouble. He hands me my coat, and steers me back into the sunny gallery where the twins are waiting to head outside in the cold to the greenhouse. I pull up the buttery-soft fur-lined hood and tie the thick embroidered belt tightly around my waist.

A nervous wave sweeps over me as we approach the queen's greenhouse. She rarely calls for me when she's with her ladies, unless it's something important—or unless some visiting dignitary wants to treat my Sight like a parlor trick.

Asher's insinuations linger in my mind, swirling with the unsettling images from my dream of the temple. I can't help but wonder if there's some truth buried within them—some piece of the puzzle I'm not seeing. I might need to call upon my Sight again, try to retrace the Vision, but that would mean telling Tobias—something I'm desperate to avoid. He'll be furious I didn't share it sooner, even though he'll try to reassure me. He'll remind me of my choices, of my duty, as if I don't already know. I'm not in the mood for a lecture, but I also know I can't face this Vision alone. It's too dangerous. My options are limited.

It's a reasonable assumption that I'd eventually accept one of the marriage offers. But why on earth would I ever consider Asher's proposal? The queen would never support him. Right? He's wealthy, powerful, and single. The queen has every right to make recommendations, but I also have the right to accept or decline, no matter the pressure or influence.

His words are nothing more than an inflated ego wrapped in

entitlement. Is he delusional enough to think I'd agree to be nothing more than a prize? No amount of pressure, flattery, or political games would ever change my mind about Asher Montcliff.

THE WALK to the greenhouse is one of my favorites in the warmer months. It's a sea of color, with azaleas gathered at the entrance. Tidy paths, lined with cherry blossoms, wisteria, and every sweet scent one can imagine, welcome me into this magical place. A bamboo maze occupies an entire side of the space, cocooning and isolating, blocking all views of the outside world with its towering shoots and leaves.

Every detail of this garden holds a memory. The soft moss will soon become a cushion beneath my bare feet, a welcome alternative to the icy stepping stones that form the hazardous, scattered pathways. In just a few months, the buzz and chirps of nature will harmonize under the warm sunshine, creating a soothing backdrop. I would miss this garden path the most if I were asked to move to another court.

Today is bare and brown, but the memory of vibrant colors is enough. The cold sinks deep into my bones, ripping through the loose gap of my coat and weighing down each step. The wind whistles through the branches, a less welcoming tune than the rustling of lush leaves in the spring and summer melodies.

We bustle down toward the queen's greenhouse, tucked into the far corner of the orchard where sunlight barely filters through the skeletal branches. It's placed away from the main buildings on purpose—out of sight, out of reach, a sanctuary hidden behind beauty and frost. The snow crunches beneath our boots, brittle and unforgiving. The sun does nothing to warm us.

The castle looms behind us—ancient and otherworldly, carved into the bones of the mountain itself. Its sweeping roofs curve like wings poised for flight, the black-tiled eaves dusted with snow.

Pale stone and warm cedar glow gold in the winter light, softened by ivy that clings stubbornly to the outer walls. It's a fusion of artistry and strength—graceful as a poem, but impossible to breach.

From the highest tower of our wing, I can see it all: the city of Saivi spilling down the mountainside in layers of tiled rooftops and smoke trails, winding streets stretching thin toward the shipyards and docks that line the frozen harbor. The sea beyond is iron-gray and restless, dotted with vessels anchored like stars caught in ice.

Closer in, gardens sleep beneath frost-covered glass. The greenhouse—half crystal, half living sculpture—hums faintly with warmth and light, like a heartbeat under snow, just as the queen envisioned. Courtyards and raised walkways thread between the estate's outbuildings: the kitchens, the directional towers at the end of each wing, the stables, the long storage barns.

Just beyond the inner wall lies the soldier compound—sharp angles and snowy training courts now quiet. But I've seen it roar to life at dawn: steel flashing, voices raised in command and camaraderie, the rhythm of discipline echoing off stone.

Two walls enclose this world. The inner, carved wood interspersed with evenly spaced stone columns. The outer, towering and stark, built to endure siege and storm. And beyond even that— beyond the back gate that faces away from the city—lies the wild. Not Saivi, but the Interior. The deep forests of Silvanisi, dense and unbroken, where the snow lies thicker and the trail vanishes into mist and shadow.

This place—this impossible, beautiful place—is both sanctuary and snare. And no matter how high the walls or how distant the sea, I know better than to believe I'm safe.

But still—this is home. The only one I've ever known.

As we cut through the orchard, with Tiernan and two other guards close on our heels, our boots crunch in the icy layer that glazes the top of the snowpack. I glance down at the smooth blanket of white. Footprints press in the other direction—from the mountains and outer wall toward the inner estate. Tiernan follows my gaze and surveys the same tracks.

"Probably the queen's guard on patrol," he mutters.

My questions are cut short as we arrive. The queen spends her limited leisure time tending to the many exotic plants from across the world. It's her passion, besides maneuvering her children. She probably realizes they give her new plants every year just to keep her out of their hair.

The massive wood-beam structure, with delicate tight-grid frames around each pane, is triple the size of the old building. High ceilings make the space feel more like a temple than a greenhouse—a place to worship Mother Nature.

A cherry blossom tree blooms in the center of the koi pond, its flowers cascading the space with a dreamy pink glow. A gift from the witches upon her marriage to King Hiro, its blooms never fade. Dozens of tiny gold and white koi swim in the surrounding pond, weaving between a few exposed roots.

In the far corner, the queen hums a soft tune to herself at the workbench, while her ladies sip tea, engage in needlework, read, or chat to pass the time. A few play cards, but they all leave her to her hobby. She's close enough to hear and enjoys staying informed about the comings and goings of her court, especially when it comes to her children. Her apron is covered in a layer of dirt over her expensive golden silk wrap dress. The broad crimson sash that cinches her narrow waist is embroidered with delicate blossoms on display all around us.

She jumps when the heavy door slams from a gust of cold wind rushing through the unseasonably humid space. The wind rustles the leaves on the many shelves lining the glass.

"Ah, there you are, my loves! You must be cold. Tea!" she says, not asking if we want tea nor waiting for a reply.

"Lydia, be a dear, and please go ahead and start without me," Queen Naomi instructs, gesturing toward the waiting tea service. She always asks me to pour.

Lady Isobel joins us, so I pour her a cup. I like her. I always have. Tobias trusts her, and that's enough for me. I think her first husband was a high-ranking Adept, but she's quiet about her connections to the Auctus. "Am I to believe the gossip that we'll have some royal guests soon?" she teases. I assume she is referring to suitors arriving for my birthday party in a few months.

At last, the queen glides into place, a portrait of poise, her fingers curling around the teacup as if the room had been waiting for her to begin. "We shall see which way the wind blows and if our invitations are accepted. If these problems continue or spread further along the coasts... Well, if we don't reach an alliance via our emissaries, it will be necessary to encourage some strategic allies to discuss the situation further in person." A slight tremor betrays her worries. I'm curious who has been invited. While the party may be in my honor, it's hardly for me.

The queen smooths the deep gold silk skirt that pools around her. None would suspect she was elbow-deep in the dirt just moments ago.

"Mother, has something happened that we should be aware of? Something we might have a right to know, perhaps?" Kira asks, dragging out the word "mother." Kira won't stop asking questions if she's brushed aside like a child. This is their home, too, and the twins hate nothing more than being coddled—or, gods forbid, managed.

Lady Isobel replies before the queen finishes another sip of tea. "Verralon is rumored to be raiding again, and Ellandelle has called for aid, my dear. Verralon's counter-argument is that they aren't raiding, but tracking and stopping raiders from hiding out in the Tyberon Islands. With their history and reputation, perhaps the truth lies somewhere in the middle. I mean, they call their king a warlord, for goodness' sake! So undignified. Can you imagine? Being called a 'war-lady'?" she replies with a pat on Kira's knee, trying and failing to keep things light.

"They're probably treasure hunting. Looking for the lost Auctus treasury," another lady interrupts, giggling as she drops a plate of cookies before the queen.

"They're little more than pirates, always treasure hunting after monsters, rumors, and myths," Kira says, biting into one of the cookies.

"Ah yes, but what treasures are they hunting? Surely not an old wives' tale of a hoard at the bottom of the sea. Gold, goods, ships, or Adepts are more their style," Isobel teases.

"Probably all of the above. My husband has asked the young warlord, Ezra, to come for a visit. It should line up nicely with a wedding here," Queen Naomi says, tilting her head toward me. Here we go.

"Has there been a new proposal that is worthy of consideration, Your Grace?" I ask, trying to keep my voice from wavering despite knowing I've failed. I take a deep breath in through my nose and slowly out through my mouth, trying to clear my mind. I fail.

Her approval means a lot more to me than it should. She's the closest thing to a mother I've ever known. She's also an excellent example of grace, decorum, and determination while being true to herself and maintaining an identity separate from her husband. Pushy and sometimes manipulative, it's a necessary part of her role, but her ambition stems from a good heart.

Isobel ignores my question. "Perhaps we could use Lord Ezra's visit to our advantage if he answers our invitation. He's new to his title since his father's unexpected passing, and at just thirty-five years old, he remains unmarried. You have two lovely daughters, and Verralon would be a fearsome ally."

For all we know about Verralon's inner workings, he could have six wives and keep them all locked together in a root cellar. We don't even know how many members there are within the Verralon line of succession. He could already be married. Already have heirs. Kira and Iris exchange glances, but they're too well-trained to let any emotion show on their porcelain faces. Kira's sharp jaw twitches, though.

Fifteen or so years ago, Ezra's father and the then-Verralon warlord, Lord Terald, came for a rare visit. I can't remember the specifics, other than being paraded before Terald and the small Verralon delegation like a doll. He patted my head, mumbled something to his wife about pathways to meet their ends, and dismissed me.

Terald was somehow insulted later during his stay. I recall Isobel later complaining that it was minor and he was having a royal tantrum. Not long after, Verralon began hammering us up and down the less-protected southern coast.

I was young and had a Vision anticipating a larger-scale attack. It was one of my earlier Visions, and my Sight still wasn't trusted. It still isn't, to my eternal frustration. So much pain and loss might have been prevented otherwise, but who trusts an army to the musings of a ten-year-old?

Tobias fought with the king to grant permission to bring me closer to the Summer Palace to enhance my Vision through proximity, but we ran out of time with the adults bickering. The need to be closer was the only reason we were there in the first place.

Witnessing Verralon's anger when mildly insulted would make anyone hesitate to not cooperate with them. Who would want to risk their wrath?

Soon after we returned, Hiro apologized for doubting me and placed greater trust in my Sight, even though I was still a child and hadn't even begun my next step of training. Yet many still doubt, despite the king's faith. Whether it's my age, my gender, or the inherent skepticism of trusting words that can't be proven until it's too late, the doubt lingers. Reaching Master level should help, but being the messenger is a thankless job—something ingrained in me from the start. Tobias has decades of experience, but he's also a man, a soldier, and a politician. By the time I reach his age, things might be different—but probably not. He's constantly challenged, doubted, and questioned, just as I will be.

Isobel continues generating ideas about how to marry one of the twins into Verralon without sparing a moment for the tension among the young ladies around her. A cousin would do in a pinch, but any connection to the crown would be acceptable in her eyes. As someone who, herself, was married off for a political match as a child, she should know better, but tradition is hard to overcome.

"He'd probably be more interested in Lydia," Isobel says, the excitement of strategy shining in her dark eyes. "You know how they're rumored to collect Adepts and weaponize them. It's the primary reason their fleet is so feared. As long as those weapons are on our side, Lydia might be the play if we're desperate for their alliance. As much as I dislike the idea, sometimes we have to make sacrifices to achieve our goals." Easy to say when she's not the one being sacrificed.

It's as though I'm not sitting right here. The huff of my breath turns every eye toward me, including Tiernan's. His eyes meet mine for a heartbeat. He heard Isobel's words. We aren't exactly whispering, but his small smile is sympathy enough to remind me that I'm more than a pawn.

"Lydia, dear," Queen Naomi interrupts. "No need to worry. We need to keep you here with us, close to the crown. No adventure across the sea for you. Kira and Iris will be the adventurers. They're much more suited to representing our interests abroad."

"Mother, you cannot be serious about one of us going to live with those people. He's old enough to be our father," Kira jumps to her feet, her hands balled into fists so tight that her knuckles are white.

"Oh, please!" Isobel chuckles. "Fifteen years is nothing! My first husband was twenty-seven years my senior, and I grew to love and appreciate him deeply and then reaped the rewards of widowhood. There are worse things than an older man. At least an older man knows where things belong." She winks.

Kira blushes.

Iris keeps her face under greater control, but the rage simmers under her jaw as it flexes and relaxes repeatedly. A waltz could start if it kept time to her clench and unclench, but she remains silent.

"Verralon is full of mercenaries with no honor. I, for one, will never agree to this." Kira stomps toward the door, making a dramatic exit.

"Kira, you will stop this outburst at once and sit back down," the queen orders calmly. She doesn't even look up from slowly stirring her tea. "Nothing has been decided, and you've never even met Lord Ezra. Let him come, and we'll see which way the wind blows. In the meantime, you will hold your tongue and do what is asked of you by your king for the benefit of your country, and you will wear a damn dress while you do it."

Naomi never raises her voice or twitches a muscle on her flaw-less, ageless face. She never changes her light or melodic tone, but the order is clear as if the king himself signed it into law. No one is above sacrifice for our country if called to serve, especially not a royal family member. They are an example to all others.

Kira seethes but settles back into her seat, a feat unto itself. Iris's jaw continues to clench, but she doesn't say a word, her eyes darting back and forth between her sister and mother. The wheels in her head are practically squeaking.

Isobel breaks the tension. "Now that we know how you feel about it, perhaps we should get back to why my queen asked you ladies to attend us today. Verralon's leadership, including the warlord himself, has been invited and will be here in about eight weeks—if he deigns to accept our invitation. We plan to throw a party for his arrival and align it with Lydia's birthday celebrations, but the truth runs deeper than that, as it often does."

Queen Naomi jumps in. "The news across the sea is, frankly, bleak. No one knows the Aperion better than the sailors of Verralon. They've caught and punished many of the slavers and... interrogated them for information. Right now, we need them more than they need us, and it would be foolish to forget that."

Lady Isobel pauses to pick out a cookie from a plate, but she looks back at me once her selection is made. "Lydia, we need your Sight, which will require you to attend multiple meetings and events to observe things we might miss. We need you to remain close to

Ezra but guard our secrets well. He might be distracted by your rare Sight and let something slip. They don't have a Visionary Seer, as far as we know. Are you up to the task, my dear, or will your birthday and possible upcoming transitions be a distraction?"

"Not distracted. Thank you for trusting me to represent Silvanisi," I say confidently, unblinking and steadfast when I'm anything but. If I'm to be a spy, I want to be prepared. If there's a chance that they need me, maybe I can use it to my advantage. Demonstrating my usefulness could bolster my case to remain here when Ryo ascends to the throne. Tobias would use this request as currency, so why can't I?

The queen nods and stands, ending the conversation. We curtsy to the queen and Lady Isobel, who looks at me sadly, leaning toward pity. She stops me before we leave, grabbing my bare hand before I can pull on my glove.

"Don't worry too much, dear. I may not be a Seer, but I know it will all work out as it should. Stay on this path," Isobel whispers cryptically, her left eye squeezing half-shut—not quite a wink, but more than a tick. This is all a game to her.

CHAPTER 11
LYDIA

Tiernan's gray eyes keep scanning me on our return to the inner wall. They swing from curious to frustrated to disappointed before returning to curious. I'm not usually uncomfortable being scrutinized. It's a reality of my birth and situation, but this is different. Or today I'm feeling different about it. Or it's possible I'm just angling for a fight.

I straighten my spine a smidge. "Why are you my shadow today, Tiernan? The truth, please." Puffs of air punctuate each word while we weave through the tidy, dormant orchard, racing the fading daylight back to the castle.

"Can I not simply enjoy your company?" He shrugs.

That's a bullshit reply. Uncomfortable silence stretches between us. I'm not going to break it until I have a real answer, and that isn't it. He fidgets as he avoids eye contact. I'll wait. "I was instructed to stay close to you up to your birthday. The crown places great value in your safety."

Tiernan is Ryo's man—this is Ryo's way of controlling. He might think it's caring, that this is how he shows love, but I know better. The prince and I are going to have some very *colorful* words later about boundaries—and about shattering them. I don't need a shadow, and I sure as hell don't need Ryo sticking his nose in my business. I wanted to spend time with Tiernan, to *really* get to know him—not as a job, not out of obligation.

Is it so much to ask for a connection outside of my position? I want love, acceptance, and friendship, just like everyone else. Is that too much to ask?

Fists clenched, I itch to scream until my voice breaks, to stomp, to punch something solid—anything to release the fury burning through me. Damn Ryo for stealing that chance. I blink hard, forcing back the tears. Self-pity won't help. Not now.

Why would Ryo assign his captain to me if he didn't have something more significant in mind than our friendship? Unless he knows of a threat that I do not. My pace quickens. I'm becoming paranoid. Veronica's words come flooding back, slapping me in the face. The minute I see him, I might slap the crown off his annoying, meddling head.

The heavy door set into the battered gate creaks open as I step through. A chill cuts through the insulated velvet and fur, seeping into my bones and freezing me from the inside out. Thankfully, the high stone walls block the worst of the wind, though my coat offers little warmth. I tug the hood tighter, burrowing into the fur.

Iris has already run inside to warm herself. She hates the cold most of all and is probably begging for a marriage that will bring her south. Kira and Ryo wait for us but are engaged in a heated discussion that involves much gesticulation. The discussion is escalating to a fight. Kira shoves Ryo's shoulders with both hands. He laughs, which only infuriates her more. With these two, the reason for the fight could range from severe and needing royal intervention to one of them taking the last biscuit at breakfast.

Circling them, I clock the look in her eyes—she's itching for a fight after that tea. She'll have to wait her turn. I need an outlet, and her brother's a safe target who won't hold a grudge. I'm mad enough not to wait.

"Kira, Ryo's in enough trouble already. I want the first crack." I step between the two. Kira breaks into a curious but satisfied smirk, bowing to give me the honors. "Setting a guard on me now, oh majestic and noble crown prince? What game are you playing, oh benevolent and glorious prince, oh honorable and *fucking overbearing asshole!*" I shove a finger hard into Ryo's chest.

A flicker of regret passes over his face, and he has the decency to wince. "It was supposed to remain subtle. I knew you'd react this way, but the reports of Adepts being taken have us all concerned, which leaves you, in particular, vulnerable. Forgive me for caring." He bows, too much flourish in his movement to make it seem sincere. I'm tempted to wipe that smugness right off his handsome face.

"Besides," he continues, "I thought it would be fun for you to have a new racing challenge. Tiernan won the Commanders Challenge Cup at the citadel on the east coast two years in a row before coming here. You can only beat me so many times before you grow bored."

Ryo's expression shifts, his condescending smirk softening into the teasing smile that always makes it hard to stay mad at him—but not today. Today, he's not getting a pass. Today, he'll have to earn my forgiveness. This is a step too far.

I glance at his pleading eyes, and I know he can't keep a secret from me—but he did. And that stings more than I'd care to admit.

Tiernan coughs from the side, a silent observer of a family squabble. "I've heard you're quite the horsewoman. I heard a rumor about a woman sneaking onto the track and racing in the Royal Stakes last summer. There was lots of gossip about who was behind that winner's mask, and then she disappeared when it was time to receive the trophy. The purse was missing, though. Quite the scandal."

That blame can be placed squarely on the twins. They were the ones who put me up to the race, not that it took a ton of convincing but they are hard to say no to. The Commanders Cup is only open to former and active guards, but the Royal Stakes is anonymous and anyone can enter so long as you are a man. I didn't grab the purse. Iris did while Kira created a distraction, but that's not the point. I should have been allowed to race in the first place.

My blush is hidden by rosy cheeks courtesy of the frosty wind. The race victory is the worst-kept secret in Saivi, probably across all of Silvanisi, but it's nonetheless a secret kept for the sanctity of decorum. Tobias knew, and while he was privately amused, it meant a lot of additional politicking to keep it quiet and not "damage the reputation of the Auctus." Someone will always scream that an Adept competing in anything must be cheating.

Kira and Iris giggle while Ryo snorts to contain his laughter. I spin on my heels and leave them all snickering at my expense, while I secretly swell with pride I'll never be able to publicize.

Tiernan catches up in a side stairwell. He must have waited a few minutes to give me space. "I was only teasing." He pulls my elbow to stop my march down the hall, turning me to meet his eyes. The smile he wears is hesitant but breathtaking. So in conflict with his usual confidence. I can't look away from his annoyingly perfect mouth. For a moment, I wishfully think I'm more than a security posting, a job, an obligation. But only for a moment.

"You should go back to Ryo. I don't need a shadow, and I certainly don't need someone questioning and judging my every move. Past or present," I say, trying to sound dismissive, but it comes out weaker than I want. I hate that.

He slides his hand from my elbow up to my shoulder and glides it to the back of my neck, the warmth permeating through the fabric of my thick collar. His eyes remain fixated on my face. He pulls me in to close the gap, and I let him despite my better judgment. He tugs on my hair just enough to lift my chin. His warm breath cascades under my jaw as he tilts my head toward him. His lips barely brush the burning skin along the exposed column.

I shiver, unable to guard my reaction, and am rewarded with a soft but searing kiss under my earlobe, lingering with the promise of more.

"Lydia! There you are!" Iris calls out. She rounds the corner with Kira. They pause at the end of the hallway, simultaneously registering my proximity to Tiernan. I step back and out of reach as he drops his hand.

Iris mouths a silent *sorry*.

No glance back as I hustle toward the twins, but I feel him still standing there—his energy crackling through the air and crawling over my skin. Their eyes stay locked on the space behind me, then flick to each other in perfect sync, then to me. Without a word, we leave together. Only once we round the corner, out of his line of sight, does the breath I've been holding finally escape. Iris bursts into laughter, but I don't join her. Not this time. I'm too wrapped up in the ache he always leaves behind—unwanted, uninvited, and impossible to shake. I don't know what I want from him. I just know I hate not having it.

"Well, well, well..." Kira teases, unable to hold back her giggle. I say nothing but keep walking away, away from whatever was or wasn't about to happen. Away from what I want to happen again and what I think he might want too.

CHAPTER 12
TIERNAN

What would I sacrifice to watch that woman race, those curls flying like a flag behind her, her cheeks pink from the wind, her throaty laugh teasing me to keep up, her thighs squeezing the saddle while she straddles it and holds on tight to stay on? In this little fantasy, she's wearing those tight leather riding pants I've seen her in, and her dark hair is always down. Wild and free. It's how I like her best. Not the polished, dangerous Auctus representative, not the treasure of the king or the doll of the prince. Only Lydia.

Damn it, why did the prince have to assign me to follow her? The change suits the commander. He shifts me seamlessly onto Seer protection. My boring post outside the prince's door was serving its purpose, free of distraction. Now I have nothing but distraction. She makes it hard to concentrate. Hard to see the risks lurking, the encroaching threats. She makes a lot of things hard. I'm so screwed.

I need to get her out of my head. She's like a blazing fire, and I'm tired of being cold. I want to feel her heat in my bones. A cold dunk in the pools is needed.

Weaving through the outbuildings toward the men's pools is

navigating a puzzle. It's tucked away over one of the many hot springs littered across Silvanisi. They are crowded today. Men mill about, some wrapped in towels, some nude, some still in their full kits, and every state in between. No women are permitted here, and the atmosphere is relaxed and friendly if a bit crude.

Multiple pools spread throughout the long building and vary in temperature. Each serves a unique purpose to the sore muscles of the fighters that dive under. There is an order to be followed for maximum benefit and recovery. Step one is to shower off any filth before entering the baths. These are not baths for washing one's body but for rejuvenation and healing.

I'm too keyed up. I need a cold plunge to get the idea of her on me, under me, straddling me like that saddle out of my head.

I grab a towel and peel off my dusty clothes, shoving them into one of the empty wall cubbies. I sit on the bench and pull off my boots. A man I recognize but can't name emerges from one of the many showers and bounces onto the bench. The wood bends enough to jolt me.

"Captain, could I have a word?" he asks. His intense focus on tying his towel around his waist is awkward.

"Give me a few minutes. I'll meet you in the cold plunge," I offer.

A grimace crosses his face. The cold plunge is not where he had hoped to talk. I don't care. It's best to keep them all a bit uncomfortable and remember rank.

I step under one of the open showers that line the wall to soap and rinse myself. The man meanders to our meeting place, stopping to chat with a few friends along the way. Not a care in the world.

I hold my breath beneath the lukewarm water, feeling the steady rush of the shower against my skin. She's in my bones now. I can't shake her.

I have a job to do, one I take seriously. I didn't rise through the ranks by being distracted or losing focus. I need to refocus on my responsibilities.

Grabbing a towel, I wrap it around my waist and step out. A few

more men are waiting for me now, huddled together, whispering—
but none of them have dared to enter the cold plunge. This is a meeting, the kind of gathering that always piques my curiosity.

As much as I loathe it, gossip is often the quickest way to gather
intel. It's unreliable, though—full of biases and half-truths. Still,
there's always a nugget of truth hidden somewhere.

"Well, I'm here. Spit it out," I growl, not bothering to mask my
foul mood. I'm pissed at my new assignment. Pissed that, for some
damn reason, I want to see her again so soon after leaving her
shadow. Pissed at the whole damn situation and the roads that led
me here.

Maybe I'll get lucky and she'll stay in her room tonight. But if she
wants to venture out into the city... I don't know if I can keep my
hands off her.

Shit, what if she sneaks out in those leggings she wears riding?
Those smooth, tight leggings that cling to her thighs in all the right
ways. I dive into the cold plunge, letting the frigid water seize my
muscles, hoping it'll freeze away these thoughts. When I break the
surface, I swim straight for the gossiping biddies.

"We felt we should warn you after word got around that you're
assigned to the Auctus Seer for the prince. You haven't been on his
guard for long, but he's edgy when one of his men gets too familiar
with Lydia. He mildly tolerates it with his sisters, but Lydia is a silent
sore spot," the man tells me. The small crowd surrounding us shuf-
fles on their feet and averts their gazes. Their various states of
undress make it more ridiculous.

I shake my head, regretting this conversation already. "So we are
here to gossip after all. Very well, you know the prince better than
myself. What am I missing? Is she a former lover?" I stretch my arms
wide over the stone edge of the pool against my back. My irritation is
growing, and my patience is waning. I had come here to stop
thinking about Lydia, and I can't escape her even in a room full
of men.

"Well..." Another soldier hesitates, "When she was... close... with

Lieutenant Maitland for a bit, sir, Captain. You know Brandon Maitland, right? Well... Prince Ryo heard about them... and... went to confirm it with Lydia and walked in on them together... and..."

"Spit it out." So she and my Lieutenant have a past. They seemed like friends when I spotted them chatting. She appears comfortable in his presence. Maybe that's why.

Irrational jealousy courses through me, and it takes significant willpower to rein it back in and keep my face impassive. I'm nothing to her, but that's beside the point. I'd be blind to miss the way she flirts with me. I can't deny that I like it and look back.

She's enchanting. Bewitching. Perhaps it's her Adept blood or her Auctus training or maybe it's just her but I'd like to find out. I'm not the first man to fall under her spell.

"Ryo put him on night watch for a month straight. The prince put in orders to have him transferred. The Seer didn't speak to him for a month and he relented. By the time Brandon's month was up, it was as if nothing had happened, and they were all friends again, out partying with the princesses. We thought you should know the history," the man finishes, his eyes glued to a spot on the stone floor.

I can appreciate his intentions. He's looking out for me. I don't have the history with the prince that many of these men do. I'm the captain of the crown prince's guard now, and someday, if everything works out, I'll be the king's captain. Some of them are jealous of my rise in station. It doesn't take a genius to figure out that some are interested in Lydia, too.

I grunt an inaudible acknowledgment of his advice and dismiss the men. They scurry away, probably to spread gossip.

It occurs to me after bracing to dive back under the cold plunge that I need to look a bit more at Lydia's past. It wasn't my business before, but staying close to her and learning more about her could be helpful down the road in my new assignment, however long this lasts. This is part of the job. It's not personal curiosity.

In the back of my mind, it grates that Brandon may not be the only one of Ryo's men with a place in Lydia's history or heart. It shouldn't matter. I'm not part of her future anyway. I need to focus on the present, keep my head down and do my job. Lydia's protection and watch are my priorities. I can't get wrapped up in whatever has been brewing between us. I need to shut it down or I'll drown in her. Distractions can get someone killed, and she's the ultimate distraction.

CHAPTER 13
LYDIA

Days of uncomfortable, awkward distance stretch between Tiernan and me. I'd like to say we've settled into some kind of pattern, but that would be a lie. Tiernan is still my shadow, and with every glance, every brush, every touch, I'm on edge.

He's stopped with the innuendos and teasing jokes, switching from light and flirtatious to nothing but professional. It shouldn't bother me, but it does. I thought we had something—something real. I thought, foolishly, that he was interested. After months of smiles and laughter, now... nothing.

I'm not proud to admit it, but I'm avoiding him. And by avoiding him, I'm avoiding everyone. Including my responsibilities.

I faked a head cold. That bought me a few days. Then I dragged out the recovery, claiming I was studying for my Master's testing. But I spent that time rolling around, not sleeping, fantasizing about a certain gray-eyed captain.

After going to bed early again to avoid seeing Tiernan, I wake up exhausted. It could be the one or two graphic dreams interspersed with a few Vision flashes I jot down in my notebook. Visions of ships crossing the sea, a snow-covered forest, a lynx leaping from a cliff. A jumble interwoven within the mist that needs to be organized.

My dreams, however, are consumed by those gray eyes—possessively watching me, never letting go. Or I'm overanalyzing every word he's ever said, every look he's ever given me, every casual touch that lingers a second too long. If he was interested, wouldn't he have made a move by now?

I want to know him. When I'm with him, I feel safe, *seen*—in a way that no one else has ever seen me, not in the castle, not as just a Seer or Ryo's friend. I like the way he looks at me, but his gaze keeps shifting, and I can't keep up.

Or maybe I'm just delusional. Maybe it's time to move on from this crush.

Colleen finally kicks me out of my room, sick of my moping. She says the place needs a deep cleaning after days of me just lying around, and that it'll keep her busy for the rest of the afternoon.

"Go on," she says, giving me a shove toward the door. "You can't brood in here all day. The room needs a good scrub, and you need to get out of this funk."

I sigh but don't argue. She's right—being cooped up isn't helping anything.

Before I leave, though, she pulls out a dress from my wardrobe— a buttery yellow gown—striking in it's simplicity. Its long, silky sleeves trail almost to the ground, wide and heavy. A deep vee neckline softens the traditional silhouette, and frames my star pendant. The sunny fabric shifts with every movement bringing a dash of springtime to this ceaseless winter.

. "This one," she says with a little smirk, "It'll do wonders for lifting that mood of yours."

I slip it on, the soft fabric brushing my skin as I glance at my reflection. The only piece of jewelry I wear is my star pendant, hanging loosely around my neck, a quiet reminder of everything weighing on me.

"How do I look?" I ask, turning toward Colleen.

She gives a satisfied nod. "Better. But you're not fooling me. I know that star is a heavier burden than you let on." She raises an eyebrow. "Ready to face the world again?"

I hesitate, the weight of her words pressing in. But she's right. I can't keep hiding forever.

The girls catch up with me after lunch, and we start walking together, their chatter filling the air. They're full of energy, eager to tell me about a fight I missed the night before. Kira practically beams as she recounts the chaos.

"So, one of the soldiers got jealous," Kira begins, laughing, "because I was dancing with a new guy, a transfer from the East Coast. That's when the fight started. They went at it like wild animals. The commander had to come down and break it up when it spilled into the streets."

"Was it Amos?" I shake my head, amazed, but Kira glares so I change the subject. "The commander had to step in?"

"Yep," Iris chimes in, a smirk playing at her lips. "Then he escorted us back, like we were his little charges."

I snort at the thought, picturing Commander Cormac trying to maintain some semblance of authority while shepherding them through the chaos.

As we round the corner back toward my room to warm up, Kira grins mischievously. "You know, the commander would be ranked high enough to be a *realistic* prospect for you."

I almost trip, catching myself just in time. "I hope you're not referring to Commander Cormac." I shudder, the image of him too absurd to entertain. "He's old enough to be my father."

Kira nudges Iris. "Hey, he's a catch for some. You can't argue with power."

"Power?" I snort, my eyebrows raised. "I'm more worried about his hip breaking than his rank."

They both burst into laughter, but Iris gives me a thoughtful look as we reach my door. "Well, there's something about an older man."

I roll my eyes, stepping inside to escape the teasing. "You two are incorrigible," I say, but there's a smile tugging at the corner of my lips. I'm not sure why, but it feels good to laugh. Even if it's at the expense of an ancient commander.

"Yuck! No, I meant if Tiernan were promoted." Kira makes a face like I'm an idiot for making that assumption.

"The commander does have that silver fox thing going for him, though. Not quite as polished as Master Tobias, but there's something to be said for an experienced man," Iris says.

"That is inappropriate on so many levels." I shake my head.

"Kira, tell me I'm wrong. Older men have time and wisdom on their side. Plenty of time to work out the kinks." Iris relaxes on my couch before the warming fire, pulling off her gloves and coat.

Kira laughs. "Not my style. I don't even want to know your thought process, sister, but I can't help but wonder why our dearest Lydia here has been hiding out for days on end. We both know you don't have a cold. You aren't that good of an actress."

We all have our masks on when in public, but when we are alone, they can sniff out my tells. It makes it challenging to hide things from them.

They wait for me to say something. Two sets of dark eyes focus on every twitch in my reactions. I lie down on the floor since they took the two chairs. I stretch out on my back and spread my limbs like a star across the carpet. They wait.

I let my response roll around in my head before I speak, choosing my words carefully or else they will lovingly but annoyingly pick them apart. "Tiernan isn't a long-term option."

"Who said anything about long-term? He won't get promoted between now and your birthday. It doesn't mean you can't 'go for a ride' between now and then. Figure out the rest later," Kira says. The wiggle of her eyebrows and shoulders shimmy are both unnecessary and overkill.

"That's not a path I should follow. Tobias would tell me I'm supposed to be keeping my head down."

Iris nods, elbowing her sister, the two egging each other on.

"Screw that. Follow the path that leads to you exploring that delicious man and pissing off Ryo at the same time. Win-win. Besides, Tobias will support you no matter what. You know that."

"I don't understand Ryo's logic, and he's pissing me off. Why would he assign a guard to me unless there's a reason?"

"Or he cares about you and simply wants to keep you safe given the rumors of missing Adepts?" Iris asks.

Not rumors. Facts. Dozens of Adepts are missing, and we have no leads. Iris probably doesn't have all the information. I'm sure some pieces are being kept from me, too. I'm so close to passing my Master exam, I can taste it, and yet I still feel like I'm kept at the children's table. I'm sure Ryo feels the same way sometimes with how his mother tries to maneuver him. All the more reason Ryo shouldn't treat me the same way.

"Oh please. Don't sympathize with your busy-body brother. He can't help but stick his nose in my business. He made a comment about my eyes on Tiernan, and now I need some quality payback," I ask. The twins will help me come up with a compelling petty revenge.

"Ryo is in enough trouble with this one." Iris nudges to her sister. I'm curious as to what the siblings are fighting about today but not enough to ask. "But, and I'd never say this to his face, Ryo never does anything without our best interests in mind. Even when he's being an ass or goes about it the wrong way."

Kira purses her lips and shrugs. "When he's king, he'll be even more overbearing, but you're right. He's always protected us, with any means at his disposal. He'd put walls around us if he could. That's why he asked Tiernan to stay close. To be the wall between you and Asher."

Ryo can't outright ostracize Asher until he's king. We may be given a long leash, but eyes are always watching and politics is a long game. Asher, while despicable, serves the crown and seems to do it well enough to stay in his seat at the table.

"Asher cornered me about his proposal to the queen a few days ago. Tiernan overheard. Asher still clutches to the illusion that I will cave and accept his proposal. Maybe Tiernan has a hero complex and wants to save me from Asher's evil clutches?" I smirk, teasing, but deep down, hope that might be the case. Asher is persistent and also seems to playing a long game. Unfortunately, he thinks I'm the prize at the end.

"Well, what if he's jealous and wants to remain by your side beyond this assignment? A blind bat at midnight can see he's interested in you," Iris says with a sigh. The romantic in her wants to see a fairy tale of unrequited love overcoming obstacles, but all three of us know the realities of our births.

"I need a hot bath. His mixed signals are scrambling my brain," I exhale, a half-whine. My mind clears more easily when immersed in water, muffling my other Senses without shutting them down completely. I walk into the bathroom and turn the hot valve wide open. I don't even ask them to leave before I close the door and slide to the cold stone floor. My head aches, and my eyelids are sandpaper, scraping and scratching with every blink.

With the steam coming off the top of the bath, I strip down and slide into the heat, letting everything wash over me. Kira and Iris are laughing about something still in my room, but the door slams open and closes, so they must be off.

A few days ago, I was with Tobias, discussing my Vision of the horse. How on earth did I end up here, fawning over a man when there are much bigger problems on the horizon? Personal and political issues—hundreds of them, to be precise.

I sink deeper into the water and hold my breath, letting the quiet come over me, clearing my mind. *Clear mind. Clear Path.*

My heart rate slows. The meditation brings me back to a calm center. The bath serves its purpose, and I feel more like myself again.

I wish...wishing is foolish, but I wish I could see my own future clearly for once. Tiernan isn't my future though. I should enjoy the present a bit more. While I can before the weight of expectations becomes my reality.

Ⓣ

THE OPEN CURTAINS let in the abundant morning sunshine of a clear winter day. It blinds me for a heartbeat before my sensitive eyes have the chance to adjust. Colleen must have already been here and decided to let me rest a bit longer. Keeping the curtains closed would have been preferable, but then I'd probably have slept the day away, snug in my bed.

A minor miracle greets me as I wake rested and refreshed. I roll over to my notebook and jot down a few details that are sharper than others. Dream-free sleep is nonexistent. Vision-free sleep is rare, but some nights are lighter than others. Last night's dream was… enticing but sadly, one hundred percent a dream and not a Vision. My groggy mind immediately floods with thoughts of Tiernan's smile and his warm hand sliding over the skin on the nape of my neck. I stretch and slap my cheeks to shake out the cobwebs.

A tray of tea and a biscuit with ham and cheese is on the table by the fire. About to take an unladylike bite, I pause at the note scribbled on a torn sheet of paper beside the tray.

> Lydia,
> I am summoned to Merthaset and left on the tide before dawn. I will return when my business is complete. Stay in the castle and wait for my return. That is an order. Keep your head down and your eyes open.
> -Tobias

There is nothing more in the borderline illegible missive. For a lifelong diplomat, Tobias has terrible penmanship.

Winter sea travel in the Aperion is fraught with dangers above, on, and below the water: pirates, slavers, Verralon's fleet, and sea creatures that pull ships below. Then there are the seasonal storms that rage this time of year, but Tobias is an experienced sailor. He would not leave this close to my birthday if it were unimportant. What do they want that cannot wait?

With Tobias's sudden departure, I now have a glorious free morning and decide to stay in my warm bed and catch up on some reading. I'm snuggling deep into my fluffy pillows, a slow and deliberate *knock, knock, knock, knock* beats from the door. Ryo saunters into my room, interrupting my peaceful lounging plans.

"Good morning. Has anything interesting happened recently?" He's a bit too chipper. "I haven't seen you for a few days. Some might think you were avoiding me." He concludes his teasing questions with half a smile pulling at the corner of his mouth. Damn those twins and their inability to mind their own business and keep their mouths shut!

"Are you here to discuss the logic of demoting a well-trained guard to babysitting duty, oh my dear glorious and benevolent crown prince?" I poke, marking my page before setting my book down. If he's here to instigate something, I'm going to push back.

He hates it when we fluff up his title, the majestic and modest crown prince that he is. He says I'm mocking him, which I am. I feel the same when people call me lady or mistakenly call me princess, but I'm choosing to poke the bear this morning. He's in my space. If he can't take some light ribbing, he needs to consider that before he barges in here to do the same.

"No, not here to talk about any of that. As a handsome and virile crown prince, I don't need to discuss my decisions with you. I came to inform you that your presence is requested at dinner tonight. You were missed last night, but I made excuses. You're welcome." He flops his long body onto my bed and stretches over the blankets. He has the decency to keep his boots hanging off the side and not on my new embroidered bedspread. I try to shove him off, but he doesn't budge.

"What are you after, Ryo? To pester me to death, or is there an actual reason?" I snap, wanting to get back to my book that was starting to get interesting.

"I heard a rumor this morning. Your name was mentioned, and I need to discuss it with someone. Well, there is more than one rumor circulating, but isn't there always? You're my closest person without a personal agenda, so..." he says cautiously, uncomfortable with broaching the mystery subject.

"What makes you think I don't have a personal agenda?" I tease.

He shifts to pull me closer, wrapping an arm around me in a half hug. "Because you are the only person who doesn't want something from me," he says with a hint of sadness to his voice. "Father is going to make an announcement tonight at dinner. He and Mother are quiet but have requested all of us to attend. No excuses will be heard short of the plague. That's a direct quote from Mother Dearest."

I sigh. "I knew this would happen eventually. I thought I would have more time. Wagers on who is the lucky man they plan on holding up in front of me to reject publicly? I hoped to do this part in private and save the man some embarrassment. Tobias is gone. Do you think they waited to push someone on me for when I'm alone?"

My attempts at keeping my tone light and indifferent are foiled by the overwhelming need to throw myself back in the bed and drag my hands down my face. If I bury my head under my pillows, I can pretend to be asleep. It worked as a child. Something tells me that won't work now.

Ryo wraps his hands behind his head, the picture of relaxation. "I didn't have the impression our attendance was about *that*. Father said we need to present a unified front politically, whatever that means. The lynx cubs must be ready to pounce, or some trite expression he loves. You know you are an honorary lynx cub in his eyes."

"Tobias sailed out this morning to Merthaset. Without warning. Do you believe it's a coincidence?"

Busy with the thoughts of what the grown-ups are keeping from the children, I throw the blankets off and jump out of bed. Suddenly, I'm ten again, sitting at the children's table, not being trusted with the truth of the risks associated with my position in the world. I was old enough to see it in my Visions, but not old enough to sit with the grown-ups. Doubted then and doubted now. Disappointing but consistent.

The golden-eyed horse drifts into my thoughts, along with the ships on the water. I am being carried across the water, and images flash before my eyes like the fanning pages of a picture book, flipping from one to the next. I shake it off. Tonight will come soon enough.

Ryo pats the vacated space beside him, and I climb back into bed. We lie in companionable silence for a few minutes, staring at the wood ceiling, studying it like it will magically reveal the truth of what is to come.

He sighs, sitting up, and the bed shifts, jostling me. He squares his broad shoulders, puffing out his chest a bit.

"Asher is up to something. I'm worried we're two steps behind. I feel like a pawn on his chessboard in a game I don't want to play and don't know the rules to." He pauses, taking a breath. "I'll accept your oath request. You were right, Lydia. I shouldn't have denied you, not when it might be well within my ability to do so someday."

He looks at me, his expression tight. "There's this pit in my stomach when I think about having your choice taken away. Too many people are trying to do just that. Everyone is pushing or pulling you, and I won't let that happen."

His voice softens slightly, the weight of his words sinking in. "I'll have to phrase this oath delicately. I can't promise things that are outside my ability. You know that. But I'll do what I can for you once I'm king."

Without another word, he pulls out a knife and drags it across his hand, hissing as a deep red line rises from his calloused skin.

"You only needed to prick your finger, ding-dong. You're always so dramatic. Try to keep the blood off my new bedspread, please." Overwhelmed with the weight of this agreement, I'll take whatever he's willing to give. This small bit of reassurance might never be needed, but it means the world to me. Twice lately, I've had to blink back tears. Tears accomplish nothing. Humor is the only emotional shield I have left. I hold out my finger. Ryo pricks the tip and holds my wound in his bloody hand.

"I, Crown Prince Ryo Rinkusu of Silvanisi, pledge this binding oath to Lydia, Adept of House Sight, Novice of the Auctus, that upon my accession to the throne, I vow to honor her choice to accept or reject anyone proposed or her choice to remain unmarried. I will defend that choice to any who challenge it. I vow to honor our friendship and alliance for the rest of my days."

"I, Lydia, Adept of House Sight, Novice of the Auctus, accept the oath of Crown Prince Ryo Rinkusu of Silvanisi. I vow always to honor our friendship and alliance for the rest of my days."

I whisper, my voice thick with emotion. "Thank you, Ryo."

Tears blur my vision. This is the last thing I expected today, and he's caught me completely off-guard. We both know this may all be for naught, but still, he came to my room. He bound himself to this commitment, knowing it would bring me comfort—if nothing else.

This is true friendship. The closest friendship I've ever had. The love I feel for him in this moment only deepens. I would do anything for him. I'd make any oath he asks, but he would never ask anything of me that I wasn't willing to give. He'd never demand something that might cause me pain or heartache.

Despite his teasing, his pushing, and his overbearing ways, he is a good man. He doesn't show it enough. Instead, he presents himself as the carefree playboy, the fun-loving prince with the dazzling smile. But this—this is the true Ryo. The one who offers the most pure promise to his friend, knowing he has nothing to gain from it.

I question what changed his mind, but the set of his jaw halts me from asking. This won't do me any good while Hiro sits on the throne, but the gesture will never be forgotten. Someone must have said something to shake him.

My eyebrows pinch, and my muscles seize. A burning sensation shoots up my arm from the small prick on my finger, rapid and furious.

I reflexively squeeze my hand tight in his. The burn subsides just as quickly as it came.

A faint swirl of the oath rises from what was once unblemished skin. The oath has been sealed.

A narrow, intricate white band now encircles my wrist, mirroring Ryo's. It weaves over and under his massive black marking, stretching to his wrist.

Though the band is no wider than a blade of grass, I can make out faint words in an unknown ancient language woven into the burned bracelet.

A faint, acrid smell of burning flesh lingers in the air.

My other oath mark is to the Auctus. That swirling spiral of raised white script on my inner forearm is no larger than a small coin, burned on when I became a novice. Once I reach Master status, I will pledge my new oath to my new position, and the swirl will expand.

We sit, the weight of the moment lies heavy between us. In classic Ryo fashion, he can't be too serious for too long. He hops off the bed, like it's burned him and he has to remove himself from the seriousness otherwise it might be catching. "Don't forget about dinner. I'm off! This was... enlightening. Let's keep it between us. Don't want my sisters getting any ideas."

"Ever think of extending this promise to them, too?" I ask. I have to. They've been raised to plan for a political marriage. They expect it but it's still not right.

He shakes his head. "I'll do what I can for the ones I love."

My room becomes a haven for everyone else hiding from their responsibilities. Kira at least has the decency to knock and enter bearing a stolen plate of cookies.

"Hiding out? This isn't like you. You can't change the future if you don't participate." She sets the plate on my nightstand and spots the note from Tobias. She holds it up to me, and a quizzical wrinkle furrows her perfect eyebrows while she reads the brief message. "Keeping my head down has never been my forte. I don't know how you manage." Kira folds the paper back up.

"I've always wanted to see Merthaset in person. See where I was born. What if there are records on where I came from or who my parents were? See the towers and the library. Meet other Seers. See more of the world than just this castle." How can I feel safe here and feel trapped at the same time? I want to stay and I want to see the world. I want to have a home and the ability to miss it.

"Perhaps your new husband will take you someday, or you'll hold a seat at the Star Table," Kira's voice has a distinct bite of disbelief. She wants to see the world, too, mythical, magical Merthaset included. I've heard countless descriptions and seen paintings of the clustered spires, bustling avenues, and entire buildings dedicated to learning, but Tobias has always been adamant I stay here.

"Time to get up and stop wallowing in self-pity or avoiding Tiernan or whatever it is you've been doing in here all day. We both know you haven't been studying. Get dressed before Colleen picks something out for you." Kira storms into my dressing room and returns, bearing a green wrap dress with golden leaves embroidered on it, and a lighten green sash. The thicker wool will keep me warmer than the flimsy silk Colleen prefers. She throws it in my face and walks out, grabbing the plate of cookies on her way.

Fine. I pout. I dress myself and leave my hair down until Colleen can help me. I've never obtained the skill of arranging my hair beyond a basic braid.

I slip on my warmest boots and step out into the bustling corridor. It's later in the day than I realized.

Asher bumps into me almost immediately upon my exit. Has he been waiting for me to emerge this whole time? He uses the contact to put his hands on my shoulders, the appearance of steading a clumsy woman. He's always a little too aware of appearances and perception until he doesn't have an audience, and then he removes his mask. "Just the person I was hoping to bump into. Are you ready for this evening, my vision?" he purrs, wrapping my arm into his crook and holding it tight enough that I can't let go.

He begins to walk. With the castle so busy, I walk, too. To pull away would cause attention I don't need or want. I'd receive a lecture about causing a scene that could reflect poorly on the Auctus from some stodgy cabinet member. This has the unfortunate effect of Asher interpreting my walk for acceptance. He steers us into an unused sitting room at the end of the hall. My eyes dart around the secluded space, and I realize I'm about to cause a scene, negative attention be damned.

"I'm pleased to hear that you're coming around to our future," he says, his voice smooth. "I thought you'd be more of a challenge. I can't deny it's been pleasurable to play this game, but tonight, I'll make my public declaration. The king will announce his choice. You, as a good girl, will accept. I've been patient, but time is up."

He still hasn't let go of my arm, but he hasn't closed the door either.

I pull away, positioning myself between him and the door.

The little sitting room is dark and cold, lacking any fire or light source. It hasn't been used for a while, and a few pieces of furniture are still covered in sheets to keep the dust away.

"We have a different understanding of what dinner tonight will be about, it seems. Excuse me, but I have better things to do with my time." I turn to move back into the hallway. I don't make it as far as I hoped before he reaches out from behind and grabs my wrist. Tiernan comes around the corner into my line of sight. Our eyes connect from the opposite end of the long hallway before I'm yanked back into the sitting room.

My back slams against the wall next to the doorframe, and my head knocks into a painting hard enough for it to fall to the floor. I'm dazed for a moment from the impact, and Asher presses his body against mine, not letting go of his tight grip on my wrist.

"Leaving so soon?" Asher asks, but it's not a question. His grip on my wrist tightens, and I wince. Pleasure spreads across his face. He squeezes a bit harder. The man dares to lick his lips and presses his pelvis into my stomach. Oh, I'm about to cause a scene alright. I'm done playing by these stupid rules, staying diplomatic, subservient, and keeping my head down.

I snap. I pull back and slam my forehead against his nose, the crack of it breaking echoing through the room. Gods, my head hurts, but he's stepped away enough so that I can shove him away. His legs catch on an ottoman, and he falls backward onto the carpet. Arms and legs flailing to grab a hold of anything.

"What is going on in..." Tiernan storms into the room the moment that disgusting man's ass hits the ground. The captain's eyes go wide; two silver moons process the scene.

Blood streams over Asher's chin and neck, down onto his crisp white shirt. He'll have two black eyes for a few weeks. He'll also need to find an Adept Healer to get his nose straightened. It is, without a doubt, broken. What a pity the old Healer might be able to patch him quicker than he deserves. Maybe I should pop by and ask her to be busy for the next few days.

"You broke my nose!" Asher screams, blood on his hands and dripping onto the carpet.

"You deserved it, you piece of shit," Tiernan says, not offering a hand to help him up. He turns to me and holds my shoulders to steady me. I'm a little dizzy from slamming my head into Asher, and the stabilization is welcome. "I guess you don't need a guard after all."

"This doesn't change anything. Your choice is an illusion I'm all too pleased to shatter," Asher sneers, but between the nasal voice, the blood, and the whimper when he tries and fails to sneer, it loses its impact. He storms out of the room, apoplectic with rage and leaving specks of blood trailing him down the hallway along with that dark promise. He shoves two gentlemen out of his way who have the nerve to ask if he needs assistance or a Healer.

I don't think this is what Tobias had in mind when he told me to keep my head down. A small giggle escapes me, and Tiernan peers over like I've lost my mind. I can't keep the giggle back, which turns into a full body-shaking laugh. I clutch my stomach and sit on the blood-speckled ottoman, my laughter slowly subsiding.

Looking down at the red stain on the carpet, I consider how Asher might get retribution. Maybe he will stay away now. I doubt it. Someone so entitled will see a greater challenge to break me—the thrill of the chase.

I'd flee on a merchant ship bound for the continent before I'd marry that man, no matter what Silvanisi needs. I glance down at the oath wrapping my wrist, still fresh and a bit sore. It's red around the edges while the burn heals. Ryo's promise holds me steady, and I take a deep breath.

The door clicks closed. Tiernan surveys me from head to toe and back up again. He didn't believe me when I told him I could defend myself. I didn't need a guard then, and I don't need one now, but his presence offers a comfort I can't deny. Someone on my side. Someone who cares about my well-being.

He takes a tentative step into the room and kneels in front of my seat on the ottoman. His face is almost even with my own. I can't stop myself from staring at his intense gray eyes that are studying my face for any sign of injury or concussion. He must think I'm crazy.

His hands cup my cheeks. "You're such a pleasant surprise," he whispers, leaning in to brush his velvety, warm lips against mine.

I pull back, a reflex I instantly regret, but one he's already registered.

"My apologies, Lydia. That was out of line." But his hands remain on my cheeks. His thumb grazes back and forth against my jaw.

I've had enough mixed signals. I've had enough pressures and pulls. Enough of hearing what everyone else wants and ignoring what I want right in front of me. Consequences and the future be damned. I grab his shirt and pull him toward me, kissing him back. He deepens the kiss with my encouragement. His hand slides to my back, resting between my shoulder blades to slowly press me closer. I go willingly. No pressure is necessary.

His body molds against mine as he leans down, wrapping his other arm around my waist and pulling me tighter. Every ridge and muscle molds against me. My back bows as we fit seamlessly together. We stand as one, a tangle of arms, with his entire form rigid and heated against me. My back arches farther as I wrap my arms around his neck, trying to regain my balance and pull myself closer to him, which is impossible, and yet I try.

Tiernan's arm around my waist may be the only thing keeping me from falling. His lips leave mine to spread kisses down my jaw and neck. My breath is fast and shallow. I grip his solid biceps, dying to be closer. What is happening? Did I just moan?

He tightens then releases and steps back, holding me at arm's length. His ragged breath is as rapid as my own. His eyes bore into mine. Confusion and heat burn in his gaze, but he lets go. The warmth that drew me in, tempting me to reach for more of his heated touch vanishes in a breath, leaving me keenly aware of icy goosebumps spreading and a crushing shiver of a moment lost. He turns around slowly, like it's a painful and monumental effort requiring much conviction. Then he leaves me alone to catch my breath. What the hell just happened?

CHAPTER 14

RYO

My newest binding oath wraps delicately around my wrist, weaving through the gaps in the contrasting larger black oath winding up my forearm. It's pretty. I can only spot the scrolling letters through the gaps. I made the right decision, and I will abide by it, even if it was a snap decision. It may all be for nothing, but I had to do it for her. My gut has never steered me wrong before, and my gut told me I needed to do this for both of us.

That list of prospective brides is burning in my pocket. Seeing her name in my mother's ornate penmanship jarred something deep within me. From a young age, I was told I'd marry for Silvanisi. I'm not surprised to be handed a list of acceptable names. I, for some reason, never expected Lydia to be one of them. Call me naive or willfully ignorant. Both are probably true. I'd been living in a bubble of my own making, enjoying the benefits of my birth while denying that my future responsibilities lie just around the corner. If I can step up, be the man, the king, my home requires. I can step up for Lydia, too. Step up for the one person who has always been on my side. Not my mother's side, the heirs side, or Silvanisi's side.

My. Side.

So I made the oath. I do not regret it. Not one bit. Will she ever need to hold me to it? Unlikely but irrelevant. It brought her comfort, and it was within my capacity to do that for her. To be the one that brings her comfort. To be on her side when she's always been on mine. To prove to myself that I'm someone to take seriously. I can step up for no greater reason than it was the right thing to do. Without expecting something in return. I'm capable. Trustworthy. Loyal.

A soft knock is the only warning before my mother slides in and closes the door behind her, not waiting for an invitation to enter. Not that she needs permission to enter any room in her home. Not that she has any issues invading her children's privacy. Here we go.

Today has had too many distractions already. I need to find Veronica before this rumor of her pregnancy spreads further and, gods forbid, reaches my parents. If it hasn't already.

"Am I to be a grandmother?" the queen asks softly. Her voice is relaxed, bordering on flippant.

Well, shit. It's too late now. "It's a baseless rumor I plan to address immediately," I reply, continuing to dress for dinner.

"I'm not such an old prude, you know. She's been a diversion enough for you, but that must now end. Things are in motion, and it's time to grow up. I spoke to your uncle. It appears his conversation with you was unsuccessful. Do we need to clarify our objectives on this matter, my son?"

If one can move beyond Mother's melodic tone and understand her steel desire to control and protect her children at all costs, then the true power of the crown becomes clear. Maneuvering and protecting are synonyms for Mother.

All too aware of the reply she wants, I say it.

"Veronica is a part of my past. It is time to look to the future." I want this talk to be over before it even starts, and the fastest way to do this is to tell her what she wants to hear.

"Good. Good," she replies, making no move to leave me in peace to finish dressing. She sits on the side of my bed and smooths out her skirts in that graceful and practiced way she's done since I was a child. She can be elbow-deep in pots and dirt, but gods forbid she has wrinkles.

"And what of the names on the list?" she asks, focusing on smoothing an invisible wrinkle on the perfect pleats of her sleeve that we both know isn't there.

"What of it? I told Uncle Oscar to invite the Renatto princess. Is that not what you wanted?" I counter. I know what she's digging for. She's going to need to stop dancing around it.

"And what of the rest of the list? I've been told you balked at Lydia's name. Quite unmistakably." She peers up through her eyelashes to study my reaction. It's not as demure as she hopes.

There it is—the real reason she came to talk to me. I'm glad my shirt covers the new mark; otherwise, there would be questions I have no plans to answer. I should have told Lydia about that list. Then again, I'm sure she's received a similar list from Tobias and the Auctus, not that she's told me. She's expecting a list from my mother and father as well. I wonder if my name is on any of them. If it was, how did she react? I should have told her. Warned her.

"Lydia is not, nor will she ever be, an option, so her name on that list was unnecessary. That's her choice, and I won't let you try to pressure her into something like everyone else in her life. She earned that freedom when she agreed to pursue her Master's class within the Auctus. I won't dishonor my closest friend or disrespect the Auctus's traditions."

"I respect that, my son. Two things I'd like to point out. I'm expected to offer guidance and input as she holds a position in my court. She knows this. The fact that I have not already done so is a work in progress. She's a smart girl and knows it's in her best interest to ally herself with someone influential and the best way to do that is through marriage. She will pick someone eventually. She's too realistic to not see the benefits."

My strings are being pulled again. She shifts smoothly, abandoning her original idea and setting her mind onto the next. By the end of dinner, she'll have formulated a new plan to steer my life and Lydia's, Kira's, and Iris's lives, too. I accepted long ago that this is her brand of love. It's how she was raised, and she knows no other way. I pray I'll never subject my children to this, someday, but never is a fool's timeline. Never doesn't belong on the lips of a leader.

"You mentioned two things," I remind her, bracing myself for an emotional chess match.

Mother scrutinizes me, with love and a dash of pity. "Step back and see how this marriage would benefit everyone. I'm honestly shocked. I thought you'd be thrilled by the idea. Oscar thought you would jump at the opportunity. The gossip is rarely this wrong. You two have always been so close. Since you were children, you've had your heads together. I assumed there would come a day when it would be more. I assumed wrong. I suppose we will have to consider alternatives for you both. Someone influential but close. Asher made an interesting proposal."

Every muscle in my back goes rigid. "I forbid you even to consider that man. Just leave her be to make her own choices."

"My dear sweet boy. None of us are truly free of the consequences of our choices. We listen, we learn, and we make decisions. Each decision leads to another and another. Sometimes we believe these decisions are our own, but they rarely are." Mother meets my eyes and studies me for a moment longer before resuming the inspection of her draping sleeve. She knows it irritates me. "You seem to forget I was once a name on a list. Perhaps it didn't start as the most romantic of stories, but I love your father and we are partners. A team. I want that for you. Is that so wrong of me?"

"I need to finish dressing for dinner, Mother. Was there something else you needed?" I ask, trying to wrap this conversation up. I am not in the mood for a lecture or a guilt trip. She is the master of those.

"Lord Strom arrived from Ellandelle and is attending dinner tonight. I need him happy, and we need to know what he knows about the North Aperion activities. Ellandelle has been keeping things closer to the vest. Bickering with Verralon over those little islets they all use to stash their stolen goods. Get Lydia on board. She's so skilled at getting others talking and seeing things others overlook. It would be a fine quality in a future queen, if you ask me," Mother smirks.

"Lord Strom is here to discuss trade and the raids, not Verralon and certainly not where they hide their ill-gotten gains."

Mother rises from my bed. "Strom is here as the Admiral of the Ellandelle Fleet. They are our allies, and it benefits us both. Ask Lydia to be her warm, charming self. People can't help but love her. Most people would be overjoyed to spend time with someone so lovely and gifted. She will be a credit to whomever she chooses to wed."

She's meddling with my head. It has the effect she hopes for, which somehow irritates me more.

CHAPTER 15
LYDIA

The prospects of tonight have Colleen tittering around the room. I'm staring into the mirror at a face drained of all color. My lips are tight and pale. Deep shadows have made a tiny home under tired eyes.

She's arranged my hair in a pretty and intricate coronet and manages to weave a few flowers from the greenhouse into it.

My jade-green silk gown sets off my pale skin and brightens my unusual eyes. Its long, draping sleeves, wide as waves and trailing nearly to the floor, mercifully conceal the bruise circling my wrist from Asher's earlier grip, as well as the faint shimmer of the binding oath with Ryo. The light, billowing fabric flows almost to the hem, each step sending a quiet ripple of grace through the folds. A straight neckline slashes across my collarbones and bare shoulders—a subtle, modern deviation from the traditional wrap style. There are no embellishments, no embroidery or sewn jewels, only the elegance of clean lines and expert tailoring that flatter my curves and enhance my coloring. My star pendant glints faintly, just barely hidden beneath the higher overlap of the robe's collar. Whatever happens tonight, I will look flawless.

A deliberately slow *knock knock knock knock* thuds at the door. Four knocks. I shout to Colleen to let Ryo in.

"Do I get a royal escort to dinner?" I follow his gaze sliding over my gown.

"You're going to make many men jealous whenever you decide to wed. Are you ready to go?" he asks. A bit heavy-handed with the compliment. I wonder what he's sweet-talking me for. He probably senses my stress and is being a friend with a comforting word. Or he's buttering me up to ask for something.

"As ready as I'll ever be." Am I telling him or myself? It doesn't matter. Tonight was going to happen eventually. Names were going to be presented whether I feel ready or not. I'm under no obligation to accept anything. I don't like being put on the spot, particularly in public. Keep my head down. I thought I'd have more time before words and suggestions, hints and conversations shifted officially to proposals and paperwork.

Ryo hesitates at the door. His mouth opens, as though he wants to talk to me about something, but then he shakes it off and is back to his charming prince persona. Yup. He's going to ask me for something and is waiting for the right moment. We link arms and make our way to the dining hall. We're a handsome pair, passing smiles to each person down the wide stairs to the dining hall below.

Tables line both sides, laden with delicious, untouched platters heaped with delicacies from across the Aperion—each dish a symbol of our trade relationships with the other islands.

The hall is vast, cavernous in a way that demands reverence, its high ceiling rising into a lattice of blackwood beams so precisely joined they seem carved from a single living thing. Lanterns hang from iron hooks, their light diffused through panes painted with the curling waves of the Aperion, casting halos across polished wood floors.

While the rest of the castle delicately balances austerity and abundance, this hall is meant for ceremony and community.

A low platform rises at the head of the room. Behind it, an enormous mural of the mountains encircling the Interior looms over the throne dais, the ink layered in delicate washes so that clouds seem to shift depending on the angle of the candlelight. Tiny lynx painted in gold shimmer and scatter out from the mural.

Attendants move silently, folding and unfolding silk screens to partition off private alcoves. Musicians tune zithers in one corner, their soft plucking almost lost beneath the low murmur of conversation.

This space is more than a dining hall. It's a theater of power.

Ceremony is baked into the bones of the room—where people sit, how they're served, when they speak. I've learned to read the language of bowls placed one inch closer to a favored guest. Of sleeves trailing a breath too long across the table. Of silences that say more than any toast.

And still, every time I enter this place, I feel like I'm walking into a shrine.

Even now, with the scent of ginger duck and citrus-glazed yams thick in the air, with silk whispering over wood and eyes tracking our every step, the weight of expectation presses down like incense smoke.We make our way up to the head table where Ryo will be seated next to his mother, and I am placed closer to the end—a treasure to be displayed prominently, but always separate. Until I'm useful.

That's unkind, but I'm feeling salty tonight, as though this is all nothing but pageantry to remind me of my place. Family but not family. A faithful subject but with divided loyalties. A trusted advisor but never believed. Unkind but not untrue.

Ryo moves toward his seat with that steady, careful grace he always wears in public—back straight, expression charming and light, but unreadable. I know how heavy that mask is. I wear it too.

I smooth my robe as I sit, spine tall—or as tall as I can make it—and gaze lowered just enough to be respectful, but not meek. Never meek.

A treasure on display. A Seer kept in a glass case.

Tobias would remind me that my skepticism is a shield necessary for what we do, who we are, and who we represent. I miss him already. He usually sits next to me but won't return for a few more days, maybe a few weeks at most. A man in elegant but foreign clothing is in his place, and I curtsy to introduce myself. Ryo hasn't let go of my arm and gives it two quick squeezes, a silent signal we've honed over years of diplomatic teamwork. *Can we trust this man? Find out why he's here. Play the game.*

"Lydia, this is Lord Lionel Strom, an old friend of my father's. He is the Ellandelle Admiral, their court representative visiting to discuss some... sensitive issues. For tonight, though, he's a welcome guest. I'm sure you'll enjoy discussing the merits of Silvanisi with him through dinner."

Ryo will be a good king someday. I see the potential in him, even if he doesn't see it in himself. There's a flicker of doubt in his eyes that he can't quite hide. He explains everything I need to know about this man, why he's here, and my role during dinner in two sentences. His tone is light and friendly, almost too casual, but the effort is there —he's putting everyone at ease, even if he's still unsure of his own strength. I believe in him anyway.

"Lady Lydia, it's truly a pleasure. I have heard a lot about you. I met you when you were still a small child, but now you're a beautiful grown woman. A treasure greater than the lost Auctus hoard," Lord Strom says, chuckling, taking my hand to give it a proprietary kiss of good manners with no hint of alternative motive or flirtation.

"Well that's quite a compliment indeed to be compared to folklore." I find myself liking this man instantly. His charm is relaxed without feeling forced or pushy. He has kind eyes, and while a bit older, I'd guess in his early forties, he's quite handsome in his black velvet jacket cut to accentuate his trim waist and square shoulders. A slash of white pops up from his collar, highlighting a strong jaw. He pulls my chair out for me.

I glance at Ryo, silently telling him to keep moving. I have this under control. We've played this game many times over the years. I'm a novelty.

"I'm sorry to have missed Tobias. I enjoy his company," Lord Strom continues, holding the chair. We sit. He pours me a glass of deep red wine before pouring one for himself, a gesture of friendship. "When do you anticipate his return from... Where did he go again in such a rush?"

Ah, a loaded question by a seasoned politician.

He takes a sip and nods appreciatively. "Silvanisi has such fine wine for being this far north. It's a shame about the distribution challenges. The loss must be hard on the vineyards and those who work there."

"Is that why you've chosen to visit us, Lord Strom? Appreciation of wine?" I keep my tone light, hinting at flirting. Most men are vain and more cooperative after a bit of banter, especially from a younger woman. I'm not proud of it, but we all use the tools at our disposal. I may not be as stunning as the twins or as seductive as Veronica and her cadre, but I have some assets.

"Among other things," he mumbles while turning to survey the tables before us.

The doors open, and the gathering stands in unison.

While Queen Naomi keeps her eyes straight ahead, her face a beautiful but cold mask of indifference, Hiro makes pointed stares along his path. Some receive smiles. It's reassuring to see the king up after his most recent illness. His skin shows a sickly pallor, but his steady gate portrays his strength. His body may challenge him, but his mind is sharp and his heart is full.

When they reach their seats, the queen doesn't wait to sit. The king, however, comes over to my end to shake Lord Strom's hand with a broad smile and a small laugh, which he doesn't bring out often at public functions. Hiro whispers something I can't hear into Strom's ear. Strom's face hardens but quickly shifts to a calm friendly mask.

We all have our masks on tonight it seems.

Ryo pops his head out over the table and looks down in my direction. He raises a single eyebrow. *Anything interesting?* I jut out my chin. *I'll tell you later. I'm busy. Piss off.*

He chuckles and bites into the chicken the queen places on his plate dotingly, only for her son. He's such a mama's boy.

His attention is back on something Iris says, pointing toward the room. My eyes follow her gesture and land on Tiernan. Oh shit. I'd hope she knows better than to tell him anything about my sex life. Or lack thereof.

The king clears his throat, drawing the attention of the chamber. A hush falls over the room as we wait with anticipation. "My loyal people of Silvanisi and honored guests, your attendance tonight on such short notice is noted and appreciated. Lydia dear, please come join us." The king says the second part loud enough to be heard, but not so loud to sound like the command it is.

A sea of eyes turns toward me, trying to interpret the frozen, confused look on my face. I didn't have time to shield my surprise. I didn't think this would be so public. I wrongly assumed I wouldn't be made a spectacle. My eyes tear up at my amateur error. My moment of self-pity and weakness cannot be visible to the room, so I refuse to blink and steel myself. I attempt and fail to calm my mind. I pull my shoulders back to appear confident when inside I'm anything but.

The king prattles on, ignorant of the war raging inside me. "She is the treasure of Silvanisi and to all who know her. Lydia, I count you as one of my own, an honorary lynx cub."

We all despise that nickname, and he knows it. He loves it. We love him, so we humor him. An honorary lynx cub is all I'll ever be. He takes my hand and places his over it, warm and kind.

"Be strong and serve to the best of your abilities. That's all I expect," he whispers for my ears only. His eyes soften with pity, and my heart drops into my stomach. I might vomit.

Asher stands from his seat at one of the lower tables and straightens his fussy, cobalt blue jacket. His eyes connect with mine, and my chest constricts. The smirk on his bruised face is enough to bring black spots across my field of sight. This cannot be my destiny.

I'm about to cause a scene.

Keep your head down.

A big scene. A scene I won't be able to come back from, and I'll have to deny my king in the process. Asher won't handle a public rejection with grace and dignity, no matter how diplomatically it's phrased.

Hiro nods and leans down to whisper in my ear, "Everything will be okay. I'm going to protect you, little cub. Stay strong." He then addresses the gathering. "I spoke to my Master Seer, Lord Tobias, before he departed. Lord Strom of Ellandelle is here tonight, an integral piece in the shifting of this Vision. Lydia, will you bless this room and permit us to witness your Vision from your lips directly? We must share this most recent Vision as you have seen it."

Wait. What? My lungs slowly fill back up. The room stops spinning as the path comes into focus. I'm just the messenger. I give a slow but affirmative nod. The pieces fall into place: Lord Strom's presence, Tobias's rushed trip, and Verralon's invitation. All the closed-door meetings over the last few days. They know more. This isn't about marriage or proposals, but it sure is about alliances.

Tobias's incomplete Visions from the last few weeks come back to me. He kept this from me! Our Sight has always been stronger when we work together. He and I will be having a chat when he returns. A loud chat that may involve throwing and shattering of things. But right now, I can't let any of that show or they'll doubt me more than they already do. Keep it clear and concise. Leave no room for interpretation. This is a test. A very public one, possibly dangerous, but a test nonetheless.

An Auctus test? Unlikely.

Unless they set this up. Unlikely.

Tobias is gone. I'm alone. I'll have to act alone when I become a Master. Yes, this is a test. A way to test myself. I can do this. I can be the messenger.

I inhale for five counts and exhale for another five. I thought I was doomed to make a public rejection of a furious and petty man. This, while vulnerable and depleting, is manageable. I'll be left defenseless for the duration, but Ryo comes right next to me, within arm's reach. There's always an inherent risk, but that's the cost of being born with this gift. Nothing about this is safe, but my best friend at my side helps.

Asher sits back down. His fists clench. He raises one, poised to smash the table before him. He pauses right before he makes contact. He takes a deep breath and pulls his mask back on, almost like tucking his claws back in.

The king squeezes my hand and brings my focus back to the task. I sit in a chair brought before the table and place my hands on my knees, sweaty palms up toward the sky. I rub my thumb across my middle finger a few times, letting the sensation ground me. There are more comfortable ways to go about this, but I am obligated to my king. I can't decline. It's literally my job. I prefer the serene privacy of Tobias's office while I re-walk. I can sink into the deep, plush lounger, not this hard wooden dining chair with a spindle digging into my back. I relax my eyes and focus on the blood coursing through my veins. The furious beating of my heart. The drumming in my ears. The strained inhales and exhales of my breath.

Clear Mind. Clear Path.

Anyone could walk up to me and slit my throat, and I wouldn't even know it. I wouldn't hear their footsteps or feel the blade. It demands an immense level of trust—trust that's difficult to build and easy to destroy. Once broken, it's nearly impossible to repair.

Someone could also distract me and pull me out before the mist releases me and my mind is ready to leave, which is painful and can take days to recover from. Hiro knows this. It explains why more guards are in the hall tonight than usual, to protect me and prevent disruptions. Five surround the table, while more are spread throughout.

Five things I can see. I look into five faces in front of me, avoiding

Asher. Four things I can touch: my dress, my clammy fingertips, the uncomfortable chair, and my necklace. Three things I can hear: my breathing, my heartbeat, the hush falling across the room. Two things I can smell: the rich brown gravy on the table and the queen's floral perfume. One thing I can taste. The tangy, coppery blood from biting the inside of my cheek.

The warm, colorful haze builds, clouding my eyes. The room fades away. People mumble and gasp in the back of my mind, but even that goes quiet as I step into the multi-colored fog enveloping me in every color of the rainbow. I can no longer see, hear, taste, touch, or smell anyone around me. My mind isn't in the dining hall. It's in a different place, at a different time.

The path is easy to retrace through the trees, tamped down after so many strolls. I repeat my Vision, word for word, following that worn trail. I describe every detail, from the weather to the phase of the moon. I operate in facts only.

As I reach the point when I see the harbor and disclose the fleet of ships approaching, someone bumps the table into me, knocking me out of the rickety chair and onto the floor. My hip lands hard, and then my head makes contact as I'm brutally pulled out of the Vision. The room is in an uproar I was numb to while within the Vision. My muscles seize from the rapid release of my locked-down Senses. My eyes can't focus. Even the dim light is too much. My head throbs, and my body shakes and shivers. I reach up to dig my knuckles against my temples and squeeze my eyes shut, unable to handle the over-whelming onslaught to my Senses. I might vomit. Yup. I'm going to vomit in the middle of an uproar. So much for keeping my head down and not causing a scene.

Ryo maneuvers me into an alcove behind the table on shaky legs to compose myself. "Stay here. I'l take care of this. I'm so sorry, Lydia." He closes a curtain, knowing the darkness will help for my eyes to recover.

No one else seems to notice I've moved. The hall is a churning wave of fear and commotion. Men shout over one another. A glass shatters. Women openly weep.

Maybe the cynics will finally believe me. A silly girl, an untrustworthy Adept, an Auctus weapon preaching about dreams. The future I laid out works against them, or for them, or they need time to figure out how to use it to their benefit. If I were a man, they'd believe me without question. No. That's not true. They doubt Tobias, too. They believe we lie and manipulate and maneuver for power, just like them.

Dizziness hits like a crashing wave, and I stumble to a bench, pressing the heels of my palms into each side of my head. A slow, deliberate breath in for five counts, out for five, but the nausea claws at my stomach, and the room keeps spinning. Struggling to steady myself, lungs desperate for air, each breath feels shallow and fleeting. The world blurs, but Tiernan's presence cuts through the fog. When did he slip behind the curtain? My fuzzy mind fights to recall, but it doesn't matter. He's here now.

"What the fuck was that?" he shouts. "How have you been able to go about your life for the last few days with *that* repeating in your mind nightly? Why the hell is this the first anyone has heard about this? The castle burning, a mass invasion, Lydia? Really?"

Tiernan's voice is growing louder and more accusatory, each question hammering a rusty nail straight into my head.

"Is this what you're trained to do? Is this how the Auctus manipulates us all? Is that where Tobias ran off? To control the situation to your advantage and leave the rest of us to die? This is my life. I'm a soldier. How could you keep this from...? I thought I knew you... trusted you. I...thought we were...Who gets *blessed* with your trust?" Tiernan throws out the word *blessed* like it's trash.

I'm exhausted and broken. I should be used to interrogations about my loyalties. I look into his eyes and see his disgust, anger, and hurt at what he interprets to be a betrayal.

"That's not how it works," I grumble, my fingers making slow circles on my temples, anything to alleviate the immense pressure. Bed. I need my bed. Is it possible to have sore eyeballs? "Sharing an incomplete Vision is dangerous. I know. I've seen the ramifications firsthand. Please forgive me for using my *blessing* when my king commands." I'm also loyal enough to my king to follow his desired protocols on using my Sight and with whom I share any Visions even if I don't have all the pieces, which frankly, I never have. I don't owe him an explanation, and I don't owe him proof of my loyalty. He wants my trust? This is not a great way to go about earning it. He's not the only one angry and disgusted right now. I can't even look at him. I need to find a dark room. Ice packs and a sedative wouldn't be remiss either.

Rising too quickly, the world tilts dangerously, and I nearly crash back down. Tiernan's hand shoots out, trying to steady me, but I jerk away from him, colliding with the wall instead. Unsteady feet scramble for balance. Dammit—add another bruise to the list.

Ryo joins us in the alcove, his eyes dancing between Tiernan and me, unable to ignore the palpable tension. He extends his hand to help me exit, and I take it, weaving my fingers between his.

"Do you want me to carry you?" Ryo murmurs, leaning into me.

"No." I wince and grind my teeth. "I'll walk out of here with my head high and on my own feet. I'm a Master, remember?" Tiernan can stew in his misplaced judgment alone. I won't have my loyalties questioned. He thought he knew me? He thought he could trust me? That goes both ways.

Ryo takes me back to my seat at the table. Not the one in front of everyone, thank goodness.

King Hiro collects the room's attention again. The ringing whine in my ear takes a few minutes to dissipate, so I miss the first half of the kings speech. "The Ellandelle fleet has made us aware that an armada amassing from the continent matches Lydia and Master Tobias's descriptions. Lord Strom and Ellandelle have asked us to ally with them. We are raising our banners to deal with any threat from the mainland. All merchant ships will be put into use to protect our shores. Thanks to Lydia and her blessed Enhanced Sight, we are granted time to prepare. Let us use this gift to our advantage. The mainlanders believe they can band together to control the sea. We will push them back to their desert cities if we work together."

The scattering of isolated cities smattered down the continent's shores have never banded together in a common goal. Or at least not anytime in recent history. They despise each other and constantly wage war over their limited resources. Their numbers are vast collectively.

But they stick to the mainland, bickering.

If every island in the Aperion gathered its fleets under the same flag, they would outnumber us easily in souls, but we have ships. We are masters of the sea. Well, Verralon are the masters but we are a close third behind Ellandelle. If the continent is cooperating to create a fleet, we need to come together.

The people and governing bodies of the Aperion islands have differences, squabbles, and skirmishes too. But all seven islands share our knowledge of the sea, our considerable natural resources, our hatred of mainlanders, and the cooperation of the Auctus to varying degrees. It seems we have a common enemy for the first time in written history.

CHAPTER 16

LYDIA

Late into the evening after the shock of the king's announcement, the lynx cubs and pertinent cabinet members gather. It might have already transitioned to the morning. A few birds chirp from my seat by the window. It's loud to my hyper-sensitive hearing while I come back down from the void of shutting down my Senses, but the tweets pierce my ringing ears.

The air is thick with tension and an undercurrent of fear. The planning had already started before tonight, hence Tobias's quick departure for Merthaset and Lord Strom's timely arrival.

Asher leans forward in his usual spot toward the center of the long stone table opposite me. His elbows rest on the table, his sharp shoulders tight, while his eyes dig into mine, and I hold his stare back. His mouth is twisted in a permanent smirk. I want to slap it off his face. I won't be the one who looks away first, no matter how painful it is to keep my eyes open.

Tobias will be back soon, but no one quite knows when we can expect him. Many hope he will return with a commitment from the Auctus to join Silvanisi and Ellandelle in the alliance against the continent. Greater numbers of Adepts can turn the tide in combat. A few in the room openly object to the Auctus's involvement in our affairs, Commander Cormac being the most vocal.

"Our intelligence gathering has discovered a link between the largest continent city, Bereg Reki, and the lucrative slave trade targeting Adepts. They're trying to build their ranks by press-ganging Adepts." Lord Strom delivers his summary.

"My information is that Verralon is working to take over the trade routes through military strength. That's the immediate problem in the Aperion," Emmanuel, the ambassador from Renatto, informs us, smirking at Commander Strom. "It's not a weak attempt at an invasion from those desert scorpions in Bereg Reki or any other backwater city. They can't build one decent warship, certainly not hundreds. We are the gateway between the continent and the Aperion, and our sources beg to differ. I'm sorry, my dear." The ambassador gestures his glass toward me by the window. "But you're either pushing an Auctus agenda, looking in the wrong place, or your Vision is plain wrong."

His accusation is a slap in the face, not just to me but to the Auctus. I should be used to this by now. It never fails to disappoint me, though.

"We know there is a threat at sea. We know it will anchor off Cerulean Bay sometime late this spring. We know they'll have to pass around or through Renatto to reach us. What more do we need? Unless we all want to be caught off guard? Who's to say Renatto doesn't aid Bereg Reki in this?" Ryo asks, taking command of the room, ready to start planning. I'm proud of him and grateful.

The ambassador mocks a gasp. I hate him. The man's lack of faith in my Sight is insulting and dangerous. Soldiers die when men in power fail to prepare and distrust a Seer. It's happened before, with dire consequences. Hubris will only lead to history repeating itself.

Ryo's hand rests on my shoulder, transferring his strength and support. Also aiding in keeping me upright. My exhausted eyes dart around the room. Asher is still staring, tracking Ryo's hand.

Asher's back straightens. There's a shift behind his eyes.

Always hunting for a new angle. He turns toward the king at the head of the table, ready to strike like the snake he is. "What we need is a more complete Vision. Send Lydia with a guard to the Bay. She can use location proximity to strengthen her Vision, correct? I humbly volunteer to escort her safely," he offers without a hint of hostility, but his hard eyes glance briefly, showing a whisper of the truth. So this is his opening to separate and surround me with men loyal to him. "We can stop in Stones Cove on the way and muster more guards to protect our treasure of Silvanisi."

Murmurs of agreement buoy up and down around the table. Ryo's hand tightens on my shoulder, but Commander Cormac, never one to let us forget he's in charge, comes to the rescue.

"Lords, I will assign my best soldiers to escort Lydia to the Bay. The royal guard will protect her. We don't need lesser trained men from Stones Cove, which would add days to the voyage with an unnecessary and dangerous detour," Commander Cormac declares. He smirks at his blatant dig at an opposing cabinet member. That's all this is to these men, volleys for the upper-hand.

Asher is vibrating. His white knuckles clutch the arms on his chair tight enough to snap the wood. Twice tonight, Asher has attempted to maneuver me, and twice tonight, he's been disappointed. I need to thank the commander later.

Hiro tips his chin up to approve the commander's plan. *Wait. What?* Tobias told me to stay in the castle. I can't go traipsing across Silvanisi while he's gone.

"You have tomorrow to prepare your men, Cormac. That gives Lydia a day to recover from this ordeal. The escort will leave at dawn the following day," Hiro announces, turning to address Asher, simmering in his seat at being outmaneuvered. "Asher, you are brilliant and irreplaceable with our nation's trade, but this is a time for soldiers. You will stay here." With a wave of his hand, Hiro dismisses the council.

"What's the rush?" Ryo asks. "Lydia needs more than a day to recover. That whole debacle should have never happened. What were you thinking?”

“Don't challenge me publicly,” Hiro orders under his breath. “We will discuss this in private. Later. That's an order.”

I'm too tired to argue knowing it won't change the plan. If I have to leave the day after tomorrow, I will take advantage of all the rest I can get between now and then. I stand too quickly. This blinding pain in my skull assaults every system in my body, making me reevaluate the mechanics of walking. My bed calls to me, the dreamy darkness of the room singing to me like a soft lullaby.

Ryo's warm hand wraps around my wrist pulling me back. He tilts his head toward the king. We four are meant to stay. I will have to power my way through in borderline delirium and try not to vomit on the council table. What's one more scene at this point?

His hand slides down, weaving his fingers into mine. We are never this affectionate in public, but his support may keep me from crumbling. We take the two seats beside the king—Ryo to his right, and me one seat over. The queen is to his left, followed by Kira and Iris. Ryo's hand, still in mine, rests on the table.

“I'm going with Lydia. She can't go alone with a bunch of soldiers she doesn't know or trust. That journey will take at least a week to get there if they go on horseback, and a ship isn't a viable option. It was dangerous for Tobias to sail. I won't risk Lydia, too,” Ryo says with a slight squeeze of my hand.

Queen Naomi speaks after being silent and watchful for the past few hours. “While your intention is noble, that's not up for discussion. Lydia, I'm sorry we surprised you and put you in this position, but Tobias's information coincides with yours. The timing was less than ideal, and we needed to act while Strom was here. We understand we put you in a terrible position, and for that, we are sorry, but your king is commanding you to go, please. Ryo, you must stay here where you belong. You are the heir. Verralon has been invited so we can feel out if they're a threat or if an alliance is possible in the face of an invasion by the continent. We have also sent word through

Lord Strom to see if Ellandelle is open to an alliance with one of their five sons. God knows they have plenty to choose from. Kira, Iris, prepare your minds for the possibility of marriage for your country if we run out of options. Marriage to the crown princess of Renatto is also on the table, as you know, Ryo. Our choices are limited, and we will *all* be expected to make sacrifices in the name of Silvanisi." Her eyes dart to me.

There is something breathtaking about her unwavering confidence that all of us will follow her instructions to the letter. There's no doubt we will do what's expected. I can't decide if I respect or resent it. It's probably a bit of both. She doesn't even wait for a response; she stands to take her husband's hand and leaves us alone.

The minute the door closes, I jump and run to a flowerpot and vomit my guts up. A Master wouldn't show weakness. A Master wouldn't puke, because a Master would have better control. A Master would have known how to handle all of that and not floundered.

"What the hell?" My forehead rests on the wall I'm leaning on for support. My voice sounds scratchy like I've been screaming into an endless void for the past few hours.

"At least it wasn't an order about *your* marriage," Kira mumbles, trying to lighten the mood and failing spectacularly. It comes out bitter. She flinches. "I'm sorry, Lydia. That was selfish." She curls up and sinks deeper into her seat.

"Well, fuck, this is all awful. Can't you have a Vision about the importance of bringing back an ancient holiday of wine and orgies or something?" Ryo asks, helping me back into my seat. He hands me a glass of water and a towel. We all look at each other, reality sinking in.

I can't muster any more energy. My body and mind are broken. I need some time to recover. Operating on zero sleep with exhausted and abused Senses isn't going to help clarify any Visions. I need to find Mabel. The Healer can speed things along, or at the very least, ease the pain.

My mind is still reeling from Tobias leaving, Tiernan's angry accusations, the night in general, and now this journey without any of my support system. I need to focus on this mission. I have tomorrow to prepare and no Tobias.

I bang my head on the table a few times in frustration. I inhale for five and exhale to give myself a moment to collect my thoughts, but instead, I fall asleep right there.

A BLINDING light slices across my face like a knife to my eyeballs. Sunlight peeks through the curtains of my bedroom. Still in my dress from that horrible dinner the night before, I'm somehow back in bed. My boots rest on the floor. Someone must have carried me back here and pulled them off.

Colleen peeks her head in through the door she left ajar. "You're up! There's much to do, and the commander has asked to see you at your earliest convenience. Lunch is on the table. You missed breakfast. Your bath is already cold, and a clean dress is hanging in your closet," she says in one breath before closing the door.

She barks incoherent orders at the maids outside, her footsteps gradually fading from the door. I collapse back into the pillows, utterly exhausted and still not recovered. My Sight struggles to make out the small clock atop the fireplace.

Colleen will keep bugging me until I get up. So I drag myself out of bed, shove a few bites of a cold chicken and arugula sandwich into my mouth, and prepare for my last day at home for a while.

After dressing in a softspun sage green wrap dress and weaving my hair into a simple braid down my back, I head to the commander's office, past the inner gate by the barracks.

Soldiers are up and about for dispatch to various posts throughout the island. Fortifications around the castle are being checked or repaired, and men clean and sharpen weaponry. The area is a flurry of activity, but the soldiers are sedate about their business.

There's no rushing or urgency. I am somehow the only one in a panic. Perhaps it's part of training to remain calm in the face of impending chaos.

I knock on the commander's door, a nicked and scratched wood that could use a fresh coat of paint or a replacement. It's been kicked in more than once. The door swings open before I can knock a second time.

"Lydia, come in. I believe you're acquainted with Captain Whitlock?" Cormac says without looking up from the scattered papers covering his desk. Tiernan sits in a too-small chair in front of the desk, probably an intimidation tactic by the commander.

Ten or so guards sit on the other chairs or lean against walls in the room, but all their eyes are fixed on me. I straighten my spine.

It's a sparse space. Packed full with this many armed and intimidating men, it's oppressive. Claustrophobia spreads up my back and across my shoulders, but I relax my face and slide into the crowded room, weaving a path through the towering soldiers to the empty seat remaining.

"Yes, Commander, the captain and I are acquainted," I deadpan. The chairs are close enough that our thighs brush. I move to slide the chair further away. The leg scraping on the floor screeches as I shift away is jarring and awkward. One man near the back chuckles. I'd be embarrassed if I wasn't still tired, aching and pissed at this whole situation. Tiernan included.

"Here's your escort," Cormac grumbles, ignoring the chuckle. He gestures, mildly disinterested, to the men crowding the office. I glance around the room. My friend Brandon is the only one I know. He gives me a small smile as my eyes land on him. At least one friend will be with me.

"You will all depart at sunrise tomorrow. Your horses are being prepared. This will be swift and hard travel. Our objective is to keep the Seer in one piece. With the threats of the rebel bands and the Adept kidnappings, we need to do this quickly and quietly. Any questions?" Cormac says to no one in particular. He doesn't even wait and leaves us all in the room. The rest of the men shuffle around. A rumble of chatter grows but no one moves to leave.

"You're dismissed back to your responsibilities until departure," Tiernan announces as the men straighten in unison.

One of the guards behind Tiernan approaches and takes my hand. He's tall and lithe with sandy brown hair, friendly chocolate eyes and dimples that probably get him into and out of a good deal of trouble. "I'm Griffin, my lady. I'm proud to have been selected to protect you." He dips down to give my hand a gallant but polite kiss before stepping back and nudging the guard next to him to do the same. Each man comes over and introduces himself. Brandon comes over and kisses my cheek before stepping back and leaving without a word. Tiernan is the only guard left not to have taken my hand.

He closes the door, leaving us alone in the commander's study. He turns, and his eyes lock into mine. I stand to leave, but he puts a hand on my shoulder. His warmth burns through the fabric and presses me back into my seat.

"You have not been dismissed."

"Excuse me? I am not under your command, Captain." I try to stand and leave, but he holds me in my chair. His other hand comes to rest on my other shoulder as he leans forward so his eyes are even with mine. He has my attention, and he holds it, searching my face for something.

"I have been placed in charge of this mission; you are indeed under my command. Your safety is the top priority. Lydia..." He pauses. "I have to keep you safe. You have no idea what's out there. You will do as you're told and follow orders like your life depends on it, which it very well may."

His orders hang in the air. The fastest route is to sail around the coast, but the seas are too dangerous, not only because it's winter and the weather poses problems, but also because we can't spare enough men to protect the ship.

"What route do you plan on following? The mountain passes and through the Interior, or will we follow the coast and wrap around?"

Following the coast on land would be more comfortable with villages to stop at overnight, but it would add multiple days there and back. Days we cannot afford. Not to mention the risks of raiders along the shore.

The faster but more treacherous route is to cut across the Interior. Small tribes loyal to no one and nothing scatter throughout. Mercenaries and criminals hide in its caves and forests. Cults worship old gods through blood sacrifice. Predators roam at night.

"We go through the Interior. Dress warm, Seer. We will be testing those riding skills of yours," he says with no kindness in his eyes. He slams the door closed behind him, leaving me alone in the quiet office.

CHAPTER 17
RYO

The tangled sheets trap my legs, and I almost fall on my face in my attempt to unravel myself, shooting out of bed.

I should be focused on handling Veronica. I should be concerned about my father. I should be worried about a potential war when I've only known peace. But Lydia's departure consumes me. Why won't they believe her? Trust her Visions?

I rest a bit easier knowing my best guards will protect her well. Captain Whitlock, well, I don't like how he eyes her but then again, that's my problem. Lydia has made it clear she wants me out of that part of her life. He may be rough around the edges, but his reputation is stellar. Commander Cormac vouched for the captain personally. I'll deal with whatever is going on there if it keeps Lydia safe.

I can't lie about in bed all day. I might as well address the most straightforward issue first. I need to find Veronica.

I sat down in the middle of the night with pen and paper and wrote out every date we spent together over the last two months and the week she refused to be with me during her cycle. I've never missed a dose of the medicine designed to prevent this exact situation, and she's always claimed to be taking the same preventative measures. Either she's not pregnant, or the child isn't mine. The math doesn't lie and the witches' medicine doesn't fail.

I splash water on my face and toss on some clothes, heading off to Veronica's room on one of the castle's lower levels, courtesy of her rich father.

Raised voices filter through from the other side of her door. Instead of knocking, I opt for the childish route and press my ear against the keyhole.

"He's going to find out, my lady!" her maid shouts. "He's going to know you're not with the child when you don't grow. He hasn't asked for you in over a week. The prince is smart and knows how to count. How do you think this is going to end? Your bleeding came right on time."

"It's going to end with me as queen, you dumb fucking commoner. Learn your place and never speak to me of this again." The crack of a palm hitting flesh follows Veronica's bark. "That damn underground Healer said this would stop my bleeding for a few months at least. Liar! I'll find her and get my money back."

My sisters were right. That particular truth tastes foul in my mouth. Her seduction blinded me, and while I knew she had her faults, I chose to overlook them, focusing on the physical and ignoring the rest. Thinking with my dick.

Fabric rustles and wood scrapes across the floor. "Get these sheets into the fireplace and help me clean up, or I'll sell you onto the next ship to the continent. I need to find someone to get me pregnant yesterday if Ryo isn't to get suspicious. The plan can still move forward. No one has to know."

I don't even bother knocking and step in to see the two women frantically pulling sheets off the bed, Veronica's nightgown covered in blood between her thighs. She freezes when our eyes meet. Realization and fear wash over her features, but a new mask drops into place.

"My love!" she says, shifting her tactic. She would have made a marvelous actress. "My love, I'm devastated. I wanted to tell you first. I've lost our child. I was going to tell you and we could celebrate together, but I'm sure many more healthy little princes will be in our bright future together."

"Veronica, I'm not stupid. I was standing outside. We had fun, and I will fondly remember our time together, but the game is over now. You played your hand." I take a deep breath to maintain a compassionate tone despite my anger at the apparent setup. The last thing I want is for anyone to overhear a shouting match from the busy hallway outside.

"Ryo, I don't understand. We love each other. We will be wed. I will be queen," she says earnestly, giant teardrops streaming down her flawless cheeks. Her plump lip shakes, but she's barely keeping the facade in place. Her fists clench around the bloody sheets.

"We've discussed this already. I couldn't marry you even if you were pregnant. I'd take care of you, love our child, and find a place of comfort for you both, but you know I have to marry for my country eventually. My choices are limited, and my duty comes before all else. You've always known that. You thought you'd be an exception, and for that misunderstanding, I am sorry." What I want to say is *How dare you behave this way? Treat your servant this way? How dare you try this stunt? You'll pay for this.* But I won't. I'll maintain my composure even if I have to crack a tooth to do so. I'll deal with this privately and thoughtfully. That's what a leader would do. The back of my mind niggles that a leader probably wouldn't have put himself in this position in the first place, but I can only move forward.

She's teetering on the edge. She throws the balled-up sheets at her maid's face and shoves her out, leaving us alone. She slams the door behind the maid and spins around to face me. All her beauty that draws men in is gone—her face in a twisted snarl of anger.

"So now I'm not good enough for you? Is that it? I was enough to distract you. Enough to wait on you. Enough to be under you but not good enough to sit beside you? Who is? Some mouse-faced princess from one of the shitty little islands? Some rich merchant's daughter from Renatto? Or is it what you've always coveted? Is it to be precious, perfect Lydia?" She hurls a glass vase across the room—a gift from me. The glass shatters against the wall, leaving a gash in the beautifully painted mural. Also a gift from me.

"I am not marrying Lydia, but even if it were true and I intended to ask her to marry me, it does not change your manipulation, deceit, or lie. It doesn't change our situation."

I struggle to keep my temper under control, focusing on my breathing like Lydia taught me. It's my greatest asset. It's hard to irritate me. I strive to be unflappable in public. It's a work in progress. I've worked hard at it over the years, knowing it will serve me when I become king. I can't blow into a rage at every person who angers me, even when I want to. What kind of king would that make me?

Veronica's shoulders sag, not quite ready to accept her loss. She sits on the edge of her bed, still in her bloody nightgown. Her golden hair is a frazzled mess. I've never seen her this unkempt. I wonder if she gets up before me when she sleeps in my room to brush her hair and comes back to bed before I wake. Is anything about her real? Was it all an illusion?

"Our time together is over. There is no child between us, and I will ask you to stop spreading the rumor that there is. You will stop speaking about my sisters or Lydia. I will be writing to your father regarding your return to his care. I suggest you start packing. An escort will bring you home by dawn tomorrow. Am I clear?" I ask, but it's not a question. She has no alternative but to agree.

"And what am I to do? I'm the discarded mistress of a prince," she whispers, the reality of her situation coming to head.

"I will ensure you marry a good man who cares for you and is kind and respectful. Gods willing, you will live a long, peaceful life, but it won't be in Saivi." A mental list of a few trusted men who have coveted her beauty for years and sought her attention begins to form. I'll do right by her despite everything.

She sits silently. Tears stream down her face. No artificial manipulations this time, but genuine tears of disappointment at the path before her.

She could still choose to make my life hell, but if she's smart, which I hope she is, she will take advantage of this offer. Her father would not grant her the same deal. He'd marry her to the wealthiest man who offered, no matter how old or terrible. I don't want to punish her for one foolish choice out of desperation to hold on to me. I kiss the top of her head, my final goodbye. She doesn't look up.

As I leave Veronica's room and return to the bustling hallway, I receive more than one sideways glance. They all gossip that she's pregnant with my child.

"I won't go quietly!" Veronica shouts behind me, standing in the center of the hallway in her bloody nightgown. So much for not causing a scene. Everyone freezes to absorb every detail to be retold to anyone willing to listen. Her golden hair is wild and tangled. Black makeup streams down her tanned face, splotchy with rage.

"You need to return to your room and start packing, Veronica. This is embarrassing for both of us. You aren't pregnant, and you never were," I say through clenched teeth, taking her elbow to steer her back into her room, but she rips herself away.

"You think you're *soooooo* above me. So much better. You're a joke. A laughingstock. No one takes you seriously. No one thinks you are fit to lead. You're a playboy. A drunk. A child playing dress up. You have no clue how many of the sycophants surrounding you plot your downfall. Go ahead and marry Lydia. The whole country already thinks you will do whatever the Auctus wants anyway. You might as well fuck your perfect little Seer. Everyone already thinks you are. Good luck to you both when the rebels come calling, and come calling, they shall. Sooner than you think. My biggest regret is that I didn't kill you when I was ordered," she growls loud enough for everyone in the hall to hear. Hushed whispers spring up around me increasing in volume.

"Have you lost your mind?" I ask, trying to keep my voice and body language relaxed. Schooling my features into the handsome, controlled, and calm prince isn't easy in a hallway full of said sycophants.

"I don't care anymore. The people are not on your side. They are out for your blood. Yours and anyone who supports the Auctus. When your father dies, what will you do? Will you keep giving away everything we have to Merthaset? Will you keep giving them our children? Our resources? Will you blindingly obey like our weak king? Place the few above the many?" Veronica accuses, standing her ground. I had no idea she even cared about anyone other than herself. Certainly not the commoners she snubs, slaps, and insults.

"I will always put Silvanisi before everything else, before my wants and needs," I thunder, pulling up my sleeve to point to my binding oath. How dare anyone question my loyalty. My life is bound to this land.

I wave to one of my men. He takes Veronica's elbow and escorts her down the corridor, pausing for no one, bumping into a few who step in their path. She threatened my life and shouted rebel sentiments within the walls of my home. Her maid still stands by the door, bloody sheets in hand.

"Please begin to pack up the lady's belongings. She will no longer be occupying these rooms. You may stay in court, if you wish. I can find you a position with my sisters," I tell the terrified girl. She can't be older than sixteen.

"Thank you, my prince. We are all lucky to have you," she declares loudly enough for the hall to hear. I'll make sure she's taken care of.

As I stomp away, I pass a dozen more people pressed against the walls, avoiding eye contact. All the men and women stand waiting for me to pass in silence, the whispers cease. The chatter will resume as soon as I turn the corner, no doubt.

I bump straight into Kira. She bends over to clutch her side, unable to control the hysterically inappropriate laughter. That isn't the emotion I expect, or perhaps I should.

"Well, you've had quite a morning!" Tears run down her reddened face. She tries and fails to regain composure.

"Have you ever taken anything seriously?"

"This is serious laughter. I came to find you and heard your former mistress commit treason. What do you plan to do?" she asks, finally controlling her inappropriate reaction. She tilts her head. I shift under the gaze as she waits for her answer.

"I'm having her removed from the situation and will investigate further. I have a thousand meetings and need to prepare for an imminent invasion before everything collapses all while suppressing a rebellion and tracking down kidnappers. Forgive me for not giving you every tiny detail. My plate is a bit full," I reply, moving to step around her, but she shifts and blocks my path.

"Are you going to tell Father about this? He's in the steam room again, trying to clear his lungs. Mother's worried. The news last night stressed his constitution. Let me know how I can help. We should work together, with Lydia leaving..."

"She will be gone and back before we know it and tell us ghost stories of the monsters she finds in the Interior. She's most likely to make a stone beast her pet and give it some silly name like Rocky," I muse, trying to lighten the mood.

"And what will we do while we wait? Knit?"

"We will prepare as best we can for any eventuality. Plan for the worst, hope for the best," I say with what little confidence I can muster.

Kira pulls me closer, leaning in. "Is Veronica a rebel sympathizer? A spy? Is someone that dumb truly an assassin mastermind?" she whispers, not wanting to be overheard. We know there have to be a certain number of rebels around us. I never thought one would be in my bed off and on for months. She could have slit my throat a thousand times.

"I had the guards escort her out. If it turns out she's just bitter, she will go home to her father, and I'll find her a good man to marry and keep her away. If that isn't the case, Amos will use his Enhanced

Taste to detect her lies, deal with her, and find out who she's been working with, if anyone."

Amos gets results. He doesn't often need to resort to torture. His methods are his own. He is the most reliable man in my arsenal at getting the truth out of someone. I don't care how he does it, so long as he remains loyal. What does a lie even taste like? I should ask.

Kira shifts. "I didn't know Amos was handling that sort of thing anymore. He didn't mention it," she grumbles.

"I don't even want to know." The women in my life will be the death of me.

CHAPTER 18
LYDIA

The door slams closed on the commander's office. The glass on the desk rattles. My skull throbs. My Sight wavers to the side, not fully recovered from the ordeal of last night's dinner—a physical manifestation of the chaos in my mind. I have difficulty finding the back of the chair to stand up. Flashing spots disturb my balance.

Breathe in deep for five, hold it, breathe out. Slow down and repeat until the ground settles. I swallow back some bile and find the balance to walk out.

I skirt the edges of the busy outbuildings, staying out of the way. Inviting warmth blasts through the blacksmith's door propped open with a box. Just needing a moment to warm my hands, I slide through and sit on a little stool behind a stack of crates. The sudden heat sends goosebumps across my skin. If the cold today were not so bone-stripping, it would be stifling here. How does someone work in this during the summer?

Commander Cormac enters the opposite side of the workshop. He's looking around for someone but doesn't spot me. The smithy is empty and quiet, except for the hiss and crackle of the fire.

As I'm about to stand and make my presence known, Tiernan storms behind the commander, slamming the door behind him. His back is to me, but I can see the commander's face through a gap.

I can't sneak out now. Tiernan will think I'm spying. *Shit. Shit. Shit.* I opt to stay, making myself small and silent. It's so hot in here that they won't last long in their heavy uniforms. Then I can sneak out the way I came with no one the wiser.

"Why am I assigned to this guard? I'm captain of the prince's guard, and my place is to watch and stay close to the prince, not run errands for the Auctus. This isn't what we agreed to," Tiernan barks, bouncing on his feet, unable to stand still. His back is tense, his shoulders are straight, and his feet are planted wide. His fists open to stretch each finger to its limit then close into a tight white-knuckle clench, again and again, at a steady pace.

"This is an opportunity, Tiernan, if you will recognize it—an opportunity to further your and *our* objectives and show your loyalty to the cause in the process. Besides, I thought you'd be pleased to leave the crowding in Saivi."

Now, I'm genuinely eavesdropping. His angry words from last night sit heavy in my head, conflicting with the memory of his kiss and his casual touches over the last few days.

"So I'm to babysit now? I understood my assignment with the prince, but Lydia? She's different. I can't do it." The frustration in his voice is palpable.

"I thought you'd be happy about it. Get closer to the girl. You think I'm blind to how you look at her? I see and know everything, boy. No matter, as your uncle and commander, I'm ordering you to do your duty. Plans are shifting, and you need to shift with them. Keep your heart and your dick out of it." Cormac walks out without waiting for a response.

The commander is his uncle? Tiernan's back remains facing me. He stands in the suffocating heat of the smithy and continues to open and close his fists. He repeats the motion a few more times in slow, methodical repetitions. Open, stretch, close. Open, stretch, close.

After an eternity has passed, Tiernan's shoulders drop before he walks out of the stifling workshop none the wiser that I now know exactly how he sees me.

The hollow ache in my stomach tightens, but it's not hunger. Perhaps I thought, foolishly, he would be different. I'm nothing more than my Sight—useful when needed, prized and precious, or a place to lay blame. A target, a burden, but never a person, never an individual.

STARING at the ceiling all night did not bring any clarity.

Colleen laid everything out last night: my favorite buttery-soft brown leather leggings and warmest wool sweater. My black riding boots have been shined, no longer caked in mud that would leave footprints all over the floor. I hold off on putting on the gloves and my thickest hunter green coat with a fur-lined hood.

I finger-comb my curly hair. Sleeping on wet hair always makes it even more unruly, but I had asked for a bath before bed, hoping it would help me sleep. It might be a few days until I can get another. Once the bigger tangles are addressed, I braid it and leave it hanging over my shoulder.

Colleen sneaks in with a breakfast tray while I shove my frozen feet into my boots. "I thought you'd want to fill your belly before you're tied to rations for the next few weeks," she whispers, trying to keep quiet even though I'm already awake and dressed. "I won't say goodbye, so instead, I'll say I'll see you soon. Try not to be feral, or maybe you'll need to be slightly feral. I don't know, but be safe and trust your Sight." She leans down, hugs me tight, and kisses my head.

Shaking off the creeping fear, I dig into a hot breakfast of scrambled eggs covered in sharp cheese, thick, crispy bacon, two fluffy biscuits with jam, and some type of lemon pastry. I'm in heaven and gobble it up with a pot of steaming tea. I wrap one of the biscuits in a napkin and stash it in my bag for later.

Having paced back and forth with nothing else to do with my restless energy, I head to the stables. Wrapped in my long coat that almost brushes the ground, I slide on my gloves against the frost biting into my hands but leave the coat open for now.

A few men are already starting their morning chores. My beloved horse, a dappled gray mare named Burya, is already saddled, and my bags are strapped to her flanks along with my bedroll and a spare blanket.

"Those leggings are going to cause problems," Tiernan says behind me. My legs poke out from the gaping coat as I walk toward him. He surveys me from head to toe, staring at their snug fit long enough to make me forget his words in the smithy. His words might have conveyed his displeasure, but his eyes say the opposite. The man is infuriating.

"I'm not riding across the Interior in a dress. You've seen me in my leggings before. These are better suited to the pace of our travel. Besides, they'll be under my coat. Wouldn't want to scandalize anyone with a woman's legs." I turn back around, checking the saddle.

A man from our meeting with the commander adds a few provisions and a full canteen. He's a towering, stocky mountain with a neatly trimmed red beard that accentuates his jaw and wide face. His bright-blue eyes sparkle, and a giddy smile spreads when he turns to me.

"A fine day for adventure!" he says, extending his hand in greeting. "We met yesterday, but you looked like you were going to vomit, so... I'm Finley, my lady. It's a true pleasure to be escorting you. I haven't been through the Interior in a few years, and it's always a roaring bundle of surprises."

"You've crossed through before?" I ask. Few soldiers are assigned to patrol the Interior. Most follow along the coast or sail in the fleet.

We simply don't have enough men to patrol both, and given the bulk of Silvanisi's population sticks to the coasts, there's little need for the mostly uninhabitable Interior. It makes sense, though, that one or two of the men assigned to this journey would be familiar with the route.

"Yes, my lady, many times. We'll get you through and back and make some friends along the way." His massive hand shakes mine, and his smile never falters. He's genuinely excited about this *adventure*. He has an accent I can't quite place, almost melodic with certain words lilting up at the end. He must be one of the few who grew up in the Interior like Colleen, but her accent is different.

"It's a pleasure to meet you, Finley. Please call me Lydia." I hope he won't stick with *my lady* for this journey. He chuckles and moves to check the other horses.

Tiernan glances over more than once. I can't shake the impression that I'm the topic of his heated conversation with two other soldiers. All three look at me in unison. I roll my eyes and walk my dappled gray mare outside and step to her side to mount up.

Tiernan is behind me in a heartbeat, his burning hot hands wrapping around my waist to lift me into the saddle. I jump away, almost tripping, but I regain my balance. I can get on my damn horse, and he's the last person I want to help me.

"I can handle myself on a horse better than most, as you know. You shouldn't feel the need to babysit an Adept," I sneer.

His eyes narrow, realization washing over him that I had overheard his conversation. Anger, fear, and concern all flash in succession. Hopefully there's a bit of regret in there too. I grab the reins, and walk my horse a few steps away.

Iris, Ryo, and Kira emerge, all three wrapped and bundled tight against the pre-dawn cold. I lean into a group hug. They each kiss their palm and then reach over to place that same hand on my cheek —a blessing.

We don't say a word; words would mean goodbye, and that feels too permanent. The silence stretches between us like a slowly forming barrier, one that will soon become impenetrable.

Ryo takes hold of my face, kissing my forehead and each cheek. His deep ebony eyes search for something. A look I don't quite recognize.

I blink away a few tears that threaten to escape. They will serve no purpose. One manages to break free, leaving a frigid track down my cheek in the cold morning air. Ryo brushes it away with his thumb.

"This isn't goodbye," he whispers.

"Then what is it?"

"It's..." He sighs, searching for the right words. "It's *I'll be here when you return.*" His lips set in a thin line. He nods, patting the back of my horse before stepping back. Granting his sisters some space.

Iris chokes out a sob before Kira elbows her in the gut. It's the tension break we all need. I hug them both, squished between their two bodies, and embrace their warmth, absorbing their love.

"Now go enjoy being surrounded by some fine guards for a few weeks, and remember, the hot springs can fit more than one person." Kira winks before one more hug.

Joining her, Iris wraps me in a tight embrace, and the sisters of my heart hold me so fiercely it feels like I might burst. When they let go, a wave of cold loneliness rushes over me, faster than I can catch my breath. Dread blooms within me as they turn, heading back into the warmth of the castle, hands linked together.

Ryo lifts me onto the saddle. Not that I need his assistance, but we both need one more minute. Reaching down to give my horse a neck scratch, I turn her toward the other men who are either ready to go or getting onto their saddles now. My shaking hands grab hold of the reins. Fatigue is catching up with me, fighting with the nervous anticipation of what is to come, making my heart pound in my chest. He pats my knee once more before he steps back but doesn't follow his sisters inside.

Tiernan commands the space, drawing the attention of his men ready for his signal. "Men, we have two objectives. First, get the Seer to the bay and back quickly and safely." *The Seer*, worth nothing more than my Sight, not even deserving of being addressed by my name. I see how it is. His mood swings could give a girl whiplash.

"Our second objective is to investigate the rumors that rebels are hiding out in the Interior and how we should proceed for the safety of our homeland. No one goes anywhere alone. We pair up at all times. No exceptions. Lydia"—Tiernan meets my stare—"you will stick with me *at all times*. No exceptions. Am I clear?"

Nodding, I remind myself that he's the captain and his men will follow his orders. Fighting with him won't help me achieve my objectives, finish this trip, and return alive. My personal, complicated feelings about Tiernan have no place here. If he continues acting like an ass, this crush will fade. That's all it is—a crush. But I'm no silly young schoolgirl. I'm about to be a Master, and Masters don't get crushes.

"Move out in pairs. Keep the Seer in the center of the line," he orders and reaches to grab my reins.

I pull away from his reach.

"Just to get you in the line, relax," he whispers, trying to be gentle and reassure me but failing spectacularly. He opens his mouth, his eyes soften, but nothing comes out. *Apologize, you ass!* He lets go a moment later.

We pass through the gate, an organized travel party heading into the terrifying wilderness, praying we all come out on the far side. Then we have to turn around and do it again to get home.

I twist on my saddle and spot Ryo, a statue, a sentinel. His eyes stay connected with mine until the gate closes behind us with a thud.

Dread sinks deeper, a lead weight in my throat, impossible to swallow. Impossible to ignore.

CHAPTER 19

TIERNAN

We weave deeper through the snow-tipped evergreens and up the rocky terrain that encircles the island. The Belt is an uninterrupted mountain chain enclosing the heavily forested and sparsely populated Interior. Jagged, high, and impassable in many places, this is where anyone who wants to be left alone goes to hide out or live outside civilization.

Having been raised deep within The Belt, I can say with confidence I've never seen one of the monsters that nursemaids whisper of to scare children into behaving. Predators, yes. Mythical beasts, no. My sister claimed she saw a one-eyed fox once. Father said the dangers came lurking at night, which is why we locked our windows at dusk. I thought he was simply done for the day and wanted us to go to bed.

Lydia is tense but steady in her saddle. Her beautiful eyes are constantly on the move, using the famed eyesight of a Seer—eyes like a hawk that can see through fog or darkness. I wonder how true this is, but I opt not to pry into the details of her Sight. I doubt she'd tell me trade secrets. The Auctus frowns on sharing anything with outsiders.

She's a natural on a horse, but I'm not surprised. Everyone knew it was her in that horse race. If I wasn't sure, her figure in those leggings is a giveaway. Every time she pulls off that long coat, they hug her curves like a second skin. Her warm breath hangs on the cold air every time she exhales. She continues to distract me and draw my attention away from tracking our surroundings. I can't decide if she's doing it intentionally.

I need to keep my eyes and ears open to any potential threat. In these dense woods, it would be easy for a group to ambush us.

On our first night, we stumble upon the remnants of an old building—half-swallowed by time but still holding strong.Dry and sheltered, it's ideal for setting up a rotation. Surprisingly, most of the roof remains intact, and the structure, though weathered, holds. It looks like it was once a hunting lodge, now abandoned and gently claimed by the wild. We move quickly, efficient in our tasks, grateful to forgo the tents for sturdier walls. Soon, a fire crackles to life, casting long, flickering shadows over the cracked stone and ivy-laced corners of our temporary refuge.

Tracking her every move, I maintain a safe distance but constant awareness. Lydia is all soft curves and fidgety energy among gruff, experienced soldiers. What takes me by surprise is her quick camaraderie with many of the men.

Cormac hand-picked each guard, but a few were pulled from Ryo's guard. Brandon is sitting next to her while they warm themselves by the fire. I don't like how close he is or how he keeps leaning toward her. I don't like his dark hand brushing against her pale cheek to brush away a stray hair. I don't like the smile she keeps giving him. It's too familiar how their heads keep tilting nearer to each other. A brick sits in the pit of my stomach.

If I hadn't been warned about their shared history, I might have passed it off. Nothing more than a friendship. Sure, men can be friends with women. I may not have any female friends, but it's possible, in theory. The pit in my stomach ignores the logical part, though. They smile and laugh about some private joke. He shouldn't be that close to her when he's already aware of his prince's implied wishes.

I'm a damned hypocrite.

Another guard sits on Lydia's other side and nudges her shoulder with his own. She gives him an equally stunning smile. It spreads across her face like sunlight across a field at dawn, reaching her beautiful eyes, somehow brightening them in the firelight. Does she share a history with him, too?

Fuck, what is wrong with me? Jealousy doesn't become me. It's not my business. She's unmarried, beautiful, and intelligent. Plus, her position with the Auctus gives her much more freedom than the average twenty-four-year-old woman in Silvanisi. It sets her apart.

She doesn't owe me anything. I've kissed her once, and she's got me in knots. Now I find myself on a journey with her ex-lovers, unable to shake the thought of how much I want to kiss her again, which is an obviously terrible idea.

"Captain, come join us! It's warm by the fire. Lydia's telling us about her first Vision." Brandon waves me over. I had liked him well enough for an Adept soldier, but that was before I knew about his history with Lydia.

I join the group. The information might come in handy at some point. That's what I tell myself when in reality I simply want to hear her speak. I want her attention back on me.

"How old were you? Did you know it was a Vision?" I ask, jumping into the conversation with genuine curiosity. Sight is so rare, and a Visionary Seer is even more so. They are so well-guarded that most people never even cross paths with one in their lifetime. The fact that Silvanisi has two is a testament to their power and alliance with the Auctus.

What did Hiro have to give up or pay to keep her and Tobias at his court for so many years? How did his people suffer due to his desire to keep two Seers close at hand?

"I was about five or six, maybe. I don't quite recall. Tobias had already been teaching me the signs for a year prior, so I had an idea of what was happening."

The large man with the red beard interrupts. "How'd ye know so young that you had this ability?" Good question, but it rubs me wrong that he interrupted her. His lilt slips in and out with each word.

"Well, being born with one green eye and one blue is a bit of a giveaway." Lydia smiles, humoring us, enthralling us with her honey voice as she continues. "I remember walking through this hazy mist, all the colors of the rainbow weaving together to form a wall, and emerging in a beautiful forest, sunlight dappled through lush summer trees. A blanket of warmth wrapped me up tight. The greatest sense of peace washed over me; I simply knew. My Sight was embracing me, welcoming me into my journey as a Seer. I woke up and ran to Tobias in the middle of the night and started jumping on his bed!" Her whole face lights up with joy at the memory. I assumed most Visions were of doom and gloom. Apparently, I can be wrong from time to time.

A few more men gather closer around the fire to listen, every set of eyes riveted by her story. She pulls them into her orbit, unconsciously demanding their full, undivided attention. I'm sure she's been trained to speak to a room and hold their attention. It's part of her job.

"That's so young to be forced to see the horrors of our world, Lydia," Brandon interjects. He's gazing at her with puppy eyes, oblivious to the iron grip she has as she weaves her beautiful tale.

"It's a part of existence, though. One can't embrace the good if one ignores the bad. How would you recognize how beautiful life can be if you focus on the ugly?" Lydia says, although it sounds like a token Auctus statement, hollow and rehearsed. She might not even realize that's the case. She delivers the line with such conviction. "Anyway, not all Visions are bad. I've had many happy, pleasant ones, but people tend to remember the bad news. It's the reality of being a Seer. The plight of the messenger. I will forever be the bearer of bad news, no matter how often I have a Vision of a healthy baby, a peace treaty, or the safe return of those I love."

The men all nod their heads in agreement. They change the subject and move on to campfire stories. What monsters might we find to be real in children's tales? How Duncan spotted a sea serpent on his last assignment along the north coast. No one believes him. The stories grow more outlandish, lost treasure and witches' curses. Gradually, the men each head to their blankets or turn as sentinels. They all take a moment to say goodnight to Lydia before dispersing.

She tugs on the loyalty of each man sent on this mission, pulling each one tighter and closer to her. It's wondrous to watch her spell settle over the gathering. The pang of jealousy that courses through my veins sits like a lump in my throat that I can't swallow. It doesn't ease until she's asleep, positioned between me and a stone wall. I become a physical barrier separating her from everyone else, and I sleep a little easier, keeping her to myself for just one night.

CHAPTER 20
LYDIA

Pairing up is a literal order. Tiernan sticks to my side, giving me privacy only when nature calls. We've been able to ignore each other, the occasional question being the exception. He keeps looking at me like I murdered a kitten, but I am at a loss. Then I remember that we are all out here in the Interior because of me and my distrusted Vision.

"We will camp here tonight."

The horses ease to a halt at Tiernan's command. The men dismount in unison and begin to set up tents, dancing and weaving between each other to accomplish their tasks.

The choreographed dance unfolds before me for a few minutes, and then I dismount, stiff from the prolonged ride. Though I ride almost every day, it's usually in a field or at the track, never for this length of time. This is a level of horsemanship that demands precision and endurance.

The temperature plummets and dusk settles around us as the sun sinks behind the mountain peaks. Splashes of pink and orange streak through the sky, casting a vibrant glow on the clouds rolling over the distant mountains.

In my distraction gazing at the sunset, the burly redhead, Finley, sneaks up behind me. He taps me on the shoulder. I spin with my hand flying to the hilt of my weapon.

"Apologies!" Finley jumps back. He's holding a steaming cup. "I thought you might want something to warm your bones while your tent is set up." He hands me the mug. My quick smile is insufficient for the kind gesture. He pats my back, chuckles, shakes his head, and leaves me alone to finish assembling the camp. I return to the sunset, useless in the middle of all this action.

Trying to stay out of the way, I settle on a log near the fire to warm up, gulping down the spiced mulled wine a little too fast. The warm liquid burns down my throat, sending me into a coughing fit.

"I've seen you handle stronger than this!" Brandon teases. Four of my guards approach, and Brandon is the sole familiar face, although I'm beginning to warm up to the other men. They settle on the cold ground, their postures relaxed. Brandon sits beside me, rubbing my back as I burst into laughter, interrupted by coughing fits. I giggle between coughs, struggling to regain my composure, which only makes me laugh harder as my eyes water.

We enjoyed each other's company for a brief period, and an experienced Handler can do wonderful things with that Touch.

It was one of my worst fights ever with Ryo. He shouted that Brandon was beneath me, which he technically was when Ryo walked in. Brandon served the prince and was missing his assignments and posts because he was wrapped up in me. It was a flimsy argument. Brandon caved easily, which stung, claiming his duty came before his desires. Is it too much to ask for a man to fight for me a little?

Being close to another Adept for a while felt comforting. We naturally gravitate toward each other, sharing things that Laymen wouldn't understand. Now, we're nothing more than friends. He remains respectful, never slipping into snide comments or flirtation since we ended things.

I turn around to wipe the tears running down my face and catch

Tiernan's eyes tracking me from the other side of the fire. His gaze is a physical touch. He's not looking at me, though. He's glaring red-hot animalistic rage at Brandon's hand on my back. I huff, annoyed that something as basic as jealousy is what finally snaps his attention. *Men!*

Brandon hands me a bowl of soup one of the men pulled together. It tastes a bit bland, but it's hot and will fill my hollow stomach.

The riding has been challenging on our way up the front range, steep and winding, at points requiring total concentration. Finley reassures me that it gets easier once we are over The Belt. The forest gets thicker, but the land flattens once we are officially in the Interior. When we reach the range on the far side of the island and have to rewind our way down to get to the East Coast, it will be no different as The Belt mountain chain encircles the whole of Silvanisi.

"Brandon and Luther, you're on the first watch." Tiernan looms over me. I didn't hear him approach. He holds a hand to help me stand as I look up. "Do whatever you need now, and then get in your tent. It's unsafe for you to wander about once it's dark."

"Grumpy tonight, I see," I mutter, letting his outstretched hand hang between us. Brandon overhears and breathes a little snicker.

Tiernan's eyes bore into me. A challenge. His jaw tightens. He might crack a tooth if he doesn't unclench. He can't tolerate a bit of humor when he's in charge. I decide to let him be cranky alone and smack his offered hand away to go about getting ready for a cold and lonely night in my tent.

Cleaning my bowl in the little creek nearby, I wash my face and body with the frosty water and soap. Only a few days in, and I would pay a lot for a warm bath. The hot springs scattered across the Interior will be a welcome sight, the sole benefit of this route. Marching back up to the tent, I pop my head in, confused by the additional bedroll beside mine.

Tiernan follows behind into my tent, pulling off his boots and untucking his shirt. A sliver of skin peeks out as my Sight adjusts to the changing light.

"What are you doing?"

"It will be an early morning and long day again tomorrow." He reaches behind his head and pulls his shirt over his back in one swift motion. All his solid masculine attributes are cast in shadows. The outline from the fire through the canvas gives me a tantalizing silhouette of his sculpted torso. He reaches down to loosen the laces holding up his leather leggings. My comically loud exhale is embarrassment enough, but his teasing bright grin in the dim intimacy of the tent snaps me back to reality. Hot and cold. How can he go from grunts, grumbles, one-word commands, and clenched fists to flirty smiles in the snap of a finger?

"Why are you getting naked in my tent?" I jump and turn around, my back now to him. I'm thankful it's darker here, and I'm hoping he doesn't notice my quick breathing and flushed cheeks with his Layman eyesight.

"I'm going to bed. I sleep hot. I'm taking my shirt off so it doesn't get sweaty and more filthy than it already is. I'm loosening my pants so I can sleep more comfortably. Relax, Lydia, they'll stay on." He leans down behind me and whispers into my ear. "Unless you'd prefer I take them off?" His warm breath spreads a cascade of tingles down my skin and settles in the pit of my stomach.

"Why are you doing that in my tent? Do it on your own," I snap and straighten. As I turn back around to kick him out, I'm frozen at the sight of him without his shirt on, his pants sitting low on his hips since he loosened the laces. A delicious V dipping under the fabric. Practically an arrow. In such a confined space, the heat is tangible. For a moment, I envision sliding my hands across his torso and slipping them below his waist, but I shake those thoughts out of my head. The whiplash from his mood swings is enough to cool my libido and remind me of everything I heard Tiernan say about me and this assignment.

"We pair up, remember? No exceptions. I've been sleeping next to you every night, and it hasn't bothered you before," Tiernan reminds me, stretching out and pulling his coat and blanket over his toned body. He rolls away from me and ends the conversation.

I huff loud enough to be childish, making an equally childish amount of noise. I remove my belt and reach under my sweater to unclasp my bra. Doing it with my shirt off would be easier, but that's not happening. I emit a satisfied sigh, releasing the constricting fabric, but it has the unwelcome effect of drawing Tiernan's undivided attention.

"Why do you wear that? It doesn't look comfortable. Women at court don't wear that," he says.

"Women at court don't ride for days through the Interior either. Riding a horse without one would be painful—all that bouncing. No, thank you. Besides, a bra is usually sewn into the slip," I explain, folding it carefully.

Lying down, I pull my blankets and coat over me, painfully aware of his proximity. My teeth start to chatter. We'll be at the harbor in a few more days. I need to conserve my energy for when we arrive and my job starts. I can't simply close my eyes and BOOM, Vision time. It takes a toll, like any physically demanding exercise. Rolling away, I curl into a tight ball.

"Goodnight, Lydia," Tiernan whispers before his breathing evens out. His warm hand slides over to rest on my lower back, pouring his heat into me. The gesture might be tender or comforting or even suggestive, but he starts snoring right in my ear. Cursing his name in my mind, I scoot closer to his heat and drift off.

THE GROUND IS SHAKING. No, that's not right. Tiernan is shaking me. My eyes crack open, adjusting to the pitch-black darkness. He puts a finger to his lips.

Something is prowling. More than one something from the crunching leaves and low growls.

Tiernan holds his hand up, his eyes darting back and forth before he holds up three fingers pointing in different directions. He pauses, shaking his head, holding up four fingers.

A rustle of canvas from another tent and the slow drag of steel being unsheathed rings into the night. The growls grow, circling closer.

"Stay here," Tiernan whispers.

"What happened to staying together?" I whisper-yell, grabbing my knives. "I'm the only one who can see whatever is out there."

"I can't protect you out there."

"I can protect myself." I wave him off and open the tent flap enough to peek out and see. I wish I hadn't.

Four, no five, hairy beasts circle the encampment. Varying in size from massive to gigantic, they are easily the size of two, if not three, Finleys. The largest and closest is jet black, with scattered scars that peek out between patches of fur. The scarred skin exposed between the fur is gray with tiny cracks and crevices. The white jagged marks aren't scars at all. Stone beasts. *These would not make good pets.* I chuckle in my head before coming back to the threat. These are terrifying predators designed to inflict maximum damage if the stories are to be believed. The elongated snout is wolf-like, but the long claws emerging from massive paws lean more bear. I've never seen a bear or wolf quite this enormous.

The other beasts spread out, taking a corner of the camp. A few soldiers stand alert but still. Brandon and Luther discretely tap each canvas tent twice that's within reach, waking their fellow soldiers up. Amazingly, none of the men rouse from sleep in a panic. Fear is palpable but training takes over. How many of these men have been to the Interior before? Surrounded by a monster from bedtime stories would shake even the most hardened warrior.

The stone beasts circle closer, each pass squeezing their prey tighter, yet they don't strike. They sniff the ground, digging their razor-sharp claws into the frozen earth.

Foolishly, I step out. I cannot stay in that tent, a doe in an open field waiting to be devoured. Tiernan follows, pulling me behind him. The protective gesture isn't quite effective. Another stone beast is behind us.

The large black beast sniffs the air, swinging his head and tracking some specific scent. The beast's solid black eyes shimmer in the moonlight as they fall on Tiernan and me before shifting leisurely to Brandon and then back to us. It sniffs again. The other beasts hold their positions. One digs its claws into the earth, catching rocks and cracking twigs and flinging them into the woods.

We hold our breaths. Snarls, growls, and huffs come from all around us. They sniff the wind. The black beast roars, booming, startling us all. I grip my pathetic knives tighter, willing a shred of bravery into my shaking body. I sharpen my Sight for a bit of additional clarity. The beast's attention returns to me, then it sniffs the air again.

The beasts grumble and paw at the ground. The black one takes one last look in our direction. Its void eyes tunnel into mine, gazing deep within me before it turns away and lumbers back into the darkness.

No one moves. No one breathes. For minutes, we stand, unwilling to question our luck. If we twitch, will they come back and charge?

"Can you still see them?" Tiernan asks, standing ready for anything that might emerge.

I turn in a slow circle. One beast trudges away from us a good distance away already. The other four are beyond my Sight. I exhale. "We are clear."

The men groan. Luther sinks to his knees. Another falls back.

"Hell yeah! The fucking Interior! Am I right or am I right? It makes a man feel alive!" Finley cheers, thumping his chest. The other men sit slack-jawed as nervous laughter slowly spreads throughout the camp.

"It looked at me," I whisper, disbelief and confusion taking over for fear.

Brandon comes beside me and rests a hand on my shoulder. "Are you okay?"

"I think so. Brandon, it *looked* at me. It *saw* me."

"It looked at me, too, like it knew me or sensed me. That'll haunt me for years," he mumbles.

Tiernan watches us, his eyes on Brandon's hand, now rubbing my shoulder. Brandon steps back, scratching the back of his neck. "I'm going to do another perimeter check." He tactfully walks off.

Tiernan pulls me close, wrapping his arms around me tightly. A long ragged exhale releases along with his coiled muscles. "This is not what I signed up for. I should be back at the castle, watching Ryo's damn door, bored and warm. Come on, let's get you to bed. I'm going to put another man on this rotation, although I doubt any of us will get decent sleep after that living nightmare."

I let him lead me back into the tent. He tucks me in, checking each blanket. "Try to get some sleep. We need to cover some distance tomorrow if we want to stay on the timeline."

"Tiernan." I pull his arm back from leaving. "It felt like it sensed me, and Brandon said the same. Did the stone beast look at you, too? Did you sense that?"

"I have no idea what you mean. It's an animal. A monster. Get some sleep."

Staring at the seam across the top of the canvas, it blurs before my eyes. A moment of rest is all I need.

THE MIST WRAPS AROUND ME, *warm, sticky, thick, and suffocating. I no longer feel the cold. The undulating colors—a rainbow of promises—float in the air, beckoning me. It whispers of a path I cannot refuse to follow, though shivers ripple over my damp skin.*

The world shifts and rolls beneath me, propelling me forward. I run, feet pounding the frozen earth. I plunge into the icy river, the water biting at my skin, pulling me down, down, deeper than it should be. The far shore is a dream, firmly out of reach. My breath catches, choked by panic, as I sink, swallowed by the dark current. My limbs flail, but the light of the surface slips farther away.

Hands—strong, unyielding—grip me from the depths and drag me onto the bank. I sputter, coughing the cold from my lungs, and look up, desperate for a savior. But there's no warmth in his eyes. Only shadow.

He seizes my ankle, jerking me deeper into the heart of the forest. My body is torn by rocks and sticks, each one slicing into me like the teeth and claws of the earth itself, drawing its own mark on my flesh. I reach for something, anything to hold onto, to stop this, but the ground offers no mercy. I fight, my free leg kicking wildly, but his grasp is iron, pulling me deeper into the dark, further away from salvation, from freedom.

I strike, my booted heel finding his side, but he only tightens his hold, his fingers digging into my ankle, a vice that will not let go. He rises, towering over me, his presence suffocating.

With a brutal grip, he seizes my throat, pinning me against the stones, moss, and soil, pressing down with a weight that steals my breath. The collar clicks around my neck—cold, unyielding metal pinching my skin, cutting into the thin flesh and drawing blood. I claw at it, my fingers slipping beneath the iron, trying to tear it off, but it will not yield.

His laughter is a low, cruel sound, echoing in my ears as he tugs on a chain connected to the collar, pulling me up before his fist connects with my temple. My skull slams against the rocks, the world spinning, and I taste the salt of blood on my tongue.

I scream, but the sound is swallowed by the sounds of the forest—birds chirping, leaves rustling, water rushing. Someone must hear me. The guards, the soldiers—they were with me, once.

But there is no answer. Only the pull of the chain, dragging me deeper into the unfeeling dark.

"She'll show us the way," he murmurs, his voice a promise—and a curse. "She'll show us the path."

"WAKE UP. It's a nightmare, Lydia. Wake up." Tiernan's gruff voice, sharp and forceful, shakes me out of my Vision. The colorful mist clears in one harsh gust of wind. My Sight adjusts too quickly to the light of dawn seeping through the thin canvas. The brightness burns as blinding pain flashes from my eyes to the back of my neck.

"There are more pleasant ways to be woken up than blinded," I growl, my voice raspy and strained.

He pushes out a solid exhale and falls back onto his bedroll, relieved. "There are more pleasant ways to start my day than hearing a woman scream in terror, alerting the entire camp to a danger only she's *privileged* enough to see. Another Vision? Will you deign to inform us lowly bodyguards of this one? It's not like our lives are on the line or anything important."

"Then why did you wake me up?" I snap.

"Because you could give away our location to anyone within hearing distance and you woke up the whole camp."

Oh. Okay then. Shit. "I'm sorry to have woken anyone," I murmur, sliding on my boots. I push down a wave of nausea as a burning heat spreads across my cheeks, a mix of embarrassment and anger. The audacity that my Sight is a privilege or that I see anyone here as lower than myself. My over-sensitive eyes and headache hurt like hell. Nausea returns, rolling up my stomach. I doubt I'll get any sympathy from Tiernan this morning. He must have used it up last night.

Hot and cold.

I talk in my sleep and sometimes yell, cry, or laugh. It never occurred to me that they might react or be able to hear me. It *should* have. I *should* have known to tell them not to wake me up unless it's a matter of life and death, and now my mind and body are screaming. My eyes are basically blind until my pupils adjust. Until then, they are dry and gritty. I have eyedrops somewhere, but I can't open my eyes enough to find the damn bottle.

"Can I have some privacy?" I ask, angered by the sound of my own weak and dejected tone. I don't have the energy to deal with his mood swings, and I want to get dressed in peace.

"So you won't be sharing this latest Vision? Why am I not

surprised?" He sits up and slowly turns his back to me, reaching over to grab his shirt.

Frustration wells up as I huff, irritated with both myself and him. We're back to back. I hear him move, rustling as he grabs something. The flap creaks, and I silently hope he's gone. Pulling off my shirt, I clutch it to my chest as the cold morning air sends a chill rippling across my exposed skin.

His radiating warmth rolls over me. I'm not alone. Reaching around, a breath away from my naked skin, he hands me the folded fabric I left on the ground. His arm grazes across my bare waist for scarcely a moment.

"Do you need a hand?" he asks, a bit softer than before.

His warm breath rushes past my ear, but he keeps his torso straight, respectfully, and deliberately detached. I can't tell if he's being flirtatious or sincerely asking if another set of hands might help secure my bra.

"No, thank you," I reply through clenched teeth. I take the linen from his outstretched hand, keeping my back to him. My body and my brain are at war. Finding a tiny remaining shred of dignity is hard when all I want is to turn around and wrap my arms around his neck, press my skin against his, and pull his head toward mine. At the same time, I want to shove his ass out of the tent with a swift kick. Maybe we are both hot and cold.

"Mount up in fifteen minutes," he says quietly, still standing behind me. The tingling sensation of his knuckles glides down my bare spine—so softly, I might have imagined it. Before registering the touch, I'm alone in the tent, holding my breath.

Rushing to dress, I pull on my sweater and coat, eager to return to the warmth. For good measure, I add a heavier sweater. The past few days of travel have been bitterly cold. Choosing a clean sweater later over warmth now feels foolish. Everything will eventually smell until we reach the bay or find a hot spring.

Every man stops their task and stares at me when I leave the tent. The steady rumble of chatter and activity a moment ago halts before my foot has even landed on the ground. The silence is its own deafening sound.

"Do I have something on my face?"

"You screamed like you were fighting for your life. It woke up every one of us and even a few farms nearby." Finley teases me with a reassuring pat on my shoulder. A friendly gesture of camaraderie he seems to do with the men in camp, too. I'm one of them now or part of their group, at least. Finally, I'm included in a world where I'm so often isolated. "No harm done, lass. It took us all a heartbeat to figure out Silvanisi's dreamer was having a bad dream. Understandable after what we saw last night."

My eyes fall to the massive paw prints circling the encampment. "My apologies. I'd like to promise it won't happen again, but then I'd risk being called a liar. If it happens again, you all have my permission to come check on me, but *please* don't wake me up unless it's an emergency. It wreaks havoc on my body, particularly my Sight, and the damage can take days to recover." I glare at Tiernan.

"Anything we should be on the lookout for?" Finley asks gently.

"Perhaps if we come to camp near a river, stay alert. There was a man. No one in this group. He was thin and angry and wanted to hurt me. I think I fell into the river or dove in to escape. He tried to take me," I quietly reply.

The men are all listening in silent attention.

"No rivers are deep enough for diving in the Interior. A web of shallow creeks and streams coming off the mountains is all we'll cross. Must have been a bad dream brought on by the stress of the stone beasts," Finley informs me, trying to be comforting. It wasn't just a dream, though. I know the difference.

The horse stands ready, slightly agitated, tied to a branch. Her ears perk up, and her wide black eyes follow me. I check her over, finding no visible issues, and secure my bedroll over my bags. Tiernan's busy with his preparations, but I'm done with his mood swings. Grabbing my canteen, I head toward the little stream. My body shakes as I approach, peering down into the water. It's too shallow for a dive. Shaking the cobwebs from my mind, I bend to fill my canteen when shouts erupt from the camp.

Shooting to my feet, I flex my Sight and scan the forest. An arrow whistles by my ear and embeds itself in the tree on the far side of the creek. Close enough to ruffle my hair. Steel against steel rings from the campsite. Instructions, shouts, and wails echo. Do I run? Hide? Go back to the camp and fight off our attackers?

"She went that way! We need her alive!" an unfamiliar voice shouts. Boots crunch on icy snowpack and dead leaves. The sound is a bit too close for my comfort, too close for me to run and not be spotted.

I duck between some boulders and make myself small, hoping my coat will disguise me in the shadows. The crunch of icy leaves slows as the hunters approach my hiding spot.

Shaking hands slowly slide to the hilts of my daggers. I can defend myself. I think. Sight won't help me in this situation. I need to open my other Senses. Trust my training will keep me alive. I'm thankful that Tobias insisted on self-defense. Clear Mind, Clear Path.

The fighting from the campsite makes it difficult to separate the sounds. I focus on my weak experience and basic knowledge of an Enhanced Listener. I listen. I wait. I can't track the footsteps of the attackers looking for me anymore. This is my chance to run.

Taking a deep breath, I bolt from my hiding spot, sprinting over rocks and fallen trees to reach the creek's far side. I leap over before someone grabs my hood, propelling me backward and throwing me to the ground. My back slams into the icy water knocking the wind from my lungs.

My head hits a rock, blood swirling in the water. I push up off the ground and try to get up.

A man in a ratty, brown cape steps over, blocking the light. The figure pushes down on my chest and holds my head under the shallow water, trying to drown me with one hand. I claw at the arm that's holding me, scratching and pushing. My legs flail to get out of the water or connect with a kick. His grip on my head is solid, unfazed by my fighting limbs. True, undeniable fear takes over. I'm going to die.

My body is lifted out as the man holding me is pushed off. I gasp for air. Another man grabs me by my braid and pulls me to the rocky shore. It stings. Two men stand over me, the one who held me under and the one holding my braid. They both look out of breath and furious from the chase deeper into the forest. Same. My eyes dart over the forest, hoping to see Tiernan or someone from our group creeping toward us to come to my rescue but there's no one. Only me and the two angry men.

"Alive, you fucking ox," the thinner one holding my braid says to the ox who smashed my head into the rocks.

I recognize the thin man from my Vision. He places a foot on my chest, holding me down on the ground, grabbing my wet hair. Tiny rocks press and dig into my back. "She better be worth this payout. We need to get moving before one of her bewitched guards comes after us." He spits on my face, smirking as it dribbles down my cheek. He pulls something out from the back of his belt.

"Hold her down. I'll do it," the thin man says to the ox. They switch places, and a heavier boot kicks my side then presses down. Panic floods my system as he grabs my neck to place a collar around it. I roll and kick to stop him to no avail. His boot presses harder, threatening to crush me with his weight.

I scream until my throat is raw, the sound desperate and broken, but his hand clamps down over my mouth, smothering the noise. His boot presses harder into my chest, forcing the air from my lungs, and the world tilts as my vision swims. My heart pounds in my ears, each thud a painful reminder of how powerless I am.

He releases my hair with a cruel yank, and I barely have time to brace myself before his hand swings back, the backhand connecting with my cheek. The sharp crack of impact echoes in the silence, my head snapping to the side with the force. The sting radiates across my skin, and my mouth fills with the bitter taste of blood as I struggle to focus, trying to fight against the wave of nausea threatening to overwhelm me.

"Fucking Adepts. Think you're better than us. Only willing to fuck others of your kind or use your pussy to control kings. I should carve your precious five-pointed star into your pretty face. Then we'll see how much he wants for your body. It's your eyes he's after anyway," the thin man sneers.

I snatch one of the daggers from my belt and drive it into the closest leg, my grip tight as I swing. The blade hits with a sickening thud, then slices through flesh with an unexpected smoothness. The sensation catches me off guard, colder than I anticipated, but then again, I've never been on this side of a blade before today.

Is this a stabbing or a slashing? The question barely registers as blood bursts from the wound, splattering across the ground, staining everything in its path. The heel jerks back, but it's too late—my strike has already landed. The air tastes of iron and desperation.

"She fucking stabbed me!" The ox falls to the rocky ground. The thin man steps off me in the chaos to help his friend, and I jump up.

"Technically, I slashed you, not stabbed." Survival and a bit of stupidity take over. Maybe I'm a bit mad. With the knife still in my hand, I reach down to slide out another one. The thin man turns back.

"I'm going to make this hurt. It will be slow. You will be conscious the entire time until I'm done with you. He told us to bring you alive, not bring you whole," the thin man says and unsheathes his battered, dull knife. That rusted piece of shit would not make a clean cut.

The thin man swings, his form sloppy and untrained, his balance all off-center. Years of self-defense practice at Tobias's insistence are put to use. I'll thank him if I survive long enough to see him again. I duck under the thin man's attack and turn upward. Using all my weight to throw myself against him, I impale my knife deep between his ribs. It's harder than the slash and must bump against a bone so I shove harder. The man trips back over a rock, drops his weapon, and crumples to the ground with a thud.

It's over before it begins. The life force leaves him before he even hits the ground. I wobble back a step then another. I bend in half and vomit.

The ox is bawling. His wide eyes dart between his dead friend next to him, and back to me, covered in blood with a knife in one hand and another impaled in his friend. My mismatched eyes connect with his, and he flinches. I probably look deranged. I never blink first. I'm in control now. I revel in his fear and let it warm me—a heat pulsing through my veins, wanting desperately to lash out. It's a new, overwhelming, and not entirely unpleasant sensation. A prickling awareness.

I want him to fear me. He believes I'm a monster. Well, I'll show him a monster. I pull my knife from the dead man and move to stand over the ox who held my head under the water.

"Lydia, stop! We need to leave someone alive to answer some questions!" Tiernan's voice cuts through a furious haze clouding my decisions. Reality punches me in the gut as I leap away. Then the shaking begins. I drop to my knees. It's over, or at least I hope it's over, but the grip on my dagger remains tight.

The cold sears through me, soaking my clothes, and the ache in my body feels like it's been carved from within. My ribs protest, stiff and sharp, the weight of something likely broken dragging my every movement down. The bruises already starting to bloom beneath my skin only add to the crushing sense of helplessness.

I try to take a deep breath, but the air feels thick, too thick, and a jagged pain sears through my chest, forcing my lungs to scream for oxygen. Panic claws at the edges of my thoughts, and soon, my breaths come in shallow, ragged gasps.

Then something cold and unyielding presses against my throat, tightening with an agonizing pinch that sends sparks of pain through my neck. My hands fly up instinctively, fumbling for the source, for the cuff choking the life out of me.

"Get it off me!" I scream, my voice raw with desperation, "GET IT OFF ME! NOW!"

The words are choked out through ragged breaths, each second more suffocating than the last.

Tiernan shifts in front of me. Brandon limps, struggling to be held up by Finley, but his crossbow scans the trees despite his injury.

Finley sets Brandon on the other side of the stream bed and jumps over to help me. Tiernan grabs the ox and pulls him deeper into the woods, away from the creek and the dead body.

"Please!" I sob, gasping for air. "Help me! I can't get it off!" I claw at the collar, slicing the delicate skin on my neck. Hot tears leave tracks down my dirty, bruised face. I gulp for air, but nothing comes. Spots begin to cloud my Sight as the world around me spins and tilts in and out of focus.

Finley's sausage fingers struggle to unclasp the cuff. He curses under his breath, reassuring me with his unique melodic accent that it will be okay. He glances down at the lifeless body of the thin man at my feet, pausing momentarily before turning his focus back to me. His soft, soothing voice conflicts with his frantic attempt to remove the collar.

"I can't get it off. Fuck! A little help, mate!" Finley's soothing tone is gone, tension creeping into his melodic accent.

Tiernan appears, kneeling in front of me, blocking out everything while he cups my cheeks. Somewhere in the muffled distance of my brain, I hear him reassure me that he will get the collar off and that the threat has passed but I need to be still.

"Shit. Okay. Focus on slowing down your breathing. This may pinch for a moment, but then it will be off," he whispers so softly it's barely audible. He holds my cheek in one warm hand and reaches behind me with his other to remove the cuff cutting into my skin. He never glances away or blinks until it's off, dropping it at his feet.

We look down. The dull gray metal is dented and worn by many other tragic people before me. I step forward to pick it up but pause before my hand makes contact. Tiernan steps back, giving me some space. I appreciate that. I pick it up and turn it over in my bloody hands a few times, studying each scratch, running my fingers over the latch Finley struggled to open. I throw it down the creek with a scream. I can't rid the world of all evils, but I can take my anger out on this single representation of it.

The metal clangs into a rock, then another, before splashing into the water. It's immensely satisfying. With that final splash, I fill my bruised lungs. It hurts like hell, but I can breathe again. I'm alive.

Tiernan checks the wound on the back of my head from where it connected with the rock. There's a little blood, but it's not too bad. "I'm sorry you were forced to take a life. Did they say anything to you?"

I shudder. "They said someone was paying them to grab me specifically, and they needed me alive."

"Let's get cleaned up. Then we can ask our new friend a few questions," Tiernan says, reaching into the stream to methodically wash off the blood coating his hands.

"Is everyone else okay? What happened at the campsite?" I ask, looking around for the rest of the men.

He heaves air into his lungs, holds it for a few seconds, and then exhales slowly. The silence stretches for too long to be good news. "It's only us left. We were more experienced but grossly outnumbered. They ambushed us. I'd question the men who were on sentinel duty but..." He sighs again, continuing to wash his hands. "We took out all the attackers but those who ran back into the woods. Some of the horses were spooked and took off, so a quick inventory of what we have is necessary, and then we need to get away from here. Do you understand?" he asks, moving me toward the creek, holding my shaking hands securely.

I flinch and pull away, not ready to go back into the stream.

"I've got you," he whispers as he walks me to the water and gently washes the blood off me. "We'll find a hot spring soon and get a proper bath."

Finley is rinsing off, too. Then he helps Brandon hobble toward the water. There's a gash across his thigh that needs to be sewn up. He's losing a lot of blood.

"I have a small sewing kit with bandages in my saddlebag. I'll go get it if my horse hasn't run off." My voice falters. Brandon glances up at me, nodding with a faint smile, barely masking the pain he's trying to hide.

Tiernan shadows close behind me while I retrieve the sewing kit. It'll do until Brandon can see a Healer. All he can do is take the edge off with his Enhanced Touch. It takes massive amounts of energy to heal, and he's pretty darn weak.

The campsite is a nightmare of destruction and bodies. It reeks. I don't know why it's only occurring to me now that death has a scent. I swallow down bile, try to breathe through my mouth and focus on the task at hand.

My horse stands, unaffected, munching on a few blades of grass poking through a bit beyond the chaos. Good girl. I pull out the thread, a needle, and a roll of bandages from my bag. I grab her lead, and she follows back to the creek. I make quick work of closing the wound on Brandon's leg with shaky hands. He stoically takes the needle, wincing and hissing a few times. It's ugly but serviceable. I won't win any embroidery awards.

Finley squats down next to me as I finish wrapping the leg. "He can't continue. He's lost too much blood."

"Lydia and I will continue to the Cerulean Bay. You take Brandon back and get him to Mabel's care as soon as possible," Tiernan orders, leaving no room for discussion from his two remaining soldiers. "Before you both head back, Finley, I need your help questioning the survivor."

"I can help," I offer.

"No, little lady. Stay with Brandon. Keep him conscious. We'll deal with this," Finley says and heads off into the woods with Tiernan, leaving me to finish wrapping Brandon's injury.

He lies back on the bank and closes his eyes as I trim off the excess bandage. I lie beside him and look up at the canopy of trees.

My legs and arms stretch out across the rocks like a star. I start to register the cold seeping into my bones along with all the aches and pains, cuts, and bruises. I need to change, find a hot spring and a warm place to sleep for a week.

Rising to my feet, I snatch a spare sweater and leggings from my bag. Hopefully, an extra will turn up during inventory, though that means heading back to the campsite. If we're pushing forward, I'll need every layer I can get.

The sweater halts halfway over my head, frozen in place as I remember I'm not alone. A glance down at Brandon reveals him still, eyes closed, body relaxed. That gash across his leg could've killed him. It might've, if he were a Layman.

"Don't worry, I won't peek. I've seen all of it before anyway," he teases, and a bare hint of his blinding smile crosses his charming face. "Thank you for patching me up. I'm glad you're still my friend." His eyes stay shut. His body tightens. Sweat beads across his ebony skin as he tries and fails to mask his pain. He doesn't look good.

"I'm going to listen to their questioning. You don't move," I order, the command coming out much more confidently than I feel.

"I couldn't if I wanted to."

Leaping back over the stream, I glance down at the water that nearly killed me—so shallow, yet deep enough to pull me under. The memory of its cold grip lingers on my skin, a reminder of how quickly everything can turn.

I weave through the trees, the underbrush crunching beneath my boots, until I reach the ox. Tied up and whimpering, his body shakes, the panic palpable in the trembling of his limbs. The sharp, distinct scent of urine hits the air, cutting through the dampness of the forest. He is no stoic warrior like Brandon. Fear pulses through him with every twitch of his muscles. He's overwhelmed, and it shows in every strained breath he takes.

Good.

"You're going to die anyway; you might as well die with a clear conscience, quickly and without additional pain. Or I can drag this out. Either way, today is your last," Tiernan growls that last part into the man's ear.

Awareness and fear drain him of the little color in his complexion. "I'm new to the crew! Fuck them. I didn't sign up for this! My brother convinced me it would be easy money," he confesses, openly weeping. I guess the thin man is his brother. *Was* his brother. "We were told to track the girl. Two front riders have been shadowing you all for days, and then we heard her screaming and decided to move in while you were all distracted with packing up. The fancy lord wanted her alive. He was willing to pay a king's ransom for us to trap the little witch." He whimpers. A twig snaps under my boot. Tiernan's and Finley's heads snap around, angry that I snuck up on their interrogation.

"I'm not a witch, you idiot. You'd shit yourself if you were ever in their presence. Who is this man sending you orders? Describe him," I demand. Finley and Tiernan make space and flank me.

"Some lord from the castle, fancy and snotty. Robbie, my brother you murdered, had been running Adepts for him for months, getting them onto ships to the continent. Robbie made a decent coin doing it, too. They needed some muscle, so he invited me on this once-in-a-lifetime payday. Said it would be an easy job. One small woman; grab her and take her to the assigned location, get paid, and be done. Robbie's done forever now, I guess." The ox doesn't meet my eyes once.

"Where was the meeting place?" I ask. This is my interrogation now. Tiernan and Finley survey the woods in case any more come behind them.

"Some fancy lord place, stone something, Stones Beach, Stones Bay, I don't remember! I wasn't the brains! I was told to bring her to his house at Stone Something."

"That fucking piece of shit fucking fucker! Stones Cove? I'm going to fucking kill him!" I scream until my throat is raw, spewing every creative curse that pops into my head. Everything comes into focus. Lord Asher Montcliff's seat is a strategic port that promotes trade and protects our northern coast from threats, hence why it was put in the hands of the Master of Trade. I'm going to kill him slowly. I'm going to make it *hurt*. This newfound bloodlust is his fault anyway. I might as well direct it at the culprit.

"And this lord is the one who has been paying you and your crew to do what?" Tiernan asks with indifferent curiosity. He might as well be asking what is on tap.

"Take Adepts, set aside any Seers and send the rest to the continent. Please don't kill me. I needed the money, and ain't no one missing one of them Adept freaks, anyway. That's what he said, but he wanted her to himself." He's sobbing now, with splotchy skin and a running nose.

"I'm going to slit his throat from ear to ear," I seethe through teeth clenched so tight my jaw starts to hurt. It might also hurt from the backhand to my face.

Asher fucking Montcliff wants my family to believe I died on this trip *he* suggested. A journey that *he* wanted to escort me on with his ever-so-loyal guards. His first plan failed, so his next plan was to hire some idiot slavers to grab me, and now that has failed. He failed, and he will continue to fail.

"Lydia," Tiernan whispers, putting a gentle hand on my arm and giving me a reassuring squeeze. It's enough to pull me back to the task at hand.

I walk back to the creek, the cool air biting at my skin as I process what just happened. No more questions linger that this man can answer—he's just hired muscle, nothing more than a pawn in someone else's game. The information I need won't come from him. The urgency to check on Brandon grows sharper. I need to make sure he's okay, see if he's stable enough to keep moving, or if we'll have to reconsider our next steps.

The whoosh of a knife meets flesh, barely a scream and then nothing. A few birds and the occasional snap of a branch and crunch of frozen leaves break the silence as Tiernan and Finley finish the job.

CHAPTER 21
TIERNAN

"Lydia and I will continue to the bay. This is an order that isn't open to discussion. She has to finish her Vision. Finley, you take Brandon back. Find a Healer before infection sets in. Convey the details of the attack and that Lydia and I are continuing forward." We step over bodies littering the campsite. Most are not my men, but enough are. Bodies of men I knew and respected. Men who signed up to serve and lost their lives needlessly. Blood thrums through my veins, a pounding beat from my heart pumping out to every heightened extremity.

Daylight passes quickly. We need to get away before night falls and the predators emerge. I'm surprised the wolves, or whatever else exists in these woods, haven't already taken an interest in the smell of the blood.

I check on Lydia, her mismatched eyes wide, taking in the devastation. She's hugging her arms, gripping her shoulders tight enough to see the white of her knuckles. She must be freezing, evidence of the emotional crash that is winding up to shut her body down. Judging by the bodies in the woods, she's capable of defending herself, but everyone copes differently in the minutes, hours, and days that follow battle and trauma. Whatever her level of defensive or hand-to-hand training, it is lacking in her mental recovery in the wake of death and destruction, especially if she blames herself. I want to blame her, but it's on me. How did I not notice we were being tracked? How did they get so close? How was I so distracted? These questions roll around in my mind but, deep down, I know the truth. I'm distracted. I'm enthralled. I struggle to see anything but her.

We don't have the tools or manpower to bury the dead. Not in this frozen ground. It hurts my soul to leave men who died fighting on the earth to be eaten by animals. But we have no choice. Heartbreaking but sometimes that's part of the battle. Recognize the loss, thank the men for their service, and try to stay alive to complete the mission. In this instance, there is no alternative.

We gather the horses that haven't run away and finish salvaging what we can. Finley and I work together to get Brandon stable onto one of the horses. I tie the reins to Finley's as he hops onto his mount. Brandon is a solid bastard, and getting him up there isn't as easy as I'd thought. We try not to jostle him and fail miserably, but he takes the pain and grunts while we get him settled.

"Captain. My lady. I'm sure we will see each other again soon." Finley nods at each of us. His warm and happy face has transformed into something stoic and terrifying. This is the face he shows his enemies. I check to ensure Brandon is secure one more time. He's wobbly, and weak but he still manages to give a small smile to Lydia.

She takes Brandon's hand and gives it a slight squeeze before returning to Finley. Fear, hesitation, and uncertainty pour out. She's usually better at masking her features, something I'm sure the Auctus instilled in her. Finley places a bare hand on the top of her head. He's not an Adept Handler, but the gesture is similar, and my muscles constrict, ready to pounce. To have fought our way through all of that for her to be wiped out by a head pat. She wouldn't be the first I've seen fall that way.

"Protect the captain, little lady. He needs a good bodyguard.

There be monsters in the Interior." His ominous words lose their effect accompanied by his teasing grin. Finley pats her head affectionately, his giant paws engulfing her skull. He could snap her neck in an instant. I don't know him. He volunteered for this assignment, and Cormac signed off on it due to his supposed knowledge of the Interior.

I relax when he releases her. I fill my lungs and exhale.

Lydia stands motionless, her chest still, eyes unblinking. The glassy sheen in her eyes vanishes as if it was never there. She watches them ride off in the direction we came then turns away, unfazed, and begins gathering supplies. A brief glimpse into the real Lydia, not the Auctus's most prized weapon, not a tool of kings and men seeking power, but a scared woman, aware of the risks but ready to face her fears.

A wave of prickly warmth washes over me, leaping my heart into my throat. My pulse beats faster. None of this is what she signed up for, not that she had ever been given much of a choice. We are all a byproduct of our upbringing.

Three horses remain from the fray: Burya and two others. My horse hasn't returned, but I strap my bag, bedroll, and tent to the third horse. I also pack additional rations, more clothes for layering if needed, and a few extra blankets.

"Let's keep moving. We lost some daylight, but I'd like to get some distance if possible." It's been hard to look at her since the interrogation. The possible realities could have been if one or two things didn't happen. *The ripple of change can, over time and space, create a mighty wave* is what my mother used to preach. I hold her words close to my heart and embrace that ripple every morning when I rise.

Lydia's eyes move across the carnage. Her skin loses its color, taking on a haunted, greenish tint. I want to reach out and brush a hand against her soft skin. I don't, but it doesn't stop the wanting. She darts behind a tree and starts retching.

Granting her a bit of privacy, I finish preparing the horses. She

can no longer hide the pain from her attack and the physical consequences in the aftermath. She killed someone. She may have killed
another had we not found her. What would have happened if we
hadn't made it to her in time? There's that ripple again, following the
Seer wherever she goes, and we are all left in her wake. Perhaps it's
unfair. She was fighting for her life, but we were all here because of
her and now only a few of us will return home.

She almost falls off trying to get on her horse. I move faster than I
ever thought capable and come behind her, helping her swing her
leg over. My hand rests on her hip, warm and solid. I can't stop
myself. I look up into her exhausted, broken face, wishing I could
take this all away for her, but I can't.

"We should go back," she pleads, her voice solid and confident, if
not for the slightest waver when she tries to catch her breath. Is she
afraid to be alone with me? She should be. I'm not good for her and
will bring her nothing but problems and trouble like she has brought
me to this point. All this death, my men, why? Why does she let
herself be used like this? Why does she never push back? They tell
her to go, and she goes. Therefore, we are forced to follow. I'm a
soldier; it's my job to be a weapon for Silvanisi, but she's not a
soldier. She's told me countless times she's not a weapon for the
Auctus, but how does she explain this?

"No, your king ordered us to go, and you need to do your job, as
do I," I bite out. Once Lydia is secure on her mount, I hoist myself
onto the last remaining horse and set out in the opposite direction of
Finley. This isn't an assignment I would have volunteered for, but it's
the one I have. I have a mission. I have orders. Failure isn't an option.
Too many people's lives hang in the balance, my own being one of
them. So much waste and violence, and it all could have been
prevented if she didn't dole out tidbits of information, picking and
choosing who gets to know what. Forgetting how it all impacts those
beneath her.

After an hour of weaving through the forest in silence, she trots
up next to me. I'm fuming, and my glances and glares are returned

with a similar hostile gaze. The air between us crackles, the tension is tangible, under pressure, and ready to blow on the slightest shift of the wind.

"Ugh! What is your problem now?" she screams, tugging at her curls.

"My problem is that many of my best men are dead. You almost died. We all almost died! Why? Because you couldn't be bothered to share your Vision that may or may not even be true or nothing more than some fucking dream! You play with your Sight like it's a fucking toy. You share what you deem important enough for the rest of us or manipulate it to your advantage. The soldiers, the people around you, they're the ones who end up paying the price. You and your Auctus control the information and the training. Who's deemed good enough to benefit from your benevolent gifts? All while my men, my soldiers, are the ones who will have to deal with the ramifications of your Sight."

Her pupils dart across my features. "I had no idea you thought so little of me," she chokes out and turns away, unable or unwilling to look at me a moment longer.

Regret washes over me. I can't take the words back. I'm not sure I would if I could. She didn't deserve that, but sometimes the truth hurts. My men are dead, and many more will die in whatever upcoming conflict she sees. They died for her, because of her, because of what she is and what she claims is coming.

She falls back a few paces, unable or unwilling to be next to me. I'm not even sure it's her that I'm angry with. I kick myself for losing my temper. I lash out and she lashes back. I push, and she pushes back. The only thing I can do to protect myself is push her away. She terrifies me—how she scrutinizes me, smells, feels, and tastes. Who she is, not who she's been raised to be, is dangerous. Both versions of her could cost me everything.

I rub my hands across the stubble on my scalp. "I saw you stab that man. I couldn't reach you in time, but I saw..." I whisper, dragging my hand down my face, trying to wipe away the memory. I sound as exhausted as she looks. "I didn't think I'd get to you in time. It was one of the most terrifying moments of my life. But then I saw how fast you moved..."

I can't play through what could have been. I lean on my training, pack it all away and refocus on the path ahead.

"Do you smell that?" she asks, sniffing the air.

I sniff. It's slightly rotten but not of decay. "Sulfur. We must be near a spring."

"Oh thank the fucking gods," she moans.

We steer the horses around a copse of trees and a tendril of steam emerges from a small pond barely large enough to not be deemed a puddle. Together, we hop off and tie the horses to a branch.

Lydia rips her clothes off faster than I can offer her privacy. Not that I want to or will. One of us needs to keep an eye out. As dusk descends, we will both need to be on alert.

Her pale curves glow in the darkness. Bruises and cuts stand out in stark contrast. She rolls up her clothes into her coat and sets the lump on a rock. Her toe dips into the steaming water, and she moans. Fucking moans, and all the blood in my brain rushes straight to my cock. If the pond were deeper, I'd think she'd do a cannonball and jump straight in, but she slowly descends into the water like a nymph, tempting me to join her. Dipping under for a moment, she breaks the surface and pushes her wet hair off her blissful face. Her smile stops my heart.

"There's a bar of soap in my bag. Do you mind handing it to me?"

I'm stunned stupid, gawking like a boy seeing a naked woman for the first time and being made aware of my body's reaction. She smiles again and dips her head back.

I root through her bag and find the soap. Lydia's hand reaches for it, but I have better plans. I shed my clothes, add them to the pile, and step into the water. It's not scalding but with the air as cold as it is, the warmth seeps into my aching muscles. Her eyes dart to my raging erection. I couldn't hide it if I wanted to. She has to be aware of the effect she has. The power she holds.

I spin my finger, indicating for her to turn, and she obeys. Her dark hair floats on the surface. I tug at it, pulling her closer until her back presses against my chest and the sweet curve of her ass brushes my cock. I have to bite my cheek to not groan.

Rubbing the bar of soap between my hands, I lather her hair and scrub away the dirt, grime, and blood. She tilts her head back. The column of her neck is so kissable; it takes every ounce of willpower not to take things further but now isn't the time or the place. What am I doing? This is all unfair to her. But life isn't fair. We could all die tomorrow and this could all have been for nothing. Might as well enjoy it while it lasts. If I've learned anything in my life, it's that tomorrow isn't guaranteed but we have to survive to see tomorrow. One of us has to be responsible. One of us has to think. The little noises she makes as my fingers work her scalp aren't helping.

I have to step back, and the absence of her skin sends shivers down my own. I dip under the water for a reprieve and vigorously scrub my own hair and body. Coming back up to the surface, she's rinses and is squeezing out excess water.

She dries off as much as she can and squeezes more water from her hair. Will it freeze in these temperatures? It's cold but not as bad as with the wind coming off the ocean at home. We are somewhat insulated here.

"We need to keep moving." I hop out. The frozen ground stings as a cold gust of wind whips through the trees, rustling the leaves. I grab a shirt and dry off. We both dress quickly, silently, stealing glances as we lace our boots and button our coats. She surveys me with a mix of hunger and skepticism. Fucking hell. Those eyes that see so much and yet are aware of so little. Stunning and haunting. A necessary and visible reminder of who she is and why we are here.

CHAPTER 22
LYDIA

"Let's make camp for the night," Tiernan says, breaking the silence. Daylight is long gone behind a mountain peak. We trudge east, and the temperature has dropped noticeably. What was chilly during the day is now a numbing cold.

Surveying our surroundings, I take in the thick forest surrounding a steep rocky ridge. "Where? There's nowhere to put a tent?"

He tips his chin toward a dark shadow hidden among the rocks to the left. "There's a small cave there. Some rain or probably snow is coming based on those clouds over that ridge. I'd rather not be so exposed to the elements."

"You know all of this based on clouds?"

"I'm a man of many talents," he teases. I'd poke back, simply because I can't help myself from taking the bait, but my chattering teeth get in the way. I spot the cave entrance, likely home to a hibernating predator. Before I can voice my concern, Tiernan enters. The wind shifts, carrying the crisp, frosty scent of snow. I clear my mind and focus, trying to listen. My hearing has never been close to an Adept Listener, but I have a few tricks if I concentrate hard enough.

Tiernan emerges unscathed. "It'll do until this storm passes. There's enough room toward the front for the horses to have some shelter, too, and we can get a fire going if we can find some dry wood. Grab a fire starter from my pack, please."

Hopping down, my legs almost give out beneath me. Pins and needles shoot up my calves, a sharp, pulsing reminder of how long I've been sitting. I flinch, trying to shake the numbness out, and take a few slow, careful steps, gradually regaining some semblance of balance. The world feels slightly off-kilter, but the dizziness fades as my body adjusts.

I rifle through my bag, my hands trembling slightly from the cold and the adrenaline. The fire starter, a few scraps of cloth, a canteen, and a dry pair of socks emerge. The socks feel like a luxury, a small comfort I'll appreciate later. I shift my focus to the limited bedding—thin blankets that offer little warmth against the biting chill of the evening air. With a grunt, I gather everything into my arms. The need to focus on the essentials cuts through the fog in my mind, the urgency clear in my every movement.

Tiernan starts a little fire while I set up our rolls. "It will keep us both warmer to be next to each other," he grumbles.

He's right. Somehow, that makes it more irritating. Sharing a tent with him last night was challenging enough, but a dozen other people surrounded us. Sharing a hot spring was temptation personified. He's teased and tempted only to halt both times. I don't need to be knocked down a third. I like to think I have a healthy dose of self-esteem. I think I'm pretty, and I like who I am. If his glances and touches are any indication, he likes those things about me, too, but every time we reach a line, he refuses to cross.

Sitting in front of the fire, I peel off my gloves and rub my tingling, half-frozen hands. Tiernan sits beside me, handing me a heel of bread and some cheese. It's a sad dinner, but we make do. I lean into him, seeking his warmth, and he doesn't pull away. My body starts to relax—or maybe it's just crashing. Probably both.

"Let's get some rest," he murmurs in my ear. His hand slides down my back, leading me to our makeshift bed. I stand up a little shaky from the longest day of my life. Tiernan's other arm comes under my legs and sweeps me up.

"I can walk."

He ignores me, places me on my bed, and pulls my coat and another blanket over my shoulders, tucking it in. I'm between him and the warmth of the fire, and he settles in behind me. His presence is magnetic, and it takes a few calming breaths to resist the urge to snuggle closer. I close my eyes, focusing on a meditation, hoping it will distract me from the temptation to roll right on top of him.

His breathing alters to match as I calm and clear my mind.

"How does that breathing pattern work? I've seen you do that before," he says. The curiosity in his voice is genuine. None of the angry edge when he usually asks about my Sight. I hesitate. Tiernan has repeatedly expressed distrust, interest, or hostility, and every reaction in between. He wants to learn, but something constantly stops him from asking without an edge. There's a war raging inside him; between his perception and the reality in front of him. I wonder if I reach out a hand, would it be smacked or held?

"It's a meditation Tobias taught me. When I was little, I didn't understand my Sight or the things I would see. It would scare me, so I'd fight it, fight my Visions, fight sleep. Being scared causes more problems, inaccuracies, or clouds my Vision. Fear can be healthy, but not when it forces my mind to think of nothing but worst-case scenarios. There's truth to be found in Panic-Visions, but it's a nightmare to dig through for the crumbs of what's probable. When I'm out of control or overwhelmed, meditation helps bring my mind back into my body so I can communicate with my Sight respectfully. *Clear mind. Clear path.* It works for other Adepts, too, in different ways. Handlers slow their minds and hearts to wield their Touch for healing instead of the weapon it's often associated with. Listeners use it to quiet the noise in their heads or separate sounds in loud environments. I've heard it's exhausting being able to hear everything. I use it to ground me in the present and clear my mind to recall a Vision, but when I'm in a *high-stress* situation—" I gesture emphatically to the space around us—"it brings my Sight into a state of peace and clarity."

I hope a better understanding might lessen Tiernan's distrust of the Auctus, and help him understand that we are individuals who never asked for these Enhanced Senses but were born this way. It's probably naive of me to think one conversation or one woman can change a person's entire notion of an institution as powerful as the Auctus, but I have to try. It's a part of who I am, and I owe them so much.

I keep my eyes closed and my breathing rhythmic, in for five counts, out for five counts. His breathing mimics mine, a warm wave of air on the back of my neck that cascades across my cheek. He's moved closer. His chest brushes against me with every inhale.

"What about the Adepts who can access all five Enhanced Senses?" he asks, his breathing relaxed now that he's synced with my pattern.

"Enhanced Complex? They keep their secrets. I guess it helps them stay at the center of the star, the strongest house, despite not having the greatest numbers. It requires significant training and willpower to maintain control, though, which can have serious ramifications for a Complex. I think that's why so many deny their gift. They fear being an Adept. Fear the Auctus or perhaps it's more accurate to say they fear the misconceptions of the Auctus. So they never learn to master it safely, which causes them to fear it all more. It's a horrible cycle."

A shudder runs through his body. I roll toward him and gaze into haunted eyes that would be black if not for the firelight and my Sight. I put my hand on his cheek and pull back when he flinches. His hand comes up to move mine back onto his scratchy stubble. I run my fingers across it, relishing in the sensation. He wants to say something, and I want to give him the space to speak or ask, so we lie together and I memorize the angle of his jaw while he struggles to find words for whatever thought is tormenting him behind those eyes.

"My family was killed when I was too young to fight back," Tiernan whispers with a hint of pain in his voice. "I saw them die at the hands of the Auctus. At the hands of an uncle I never knew. Rupert is his name. He's…influential. My mother was a Complex. My sister and I were the only survivors of the ambush. We fled during the massacre, found my uncle who was a part of our lives, and changed our names. She and I are both unregistered. She ran away a few years ago. She wanted to learn about her 'gift' and study at Merthaset. We fought, and she left, abandoning her only surviving family. She was too young to remember watching our parents, our half-brothers, die at their hands. My mother tried to hide us. Her family was, and still is, in a seat of power within the Auctus. Mother turned her back on them, so they killed her and came after us. They didn't hesitate to kill my father, who they thought was lower than scum, a Layman. He could do nothing for the bloodline. They also slaughtered my two older half-brothers. They came for my sister Fiona and me, so we ran while they burned down my home with my family lying dead in the dirt. I will never forgive them. No excuse could justify what they did."

A stone drops into the pit of my stomach, and I swallow hard, but it doesn't go down easy. Tiernan is a Complex. It makes sense now, looking back at moments when he likely used his gifts without realizing it. But where do we go from here? How can I help him? He carries so much hatred—for the Auctus and for himself. Grandmaster Rupert is his uncle, and every Adept knows his name and the consequences of crossing him. I can show Tiernan a different path, a way to move forward. It may not work, but I have to try.

"I won't pretend to understand everything about the Auctus or agree with their policies or actions blindly. I would never divulge your secret, but please don't think of it with hatred or shame. Understanding your Enhanced Senses will help you control it. I'll help you with whatever knowledge I have. No one should have to experience this alone. That's why we stick together. It's part of our oath. To help other Adepts in need. Let me help you." I move my thumb over his sharp jaw, brushing the rough scratch of his blond stubble underneath. The motion seems to soothe him a bit. I guess sometimes what we dislike in others is the parts that we hate about ourselves.

"I hate that this *thing* is inside me, controlling me. I hate using it without realizing it. It's like the choice is stripped from me."

"Too many hate Adepts because they don't know or want to know that we are simply people trying to use our gifts to help. Don't hate yourself, too, Tiernan. The world has enough hate already. We don't need to add to it." I don't push as much as I want. I tread carefully. His pain, both physical and emotional, cannot be cured tonight, but if I can give him a shred of empathy, I will try. I can't force him to embrace this gift. It has to be him. Otherwise, I'm what he fears most: a tool of the Auctus trying to take away his choice.

"I could never hate you. I tried. I wanted to for no other reason than what you represent. Who you represent, but I can't hate you and I can't keep trying. Another thing I've failed at." Tiernan moves his hand down and rests it on my lower back, pulling me closer. His other arm comes under my head, a makeshift pillow.

"It's never a failure to change your path and turn away from hate."

"You are impossible to hate. I'd know." He kisses my forehead and squeezes me tighter into his cocoon of warmth. A door between us has opened. I want to step through it and see what's on the other side.

CHAPTER 23
TIERNAN

Stay hidden. Stay quiet.

We had been happy only hours ago. We had left the world alone, and it had mostly left us alone in return. Had any of my thoughts summoned them? No—they couldn't read minds.

Right?

My temple throbbed in rhythm with my pounding heart. I struggled to focus, but the pulsing in my head was relentless. Everything was cloudy. A dull ringing echoed in my ear. My eyeball twitched. I was losing control of my Senses.

It was so loud. I needed to listen. I couldn't lose control now.

With every crack and spark, the ash and smoke crept closer—thick and suffocating. My sister wanted to cough, but we both knew better than to make a sound. Not until we could move.

Stay hidden. Stay quiet. Just a bit longer, and then we could run.

Through the splintering window, I saw a soldier appear behind my mother and shove her to her knees. My eyes stung and watered. I blinked to clear them.

A man in a cape stood tall. There was something familiar in his face—

his eyes, perhaps. His gaze fixed on my mother, softening briefly before an indifferent mask fell over it: cold and lifeless.

"What have we done to deserve such disloyalty? You made me an oath," he hissed into her ear. Tearing at her sleeve, he exposed the white spiral scar on her arm. "Yet you betrayed us. Your brethren. How many of us were you willing to sacrifice for your own ambition?"

My father lay on the ground before her. He wasn't moving anymore. Neither were my brothers.

Stay hidden. Stay quiet. Keep Fiona safe.

I was all she had left.

The wind shifted, pushing the smoke downwind. The man's cape billowed in the gust, revealing his armor. The dark star crest emblazoned on his pauldrons marked him as one who believed his existence more valuable than the masses. Even the king had been manipulated into placing them above his own people.

"Hiro is a puppet," my father would say—a truth carved into us from the cradle.

The five-pointed star, set in a golden-haloed sun, rested on each shoulder. Its black tips pierced beyond the sun's warming rays. The darkness overwhelmed the light, blocking it from the people who needed its warmth to survive. The dark star will eventually cover the light completely, my mother had warned us, casting the world into permanent darkness if they are left unchecked.

"You speak of ambition, Rupert. You are part of the problem," Mother said, wrenching herself from his grip and spitting in his face. "I am part of the solution."

A moment later, her cheek was pressed into the dirt. He shook his head at her defiance.

Mother was not deterred. "You've seen who they are, what they value, what they're capable of. You've followed along like a good little sheep, hoping for discarded scraps. Will you sacrifice your sister on the altar of ambition?"

Sister?

This man who came to take my family from me was my family, too?

"I'll do what I must to protect this family and our seat at the table—something you should have done long ago, Lili. Where are your Adept children? They deserve the truth, not your twisted lies. You've brainwashed them. This is for their protection. Do they even know what you've done?"

Mother reached behind her and grabbed his leg. He jumped back with a hiss. Another soldier stepped in and pinned her hands to the ground.

"I'll do my duty, Lili—distasteful though it is. I will live and die by my oath. Unlike you, who will merely die. Was it worth it? Turning your back on who you are? The Auctus will not forgive your crimes. The good you could have done for your kind—wasted. This is a mercy, to kill you now."

Her eyes flicked toward our hiding place for less than a second—so quick I would've missed it if I'd blinked. In that moment, I saw her love. Her sacrifice. All the fireside stories, the lessons whispered under blankets—they were no longer parables.

They were prophecy.

"So be it. I love you, Lili. I'm sorry it had to come to this. Here is your mercy."

He kissed her temple and placed his fingers on the same spot.

She crumpled to the ground without a sound.

There—and then gone—with one Touch.

I held Fiona tighter and squeezed my eyes shut, praying this was only a nightmare. That when I opened them, I'd be back in my bed, listening to our dog snore at my feet.

Our Senses had cursed us. It wasn't a gift. It was a scourge—raging in our blood. The blood we shared with him.

"Fiona, we have to get a horse. Be silent and follow my every step," I whispered in her ear, praying there wasn't an Enhanced Listener nearby.

"Mama said we can't take a horse without asking," she scolded, her little lisp still intact. "We aren't old enough to take one without permission."

I brushed her tangled blonde hair from her face and looked into her pale gray eyes, so wide they filled half her face. I squeezed her tiny hand—now somehow even smaller.

"We're going to have to break a few rules tonight. Do you understand, little lamb?"

She nodded vigorously.

We made it to the stable. The smoke and chaos worked in our favor—a small blessing, if one could be found. I threw Fiona onto the first horse we reached. I slid the door open carefully, trying not to squeak the rusty hinges, then climbed up behind her. I sank my fingers into the horse's mane and kicked—probably too hard—as we rode toward safety.

If such a thing even existed.

I would stay hidden. I would remain quiet. I would keep her safe.

A DRUM SOUNDS in the distance. The steady beat rouses me from sleep. My eyes...hurt. They don't want to open, and I can't contemplate why. Eyes open when you want them to. You just think it and it happens. Eyes open. Done.

And yet, it takes immense concentration to will them open.

Like I'm her personal pillow, Lydia's head rests on my arm. Said arm is completely asleep. I gently slide it out from under her head and immediately regret that decision. A thousand pins stab into me from shoulder to fingertip. The jagged walls of our cave spin and tilt in my sight. I shake my head, and it again takes more effort than it should to focus, to see.

I clench my fist. The tingling is bearable now, but the sting lingers, as does the rhythmic tempo of the beating drum.

Typically, my dreams are abstract, with no clear beginning or end. But this isn't a dream; it's a vivid memory, as if I'm standing in that spot again. The scent of my charred home lingers in my nose, the crackling beams and shattered glass echo in my ears. The softness and heat of my sister's warm hand, her chubby fingers linked with mine. It's all so tangible.

I flex my arm, bend it, and shake out the last of the needles as the sensation dulls to an ache in the background.

Lydia stirs. Without thinking, I pull the blankets over her shoulder, tucking her in. What is she doing to me? Why is this happening? She's awakened something that had been shoved down deep in my soul. Something I never wanted to emerge.

Years have been spent on rigorous practice and discipline to keep these senses dulled.

My mother's lessons are all I have left of her. It never occurred to me to question them.

I huff over the cold night air and watch the warm tendrils of my breath float away. Tossing a few more logs onto our dwindling fire, I warm my palms but the sensation of little Fiona's hand holding mine lingers. A ghost of the past.

Will I be forced to relive the night she ran away from me? From some man who claims to be our uncle from a family we never knew?

Cormac spent years patiently and diligently hiding, training, and instilling in us how to rebuild ourselves. His methods may have been harsh sometimes, but it was always in our best interest. His brother and his nephews died at the hands of the family. All for an oath to a vile and corrupt elite. No, not elite.

Fiona thought differently. She wouldn't listen to reason. She refused to fall in line. She left me alone. Was she always supposed to leave? Would Lydia have seen her skulk away under a new moon? Was Fiona's path clear long before she dishonored and abandoned the memory of her family?

Lydia says the future isn't clear. She sees possibilities and likelihoods. But the future can shift. One decision can show a new path. This is what she's been taught to say, trained to preach. We have no control. No matter what decisions we make, they won't change anything. Let the people think they are in control of their futures. But it's not true. Control is taken from us before we even recognize it was never ours to begin with.

I see it now. This was meant to happen. She is meant to be on my path, and no matter what I do, I can't change that.

This woman, with her mismatched eyes that belong to Visionary Seers and gentle touch, her quiet power and determined spirit, leads me down a path I cannot control. I can only take one step forward. Pulling me forward toward whatever destiny lies ahead.

This moment is meant to be. Every action was not a choice; it was a nudge, leading me to her, to this.

Her wild hair spreads out, a dark halo that beckons me to fall to my knees. She rolls over, pulling the blanket up as she scoots closer for whatever warmth she can grab. Her gold chain slides down her creamy skin, and the five-pointed pendant rests. A flash to the five-pointed crest emblazoned on Rupert.

If the future is a choice, and we can change our path, why does she not change her own? Why stay loyal when she knows the dark star wants to cast its shadow over us all? She's wrong. I'll show her. She'll believe me. We'll work together.

Maybe I'm wrong. Stranger things have happened. Fiona wanted to know her Senses. Lydia wants to be a Master. The unrelenting pursuit of knowledge, of power or control over one's Enhanced Senses is a force strong enough to separate families. It's strong enough to kill. It's powerful enough to pull those of us born with it together and draw us to one another. Whether that's fate or attraction or nothing more than a continuation of those bloodlines, it doesn't deny that Adepts draw towards Adepts. I draw toward Lydia, a pull I can no longer deny. A chain I no longer wish to break.

She is the fire, thawing something I tried to keep frozen. She is the star, shining above me. She is a light emerging from the Auctus's darkness.

I've opened myself to her, and she's opened my Senses. Locking them back down now is impossible. All I can do is move forward, perhaps learn restraint and follow the path to my destiny. Lydia wants to master her Sight, explore its possibilities, and push its limits. She can show me the way, and then I can show her an escape from it all. I can be her light. I can show her the truth.

Exhaustion settles over me, a heavy blanket weighing me down. I curl back down and nestle Lydia into my chest as I warm my arm around her waist and let her warmth soak into my bones. She scoots back, snuggling closer. She takes my hand in hers, linking our fingers together unconsciously. Her curls smother my face, but I brush them down and tuck her head under my chin.

CHAPTER 24

RYO

Shit goes from bad to worse in just a few short days. The universe is testing me. I'll be damned if I fail.

Amos shifts his hulking body back and forth at the end of the table, edgy but ready to summarize his interrogation with Veronica. My mother, sisters, and Uncle Oscar demanded to be present for the report. I want to keep the depth of Veronica's betrayal and my blindness hidden from the masses. I had wanted to do this privately, but my sisters insisted that if a potential rebel assassin could get so close to me, who is to say one couldn't be a step away from them, too? They have a point much as I'd never tell them that.

But even worse is that Veronica isn't just a sympathizer. She is an active member of the rebellion. She was in my bed by design. Her original orders were to kill me at the first available opportunity. She thought being queen would grant her more power to steer things. She hasn't divulged any high-level names. She has given some locations. She has also confirmed that the rebels are behind the missing Adepts. Some are being sold to the continent, but most are taken elsewhere. She doesn't know where, and she doesn't know why.

Getting close to me, killing me, was considered a promotion for her, but she's fairly mid-level.

Amos walks us through the other details of their conversation. His eyes slide to Kira's more than once.

Kira glances at me and narrows her eyes, challenging me to say something. Amos never pauses, running us through the rest of his interrogation from start to finish.

"How did you collect so much from her in such a short period? Why would she sing away the secrets of the rebels so easily?" Oscar asks.

"My Taste for lies is quite strong, my lord. And I have slightly Enhanced Hearing," Amos replies. His superior Enhanced Taste is why he has been such an asset to us. Amos is quiet, always observing, listening, and absorbing information. He's not flashy or boastful, but efficient and strategic.

"Amos, you were born and raised in Silvanisi, correct?" Oscar asks the simple question.

Kira's eyes snap to our uncle, harsh and challenging. She knows where this line of questioning usually leads. I give Oscar the benefit of the doubt. My lover is a rebel assassin, apparently, and I had no idea. Who's to say Kira's crush isn't working an angle too for a different end?

"Yes, my lord," Amos replies. "Born and raised. Trained at Merthaset under Grandmaster Caspian himself. Of course, he wasn't the Grandmaster at the time. When it became clear I could not obtain a Master's rank, I returned home to be closer to my mother and serve as a translator for my king. However, it better served the crown to wield my Enhanced Taste in a narrower capacity, dealing with one-on-one questioning."

"Thank you for sharing your gift with us, Amos," Oscar says, waving to one of the empty chairs. Amos accepts the apologetic gesture and takes a seat.

Kira stands abruptly, and Amos shoots back up to stand at attention. She walks over to a side table, pours a glass of wine, and drinks it down. He doesn't sit back down again until she's back in her seat, his eyes never leaving hers. This will become awkward when Mother decides if Kira will marry Verralon or Ellandelle, but it does something to reassure me that her crush may not be one-sided. Then again, I'm a terrible judge of character, apparently. What the hell do I know?

I knock on the table, returning my attention to the task. "So she was a secret assassin sent to seduce and kill me, but her ambition got in the way and thwarted her plans. Do I have the gist of it?"

"Correct, my prince," Amos replies. "She wasn't good at hiding her lies. They were easy to taste—bitter and sharp. She was much more forthcoming once she was reminded I could taste the lie. What do you want to do with her?"

"She will remain where she is, under guard, until her father can sail here and we can determine his involvement," Iris orders. She'd been quiet and stoic, but now her claws are out.

Amos nods and rises to leave, bowing to each of us and Kira last. She blushes as he departs. I don't think I've ever seen Kira blush. It's unnerving.

I pour another glass for myself and start to refill my sister's glasses. To my surprise, Iris places her hand over her glass, blocking me. It's unexpected, especially since they can both drink like sailors on shore. A knock rasps on the door, and one of my father's guards pokes his head inside.

"My prince, princesses," the man says, addressing my sisters. "There's a development, and Commander Cormac is requesting a moment of your time."

Cormac barrels into the room. "A ship from Verralon has requested to enter the harbor. It will dock in a few minutes. The ship is tethered to a captured slaver. I'll take care of it. No need for you to be bothered."

"No, I'd like to hear. let's all see what is being dragged back and find out how a Verralon ship got so close to our harbor unannounced." I stand and grab my coat. I don't wait for him to follow.

My sisters sit back at the table with Uncle Oscar and my mother, presumably to discuss the repercussions of our new guests, while the rest stand or follow me out to deal with our new guests.

We weave our way through the narrow city streets down toward the harbor, avoiding the central avenue and the attention that comes with traveling the obvious path. A few skeptical glances emerge from some doorways, but a greater number smile and wave. How widespread is this distrust for my family, for the Auctus, for Adepts? How long has this been brewing?

The harbor greets us at the bottom of the steep avenue. A formidable sailing ship with dozens of men running around prepares to dock. A smaller but still sizable vessel is tethered to it. A few men stand on that deck.

"Perhaps it is safest for you to return to the castle, Prince. Let me deal with the Verralon barbarians. I'll get the information and kick them out of our harbor before anything escalates," Cormac leans and whispers in my ear, careful not to let the rest of the guard overhear.

"No, we need to address this; time is essential. Amos, stick close," I order. Cormac follows behind, grumbling his frustration.

We wait for the sailors to disembark. They ignore us, aside from a few curious glares, until Cormac gets their attention. "Who is in command of this vessel? This is an unauthorized breach of our waters. I will speak with your captain immediately," he barks.

"That would be me, Commander," a bearded bear of a man replies, landing on the dock with a thud. His smooth, almost graceful leap contrasts his bulk. He ignores the commander and stops in front of me.

"Prince Ryo. I haven't seen you since you were a horny teen lusting after one of my mother's ladies." The stone wall of a man smirks, reaching out a giant hand to clap me on the shoulder a bit too firmly. He's friendly, perhaps a bit too familiar. It takes me a moment to place him.

"E... Ezra ... King Ezra. We were not expecting you. This is a surprising turn of events," Cormac sputters, attempting to regain control while processing the implications for our royal guest.

"Yes, Lord Ezra now. There are no kings in Verralon, or so they keep preaching. Why can't I be called king, but my siblings are prince and princess, and my mother is the dowager queen? Hardly seems fair." He waves the air, brushing aside his ramblings. "I brought your ship back to you. I thought you'd want it returned before it reached its destination," he says, wrapping a too-familiar arm around my shoulder as if we are old friends. His presence is so jarring and unexpected that it throws me off my game momentarily. I school my face.

"Our ship? I was told you were towing in a slaver vessel caught off the coast. We've been trying to track and intercept them for weeks, and here you are, with no notice and one in tow. It seems you have a story to tell," I prod in the most polite way possible.

"Manned by men of Silvanisi, full of enslaved Adepts on their way to the continent. That won't be happening anymore," Ezra replies, shaking his head. He steers me toward the tethered ship. His men have set down a gangplank.

"Men of Silvanisi are not slavers. Where are all the rescued enslaved? Did you leave anyone alive to question?" I challenge. It's too quiet if the ship were full of people.

"The ship was floating dead in the water when we approached. I'll show you. Then I'd like to have a word with your father," Ezra says while walking down a set of steep, narrow stairs into an open holding area, expecting me to follow.

Bodies line the walls, rough metal cuffs around their necks tied to chains attached to hooks in the ceiling. We weave our way through what appears to be the holding bay. The smell is oppressive, making my eyes water and nose burn, but I power through. It would take a few days for the bodies to reach this state.

"What happened here?" I whisper, disbelief in the situation before me. "Where are the survivors?"

"There are none," he replies. "When we boarded, a few of the men guarding the enslaved people remained alive, but they were not in control. They were rabid, screaming about how their blood was attacking them from the inside. How they went after the treasure, but the curse took hold and made them mad. The Adepts steered them in the wrong direction so the remaining crew slaughtered the Adepts before succumbing to whatever madness was inflicted upon them. It wasn't pretty nor was it quick. We don't know how long they were at sea."

"Let me take you to my father. My men will see to their burial. I need you to share everything you know."

Ezra doesn't agree or disagree. He gestures toward the exit, and we proceed to the castle, some of his entourage in tow. My mother stands at the door. My sisters flank her, awaiting our return. They've changed into something more presentable for a visiting monarch.

"Welcome, Lord Ezra. What a fortunate turn of events. When we sent you an invitation to visit a few days ago, we were not expecting a reply so quickly. We look forward to a continued positive relationship between our two nations. Perhaps even a greater alliance could be in our future," my mother says, dipping into a graceful curtsy. My sisters barely incline their heads, the most minor show of respect they can muster. She's laying it on a bit thick, but now isn't the time to tell her.

"A pleasure to behold the beauties of Silvanisi. I recall a third always at their side, your Visionary. Where might she be? If it's the future we speak of, surely a Seer is useful," Ezra prods.

"Lydia isn't available. Please let us welcome you and your attaché to Silvanisi properly. The king is indisposed but will make himself available to you shortly. Let me set you up in rooms befitting your station," my mother says, gesturing the men and women who make up Ezra's guard into the castle. She glances at me for less than a moment, her eyebrow ticking up fractionally, but it's long enough. A plea to step up and handle this while my father is unavailable.

"I look forward to an open line of communication, Naomi," Ezra replies casually, using her name instead of her title. He kisses her hand politely, but the toothy grin reminds us all that he isn't an old friend; he's the warlord of one of our greatest threats, and we must tread carefully.

"Indeed," she mumbles, escorting him down a corridor and into a small dining room where refreshments are already waiting. How she had the time to prepare all of this in the brief walk from the harbor back to the castle astounds me.

Mother settles into a seat at the head of the table, smoothing her skirts around her before placing her hands artfully in her lap. She observes our guests until we are all seated.

Ezra has chosen to sit at the head on the opposite side, while three guards and two women flank him. The women are dressed in leather armor, similar to the guards. It is unheard of to have a female guard in Silvanisi. Kira must be seething with jealousy.

"Perhaps, given that time is of the essence, we should discuss the reason behind your visit, and my father can be updated when he is available," I suggest. I should have sat at the head of the table. It would look weak to move now.

"How long until the king is well enough to join us? Or are you, prince, handling foreign affairs now?" Ezra asks, raising an eyebrow at the man on his left. He takes a few large gulps of the wine, empties the glass, and sets it down on the table to be refilled. We've been trying to keep my father's deteriorating health quiet, but I have no doubt Verralon has spies on every island in the Aperion.

Ezra doesn't wait for an answer.

"My deepest and most sincere apologies for the lack of formality, but your slave trade is becoming quite the problem beyond your island. I've been tracking it for months, and it keeps circling back here. Now, shall we discuss how Silvanisi, a most loyal ally of the Auctus, a friend and haven for Adepts, is going to handle this on your own when the Auctus fleet comes knocking, or should we all wait for your rebellion powder keg to explode? Or should we wait for your two absent Seers? Master Tobias is unavailable, too, correct?" Ezra asks no one in particular, laying his cards on the table. He downs another glass of the refilled wine. He's going to get drunk at the rate he's going.

Wait. How does he know we have two absent Seers?

CHAPTER 25

LYDIA

The cracking of a tree jolts me awake. It's still dark, and the storm outside howls. Rain, not snow, comes down in horizontal sheets.

As if we both realize in unison that our arms and legs are tangled, we tense, but neither of us is quite ready to separate. I try to shift away slowly, but Tiernan pulls me tighter into his warm embrace.

"Could you walk me through one of your meditations? I want to try it," he says so softly. He doesn't appear to want to let go of me any time soon, and I don't either. This cracked door between us opens a little wider. Maybe I'm foolish or naive, but he's been alone in this for so long, whether by choice or by conditioning. But he doesn't have to be alone any longer. I have the ability to help him, and so I am oath-bound to do so. I'll never regret helping a fellow Adept, but I would regret abandoning one.

"Of course. Clearing the way for your Senses to flow can enhance them. *Clear mind. Clear path.* I should warn you that if you aren't used to it, it can feel overwhelming the first time you open your Enhanced Senses. Your house would teach you—"

He squeezes tight, halting my words.

"I'm not of any of your houses, nor will I ever join one, but I would like to gain some...*control*. If such a thing exists." His arms relax a bit.

I smooth my hand down his back, drawing his attention back to me. Snapping at him won't help. "I'll rephrase: You can enhance all five Senses, but it's best to focus on one at a time to avoid getting overwhelmed and possibly losing control. Let's focus on Enhanced Hearing first—it could be useful in a forest full of things trying to kidnap or kill us. After that, we can move on to Scent to find something to eat." My stomach growls. "I can't guarantee this will work the same for a Complex, but it won't hurt to try it the Seer way. Close your eyes. Relax your shoulders and neck. Let your mind sweep away any stray thoughts, like clearing the floor of your head, leaving a clean space free of debris. Focus on hearing the world around you. Narrow it down to the sound of my voice. Try to isolate it."

My fingers glide up and down his spine, synchronized with my breathing. In for five, out for five. He's so solid and warm beneath my touch. Desire stirs, and I selfishly use this moment to my advantage. "Follow the rhythm of my hand and match it to your breath, in and out. Good. Keep breathing like that. Now, ground yourself in your gift. Find five things you can see, four things you can touch, three things you can hear, two things you can smell, and one thing you can taste. Once you've done that, refocus on following the path of my hand and matching it to your breath. Listen to the sounds in the cave, and quiet the noise from outside. Narrow it down. Focus on one sound, like your heartbeat. Silence the rest."

Tiernan starts to mimic my hand gliding on my lower back, and it shoots delightful tingles through me. He's. So. Warm. I focus on keeping my hand in rhythm to help him. Concentrating on anything is challenging when his hand brushes lower, dropping to the base of my back, feeling less like a brush and more like a caress with every pass.

"There's a heartbeat, but I don't think it's mine. Is that you? Am I listening to your heartbeat?" he asks, keeping his eyes closed. The corners of his mouth twitch up, showing the barest of smiles. His hand slips lower over my backside and down to my hip. He squeezes just tight enough to make my breath hitch. "Yes, that's absolutely your heartbeat. Anything making your heart race a bit?"

"Keep your eyes closed. Focus on your breathing and be conscious of how your body is responding. This is supposed to be a meditation, remember?" I chastise while grappling to regain control of my heartbeat. The fact that he could separate the sounds so quickly shows he's been testing the limits of his Senses for years, even if he wasn't aware.

"I'm feeling relaxed and am very aware of my body responding. I'm also exceedingly aware of your body," he whispers, leaning closer into the shell of my ear. Goosebumps cascade across my skin. He kisses the spot right behind my earlobe, and a small breath escapes my lips before I can stop it.

Fingers tighten on my hip, dragging me closer as warm lips find the curve of my neck. Our breathing deepens, each exhale rougher than the last. My hand slips beneath his untucked shirt, spreading across heated skin—smooth and soft over muscle tense with restraint. The contradiction stuns me. Reason slips through my fingers like water, drowned by sensation. Breathing becomes impossible to track. Rational thought? Gone.

His nose brushes under my jaw, pushing it up to expose my neck. "I want you. So. Badly." He inhales deeply, filling his lungs and dragging me flush against him. "Fuck. You make me forget everything. All I see is you. All I hear is you. Let me taste you. Feel you." There's not an inch of open space between us. He shifts his leg in between my thighs, applying a slight pressure on the building tension at my apex that is screaming for more attention, more everything.

He presses his thigh into my center, the heat pouring from me. I roll my hips. Before I even realize my reaction, he growls into my neck. Empowered and chasing the source of that building tension, I swivel my hips again, increasing the pressure where I need it most. I'm lost. I'll regret this later, but I'm chasing this and I want more.

He pushes me onto my back and positions his hips between my thighs, spreading them wide to accommodate him. I keep my rhythmic movement, not wanting to stop this rising sensation, feeling his arousal slide along my increasingly tense center. A moan comes from somewhere. Was it from him or me? It didn't sound like my voice. I wrap my legs around his waist as he bites down on my neck, not enough to hurt, but the sharp sensation rockets through me. I gasp and open my eyes for the first time since we began our meditation.

Eyes lock, freezing us in place. Breath halts. Stillness stretches between us until Tiernan looks away, shattering whatever spell held us suspended. "You were right. That was a bit... overwhelming. Wow."

He brushes some hair away from my face and moves to roll off. "I can still hear your heartbeat." He smirks, settling onto his bedroll.

I can't think. I don't want to think. I want to forget everything else. I only want to feel. My body throbs for the release I crave.

"Good. Keep listening," I sigh. My voice is unfamiliar and desperate as I climb on top of him, straddling his waist and pressing down, desperate for some friction. I kiss him before he has a moment to react, but he doesn't miss a beat.

His lips are so soft, so warm. His exhale into my kiss flows through my coiled body. His hands slide onto my hips, holding me in place. He starts to move me in tempo. The overwhelming sensation builds as the heat rises up my spine again. He deepens our kiss, his tongue sliding between my lips to open my mouth, but it's still not enough.

I break the kiss and reach up to rip off my sweater, leaving me straddling him in nothing more than my breast support.

"I want more. Need more. I need you," I breathe the words, panting and desperate.

He lifts his gaze and freezes. Fingers trace beneath the edge of the thin linen garment, sliding around to find the clasp that holds it in place. I raise my arms, and he slips it off in one smooth motion. His pupils dilate, eyes flicking across my face and bare skin. The intensity of his gaze scorches like a brand, leaving heat in its wake wherever it lingers.

Tiernan's hips thankfully return to their rhythmic movement, and so do mine. Our bodies undulate together in a perfect song. I want to feel every bit of him against me, deep inside me. The need is intense and building with every second.

Muscles flex as he yanks off his shirt in one swift motion, thrusting his hips upward to wriggle free of his pants with one hand while the other stays anchored to my side, keeping our bodies flush. Awkward but determined, the effort speaks volumes—he won't let go. Fingers trail across bruises and scrapes scattered over my skin, reverent in their touch. A kiss lands on the cut along my neck, tender and aching, the same wound I earned trying to rip off the collar.

Tiernan continues his exploration down and reaches his hand into my leggings to cup me, one finger slowly sliding through my wetness, placing the slightest bit of pressure. It's not enough. He moves his finger around a few times in patient and methodical circles. I throw my head back, letting out a frustrated groan that echoes against the stone.

Erratic breathing cuts through the haze, registering at the edge of my awareness. The sudden absence of his hand, cold and abrupt, freezes me in place.

He rolls me onto my back, pulling down my leggings on the way. His hands slide back up my bare legs as he spreads them and nestles his body on top of mine. His rigid head brushes against my core, sending tantalizing shockwaves. I arch my back, leaning into him, begging for him to stop teasing. Urging him to slide into me where I need him the most. The tension within me is so intense I can't think about anything but relief. Consequences be damned. I *need* this.

He takes his cock in his hand and brushes against my sensitive nub a few agonizing times. I reach my hands around to grab the back of his neck, his teasing becoming more than I can stand. I'm hot, burning, wound too tight. Before I can tell him exactly what I want in the most explicit way possible, he slides deep into me and lets out a harsh exhale as I inhale sharply. I'm so ready for him, but his size is still startling, stretching me with intense pressure.

Holding himself still deep inside me he gazes into my eyes. I focus on my Enhanced Sight to appreciate his beautiful gaze in the cave's dim light, the fire casting us in harsh shadows. He gives me a moment to adjust, but I can't wait and roll my hips against him. His pupils grow so large that there's barely a ring of gray left. The slightest hint of a smile forms in the corner of Tiernan's perfect mouth, and he slides smoothly out before coming back in so slowly I might scream.

"I've been dreaming about this for weeks, months even," he groans. "Ever since the first time I saw you walk down that hallway." *Thrust.* "Fuck! You feel better than I could have ever imagined." He bites my shoulder. "Like you were made for me, like we were made for each other," he whispers into my neck. His words flood my Senses as he increases the speed and pressure. He slides his hands under me, lifting my ass off the ground, letting him go deeper. The moan I have been holding escapes at the new sensation as he glides over just the right spot.

"Yes, like that. Don't hold back. I want to feel you come around me. It's all I've been able to think about," he practically growls while he leans over me, pressing his chest into mine, murmuring those sweet words into my neck. He licks up the column of my throat and tugs on my ear with his teeth. The heat and tension build inside me, so close to the surface, begging to be released.

So close.

"Please don't stop, Tiernan. Whatever you do, don't stop," I beg, barely recognizing my voice. Something shifts in him. A determination that was locked is now set free. He pulls back and slides his hand across my chest. He strokes the hot skin between my breasts and down my stomach, until he rubs over my clit.

The combination of his hand on me with him so deep inside me, moving in unison, is too much. An inferno spreads up my stomach to my chest before burning my cheeks. It engulfs me. I let out a scream. Heat rushes through my body, burning me to my core. The unbearable tension inside me snaps in one fiery explosion as I moan his name, pulling his weight onto me. My teeth clench down into his meaty shoulder.

"Gods, you're so different than how I thought you would be," he grits out through clenched teeth, his thrusts growing harder, faster, less controlled as he chases his release. Pushing deep into me, he lets out a guttural rumble. His body shudders and then stills.

Silent except for the rapid breathing between us, we don't roll apart. The freezing air on our sticky skin sends shivers down my exposed flesh. I'll hold on to this feeling for as long as I can.

Tiernan dips his forehead against my temple and grazes his lips across my cheek before pulling away. I shiver, cold and empty, but my muscles are relaxed. My limbs still tingle from the intense high of my climax.

Walking over to his bag, he grabs a towel, naked and glorious, and I unabashedly enjoy the harsh lines of his body, the way his muscles flex and shift as he moves. I send a silent thank you to my Sight for the ability to appreciate this view even in the darkness. His long legs and tight ass lead up to his broad solid back and strong shoulders. I want to run my hands over his skin until I know each scar, indent, and muscle.

When I reach for my sweater, he moves fast and throws it out of reach. He doesn't bother putting his clothes back on. A wide smile spreads across his beautiful, angular face. He doesn't smile enough. He might smirk, tease, or grin, but this is a true smile that crinkles the corners of his eyes.

Tiernan kneels and cleans us both up, grinning the entire time. It's a good look, one I'd like to see more. He lays back, relaxed for the first time since we met and opens his arms. "I'll keep you warm tonight. Body heat is more efficient anyway."

"Is this taught in guard training?" I tease as I slide into the nook of his shoulder. He wraps his arm around me, rolling me onto my side facing him as he pulls one leg over his. He maneuvers and adjusts me until we're both comfortable then pulls the blankets and coats back over our naked bodies to trap and share our warmth.

I can't keep my eyes open any longer as my sated body drifts off. Warm, safe, and relaxed.

CHAPTER 26
LYDIA

Sunshine peeps through the trees at the cave entrance. I shoot up from deep sleep. My eyes dart around, but I'm alone. *Where am I?* My heart pounds.

Ba-dum. Ba-dum. Ba-dum. Too fast. The pounding gets louder, blocking out my ability to quiet my mind. Faster and faster.

Ba-dum. Ba-dum. Ba-dum. Ba-dum.

The fire still burns. Tiernan must have put some fresh logs on, but he's nowhere to be seen. I need to ground myself, but I struggle to hold on to a single solid thought. It's gone before another takes its place.

Severely lightheaded, everything from the last few days floods through my mind at once.

I was almost kidnapped.

Deep breath.

I almost died yesterday.

Need air.

So many men lost their lives because they were charged with protecting me.

Slow down.

Their deaths are on me.

I can't breathe.

If I had been better, my Sight had been trusted, and we hadn't been on this journey, those men might still be alive.

A total stranger—multiple strangers, to be accurate—wanted to hurt me, made a plan to do so. Men who a council member hired. Asher, who proposed to marry me weekly, tried to kidnap me. I underestimated him, interpreting this all as a bruise on his ego and not part of a larger, more nefarious plot. Even I didn't think he'd go quite this far. I should have. He offered to escort me with his own men. I won't underestimate him again.

Lest I forget, I killed a man and would have killed another. I killed someone. He's dead by my hand. Rapid, shallow, and uneven breaths are all I can manage. My airway constricts. I concentrate on clearing my mind and focusing on my breathing, but I'm too late to close these floodgates.

I killed someone. *Gasp.* I almost died. *Gasp.* I had a collar around my throat. *Slow down!*

My Sight is out of control, pouring out of me. Blinding, bright rainbows interspersed with clear vignettes flash and flicker into my mind rapidly, one after another after another. The cave around me distorts and then vanishes, throwing me violently into the forest of my mind.

Unlike in a Vision, I'm ungrounded and uncentered. I'm aware of my surroundings but unable to do anything about it. It's so much worse. Equally vulnerable, I'm alone, naked and exposed to anything that may come in here. It's terrifying, but the flashes keep coming, unrelenting in the assault on my Senses.

My fingers claw blindly at the dirt, desperately searching for something to cling to. Images of what could have been and glimpses of a horrific future flash through my mind. Waves of panic crash over me relentlessly, beating me into the ground with no reprieve.

I'm awake and aware, but I have no control. This is harsh, brutal and painful, and it won't relinquish my Sight back to me. I can't find my path out of the Vision or get enough air into my lungs.

Black, spotty voids mix among the bright, colorful flashes that weave through my Vision. I'm vaguely aware of my body being lifted off the ground. A firm, warm pressure squeezes around me. My mind catches up and registers that it's Tiernan. He's holding me, but my Sight refuses to be pushed back.

His deep, soothing voice is a gentle whisper in my ear. "Breathe in, hold it, breathe out. Do it again, breathe in, hold it—five things you can see. Let's start there." A palm presses into my back. His fingers spread wide, spanning across as much skin as he can. He squeezes me in his arms, holding me tight against his chest, engulfing me in the comforting pressure of his embrace. "Breathe, Lydia. Feel my chest and follow my breathing."

I push every bit of my remaining energy into connecting my lungs with my mind. Warm tears run down my cheeks. My body starts to shiver uncontrollably. The constant, even pressure of his arms banding around me along with his hushed instructions are a soothing map that guides me back to control. After what feels like an eternity, my Sight finally provides a path back out.

He grins, but it doesn't reach his eyes. "I leave for a few minutes to piss, and you lose control of your Senses? I should stick closer moving forward."

I step away and walk over to my sweater crumpled on the cold ground where it landed last night. I slide on the chilly knit and rub my arms to get warm. I bend over to put on my pants and try to untangle my hair with shaking fingers before throwing it into a loose and messy braid. It'll have to do.

I inhale as I process the panic attacks and compare them to those of my adolescence. "Sorry about that. I haven't had that happen since I was young, fifteen or sixteen. It's been a while."

My mind whirls with all the worst-case scenarios I witnessed. They were glimpses of a future that's no longer possible but could have been true if not for some tiny shift in action or choice leading to a divergent path. It could be anything, some small change that has already happened or a change yet to come.

Tobias always said that the most challenging part of experiencing Panic-Visions is to understand and accept that these nightmares of the future are no longer possible. Visions in general are interpretations of pathways, but Visions that center around the Seer are inherently suspect. Hence, why we keep things to ourselves until we have a clear picture. Uncontrolled emotions, extreme stress, or trauma can trigger something like this. Well, the last few weeks of my life have checked all those boxes.

The path ahead has diverged from those futures, but there are still pieces to glean. Aspects of those images hold truth, impact the present, and contain elements of a possible future.

One in particular keeps drawing my attention.

Locked in a tomb, the air is rank—metallic with blood, sour with sweat, and damp.

I'm beaten and bloodied, my skin a canvas of bruises.

Asher looms above me, a towering shadow that swallows what little light dares enter the room. His presence chokes the space—and still, he steps closer.

I curl into a ball on the cold, wet stone. It leeches warmth like it means to take something more permanent. I hid something from him. An object he wants desperately.

"This is how you thank me for saving your life? You're the only one who can give it to me. Tell me where it is!" He kicks me hard. I curl tighter, collapsing further into the dark, my mouth open in a silent scream.

A kaleidoscope of color bursts in the corner of my eye—too sharp to be real, too bright for this place. The Vision claws its way in again, peeling me from the present like torn skin.

. . .

THAT POSSIBLE FUTURE no longer exists, but it doesn't mean it wasn't a plausible thread in the tapestry of possibilities. A nugget of truth. Something wiggles in the deepest recess of my mind. A rattle shaking for my attention. What did I hide from him?

After a lifetime of training, a lifetime of secrets, a leap of faith and trust is necessary. There's no viable alternative. I certainly don't see one. My blind trust could be my end, and I wouldn't even be conscious. But trust could also save me. Save us all.

"I need your help. I need to walk through those images again but holding on to the control this time. To do that, I need you to guard me, trust me, and, for the love of god, don't wake me up unless I'm in danger. I won't be able to listen, speak, smell, or feel anything. Can you take watch for me? I'm trusting you."

He stiffens and starts folding our blankets. "This is a bad idea. If that wasn't a Vision and was just some kind of panic attack, is that something you want to relive? This feels different from what you did in the dining hall. Is it safe to go back in there? Let your mind see that again? I don't know…"

I look around the cave and laugh. This is ridiculous. How did I get here? "In a perfect world, I would be doing this in the safety of Tobias's study, but we don't live in a perfect world, Tiernan. I'm not denying that it will be painful, but I *know* I saw something important. I can see deeper, and I need to try. You're all I have out here so please, help me." I straighten my shoulders. My Sight whispers to me that this needs to be done *now*.

Tiernan sighs. His shoulders sag as he positions himself facing the cave entrance, far enough away that he won't distract me but close enough that his presence is a wall of protection.

Breathe in.

Five, four, three, two, one.

Breathe out.

Five, four, three, two, one.

Repeat.

Five things I can see, four things I can touch, three things I can hear, two things I can smell, and one thing I can taste. I clear the path for the rainbow mist. Its heavy, humid warmth envelopes me. I step into its familiar embrace as my eyes glaze over and I step into the misty forest. It takes a few minutes to find the path I need. It's hidden, barely recognizable if not for my training, but the mist pulls me deeper.

I FIND MYSELF ALONE, *adrift at sea. The walls around me groan like something ancient and dying, whispering secrets in a language I don't understand. Outside the salt-smeared window, storm clouds churn in the distance—black, swollen things with bellies full of rain and ruin. A harbor glimmers faintly on the horizon, too far to touch. Closer still, another boat slices through the water like a blade, swift and silent.*

The collar around my neck is a shackle forged of possession and jealousy. It bites at my skin with every breath.

Then the door crashes open, slamming against the wall with a sharp report.

Something darker than the storm has come to collect its due.

FLASH. Pure white light, void of any color, blinds me.

A MUSTY STENCH *curls into my nose, sharp and pungent, sending phantom itches crawling across my skin. The iron collar at my throat is tethered to a hook buried deep in the rotting wood beneath me—like a beast leashed at the altar of its hunter. Asher looms above, his shadow long and stretching, swallowing the light as though the world itself has been torn open. Behind him, a figure lingers in the darkness—a presence I cannot see but feel, an undercurrent of hatred flowing through the air like poison.*

"I gave you my devotion," Asher says, his voice low and coiled with simmering rage, "my undivided attention, for years. I waited for you to

understand what we could be. I played your little games. You should have given me what I wanted—what I've earned."

He grabs my leg and yanks, pulling me closer with the cold precision of a butcher. The shadow behind him remains still, its malice simmering like the calm before a storm.

"I could have given you everything. But you—" he spits the word— "you think you're better than me. Above me. Once you show me the path, once you open the door, I'll be the most powerful man in the Aperion. And then, finally, you'll give me the one thing I've always deserved."

His hand tightens, and I feel his grip like an iron vise.

"Your respect."

FLASH. Shooting, blinding pain sears my Sight. My body recoils from the overwhelming brightness, but the Vision refuses to release me.

AN OLDER MAN sits across from me, his eyes flicking over my bruised, malnourished body. Disdain and pity wrestle in his gaze. His bony fingers clutch a small copper key. "That thing is cursed. It will lead you to madness, a slow, painful death." He hands it to Asher, but Asher recoils before accepting it, hesitantly.

Asher schools his features, then slams the key down. "You told me she could find it. You sold me a lie."

The old man shrugs. "I don't know how many more Panic-Visions we can force before she breaks. The last three ships never returned. The witch's curse is doing its job. We may need to bring her—she cannot find the path if she isn't on it."

"No," Asher snarls. "She will never be free of this prison. The risk of someone else capturing her is too great. Force another Vision. Make her understand the consequences." He storms out, leaving only the old man and me.

A small notebook cracks open, and the old man begins to write, his movements mechanical. "Let's begin."

Terror surges through me, cold and crawling. The path, just out of reach, simmers beneath my mind, its secrets slipping further away.

The path to what?

FLASH. The pure light is so bright it cuts through my eyes, burning the back of my skull with its intensity.

I CRAWL from the frigid water onto a beach of pitch-black sand, debris floating in the surf. I search for someone, but the shore is empty.

A cold key presses against my skin, its chain tight around my neck. I know this key. I squeeze it, sharp edges cutting into my palm.

I struggle to steady my breath, but my legs give way, and I fall. My swollen belly contracts violently, pain shooting through my back before fading. Fear coils in my gut. Another wave of agony crashes over me.

A dilapidated hut stands among the trees, its sagging roof barely intact.

Shelter. Blessed Shelter.

I clutch my stomach, pain crawling down my spine, and the darkness tightens around me.

FLASH. The white light is an impenetrable wall, so stark and piercing it swallows everything around it, leaving me dizzy, nauseous and disoriented.

THE FLASHES ARE COMING FASTER NOW: images, scenes, and vignettes with little to no context. A book on a library shelf. A mask discarded on a grassy lawn. The prick of blood on a fingertip. Exhaustion sets in. The Panic-Visions when I first woke up took too much from me. I need to sleep, so I relax and force what little energy I have remaining.

I close off my Sight and walk back out through the haze.

Five, four, three, two, one.

I push my way through the mist, which feels thicker and harder to navigate than usual, the colors more saturated and vibrant. It's trying to hold me back, and I can't endure much more.

Five, four, three, two, one.

My heavy feet resist, but I drag myself forward. Step by agonizing step.

Five, four, three, two, one.

Slowly, my eyes flutter back to their normal green and blue.

Tiernan hasn't moved, focused on the cave's entrance. He holds the canteen of water out to me, never taking his eyes off any potential threat until I regain control of my Sight. I drink half the water in one go.

"I know it's daylight, and we need to get moving, but I simply can't. I need to rest and might fall off my horse if I try to ride right now. I understand this affects our timeline, but it's unsafe until I've had time to recover." I curl into a tight ball on my bedroll, not waiting for a response. My eyes feel like someone rubbed sand in them. I'm so cold and tired I might throw up. This is a different kind of cold. This is a chill from the inside.

Tiernan's bedroll and bag are packed and ready to go, but he lies down next to me and wraps his arms around me. He doesn't ask me any questions, he doesn't push, he holds me as sleep takes over. I finally feel safe. If such a thing exists for someone like me.

How long have I been asleep? I pull the blanket tighter around me and reach out for Tiernan, who isn't beside me. I roll over. Dusk begins to peek through the trees. He's standing against the jagged side of the entrance. His back is to me, and his impressive silhouette in the setting sun calms me instantly.

"There's another hot spring I found not far from here when I went to find dry wood, if you want to wash off, well, everything. It'll soothe your muscles too," Tiernan says, keeping his back to me. I don't know how he senses that I'm finally awake.

"A hot spring sounds amazing. Thank you," I mumble, rolling over the stand.

"I won't peek, but you can't go alone," he teases, finally turning to me. He holds out a hand, and I take it willingly.

We link our fingers on the short walk. Steam wafts from a tiny pool tucked under a waterfall. Not even sure this counts as a waterfall. It's more of a drip collecting at the bottom of a rocky cliff.

I step out of my clothes, shivering as I fold them before placing the tidy pile on a bare but damp stone. It'll have to do. Stepping into the steaming water is divine. My sigh makes me blush. Tiernan blushes, too, as he spins on his heels, turning his back to me.

"You are welcome to join me."

"I'll stand guard. It's safer for both of us." I'm unsure how to interpret that remark, but I don't want to fight and ruin this temporary bliss. I scrub myself down instead, embracing the silence interrupted by the constant drip.

"All done. Do you want a dip while I stand watch? I can't promise I won't peek, though." I grin, stepping out of the hot spring. I dry myself off and throw my clothes back on.

The sky fades to night. Tiernan makes quick work of the hot spring, but I am able to adjust my Sight enough to appreciate every ridge of his abdomen, every scar on his biceps. His heated gaze doesn't go unnoticed either.

He steps from the hot spring like a god emerging from creation itself. Steam wafts off his bronzed skin as water droplets cling before sliding down. Tiernan's lip tugs up in the corner at my perusal. He pulls his pants back on before throwing a shirt over. The damp fabric now clinging to the ridges of his abs. I sigh and suppress a giggle realizing I'm jealous of fabric now.

He holds out a hand. "Let's get some sleep. I'll find us something to eat after you've had some rest." He eyes me skeptically. I want him to ask, to talk to me, but I don't know how to answer if he does. He opens his mouth, but nothing comes out. Concern mixes with curiosity, but something stops him from pushing for answers. Either he's giving me space or he thinks I'm nuts.

I let him entwine our fingers again and follow him back into the cave. He adds some more wood to the fire and settles into sleep quickly without a word. Okay then. The Panic-Vision probably scared him. Made him realize I'm not worth the trouble. I lie down quietly, not wanting to disturb him, and drift back to sleep.

The mist surrounds me the moment my eyes close. Not this again. Can I please just sleep?

It's calling me, tempting me to feel the warm haze wash over me. A siren's song. I can't deny its pull. I shouldn't. This is the price I pay for such a gift.

There's no flashing this time. The familiar, steady, and vaguely damp multi-colored fog is muted. Even the fog is exhausted.

*S*HOUTS CRACK *the air beyond my door—panicked, primal. I snatch my knives and ease it open. Blood clings to Iris like a second skin. Not hers. Thank the gods.*

Her obsidian eyes are wide and unblinking. "They're dead," she whispers, holding out trembling red hands. Her midnight hair is tangled, matted with gore.

The words don't land at first. They hover, unreal.

"Who?"

"Mother and Father. The rebels—they let them in. Someone let them in. They're dead!" Her knees buckle, crashing to the floor like her legs have forgotten how to hold her.

For a breath, I can't move. Something cold threads through my spine, coils around my lungs.

"Stay here." My voice sounds distant, hollow. I don't wait for a reply. The door slams behind me as I bolt into the hall.

The castle groans like a mourner's wail. Familiar corridors warp into something monstrous. Around the gallery corner, the dining hall comes into view—metal clashing, glass shattering, the very bones of the keep collapsing in protest. Ryo fights on the far side, blood-slick and limping. He's losing.

No. No, no, no.

I sprint—but the floor beneath me is treacherous. I slip on something slick. Pain explodes through my back as I slam into the stone.

Then—shadow. Movement. A man steps into my vision, sword wet with blood. His eyes burn with certainty. His gaze locks on mine.

"There you are."

I kick out, wild, but he dodges. "No time," he snaps—his voice foreign, strange. "You're coming with me."

I don't recognize him. That terrifies me more than if I had. He grabs my arm, gloved and unyielding, and drags me down the hall. I scream, scratch, fight—but no one notices. No one comes. It's like I've been swallowed whole by the chaos.

He stops abruptly, breathless, glaring down at me. "You'd better be worth this." His tone isn't angry—it's exhausted, irritated. Like kidnapping me was a chore on his list.

He sheathes his sword, rips off his glove with his teeth, and presses a bare hand to my head.

A black tattoo snakes from his wrist, branching like roots over his fingers. It pulses. Cold. Ancient. Hungry.

He exhales.

The world fractures.

I wake in a rowboat slicing through black water. Saivi shrinks behind us, a silhouette of stone and ruin. The north tower burns like a pyre—my home, my life, my family's bodies turning to ash.

I don't cry. I can't. Grief lodges in my throat like a shard of glass. Too sharp to swallow. Too deep to pull free.

Another boat follows—Tiernan at the helm.

The Handler keeps me close. His gloves are back on. He's young. Not much older than me. Boyish, almost beautiful. Brown curls fall into furious dark eyes. A face that shouldn't belong to a monster. That's the worst kind.

I burn his face into my memory: sharp cheekbones, full mouth. The kind of face that lies with a smile. The kind of face I will never forget. I will make this face pay.

His lips are moving, but the ringing in my ears drowns out the words.

Then clarity pierces through: "Do you have the key?"

He's shouting now. "Lydia. The fucking key."

He paws at my dress. His hands are rough, frantic. Then he finds the chain at my neck. Yanks it. The copper key swings free, glinting dull in the moonlight.

He drops it like it burns him. His breath catches, then releases. He doesn't reach for it again.

Behind us, Tiernan's boat gains. I reach through the ringing, through the dark, and stretch my Sight. His fury is a flame cutting through the fog. He's coming for me. For the key.

But the harbor slips away. We cross the threshold into open sea.

The mist thickens—soft, alive, sentient. It curls around me like breath, like memory. The key hums against my chest.

And the mist grants me a path.

And lets me go.

I sit straight up, gasping for air. Tiernan shoots up onto his feet, his hand on his hilt. He scans our surroundings. Finding no visible threat, he glares down at me on the floor.

"We need to get back to Silvanisi as soon as possible." My words shake. My legs are wobbly, but I shoot up and pack what's left and pull my boots on.

It's dawn again. I must have slept through the night. We can get a good amount of distance if we push ourselves. I'm still exhausted and I'd take longer to regain my strength in an ideal world, but something about this felt urgent. The cold felt recent. The moon looked similar to last night. This isn't something that may happen in the spring or even a few months away. This is a time-sensitive problem, and time isn't on our side. Even if we only break for short rests, it'll still take a few days to get back home.

"No. One thing at a time. We need to continue onto the bay. That's the mission. Then we can get into whatever else you see coming."

"Fuck this mission! It's bullshit anyway. The Vision of the ships from the bay was in springtime. This one, it was freezing. This is present or imminent. We have to go now. There's no time to waste. If we go to the bay and back, we may be too late," I plead. Please listen to me! Trust me!

"No, I have my orders. Now, get on your horse and get moving. That's an order."

We don't have time for this, and I'm not one of his soldiers. I cross my arms. "I'm going back with or without you."

"Like hell you are! I'm in command here," he seethes.

"I'm asking you to trust me. Haven't I earned at least that? Please, Tiernan. Trust me."

We stare each other down, a dual ready to commence. He could force me, tie me to the horse and continue. I'd not be able to stop him, but I can make it difficult. I disperse my weight, readying myself. His eyes trace down my stance. As though he could hear my innermost thoughts, Tiernan softens. "Okay, I'm choosing to trust you. Don't make me regret this."

CHAPTER 27

RYO

Kira growls at Ezra, a feral throaty non-verbal threat. This to a man who could one day be her husband. "Silvanisi has never and will never operate in any capacity to support any slavery. Your accusation is deeply offensive and won't soon be forgiven or forgotten." Annnnnnd there's the verbal threat. Kira held her tongue for longer than I anticipated, so I don't know why I'm surprised. Mother's side-eye gives nothing away to a stranger, but her children know what that look means. Kira is perfectly capable of looking like a graceful, well-bred princess, but she's incapable of sounding like one for very long to Mother's chagrin.

Ezra doesn't jump to respond. He merely tilts his head to the side from the end of the table and lets the silence spread across the room. He could be thinking about the implications of Kira's statement or what he wants for dinner. He jumps from cold and serious to friendly and carefree with the snap of a finger. We pose no threat to him, in his mind, so are therefore insignificant. Or I'm completely wrong because the man is unreadable and unflappable. Or fickle, which is just as problematic. It's infuriating.

Too comfortable, he leans back in his chair, one ankle crossed over his knee, a full glass of red wine resting there. Kira's anger builds with every second as his casual indifference to her accusation fuels the fire. He checks his nails, then leans over to whisper something in the ear of the intimidating woman beside him. Their inaudible murmurs stretch across the silence. She nods, and after a moment, he finally returns to the conversation, unbothered by the collective discomfort.

Or it's possible that's the point.

"I am simply sharing the information I've been able to collect—in the name of friendship, of course. Silvanisi has always been a known ally and a haven for all Sense Adepts. Your conveniently missing Seer is proof of that." He grins. "Now, we know Master Tobias is on Merthaset. Where is Lydia again? She should be present for this discussion as the highest ranking Auctus representative." That's now the third time Ezra has asked about Lydia. Alarms trumpet in my mind.

Iris's carefully crafted façade of serenity is crumbling by the minute. The inside of her cheek must be raw by now. "Lydia is not your concern. Do you plan to keep us in suspense, your majesty? Why are you here?"

"Very well, my beautiful princess." He grins wolfishly, elongating each syllable. *Beau-ti-ful.* His slight accent draws out the vowels. The shallow, insincere compliment makes Iris even more agitated. Her mask slips a bit further as she gathers and clutches the fabric of her long, billowing sleeves in her tight fists. "We've been able to intercept a handful of slave ships over the last two months or so, in varying degrees of cooperation. The majority have been average, nondescript slavers heading for the workshops, farms, and quarries on the continent. We have a few surviving refugees on Verralon and have received conflicting information but this one was different. They were separating the Seers from the other Adepts."

"And this is different how?" Commander Cormac asks. "I would assume it is standard procedure to separate Adepts from Laymen as morally abhorrent as this all is."

"Yes. You are correct in that on many counts. However they don't separate by Enhanced Sense, only by those who have or have not. The Seers were removed to a separate cell. Despite their small numbers, the Seers were isolated, and it was clear they had been tortured. We haven't come across one alive."

Eyes connect and dart across the table, bouncing like a ball. Each person seated at this end knows where Lydia is, and the reality that we may have put her in further danger begins to settle in. A brick on top of a brick, getting heavier by the second. I need to think. I can't lose myself to panic at this table. In front of these people. They already question our strength. How much will that grow when we can't hide father's diminishing health? They probably already know and are making plans. This is probably a scouting mission for them. *Fuck!*

"I need a moment with Amos." I turn to Amos and wait for verification of the statement from my Enhanced Translator.

"He speaks the truth as it is known to him," Amos confirms.

"Ah! You're an Enhanced Judge, too! That's fantastic! Always nice to meet a fellow lie-detector." One of the younger men in Ezra's entourage jumps up to embrace Amos. Amos jumps back, with his knife half drawn, ready to injure if needed.

Ezra gestures toward the young man, unamused. "My brother, Leif. He's also an Enhanced Taste Adept."

Leif chuckles, giving Amos some space. "Let's meet for a beer later and swap tips. I'm having a hard time deciphering the difference between a lie and a fake orgasm. I have my suspicions, but confirmation is always appreciated."

The Verralon prince appears to be of a similar age to my sisters. He's tall and lean, having not filled out yet with the same unique auburn wavy hair denoting his relation to Ezra. His hair is unbound, cropped to right below the sharp jaw and tucked behind his ears. He must constantly brush it back from falling into his eyes, a similar golden amber to Ezra's. His smooth face is tanned like his brothers, but his isn't hiding behind a thick reddish beard.

"And the rest of your companions? We would love an introduction to help them feel more welcome," Mother probes. After observing quietly, she's now choosing to make her presence known. Her mind must be processing a thousand scenarios to turn this into an opportunity for... something. Mother may have no Enhanced Sense, but she does have her gifts—a sense of finding a way to work everything to her family's advantage.

Ezra waves to the imposing group. "Friends, family, and trusted guards. Names can wait. They aren't the priority." He elaborates no further and makes no individual introductions. I'm not convinced he would have introduced the prince had he not needed to de-escalate the incident with Amos.

"Now," Ezra continues, "after tracking the slave ships back to Silvanisi through records kept on-board, we have discovered through... *strategic conversations*... that the ships were being funded and operated off the northeastern coast of your country, right under your nose apparently."

He pauses to study our faces, letting the accusation sink in. "How embarrassing to find out from the crude Verralon barbarians that your people are the ones kidnapping and selling their fellow citizens. However disturbing that may be, it was even more problematic to find a journal some half-witch left noting, in detail, that they experimented on any Seers they found to the point of killing them. Dwindling an already endangered Enhanced Sense. Horrible. We were unable to discover the goal of such abominable experiments. We believe they were trying to induce Visions. The Laymen crew became unwilling to elaborate when they went mad from what they described as a 'curse.' Gruesome to witness, but they would have met their fate regardless." He shrugs.

"You mean to tell us that you learned, through *strategic conversations*, that some rouge half-witch is killing Sight Adepts and selling any other Adepts they come across into slavery? Do I have that correct?" I blink slowly, baffled at the implications. I look over the faces of my cabinet, hoping someone will say something. I piece together the jumble of information over the past few months. Adepts missing. Rumors of slavers. Rebel bands roaming the coast.

What does the Auctus know? What of Tobias? Is that why he jumped when Merthaset called? He left Lydia here alone. That must stand for something if he felt she was safer here than going to Merthaset with him. But she's not here and she's not safe.

"The shipping records onboard note multiple Silvanisi ports as frequent stops. My apologies if your commander has not been keeping you updated on the latest information surrounding your shores. It hasn't been quite out on the water between our two islands by any stretch, but who am I to say?" Ezra shrugs like he didn't accuse the commander of the Silvanisi forces of gross incompetence.

Seething in the corner, Cormac miraculously holds his tounge and stays in his seat. I would have expected chairs to be thrown or fists, not this quiet simmering rage coming from him.

"And these *strategic conversations*—I assume the people you conversed with can no longer corroborate this information?" Iris pushes. The steel edge in her voice is present but softened to be more diplomatic.

Ezra nods to his surrounding guard. "My present companions stand as witnesses." He avoids introducing them. Again.

The giant man to his side with shoulders like shelves tosses a notebook and a folder of papers, letting it slide down the table until it rests on the Silvanisi end. He doesn't say anything and sits back down.

"We were also able to discover a link between the slave trade and this little rebellion you've been deliberately ignoring on your island. The two appear to be funded by the same person or people. We also have credible information that your precious and mysteriously absent Sight Adept is their top target with quite the bounty on her head should she be brought in alive. Interesting that the person with the highest value to them isn't here," Ezra continues, gesturing to the papers. Daring us to challenge or doubt the proof he's literally thrown in our faces.

All the blood drains from my face. I *knew* sending her to the Cerulean Bay was a bad idea. I *knew* it was dangerous, and we all *knew* it was a risk given the missing Adepts. She could already be captured. She could be dead. What if someone experiments on her and it kills her? Will she be found on a ship months from now? I should have fought against it harder. Should have pushed back. I should have been better.

I want to grab a horse and go after her. Bring her home where she's safe and protected. Never have I objected to the burdens of this chair, this position, this duty more than I do at this moment, but the crown must come first. With every thought of abandoning my seat, my oath brand burns from the eyes of the lynx spreading outward, a tangible reminder that my choices are not my own, and the resentment is thick and difficult to swallow.

"Where is she? Do you even know?" Ezra demands answers. His charming, casual persona is gone, and only the impatient, angry warlord remains. His eyes practically glow with fire and fury. "I'm done fucking about with this. Your bullshit won't bleed across the Aperion Sea. Your inability to control your people won't hurt Verralon. She needs protection from someone capable of getting the job done, which clearly, you are not."

"She is safe and in good hands, doing her duty to her king. Tobias should return any day now. We know no more than that," my mother replies with the bare minimum of details.

Amos's eye twitches at her statement. He bites the inside of his cheek and swallows. His face sours, but he neutralizes his expression again quickly.

Ezra glances at his brother Leif. The young Verralon prince purses his lips, winks, but says nothing. The two aren't even bothering with subtlety.

"Then we kindly request to stay until we can relay this information to the two Seers most impacted. Honored guests until his return and all such diplomatic nonsense. Ryo. Walk with me for a bit." He rises from the table, his guard following suit.

My mother and sisters catch my gaze. Amos shifts behind Kira's chair, taking up a protective stance as Ezra's entourage files out of the chamber. We need every scrap of information he holds. With no practical choice but to follow, I brace myself. To protect Lydia, I'll do whatever is necessary, even if it means building trust with an island known for its treachery. It's a risk we have to take.

Ezra saunters to the end of the guest hall reserved for the highest-ranked visitors to Silvanisi. He pauses at the door and holds it open to invite me inside. Making himself quite at home in my castle.

"Let's have a more private conversation, shall we?" he says loud enough for my guards to hear.

I nod them off to wait in the hall and follow him into his suite.

He removes his coat and flings it onto a table. He falls back into a chair by the fire warming the slightly musty space. Leaning over, he removes his boots and untucks his shirt before sinking back into the chair with a weary sigh. It's less intimidating, but I'd be a fool to relax right now.

"Don't tiptoe, Ryo. It's unbecoming of a leader. Say what you mean to say. You'll be king soon enough if my spies are any good, which they are. It's time to sack up and take this problem by the balls. I'm here to help you. You may not see it. It won't be pretty and it won't be the alliance you want, but it will get the job done. You have a rebellion you've been unable to contain spreading like herpes through a war camp. Your people hate the Auctus and are tightening the noose around your neck for allowing them to have a foothold. Let's ignore for a moment everything the Auctus has done for them and everything anyone with an Enhanced Sense continues to do to help. The Healers, the Hunters and Trackers, the Tasters, the Judges and Translators. They are blamed for any little problem, because society is stabilized on scapegoats. But unfortunately for you, that blame is now being pointed at your head. Anti-Auctus vitriol is shifting from words to action. What do you plan to do about it?"

"It's being addressed," I seethe through clenched teeth. He really does think we are weak, incompetent, and inferior. He may be the most condescending man I've ever met, and I grew up fluent in the language of politics! I'm not blind to the sentiment or where it comes from. The difference lies in how we address it. Perhaps my father could have been more outspoken or aggressive, but hindsight is unfair and we have to move forward. Also, my hands are tied. I am not king.

"Clearly. It's a matter of time until these Anti-Auctus groups come after you if they haven't started already. Words today are wounds tomorrow. You are no longer the haven you once were, and the Auctus has noticed. They are recalling all ESAs from Silvanisi to Merthaset, starting with your Seers. Is she your mistress?" Ezra asks bluntly.

"Who?" I need a moment to figure out his train of thought.

"Who! The Visionary, Lydia. My intel doesn't usually wade into the murky waters of gossip, but this one... Are you planning on marrying her or just trapping her here permanently for her Sight? Or are you going to use her to go after it yourself?" He crosses his legs and leans one arm over the back of the chair. His body is relaxed and open, but it's a ruse. He's a predator waiting for me to show weakness before he strikes. He's hunting, and Lydia is his prey.

CHAPTER 28

LYDIA

It's been two long days. I'm bone tired and freezing cold. Why does it feel like time is moving slower? What would I give for a hot spring right now? What wouldn't I give?

By the time we stop to set up a little camp, it's already dark. The area we choose is flat and dry enough, but smoke would be visible for miles, sitting high on a cliff. We opt against a fire lest we risk drawing unwanted attention. We push our bedrolls beside each other and hug for warmth, pulling up every spare blanket and coat.

"Will you tell me what you saw? When you panicked? You don't need to risk the stress of walking me through it, but maybe a summary so I can understand? I want to understand," Tiernan pleads. His warm breath caresses my hair as we shiver in the dark tent. His arms wrap around me, keeping me secure and safe. A gentle kiss presses onto my forehead. I burrow farther into his warmth, hoping to give him some in return.

"There will be a brutal attack on the castle. The king and queen will be killed, and everyone will be fighting. Someone I don't know, someone with Enhanced Touch, will grab me and knock me unconscious; I'll wake up on a rowboat. The castle burns, just like it was in the Vision I spoke of at dinner before we left that caused such an uproar. The Handler's looking for something, though. The pieces fit together with the flashes I had during my panic attack." I bite my lip, muttering, "they have to be connected."

I decide to keep the key to myself for now. It keeps appearing, but it's hazy and unclear, and a lifetime of training has taught me to keep it simple and straightforward. Clarity is essential, so I'll share only the basics until I know more or can talk to Tobias.

"Is that how it works? You piece things together until it fits?" Tiernan's body starts to relax against mine as we warm up a bit. His hand reaches up to brush the hair away from my face.

"Most of the time, yes. It's like a large puzzle. I get some pieces and a few more, then a few more until I create a whole picture. Sometimes, Tobias sees part of it, and we work together to make sense of it. His Enhanced Sight is nowhere near the level of detail or frequency as mine, but he's studied for so long that he can squeeze a lot out of a little. He achieved his Master rank through practice, study, and determination, not necessarily a wealth of ability. Sometimes but not often, we receive a letter from a Seer in another court or from Grandmaster Morgan on Merthaset. We all work together to enhance our Sight, but proximity to the people or location helps boost it. Hence why we were sent to the Bay, in hopes that it would gain clarity or add an integral piece."

My frozen body eases while his hand makes slow circles across my back. I nuzzle my head into the crook where his shoulder meets his neck, soaking in his warmth.

"You know, we would get warm faster without clothes on. Skin on skin is the best way to share body heat." His eyebrow tips up along with the corner of his full lips. His hand reaches under my sweater and brushes against my bare skin along my ribs, sending butterflies straight to my stomach. A tingly warmth spreads through my limbs, and yet I shiver at the same time.

"Shouldn't we be resting? Tomorrow will be a long, hard ride." I kick myself and blush when I realize the innuendo.

"Tonight could be one, too," he whispers into my ear before biting my earlobe. I've lost all ability to rationalize. That's what this man does to me. He takes away all distractions, demanding my full attention.

"That is a terrible line."

"But did it work?" He leaves a trail of kisses down my neck.

My body takes over, and my mind is no longer in control. My hands slide under his shirt and pull it off. I reach down to undo the laces on his pants. His hands are tantalizingly caressing my ribs, incrementally going higher until he's brushing against the sensitive skin under my breasts. A soft moan escapes my lips as I lean my chest forward, silently pleading for more. I fumble to loosen the knot in his laces that strains against his hardness, blocking me from what I'm after.

"Your skin feels like silk. I want to touch you everywhere." Tiernan's voice is husky when his hand finally cups my breast and his thumb brushes across my nipple, back and forth in torturous, lazy strums. His other hand slides behind and into my leggings to squeeze my bare ass, his hips press into mine.

Our moment is interrupted by muffled voices. We both freeze, hearing the same sound. They don't sound close, but they also don't sound far enough away to not raise our hackles.

"Don't move," Tiernan whispers. "Stay in here."

"Like hell," I hiss. "I can see in the dark, remember?"

I grab my belt, tie it back on, and wrap my dark coat around my shoulders. We tiptoe out of the tent.

"If this turns ugly and we get separated, run into the woods and hide. I'll find you," he murmurs, squeezing my hand and pulling us deeper into the darkness. The horses' heads are up, ears twitching.

We creep toward the voices, his hand gripping tight to mine. Tiernan must use his own untrained Enhanced Senses to see in the dark. With the speed with which he weaves around underbrush and avoids stepping on twigs, any Layman would have crashed over a rock multiple times.

Branches snap below us, and hushed voices grow louder.

"Stay low," Tiernan orders, and we both drop silently. We crawl toward the edge of a small cliff overhang and spot a group of men below in a well-established campsite. They've been here for a few days, most likely, given their setup. They've moved logs to make benches around the fire and assembled a little makeshift kitchen.

A portly man sinks onto one of the logs. "Only a few more days. I'm so fucking tired of these woods. Fucking tired of being cold."

A young man who cannot be older than fifteen pokes a stick into the fire. "And then what?" he asks.

"And then we move in. Make them all bend over, get our hands on a healthy batch to sell, find the treasure and get the fuck off this frozen rock and get our riches," he replies to the boy, a crude humping gesture accompanying his words. The men all laugh at his vulgarity.

"The rich lord needs to get the girl he's after first. We can't get paid until she does her job," an older man says, his voice gravelly, deep, and distinctive. He's sharpening a knife. Everything about him screams professionally menacing. He's frankly succeeding.

Tiernan's hand falls on my shoulder, startling me. His head nods to move, and we create much-needed distance. Tiernan holds my hand for the rest of the trek to our campsite.

"Mercenaries? Just great. Slavers, too? Or a whole new brand of crazy? Or do we add this to the growing pile of shit that's trying to kill me?" My rage-whisper is not as quiet as it should be, but a girl can only handle so much.

"These men are not rebels. The rebellion doesn't support or condone slavery. Don't merge the two. It's possible both are financed by Montcliff. He seems to have his hand in multiple grabs for power." He slides his boots on. I hadn't even noticed he left the tent barefoot. He didn't bother to put his shirt back on, either. His golden muscles, which I take an inappropriate moment to appreciate, are covered in goosebumps. He must be freezing.

"We need to keep moving tonight in the dark. Create some

distance. They're targeting you, not the crown," he says. Once we are farther away, he steps close and draws me in. He wraps his arms around me and presses his lips hard into mine. His hand slides into my hair as he tilts my head back to deepen the kiss. My arms wrap around his waist, and my back arches to bring him in closer.

He pulls back abruptly, his arms holding me straight before him. He inhales and lets go to adjust himself. "I want to finish what we started earlier, but it has to wait. Let's get going."

CHAPTER 29
LYDIA

We ride hard, swiftly and silently in the moonlight. Both of us are experienced riders, both using Enhanced Sight to some degree. The quiet in the mountains is peaceful while the snow starts falling in soft, fluffy snowflakes. This is my favorite kind of snowfall. It muffles the sounds of the forest to the point where I think I can hear the clinking of the ice crystals colliding.

"Are you planning on retelling your adventures when we arrive? Or will you be keeping parts of it to yourself?" Tiernan asks, breaking the silence. Interesting question, given the time and circumstances, but if it's what's been on his mind, we should discuss it. Given his suspicions and reaction in the dining hall after I retold the Vision at dinner, it's understandable but annoying. It's what set off this whole journey. He lost good men because of me.

"There are certain parts of the last few days that I plan on keeping to myself, but I do intend to expose Asher and hope to stop any attack on my family." My stomach twists into a knot then twists tighter.

"That's...good. Do you intend to continue this, *us*, once you return home?" His voice is so calm and unaffected that it takes me a moment to register his question.

"I'd like that."

"What about your *prince*?" he asks with an unmistakable hint of hostility.

"What about Ryo? I'm free to spend time with anyone I wish. If he has a problem, that's on him," I answer, shrugging my shoulders. Ryo will be happy for me when I explain that Tiernan is important. This is something special. I can feel it.

"What about me being an unregistered Adept? Is that going to cause me problems with your boss?" he asks, a harder edge to his voice.

"Tobias isn't my boss. He's my mentor. There's a difference. I told you I would keep your secret. Nothing has changed in that regard. But consider for a moment the possibility that the Auctus can help you. You could use your Enhanced Senses to help people, help yourself, too." His prejudice has hindered him. It's dangerous and irresponsible.

He stops his horse suddenly. I'm a few steps in front of him before I pull my horse to a stop. "Did you hear something?" I survey the dark woods. I clear my mind to unleash my full Sight in the forest, spotting a few birds and a squirrel through the shadows cast by the moonlight.

Shaking his head, he looks down at me. "You've been fed the same lies for so long that you don't even see them for what they are. I pity you, Lydia. They own you, and you're grateful for it. You escape one slave collar to embrace another. Look at that oath on your arm that you're so proud to bear and tell me I'm wrong."

His words hit me like a whip across my body. "You have no idea what this oath means or what it says, much less what it represents. How dare you!"

"Tell me, then. Explain to me, because I got a good look at it up close the other night." My head snaps back like I'd been struck. How dare he throw our night together in my face like that. "All I see is a brand that puts the Auctus first. Right? *Auctus Primum.* Auctus First. That's what that means. Tell me I'm wrong."

"You have a horrible history with the Auctus, and I can't begin to relate to the depth of your anger or pain, but my experience isn't yours. My oath is about cooperation. If you had bothered to be trained, you'd understand that."

"What is the oath, then? The one they force on children too young to understand the ramifications of."

I stretch out of arm, pushing up my sleeve to expose the white spiral. "*Clear mind. Clear path. Open your Senses to show you the way. Together, we stand. Together, we follow the path. Together, we thrive. Together, we survive. Auctus Primum. Together in strength to bless the world with our gift.* I don't want your pity, misplaced as it is. Do you hate me because of my Sight? Because of my upbringing? Or do you just hate that you want to fuck a member of the Auctus?" I throw out the harsh words before I can think or take them back but they're out there now. Hanging between us.

"I never wanted to want you!" he bellows, leaping off his horse. I jump in my saddle but keep my seat. Birds squawk and wings rustle to fly away from the sudden noise. Our attempt at stealth travel is over. Anyone within a few miles of us heard him. He squats down on the ground, his elbows balancing on his knees and his head hanging low. "None of this was part of the plan," he whispers so softly I almost don't catch it.

I hop off Burya, walk to him, and touch his back. He shudders at the contact and steps away from me. "I'm sorry about what happened to your family. I'm sorry that you associate me with that trauma. I can't change your past, but I'd like to help you move forward if you'll let me. What do you want from me?" I plead, searching his face for the affection and passion I felt a few hours ago.

"For months I tried to keep my distance, keep you at arms-length. Months. And you drew me in, bewitched me, made me forget everything. I want nothing from you, and it *kills* me that I also want everything," Tiernan growls, stepping into my space. He grips the back of my head and pulls me toward him in a punishing kiss.

The grip he has on my head teeters on the edge of pain. I sense his need, his conflict. I put my hands on his chest to push him away, but he holds firm, wrapping his arm around my waist, holding me against him so tight that I struggle to get air into my lungs.

I try to push him again. He lets go, practically shoving me away like I might burn him. I take a few steps back to catch my balance. His eyes widen, and he falls to his knees in the snow.

"I'm so sorry, Lydia. I don't know what else to say. I'm so sorry. I never intended for any of this to happen. This wasn't part of the plan," he says more to himself than me. "Forgive me. Please."

I say nothing and slowly back away from him as he studies my reaction. "We need to keep moving," I reply after a minute.

"What if we didn't go back?" Those gray eyes look up at me with longing and perhaps a bit of desperation. He stands, slowly stepping toward me like he's approaching a skittish colt.

I gape. No words form as my brain freezes for a moment before I can collect myself. "And go where?"

"I don't know. Away from here. Away from the Auctus. Find our own adventure away from all of this. Just us."

"You mean run away. Run away from my family, from my duty. Run from what I've seen without giving anyone a warning?"

"Would it be so bad to want to run away with me?" Tiernan tucks a loose curl behind my ear. "We can choose a different path. We could be together. Find the way together. Just you and me?"

Hot and cold.

"I will not abandon my duty or my family." I plant my foot in the stirrup with a little more force than necessary and throw my leg over Burya.

Tiernan hangs his head. Silence builds a wall between us. Each brick a decision stacked on top of another. He stands up and marches toward me, never breaking eye contact. He nods and places his hand on my knee. "I can't change what happened. I can't change that I've hurt you. I can't change what might happen when we return. For that and more, I am sorry. I hope you will forgive me."

Adjusting in my saddle, I notice his grimace. His thumb traces a gentle circle on my leg. When he moves to remount his horse, the cold absence of his hand rips through my bones.

Changing his mind about the Auctus tonight isn't possible, nor can I convince him to embrace his abilities, to see his gift as anything but a curse. Perhaps, in time, when we're home and have the space to breathe, we can work toward understanding it together.

Patience.

My heart hurts at the bumpy emotional road ahead. I'll fight for a future with the man who fills me with warmth and passion, opens my eyes to other perspectives, and challenges the preconceived notions of my life. A man I still want against my better judgment, a man I need to convince to trust in me and trust in his gift to embrace the man he could be.

THE SNOW PICKS UP. Even with my Enhanced Vision, seeing through the storm teetering toward a blizzard is becoming a challenge.

Tiernan pulls the horses to a stop in a tight cluster of evergreens. We both slide off, tired and drained, and begin to set up our little camp to ride out the worst of the storm. The wood is too wet for a fire, but sharing body heat with Tiernan leaves me...unsteady.

I can't lie to myself and say I no longer want him, but we look at each other differently than we did this morning. An unspoken gully has formed between us, and neither knows how to build a bridge. Even if he doesn't hate me personally, he most certainly hates everything I've worked toward, every loyalty I have.

"Lydia," he pleads, interrupting my thoughts. He places a chilly hand on my back and guides me into the tent tucked between the evergreens. We sit inside our little frozen shelter, facing each other to share some of the cheese and jerky we could salvage for the return journey. He takes my hands in his and rubs them, warming us both a little, but it's not enough. A fire would have been nice.

"Lydia," he repeats, my name like the most decadent dessert on his lips. He shifts closer. Close but not close enough. His muscles contract, and I make the mistake of looking into his eyes. He's so handsome, all hard angles, except those full lips.

Against my better judgment, I trace his face with a finger, running it along his sharp jaw, over his eyebrow, and down his nose. He doesn't blink those gray eyes. I memorize his features. His hand comes up to hold mine and stops me, pressing my palm to his warm neck. The only sound is our shared breathing before I roll away and slide under the blankets.

I don't trust myself to face him and not give in to this feeling, and yet that's exactly what I do. My eyes see too clearly, even in the dark tent. My body and my mind conflict as my stomach tightens, longing for his bare skin to slide against mine.

His arm comes around my waist and pulls me toward him, rolling me over. My back presses into his hard chest, and we lie together with no words spoken, silent but for the wind whipping through the trees and the crackle of frozen snow hitting the branches and ground.

The tension is too great, and I snap. "If you hate me so much, hate what I am and what I can do, why do any of the things you've done with me? Why did you kiss me in the first place? Why did you have sex with me? Why make me care about you? Trust you?" Hurt and sadness leak through my dejected tone. I shouldn't ask, but I can't bite my tongue. Straight and to the point, like when I retell my Visions. Only facts.

"You are the flame, and I am the moth, willing to be burned. I can't help it nor resist it. I tried and failed. I can't stop myself from touching you. I can't not want you, even though this path will lead to nothing but heartache. And even knowing that, I still want to be burned just to feel your heat for one more moment." His hand slides down my stomach while he whispers these words. He presses his hips into my back. A burning, tingling need glides down my body and settles in between my thighs.

His hand continues to slide lower and he pulls up my sweater. "For this moment, at least, let's pretend the past doesn't matter and the future doesn't exist. We can't see it. Let's be here, together, in the present," he whispers with a soft kiss right behind my ear that he knows will send shivers across my skin. He knows my body and plays it so well.

Tiernan's warm hand finds my pebbled skin and loosens the laces on my leggings. I don't move to stop him. My desire is in control now, my logic discarded. I'll find it later. Now isn't the time for thinking. It's a time for feeling. Nothing that feels this good can hurt me.

His lips travel leisurely down my neck, and I tilt my head back, giving him greater access. I reach behind me and run my fingers through his scruff along his jaw. Tiernan's growl of approval flutters across my ear, sending tingles down my neck. His hand slips into my loosened leggings, sliding down to where I want him the most.

"So wet for me." Tiernan keeps my back snug against his chest. His fingers begin to explore. I want more and push my hips back into him. "So greedy, too. Tell me what you want."

My body is speaking the words I cannot. Singing. My breathing becomes harsh as one finger slides deep. A gasp escapes, followed by a moan as he slides it out and back in again. Our heavy breaths break the quiet.

He bites my neck. His leg folds in between mine, pulling one leg back and over to spread me wider. My legs spread out as he adds another finger and plunges deeper while his thumb presses down with every thrust. His breathing is as labored as mine. His thorough exploration starts a rhythm my hips have no choice but to match as I grind down on his hand, wanting more.

"Let me love you. Please. I can't hate you. I can't do it. If this is the only way I can have you, let me love you." His words are more of a soft breath in my ear. I turn toward him and take his beautiful, harsh face in my hands, kissing him deeper while his fingers continue their torture. I don't say anything as I chase my release.

His hand stops. I pull my sweater off and lift my hips to slide my leggings down the rest of the way. My flushed skin burns from head to toe.

In the distant recesses of my mind, a faint shout is trapped behind muffled glass, screaming that this may not be the best idea. It vaguely sounds like my own voice. We have so much dividing us, insurmountable problems that will not go away. Deep conflicts and lifelong prejudices. My mind and my body are far from communicating at this point. I don't care. We can worry about that tomorrow. *Don't share tomorrow's problems with today*, as Colleen would preach. I shut it all out, chasing the rush, the high, of his body against mine.

"Why did you stop?" I reach for him. He pulls away, and I almost whimper at the loss.

"I want to feel you let go on my cock. I want your pussy to hug me tight with every pulse I'm about to give you. Let me." He makes quick work of his remaining clothes, and a moment later, our naked bodies fuse once more. He slips between my thighs, gazing down at me with those steel-gray eyes. We both hesitate. One of us has to jump first. I reach out and take his length in my hand, stroke him, and relish when he groans. Encouraged, I stroke him again.

Tiernan's mouth curves into a wolfish grin, his tongue running across his top row of teeth. He leans down onto his elbows and frames my face. I'm so turned on that he slides in smoothly with one agonizingly slow push. My moan could be heard for miles when he slowly drags himself out and thrusts back into me. I wrap my legs around his waist, encouraging him to go deeper, wanting more.

Oh so slowly, he almost slides out fully before pushing harder back into my center. The slam of his contact, seating him to his hilt, sends a shockwave of pleasure through my body. I tip my hips up, begging for more. My hands have a steel grip on his tense biceps as he picks up the pace, slamming in hard and fast and stroking out excruciatingly slowly, letting me enjoy every ridge as he withdraws.

A delicate line between pleasure and pain. The angle is divine, reaching and pressing at just the right spots.

"I can feel how close you are. I want you to come around my cock. Squeeze me. I can hear your heartbeat. I can sense everything. Gods, you're incredible. This feels like nothing I've ever experienced. I feel it all. Sense it all." His words course through me, lighting me on fire. He slides in and out, so deep, so hard, in such a steady rhythm. His chest presses tight against mine, hot and sticky skin rubs against my sensitive nipples.

"Forget about everything that was before." Thrust. "Forget about what will be. Tomorrow doesn't matter." He bites my neck. *Hard.* "Yesterday didn't matter. It's just us here right now." *Yes. More.* "Two people. No Visions. No missions." Thrust. "No one but us. Fuck!" he growls into my ear, and I hold him tighter, unable to form words of my own but basking in his.

He sits up without changing his pace, pulling my leg over his shoulder, my other staying wrapped around his waist. He can go so much deeper now with this position, and he does. His hand lets go of my leg to play with my nipples. He pinches it harder, and I cry out.

Before I can register that sensation, he's flipping me over onto my stomach and gripping my hips so hard it will leave bruises. Pulling me up onto my knees, he spreads my legs wider and slides into me from behind. It's such a different sensation. His hands on my hips squeeze tight, and he pounds in again, a rhythm I can't match in this position. I lose myself to his control.

"I'm so hot. My body is so hot. I can sense everything. I can feel everything. I burn for you," he repeats like a mantra, pushing into me faster, his own control slipping. "I burn for you. I burn for you."

"Tiernan! Holy Shit! Yes!" I scream. My body contracts with an explosive release, and all the problems of the world, everything following us, everything to come drifts away on the wave of fleeting bliss.

I almost collapse, but he holds me up. My skin stings under his bruising grip. He's too lost in his overwhelmed Senses. I don't even know if he heard me. My body begins to sag, but his grip on my hips keeps me in place. His grip is an iron vise holding me in place, pressing into my flesh.

"Fuuuuuuuuck!" He roars and slams into me with an agonizing groan. His fingers clench into my skin, and my foggy, sated mind processes a sharp, burning pain.

"Tiernan! Let go!" I shout loud enough that he can't miss my words, I shove hard at his elbow. He releases me and pulls out. His spent body collapses on the ground. I roll away, but he's unaware. His eyes are closed as he tries to recover his breathing.

"What was that? I felt like I wasn't in control of my body. I could sense everything around me so strongly. My body felt on fire but in the best way imaginable. Was that you? Did you do something to me?" He's staring at the roof of our tent. I sit up and square my shoulders, pulling the blanket over my naked, sweaty body. My hips burn from where his Enhanced Touch seared my skin, tiny painful welts forming a curved line across each side.

"That was your Touch, Tiernan. You hurt me. You burned me with your Enhanced Touch," I accuse him, my voice sounding pathetic, like a wounded animal. I stand up to check my burns. His uncontrolled Senses ruined the beautiful moment of togetherness and passion. I warned him that he could be hurt or he could hurt someone. I didn't calculate that someone could be me.

"What are you talking about?" he barks, grabbing my shoulder and turning me toward him. He pushes the blanket off my shoulders and scans me for injuries, concern mixed with doubt.

"You burned me! Use your Sight to see closer if you need to. I know you can." I point at the burns and bruises on my hips, the exact spread and size of his finger pads.

"Fuck, what have I done?" he whispers to the tent, to himself. He shrinks away from me. "What have you woken up in me?"

"This is my fault? That's rich!" I can't help but shout. Damn him, and damn anyone who may be close enough to hear us.

"I could feel every Sense. They were all so heightened. Is it because you're also an Adept? Why would you do this to me after everything I told you? I told you all my secrets, Lydia. Why would you do this to me? I trusted you." His eyes dart back and forth, trying to make sense of what happened.

"This is your fault. Don't you dare blame the victim. You made a choice not to learn about your Senses. I warned you someone could get hurt, but you chose to wrap yourself in hate instead of mastering your powers. Being a Complex is a gift, not a curse. *You* chose to lose control, and you hurt me, so fuck you, Tiernan. Fuck. You." I don't attempt to soften the blow or empathize with his reasons for choosing to reject what was given to him at birth. He hurt me. More than physically.

I stare him straight in the eye, unblinking. I'm a Seer. I'm inherently capable of winning any stare-down. He did this to me. He did this to himself. He needs to take responsibility.

My hips ache with the burns and bruises forming, merging with my already bruised body from the last few days. I can't even lie on my hips. The burns will be even uglier come morning. I find my clothes and pull them on carefully. The silence is broken by the sounds of us dressing.

"Lydia, I had no idea I could even do that. You have to believe me. Are you okay?" Tiernan asks softly, concern and hesitation evident in his voice—maybe even a dash of regret. He asks, but he's not looking at me. His eyes are locked on my injured hips.

"No, I'm not fucking okay! What makes you think I'd be okay? You were so out of control that you couldn't even realize that you were hurting me, and then you blamed me for your inability to control your Senses!" My body shakes with rage. I drag my sleeping roll across the small tent, far from him and slide under the blankets. It barely gives me more distance, but it's enough to show my point. I'd freeze before I let him touch me again. The sting from my burns is a harsh reminder of the risks in trusting an Adept who refuses to be trained. An Adept who hates other Adepts, who hates the very institution that could have helped him, who could have prevented all of this.

He watches me with wide eyes as I pull away. His hands remain out front, away from him. They no longer belong to him. His own hands are strangers, capable of so much more than he ever thought. He didn't even apologize, and I hate him for it. I mourn for the warmth, passion, and longing of a few minutes ago.

I hate the loss of what could have been between us and how empty that makes me feel.

<h1 style="text-align:center">CHAPTER 30
TIERNAN</h1>

ydia falls asleep after a while. I can't go back to sleep. Her even breathing is disturbed by her unconscious winces and whimpers every time she rolls over. It's a painful reminder of what happened, what I did. How did it get so out of control? Guilt creeps in along with a heavy layer of shame. Shame at being weak, at letting my Senses win, at hurting her.

One minute, we're blissfully wrapped up in each other's bodies; the next, I'm burning from the inside and unable to focus on any individual thing around me. I could feel every Enhanced Sense intensely, but failed to narrow those Senses down, letting them take control. It was exhilarating, overwhelming, and terrifying all at the same time. It was the best orgasm of my life. It was power in its purest form.

I ache to pull her closer, to wrap my arms around her and offer the comfort she so desperately needs. Comfort I never intended to strip away. But I know better. I feel the weight of my actions, they have consequences; the consequences of letting things between us spiral this far. I hesitate, uncertain of how she'd take it if I tried to offer comfort, knowing deep down I've let this mess grow beyond my control.

I never intended things to escalate to this point with the beautiful Seer. That wasn't my job, and that wasn't my mission. My lack of control is failing everyone.

When Cormac first assigned me to Ryo, it was with a specific set of tasks: keep an eye on him, on anyone who might be a threat, and keep Cormac informed of his interactions with anyone who would pose a risk. The little Seer was a surprise. I never thought she'd sneak under my armor like she has.

How did this all get so out of control? I shake my head, trying to connect the dots and figure out how I got here. I don't know what the next step is. The mission has changed. There's no doubt about that. Now... Well, now I don't know anything. Do I stick to my mission? Do I risk failing Cormac? His disappointment? No, that's not an option. I can't fail. I have to stay the course, even if it means a change in plans. I can keep her at my side. I don't have to sacrifice Lydia in order to achieve my goals. I've already had to sacrifice so much to be where I am today, who I am today. I can have it all. I can be adaptable.

I look around the dark tent, and realization settles over me that I can make out every shape and feature. My eyes have shifted to adjust to the darkness. I've always had decent night Vision, but this is a new level. A fog over my world has been lifted that I wasn't aware existed. It's terrifying and exciting to realize I've been using crumbs of my Enhanced Senses for years without realizing it but now, recognizing the full force of unleashing my Complex Senses, the possibilities are endless and yet horrifying, wondrous and yet overwhelming.

I hold my hands out in front of me, flipping them palm side up and back. How did my touch bruise her, burn her flesh? I know little about utilizing my Enhanced Senses beyond the suppression techniques that my mother tried to instill in me before she died. I focus on the few lessons I can remember.

Control. Calm. Don't let my emotions gain power. Clear my

mind. That's what my mother always told me and what Lydia tried to teach me, too. If I can control it, I can stop it from ever happening again, right? I can shut it down permanently.

I focus on the breathing Lydia showed me. My skin starts to feel warmer, too hot. I know what that means now. Fear shoots through my mind, increasing the temperature of my hands. Breathe in, breathe out. I don't know if I can do this alone. Panic wrestles for control.

How will Cormac react when we return and I've failed in so many ways? Will he reject me? How will those under my command react to finding out I'm an Adept if I can't hide it? How will those who depend on me for safety and protection react? Will the Auctus hunt me or try to kill me like they did my family? I'd like to see them try.

After so many years of being careful and hiding, why is this all coming to the surface now? Did Lydia do something to me? She wouldn't admit it if she did. She knows the Auctus's secrets. She's a few weeks away from becoming a Master. In all likelihood, she'll become a Grand Master someday if she survives whatever Asher planned for her. She won't survive the rebellion at her doorstep. She'll be one of the first to go if they get their hands on her, which would be a shame, a waste, and something I won't let happen.

I need to get her out of Silvanisi until I know more. Where would be safe for a Visionary Seer? They're so valuable and sought after. Her eyes are a dead giveaway. She wouldn't be able to hide. She tried to help me, and I hurt her. She warned me, but I couldn't hear her over the cacophony of sounds exploding around me. I owe her. I owe her something. We could help each other.

Unless she intended to awaken my abilities, she's been pushing me for a week now about how I should accept this *gift* and learn to make the most of it.

This is the Auctus proselytizing, trying to convince everyone of their good work and denying their role in breaking apart families; turning children into weapons. Why else would they require a binding oath in exchange for education? *Auctus Primum.* Auctus First.

Something isn't adding up. Using a woman isn't beneath the Auctus. They'd use Lydia or anyone else to achieve their objective. They and the rebels have that in common. Would Lydia go along and do as she's told? Would she manipulate me to get an Enhanced Complex into their army? My mind says yes, but my heart begs me to say no.

CHAPTER 31
LYDIA

Dawn sneaks across the sky, painting the world in a muted light that makes everything feel sharper, more real. The burns seem worse in the daylight—ten raw, angry ovals scattered across my hips and butt, each one a reminder of what happened. A faint red handprint stares back at me from one side, with its matching twin on the other, speaking volumes without a single word. In the harsh clarity of morning, regret hangs thick in the air, blending with a deep sense of loss and the weight of disappointment that settles into my soul.

I sneak a glance at the injuries in the privacy of the tent while Tiernan steps out to fetch us some water. He doesn't look at me, doesn't meet my eyes, just mumbles something about needing direction before rushing off without a word, leaving me behind with a cold silence in his wake.

When we get back home, Mabel can tend to it. It'll sting like hell for the rest of the journey, and I can't even bring myself to guess how much farther we have to go. If the weather turns on us again, it could be another day or two. I shudder at the thought. Thank god we decided to turn back instead of going all the way to the bay. The thought of how much more time we would have lost twists my stomach.

I need to get home for so many reasons. The least of which is the gaping wound in my heart, torn open by the shift in what once was a blooming relationship with Tiernan, now withered and dead. My body aches, but it's the pain of his refusal to even look at me that cuts deeper.

How will I ever explain all of this to Iris and Kira? Secrets breed secrets, but they'll see the marks. They'll have questions. Questions I can't and won't answer. Or Colleen? She won't tell a soul, but she has never avoided making her opinions abundantly clear. Or haranguing me into answers comparable to the interrogation skills of an Enhanced Judge.

Who the hell am I even protecting? Why should I cover for Tiernan? I promised to keep his Adept status a secret, but now it feels like a burden I don't know how to carry. Explaining these fingerprint burns? That's going to be impossible. I've got a day or two to come up with a lie, and I'm furious that I have to. Furious that he put me in this position and furious that this all could have been avoided if he chose to understand his Senses instead of reject them.

I lift my bag and bedroll, and the sharp sting of pain shoots through my hip. I can't help but wince. I see Tiernan stop dead in his tracks, like he's going to do something—maybe help or actually show some damn care—but then his eyes flicker with something else. Hesitation. Withdrawal. Regret. I don't need his pity. Instead of helping, he ties a full canteen to our supplies, like that's going to fix anything.

Despite the ache in my body, I throw myself up onto Burya's back, but he doesn't come to help me like he always has. He doesn't reach out, doesn't let his warm hands linger on me for just a second longer than necessary. I had come to look forward to those touches, those moments of warmth, but now—now it's like they never existed. Just another thing he's taken from me without a second thought.

He puts on his gloves and gets on his horse, grabbing the reins of our packhorse we were able to salvage after the attack, barely making a sound. We move out into the frigid sunshine of the early morning. I keep a few paces behind him. He peeks back to ensure I'm still there. The only sounds are the hooves clomping on the icy snow and the birds in the mountains.

The chilly air cuts through me, every ache feels sharper, more unbearable. But I won't shy away from it. I welcome the pain, knowing it's a startling and necessary reminder of my misplaced trust. Every flinch, every knot, every painful twist in my muscles is a lesson carved into me. A reminder. We're not the same people we were just a day ago. Each day in this harsh world pulls us further apart, but it also pushes us closer to the people we're meant to become—even if those people aren't the ones we thought we'd be.

He didn't stop. He didn't even know how to halt or pull his Senses back into him. He was overwhelmed, feeling everything— smelling, seeing, hearing—for the first time all at once. It unleashed a wave of sensations that he wasn't prepared for. He lost control, and I paid the price. It's my own fault for pushing reason and logic aside and dancing blindly toward temptation. He didn't know better. He didn't know the risks, but I did. I should have known better.

I shift in my saddle, trying to settle with no luck. The trail for our journey back is an icy sheet guiding us home. It's a steep part of the decline from the mountain, and we proceed slowly. Tiernan's horse slips a bit, so he gets down and walks instead. It's a safer idea.

I pull back to stop Burya, gingerly easing off her back, but her ears prick up halfway down.

Silence for a heartbeat before a hidden lynx pounces above our heads and lands on the packhorse before me. We're thrown into chaos. The predator's claws dig into the horse's flesh, and it rears up. Tiernan lets go of the lead, diving out of the path of danger but keeps a tight hold of his riding horses reigns.

Burya jumps, and with my half-off dismount, I'm thrown through the air and onto the ice. My back slams too hard into the frozen ground. The air is forced out of my lungs. Panic sets in. I fail to breathe, gasping desperately, attempting to swallow some air and unable to get enough back in. I'm going to get trampled. Spots cloud and dance in my eyes. My chest burns and constricts. One lungful is all I need.

Burya and the injured packhorse run off into the forest, the lynx on their trail. At least Tiernan has a death grip on his horse. I pound on my chest, aching to get more air into me. Finally, I'm able to breathe again and start coughing. I drag in a ragged, rattling breath and blink away the spots in my eyes.

"Fuck! That hurt. Add it to the list of injuries." I wince and slowly ease myself up, lightheaded. The pounding in the back of my head is unbearable. I reach up and feel warm, sticky blood. My head must have hit the ice. Tiernan's wide eyes are the last thing I see before darkness takes over.

I WAKE up on a blanket next to a small fire. Tiernan's gaze is steady on mine, weighted with concern.

"How long was I out?" I grumble, reaching behind my head and hissing. Blood cakes my hair, slightly tacky. I'm so sore, I struggle to sit upright. How much more of this can my body handle? This journey was a terrible idea. Why couldn't my Sight have warned me about this? Useless, inconvenient Sight. Never working to show me my own future. Only the future of others. Only nightmares for me. Bullshit.

"Not too long. We can rest a bit, but we need to find the horses. We can ride together on mine until we can track them down. Hopefully the mountain lion didn't kill them. We can hunt it down and have a hot meal before returning. Its pelt would be worth a fortune."

"It wasn't a mountain lion. It was a lynx. They're right on your Silvanisi crest. The difference is obvious. Lynx are revered, sacred even. You can't kill it. It's illegal." I don't know why I'm picking a fight about this, but I'm mad, in pain, and lashing out. Add in cold, tired, and plain old sad.

I move to stand up a bit too quickly. The world wobbles before my eyes. The trees tilt and my stomach rolls. Tiernan shoots out to catch me from falling, grabbing my arm to hold me steady. I look down at his hand on my waist, and he rears back, almost dropping me.

"If you put your gloves back on, it helps. That's one of the first things Handler and Healer children learn until they can control their Enhanced Touch. The stronger the Touch, the more it's necessary. The gloves work as a physical barrier until you harness the mental barrier of skin to skin. Plus, they'll keep your hands warm."

He says nothing but slides his gloves on. I pick up the blanket that fell off Burya when she bolted and wrap it around me for an extra layer of warmth and separation since we now have to ride together.

We saddle up onto our single remaining horse with me in the front so I can see better. Ordinarily I'd swoon at having to share a horse with Tiernan. Well, not swoon, but I'd be giddy. In between his legs now, though, I'm painfully aware of each bruise and burn when his thigh brushes against my hips. A hiss escapes me and his body flinches, but we move forward in silence.

"You could try to use your Enhanced Touch to help heal me a bit or at least take some of the sting away. I could walk you through what little I know about Healers. It's risky but—"

He interrupts. "What would you know about Healers? Did you learn from fucking Brandon? How's his Enhanced Touch?"

"Wow. Well, that was wildly out of line, not that my past is any of your business. If you had ever bothered going through any type of basic Adept training, you'd be given a rudimentary understanding of how each Sense functions. I may not be able to heal a paper cut, but I understand the fundamental process. It's so we can help fellow Adepts if they're injured or weakened from overuse."

Tiernan scoffs. "You mean Adepts are taught to bend to the will of the Auctus and learn how to use their Senses for power and control. Build the Auctus army."

Fuming, I take a page out of his book. I pride myself on being thoughtful, patient, to see the forest through the trees—pun intended. I can only handle so many accusations, and I've officially reached my limit. I pull on the reins to stop and slide off, wincing when my boots meet the frozen ground.

"I see what you're trying to do. Lashing out. Hot and cold. Push me away because I don't fit neatly into your well-constructed argument against the Auctus. Well, too damn bad. Make up your mind or leave me be. If you took five minutes to *listen*, you'd understand that Adepts rely on each other. To reach out a hand, even if that hand is slapped away in anger, misunderstanding, fear, or hatred, even if that puts a target on our backs. You may not want to be a part of that, Tiernan, but that oath we take? The one you loathe without understanding? There's a little part in the middle. *Together, we stand. Together, we follow the path. Together, we thrive. Together, we survive.* It's to help each other, always. Registered or unregistered. Trained or untrained." I'm exhausted. We keep speaking in circles around each other, neither really listening, but something deep inside me can't seem to quit. I have to try. "You are an Adept. You are a part of this community, even if you don't want to acknowledge your gift."

"This is a curse, not a gift. I won't risk hurting you more than I already have," Tiernan whispers.

I'm beyond frustrated and have settled right into lividness. My patience has reached its limit. "So you'd rather stay in the dark, risk hurting someone else, risk hurting yourself, over what?" The pain, combined with the cold, hunger, and exhaustion, makes me short-tempered. Overusing my Sight is giving me a headache. My sympathy diminishes by the second. "That's dumb and foolish and willfully ignorant and many other words you deserve right now. You're too wrapped up in your hatred, in your blind ignorance, to open your mind and learn simply because you fear what has been inside you your whole life. You've chosen to let that fear be your master."

He steps onto the ground and towers over me at his full height. "Better that than the Auctus. You expect me to blindly trust them? Trust the people who killed my family, the people who hunted me? The people who tried to take me and turn me into a weapon? The people who took my sister away from me? They took everything. How am I supposed to trust them? Trust you? You keep all your precious secrets until it's convenient. You've been a weapon since you were born. How can I ever trust you?"

I step back as though i've been struck. My jaw drops. My heart hurts more than the injuries on my skin. After everything we've said, everything we've been through together, he still can't trust me? He still denies who he is, what he's capable of if he'd just get out of his own way. How can someone live every day knowing they have the potential to be more, and choose to deny that? I pity him. "You become a weapon if you choose to be one."

"What was in your Vision? The panic flashes? Are you hiding more? I have a right to know. I know you didn't share everything. You never do."

He grabs my waist, not letting me get some much-needed space before I take a swing at him. I take a deep, calming breath.

It doesn't work.

"Visions are never a tidy little package simply because that would be easier for you. Wouldn't it be easier if I could close my eyes and have all the answers? I don't expect you to understand." I grind my teeth, trying to keep my emotions under control. "I hope... probably naive of me...that you would at least acknowledge there's a risk with misinterpretation and its inevitable consequences." I wave wildly around us and our current circumstances. My jaw hurts. Everything hurts.

Tiernan sinks onto his heels, his head drops between his shoulders. "I never asked for any of this. I never asked to guard you, to want you, to care about one of you." His words feel deeper than an attack on me. "He'll be so disappointed in me. I've failed him. I've failed them all. I hate myself for that."

"Ryo won't be disappointed in you. I'm not even sure I understand why he assigned you to guard me in the first place. I'm sure he'll be pissed that I got hurt, but he'll get over that. He doesn't need to know all the details."

Wide but hesitant eyes meet mine as his brow furrows and his mouth hangs open. He's looking at me like I'm crazy. His shoulders tighten, and he stands to back away with clenched fists. "I don't care about your fucking prince. He and his whole family are part of the problem. They're just using you, and you don't even see it."

"What are you talking about? Ryo *is* my family." I reach out for him, but he pulls away as if my touch means pain and not the other way around.

We stand locked in place for a long time—no more angry words hang between us on each exhale in the frigid air.

"Forget I said anything. I'm sorry this hurt you. This Touch… Fuck…I'm sorry. I don't know if I said that before. I don't know what I was saying. I'm sorry. Forget about it. We need to keep moving," Tiernan mumbles, extending a gloved hand to help me back onto the horse.

"This thing. This Touch. That isn't what hurt me. You hurt me. You. No one but you. Touch can't hurt unless you make it hurt. You control it. Not the other way around. Take responsibility; otherwise, your apology means nothing."

We stare each other down. Anger, rage, disappointment, longing, passion, and more hang between us. None of it matters right now. I place a myriad of feelings in a box and will unpack it later. We need to get home. Everything else can wait.

I grab his outstretched hand, and he pulls me up to retrace our path back home.

CHAPTER 32
LYDIA

My Sight is the only thing that guides us safely through the dark, but it takes a physical toll. The prolonged hyper-focus leaves my eyes dry and aching. The risks associated with Sense overuse outweigh my desire to get home as soon as possible, so we move slowly as I struggle to find the balance.

"Being a Complex would be an advantage as a Captain. I suspect you've been using your Enhanced Senses for years without realizing it." I know my words fall on deaf ears. It's ironic. He could also have Enhanced Hearing if he made the slightest effort.

He begins scanning the forest and rocks. Without control of the reins, his gloved hands don't know where to rest, so he puts them awkwardly on his thighs, avoiding any more contact with me than necessary.

The moon glides higher in the sky while we trudge along. The twinkle of stars through the trees shines on us, guiding me home at a snail's pace. The rock of the horse's gait begins to lull me to sleep, and I start to sink back. Tiernan reluctantly wraps an arm around my waist to keep me steady.

I spot the soft glow of lights through the trees off in the distance

—my city, my home. Tiernan sees the lights, too, and straightens, giving my waist an encouraging squeeze.

"This isn't what I want. I don't want to fight with you. Can't we move past this? We could turn around before they spot us. We could point this horse in the opposite direction and leave it all behind. Sail off. Become pirates or treasure hunters. Hide out in the Tyberon Islets." His gentle kiss presses against my temple, a silent olive branch. Shocking in its timing and equally confusing. I've never wished to be able to taste lies so much in my life, but I wonder if his words would be salty or sweet, bitter or tart.

"I'm not much of a sailor but no. This is bigger than me. Bigger than us. This is my family. My home. My duty."

"I can't save you if you refuse to see the danger lurking behind you."

"I don't need to be saved."

"That is where you are very wrong," he murmurs. "I'll take you if it comes to that," he whispers more to himself than to me, gripping me tighter before dropping his arm. A shiver rolls up my spine, but I shake it off as nervous anticipation to be home.

The lights of the outer city gate grow closer. Tiernan waves at the soldiers on duty, and they give a curious wave back. Understandable. We weren't expected to return for another week at the earliest, along with about ten more men. Hopefully Finley and Brandon made it back safely. I'll check on them once I've seen Mabel and had a bath.

The guards open the gate and let us through, but we don't stop to make pleasantries. It's the middle of the night, and they need to focus on their posts. They can't see in the dark like we can.

Saivi is too quiet, too still. The wall is lined with more guards than usual. A weight in my stomach grows heavier, but everything seems...well, not normal but cautiously tense.

A bleary-eyed Commander Cormac spots us. "Welcome back. Care to explain yourself?" Quite a warm welcome, indeed.

Tiernan slides off the back of the horse, leaving me on top alone. The two men grasp forearms in a loving handshake and embrace.

They slap shoulders and begin to walk away. Neither gives me a second glance. Do they expect me to wait quietly in the corner and wait to be questioned? I don't owe either of them any favors. Fine, pretend I'm not here, covered in blood and bruises, looking half-dead and half-feral.

"I'm going to bed," I mutter to no one in particular as I guide the horse to the stables.

The inner gate is already open. Ryo stands patiently. Someone must have run to alert him of our return. His eyes connect with mine, and a crack in the dam widens, letting a single tear through. A look of fear and sadness washes over his beautiful face that I missed so much.

"What the fuck happened to you? I was alerted when you came through the city gate and ran down here." He pulls me off the horse and wraps his arms around me. My feet never touch the ground as he holds me up, hugging me tight. The dam bursts, unleashing ugly, snotty, shaking sobs all over his shoulder.

Finley runs out to take the reins. A sight for sore eyes. Relief washes over me. Tears of joy that they returned merge with so many other emotions I'm not prepared to process. "I'm so glad you made it back safely. Is Brandon okay?" I laugh-cry, so happy to see his infectious smile through his bright red beard.

"We only got back a few hours ahead of you. Had to move slow to keep the poor man breathing. I took him straight to the Healer and heard the news of your swift return. Brandon is recovering, but it will take a while. It's a good thing we returned. By the time we got back, his infection had spread. Don't worry about us. Worry about your recovery. You don't look so great. I'll take care of the rest," Finley reassures me in his own way, patting my cheek. His eyes survey my face, looking for something. Whatever it is, he sees what he was looking for, nods and takes the horse to the stables.

Ryo sets me down, wrapping me in his warm coat. "Lydia, what the hell happened? You look like you've been through a war. That's not your horse. Where's Tiernan? Finley told us a little of your attack, but…" Ryo trails off. I can't hold back the exhaustion any longer. I sway on my feet. He sweeps his arm under my legs and lifts me off the ground. When his hand connects with my hip, I cry out at the sharp sensation I had been so determined to hide.

"Shit, okay, I'll get you to Colleen and we'll call Mabel. Rest now, you're safe. There's plenty of time to trade updates tomorrow. You've missed a lot."

Ryo kisses my forehead and carries me into the castle. I look over his shoulder and spy Tiernan, deep in a heated conversation with Cormac. He looks over. His shoulders tense, and his jaw clenches. He crosses his arms, resuming his talk with his commander, but his eyes remain on me. I don't look away or even blink until the door closes behind us. Exhaustion hits me like a wave, crashing over every part of me, dragging my consciousness down with it.

I'M GROGGY AND DISORIENTED, and the room tilts to the left. I float over waves, a lifeboat drifting over a stormy sea.

Ryo and Kira bark instructions in hushed voices. They fail as each order pierces my temple. It's the thought that counts as Ryo carries me inside.

The hall is active given the hour, but I can't keep my eyes open. Faces flash by, some concerned, most curious. Why is everyone up? Am I missing a party or a problem?

DEEP SHADOWS STRETCH across the carpet as Kira and Iris lean over me, peeling off my frozen, filthy sweater. Their silhouettes glow in the darkness, illuminated only by the flickering light of the fireplace. Colleen yells something about a bath almost ready, and I sigh with relief and gratitude. Ryo's muffled voice growls incoherent questions from behind a closed door.

"We need to get your pants off you. Your back is pretty badly bruised. Did she fall?" Iris brushes hair off my face.

"Down a cliff? Yikes. Roll her over." I recognize Kira's voice but can't find the strength to open my eyes. I over-extended and spent too long in hyper-focus, and now I'm going to pay the price. Hopefully, no permanent damage is done.

One of them pushes to roll me onto my side, probably not as gently as she'd hoped. The other one pulls my pants off, rubbing against my injuries. An uncontrollable scream snaps me back from the edge of sleep as my eyes snap open.

"Stop!" I shout, but it leans more toward a whimper. I tuck my knees up into a ball.

"What the hell!" Iris shouts back. My tired eyes blink and clear the drowsy haze to see them staring wide-eyed at my hips. The glow from the fire illuminates my injuries perfectly. It's a melodramatic tableau. My pale skin enhances the contrast. The bruises have had a little time to darken to ugly shades of purple and red. The burns dotting my hips in evenly spaced curves are nasty. A gruesome sight I had planned on hiding, but I can't hide anything. I don't have the energy.

"I'm fine. Just. Please. I need…I'll talk about it later. I need a minute," I mumble incoherently. I fall back, pulling a blanket over my dirty, naked body and close my eyes, sleep taking over. I can bathe in the morning.

SOMEONE MUST HAVE BATHED ME. Hopefully Colleen, otherwise that would be embarrassing. In my bed with clean sheets, I'm in a pristine nightgown that doesn't belong to me, and I have clean but tangled hair. Salves and bandages cover my burns, and something that smells a bit like arnica coats my back and various spots on my arms, legs, and around my neck. It's insane that I forgot about my neck. The bandage on my head is snug enough to help with the painful headache, putting a slight pressure on my pounding temple. The curtains are shut tight, thank the gods. I'm not sure my weakened Sight could adjust enough to daylight. I need to sleep for a year.

Rustling by the door draws my attention. With a few grunts and groans, I manage to inelegantly sit upright. Colleen carries a tray and sets it on the table next to me.

"I thought you might be hungry," she whispers, sitting on the side of my bed. She brushes a few hairs off my face, cupping my cheek. A tear slides down her plump cheek, but she quickly wipes it away. "I won't press for now, but they'll be here soon with questions. Get some rest. I'll keep them at bay for as long as I can." She kisses my forehead, transporting me back to a time when I would scrape my knee as a child. Gently, she tucks me back in and closes the door behind her. My eyes slip shut, and the soft click is the only indication that I'm alone again.

I take her advice for once in my life, roll over onto my stomach, the only part of me not battered, or at least less battered, and go back to sleep.

WHISPERS COME FROM THE FIREPLACE. Whoever is trying to stay quiet needs to work harder.

"I can hear you," I grumble, rolling over onto my back. A garble of incoherent curses comes out of my throat at the contact with my bandages. Everything hurts. Even my eyelids are sore.

"Sorry!" three voices whisper in unison, the effect not as hushed as they think.

Iris, Kira, and Ryo join me on the edge of the bed. The twins sit down near my feet. Ryo kneels on the floor beside my pillow and brushes my tangled hair away from my face. His eyes are awash with concern and curiosity, but he knows better than to push me. He'll wait for as long as I need while the twins will jump in and interrogate me.

"How long have I been asleep?" The tiredness in my voice comes across weak and brittle.

"Three days since you passed out. Master Healer Mable said you needed rest," Ryo says, combing my hair with his fingers.

"How is Mable still alive?" I ask. "She has to be over one hundred. Is Tobias back?"

A hint of a smile emerges from Ryo's sad face. "Missing the point. Tobias isn't back yet, but he sent you a message. He's on his way and will be here in a few days to turn around and take you back to Merthaset. He didn't say why, only that you must be prepared to go when he arrives. Adepts are fleeing all over the island. Father is furious. There are things you need to know. Things I need to explain." Ryo's gentle voice counteracts the seriousness of the message. Tobias has always done his utmost to keep me from politics on Merthaset. He told me to stay put in the castle.

"I need to speak to Hiro." I try to steel my voice while I push to sit upright. My face contorts with the pain of the most minor movement. Nausea creeps up my stomach, but I swallow it back down.

"He's in a meeting but wants to see you after. Lydia, there's something else," Ryo continues, hesitating in a way unlike him. "The Verralon warlord is here. Ezra. The city is tense. They tracked the slaver's operation to the north side of the island. He knows a lot more than we do at the moment and is selective in what he's willing to share. They claim to be allies, but you never quite know with them. Mother will push for an alliance, but..." He hesitates again, his eyes darting back and forth between his sisters.

"Just spit it out already!" I bark.

"He's been asking questions about you specifically. A lot of questions," Kira interjects.

Iris interrupts, receiving a glare from her sister. "He said he won't go into it further until he can see you or Tobias but we think he's more interested in you. He also confirmed that Seers are being targeted."

"I could have told you that myself." I wave down at my array of bandages and bruises. Quite the turn of events. I muster what little strength I have and commit to faking the rest. "I need help getting dressed. Ryo, wait outside. I need you three in case I need reinforcements."

Ryo opens his mouth to ask something, but I hold up my hand. "You deserve answers. You'll get them, I promise, but I'm only retelling this once." He nods and steps out of the room.

Colleen sweeps in. She must have been waiting in the hall, guarding the door to prevent any possible interruptions. That or hoping to eavesdrop on what the hell happened and why I returned a week early with one guard and injured from head to toe.

I dress with the twins' help then Colleen works on my hair. She braids and twists my curls around each other and sweeps the whole mass into an elegant effect at the base of my neck. She pats some makeup to attempt a cover-up of the cut on my cheekbone, the scrapes along my neck and my black eye. The silky sky blue dress she's selected is a bit looser now after days of stress, exhaustion and little food. It dips off my shoulders dangerously low. She clasps my Auctus star pendant around my neck, turning it until she's pleased with the placement.

"Don't bend over too far, or someone might see way more of you than you intended." Colleen tries to tease, but the words sound watery and sad. Her eyes full of concern and, ugh, pity. She comes behind me, gathers some of the loose fabric and the small of my back, pleats it, and wraps a wide sash of navy blue around my waist twice, cinching it tight, and making the dress more fitted without looking sloppy. "We need to get some meat back on these bones."

A shiver climbs up my spine. I haven't seen Tiernan since we returned three days ago. Not that I miss him or *want* to see him, but has he asked after me or come to see me? No, I need to get my thoughts organized and do my job. I didn't claw my way back here only to waste precious time on finding a man who loathes everything about me but my body. Thinking he might have a change of heart is naïve, and I'm done being naïve. I straighten my spine and lift my chin.

I'm a damn Auctus Master. I'm one of the last surviving Visionaries, or I will be. If I can make it.

Ryo waits for us outside and offers an elbow. We four walk down the hall as a united front. I lean heavily into Ryo, letting him literally and metaphorically prop me up. I clench my jaw to appear composed and casual against the pain and stiffness coursing through me. This isn't the time to show weakness. I'm already doubted, seen as a weak little girl playing at being a Visionary by many on the kings council. I refuse to let those men see me wince.

As we approach the king's council chamber, the guards inform us that the meeting with Verralon has not ended yet, so we slide quietly into the back of the room.

We aren't that discreet at our entrance because conversation ceases and eyes shift to me. Ryo sets me down in the closest chair along the wall. Iris and Kira sit on my left while Ryo stands on my right. He crosses his arms and leans against the wall. His casual stance is a ruse. I follow his glare to a bear of a man sitting to the king's left.

An unpredictable energy radiates from him. He's striking, not quite conventionally handsome. He's rough and intense, with wavy auburn hair pulled back in a knot. His thick but trim beard has prominent flecks of red that shine in the golden late-afternoon sunlight streaming through the windows. He sucks all the air from the room. He's imposing. There's no other word that comes to mind. Broad shoulders and thick arms. It's a stark contrast next to King Hiro. I hold my breath when the man's amber eyes connect unblinking with mine. They're so rich they almost glow.

"Lydia, my treasure, I'm glad you are safely returned to us. To your home, where you should be. We missed you. Captain Whitlock has updated us on most of the misadventures while you were recovering from your harrowing ordeal. I understand you wish to speak with me privately." Hiro nods at the door, finishing the meeting and dismissing the gathering.

Everyone stands in unison. Ezra rises a bit slower than would be considered polite. He won't be rushed anywhere. The various cabinet members bow to their king and make their exits. On their way out the door, each gives Ryo and the twins a bow and me a polite nod, a quizzical stare, or a glare.

Ezra holds himself back and stops in front of me. He doesn't acknowledge Ryo or the twins at all. He's a bit taller than Ryo, though not by much, and so much broader. There's an informal edge to his mannerisms—none of the smooth grace typical of someone raised a crown prince, but it seems like a deliberate choice. One designed to throw off perceptions or let down a guard.

Ryo steps a bit in front of me, placing himself between us. The physical and temperamental difference between the two men is jarring. While Ryo exudes masculine beauty and sleek, elegant confidence, Ezra appears unaffected and unbothered. He's not bored. He's studying, waiting patiently. He's coiled strength, ready to fight, if provoked, and has the scars to show that this is not his first battle.

I hesitate at the painful thought of having to stand and curtsy right now, unwilling to reach out to Ryo for help. Kira and Iris both rise, performing their well-trained curtsies to the visiting royal, who is a potential husband for one of them. He barely nods in their direction. His curious amber gaze is fixed on me, but I'm too tired to care. No, that's not true. All my energy is into appearing composed. I will not let this stranger ruffle me. Not right now. Ezra's eyes slide down to Ryo's fingers lacing through mine. It's a bit overwhelming to be the subject of such intense, prolonged focus.

Deciding to stay seated, I stare right back. I'm done keeping my head down, especially to a potential enemy, even if they claim to be here to help us. Instead, I give a slight head bow from my chair.

We stare at one another for a few heartbeats until Ryo shifts his weight, pulling Ezra's attention. Ryo squares his shoulders, the perfect image of a gallant prince protecting the fair damsel. I can't decide whether to shove him aside or laugh. I can't choose, so I grab his hand and try to stand.

Slow and gentle, Ryo takes my elbow and helps me stand. Aware of every nick, bruise, burn, and cut that riddles my body. I hate it.

"Lady Lydia, a pleasure worth the wait. I've heard an awful lot about you from a great many sources. I'm looking forward to hearing about your journey at dinner this evening. Would you do me the honor of sitting next to you?" Ezra asks. Does he not know about seating etiquette? There's protocol. He may call himself a warlord, but I can't just shuffle down the table and sit next to a king. I like to think if Hiro were aware of the mask I'm bearing to shield my injuries he wouldn't push me to entertain, but I force a smile I doubt meets my eyes and do my duty to represent both my king and the Auctus.

"Lydia would be honored," Hiro replies, and my shocked reaction resonates before I can mask it. Ezra's jaw twitches before shifting, smoothing his features into a smug smile at Hiro's approval and my unfiltered reaction. He's pleased to have gotten his way more than someone plotting menacing political intrigue.

He gives the twins a perfunctory peck on each outstretched hand and a dismissive nod to me, departs the room and slams the door behind him. Dinner should be entertaining.

"Children, come sit." King Hiro gestures to the emptied chairs. Queen Naomi remains seated, serene as ever at his right. The rest of us take our usual places. Ryo sits on Hiro's left, and I slip into the seat beside him. One day I'll be moved down the table for Ryo's wife, but for now, I draw what comfort I can from being near my friend. Across from us, Kira and Iris settle next to their mother.

"First things first, Lydia—how are you?" Hiro's voice is tired, carefully measured. His brows furrow, eyes skimming over the scrapes and bruises on my skin. He winces at each one, concern that doesn't quite reach his eyes. I wonder if anyone's told him about the other injuries, the ones I still feel deep in my bones.

"I'll heal. Bruises fade. But that's not what turned us around.

Mercenaries are on their way, likely already in the outlying woods. We stopped the first band that attacked—they nearly had me. The second group was faster. Smarter. They knew exactly who they were after." I take a sip of water, steadying my voice. "Did the commander or Captain Whitlock update you?"

Hiro's mouth quirks at the corner, something too tight to be a smile.

Naomi responds instead, cool and smooth. "The commander was called away for an emergency. Captain Whitlock's report lacked specifics—he said you'd explain in greater detail." She always knows more than she says.

Of course he did. No one wants to carry the weight. Let the Seer bleed it out at the table.

"I had a Vision. Multiple, actually. But common threads all pointed here, not the bay. I'm confident in my assessment. I wish Tobias were here—we may need backup when facing the council."

"Do you have the strength to walk us through it?" Hiro asks, tone gentle—but the words are edged with something pointed. Testing. Hopeful that I'll perform. It's worked before.

"Of course she doesn't! Look at her!" Kira snaps before I can respond.

"There will be an attack on the castle. Soon. The snow, the moon phase—this isn't some distant threat. It's coming within days. There's still time to strengthen the wall, the gates, maybe even evacuate key leadership. Because what I saw—" I stop, swallowing down the stone in my throat. "You don't survive this, my king. Nor you, my queen. That much was clear."

The silence that follows is crushing. Heavy. As if the room itself holds its breath.

No one moves. No one speaks. The Vision's memory settles over them like ash after fire. Suffocating. Final.

"My dear," Hiro says with a bit of a patronizing tone, "perhaps your Vision saw something else and you misinterpreted it." I tell him he's going to die if he doesn't listen to me so his response is to not listen.

"We need to take this seriously—take Lydia seriously." Ryo snaps "We know the rebels are planning something large. What we don't know is why. Ezra thinks they're targeting Adepts."

"I think they're after a key," I say.

Hiro's head snaps to me. "A key? Describe it," he snaps. The sharpness surprises me—it's the first time I've ever heard him slightly raise his voice at one of us.

Then, quickly, he softens. Reins it in. "Please, Lydia. Describe the key."

"Small. Copper, maybe. Plain. It shows up in every Vision, always circling back. It's the common thread."

"Well, a key and you, apparently," Kira mutters, raising her glass to me before downing it.

Another silence. This one colder. The king and queen lock eyes. It's the kind of exchange we all remember from childhood—the silent language of people who have already decided things without us. It used to make us feel small. Now it just makes me angry.

That instinct to keep us in the dark? It's going to get us all killed.

"There's more. We need to move you—tonight, if possible. The rebels breach the castle. Asher is working—"

Hiro holds up a hand, silencing me mid-sentence, then succumbs to a wet, rattling cough. He reaches into the folds of his embroidered coat, pulls out a long chain with a simple copper key hanging from it. "Don't ask what it unlocks—I haven't a clue. It's been passed down nine generations. Entrusted by the Witches at Rune Loren, supposedly. I used to think it was just a family legend. A lucky charm. Still wore it—superstition and all that."

He coughs again, winces, and takes a long sip of water. Then, with great ceremony, he lifts the long chain over his head. For a moment, he clutches the key in a tight fist, as if something grand and ancient were being bestowed. Something he doesn't want to relinquish but knows the time has come.

Then he offers it to me.

I take it. I have no choice. Duty, manners and my Sight command it.

The key is warmer than it should be, pulsing softly in my palm. I tuck it into my bodice, the weight grounding me in a strange way—like something has finally clicked into place.

"Keep it safe," Hiro says. "Tobias should be back soon. He asked after it before left. We always joked it might unlock a hidden wine cellar."

"Father, please," Ryo says, leaning forward, voice low and urgent. "Take a ship. Go to the Summer Palace. Just until this blows over. We can cover your absence. Let us protect you."

Hiro scoffs. "I will *not* abandon my home." He slams a palm on the table, and his voice—raw, strained—rises. "I am the king! I will not hide like some coward in exile. If that means I will meet my fate sooner than I intended, then I will meet it with my head held high. If death finds me, it will find me in my chair, wearing my crown."

Then he looks at me. His eyes soften, but the exhaustion beneath them is too honest to ignore.

"There will always be those who question your Sight, Lydia. Doubt you. Fear what you reveal. Who will challenge your Sight because they do not like what the future holds. I've fought to stay alive long enough to see my children be ready to lead. That is enough. It will have to be enough. I knew my time was short but now... now I must accept my fate or pray that you are wrong."

Naomi brushes away a tear. Hiro wipes it from her cheek with a practiced tenderness that feels almost rehearsed.

"If this key means something," he continues, "then perhaps giving it to you was always the point. Perhaps that's the story. We should all be so lucky to meet our end with a heart full of love and pride for this home and our duty. An honorable death." His coughs shake his shoulders and blood splatters tiny dots across his handkerchief. "Hopefully giving you this key will be enough to change the future. Keep this secret close. If this Vision holds truth, you may only have each other to rely on. You may all need to grow up a bit faster than we planned."

His words land, soft like the snowfall, but just as cold. He's not going to do anything. How can he simply accept this fate?

He stands, taking Naomi's hand. Together, they walk the table's length, kissing each of us on the head like fragile children. "Trust each other. Rely on each other. Keep your circle tight."

"There's more," I say, louder this time. "My Vision—Asher is part of this. He's still in the castle, he needs to be found—"

But Hiro cuts me off again. He pats my cheek like a nursemaid. "Later, my treasure. I must update my guards immediately. Shift rotations. There's time, yes? A few days, you said."

He smiles. Tired. Distant. "I want to hear you re-tell the council yourself. I want to see their faces."

"Mother," Iris pleads, "do something. This is madness."

"Your father is still the king—for now—and his word is law," Naomi says gently, though I see the tears she refuses to shed glinting like glass. Her voice doesn't tremble. It never does. Not when it matters. "You think I don't feel the weight of this too? That I haven't looked at that throne and seen all the ways it could ruin him... or you?"

She steps closer, the silk of her sleeves brushing against her daughters like a promise not to let go. "Visions are powerful, but they are not commands. They are possibilities. And possibilities are delicate things. One decision, one moment of hesitation or boldness, can redirect the entire shape of what's to come."

She steps to Ryo. Her hand reaches out, fingers brushing over his hair. "Bravery isn't always defiance, child. Sometimes it's strategy. Sometimes it's knowing when to act—and when to wait. Is it noble to spit in fate's eye? Perhaps. But a wise ruler learns when to listen and when to lead."

She straightens, regal even in her tenderness. "You may not like the choices being made, but do not mistake patience for passivity.

We are not surrendering. We are preparing. And when the time comes, you will not face the future alone."

Hiro clenches his jaw but says nothing. He turns, his cloak brushing the floor as he retreats with Naomi on his arm. Regal. Hollow. Every step a study in appearances of strength in a frail body. Pity perhaps or regret flashes in his eyes as he surveys each of our shocked faces. Unblinking, defeated and worn down. His thin shoulders drop. His ragged breathing struggles, and his lungs softly whistle with each exhale.

We have time. He needs rest for what is to come.

CHAPTER 33
RYO

"Why do I get the impression I'm missing something?" Kira asks, breaking the silence. With white knuckles gripped to the arms of her seat, she unclenches and stretches her cramped fingers.

"Because you are," Iris mutters staring at the table like it will give her the answers she seeks.

"Why is there always a *key*?" Lydia bangs her forehead onto the table twice.

I pat Lydia on the back. "Literal key this time, at least. Possibly also metaphorical but yes, in every legend, there's a key that opens something that should *never* be opened."

"It's like a harbinger of doom," Kira says.

"Me or the key?" Lydia asks.

"Both?" I shrug with a small smile that I know doesn't quite reach my eyes.

"Why do they never listen?" She's grumbling to herself. "Asher... where is Asher?"

"Rumor has it he's been ill," Kira says. "Maybe it's fatal and we'll never have to deal with him again."

"Would be a pity," Iris deadpans.

"Rest before dinner. It will be a long night. They'll listen to the rest. I'll make them listen." I stand and reach out a hand to help Lydia rise. She seems so fragile with her scrapes and bruises when she's anything but. That black eye against her freckles. I failed her. I should have never let her leave. I wonder if she'll ever tell me everything that happened in the Interior. I have no doubt she's keeping parts of it to herself. Tiernan gave a summary of events to the council but...I want to hear what happened from her.

I take her hand, and she weaves her fingers between mine. We squeeze. This feels right. Her hand is in mine. We're working together like the team we are. Maybe Oscar, my mother, and all the rumors were right all along. Lydia fits me too well to ignore. Perhaps I've always been a little in love with her, and it's taken the thought of losing her to wake me up and see her as more than my friend. Perhaps I've used other women as a distraction from the one in front of me.

Exiting the council chamber, still holding hands, we almost knock into Tiernan. I pull Lydia back against me before she makes contact. She flinches, and her back tightens. Her shoulders pull back like she's preparing for a standoff. Her recoil doesn't go unnoticed, nor does Tiernan's tense glance downward when I don't relinquish her hand.

My eyes volley between them. An angry, protective monster simmers beneath my skin. Something happened between Tiernan and Lydia, and I'll learn the truth of it. She's hurt physically and emotionally, and he was the only one with her for days. That cannot be tolerated.

"Ryo, I'll see you at dinner," Lydia mumbles. She looks up with her vivid blue and green eyes, but I hesitate, gripping her hand tighter. She's not seriously wanting to be alone with him right now?

He let this happen to her. "I'm not leaving you alone with him." I glare at Tiernan. He glares back, no deference for his prince.

"I'll. See. You. At. Dinner." She pauses in between each word for emphasis.

"No."

"Yes." She drops my hand.

"No."

"Ryo," Lydia warns with hands on her hips. "I'll see you at dinner," she repeats, softer this time.

I shake my head and walk down the hall, glancing back a few times. She squares her shoulders, facing off against Tiernan. Despite her small stature next to his warrior frame, I know better than to be on the receiving end of the fierce look she just unleashed.

I hang around the corner in case I'm needed. It's not spying, I convince myself as I peek around the wall no better than a toddler. Cringing but unable to stop myself. I'm protecting the most important person in my world.

Tiernan pulls her back into the council chamber. Fortunately, he doesn't close the door, so I tip-toe closer. It's adjacent to spying. Lydia will never let me live this down if I'm caught. I check the hall, and it's surprisingly empty—no witnesses to my eavesdropping.

"Are you okay? You told them about me. Didn't you? What did you tell them?" he asks, looking her up and down. He's still holding onto her arm.

Lydia pulls away. "Don't worry. I said I'd keep your secret and I am not an oath breaker. Not that you care or trust me. You forgot all about me the moment you saw your uncle. Three. Fucking. Days. Ago. What did you tell him?" She shoves him away with both hands.

"Is the Verralon lord here for you?" He's ignoring her question. What happened? Tiernan's tone hits an edge of bitter sharpness. "He's been asking questions about you since his arrival, apparently. I bet that would be quite the feather in your cap—a king in the Auctus's pocket!" His words hit his intended mark with Lydia's sharp inhale. I know that breath. I know all her ticks. She's *mad*. And Tiernan is about to bear the full brunt of that anger. I'd say I pity the man, but fuck him. I'll be having words with the commander, ready to assign his ass to the furthest outpost possible.

"Why do you care? You got what you wanted, you fucked me, you learned how to weaponize your Senses, and then you blamed me when you lost control. And somehow, it's all my fault because I was dumb enough to care about you. I ignored my intuition and let you in. No one ever trusts me, believes me. It's understandable then that I didn't even trust myself. I wanted you over my better judgment."

I bite back my shock. My captain is an untrained Adept, and he's been sleeping with Lydia for who knows how long. I thought he seemed a bit too eager when I asked him to protect her.

Tiernan steps toward her, and she chooses to stand her ground. Refuses to drop her gaze. Good for her. But then her chin wobbles, and she purses her lips. Lydia wants to forgive him. Fuck. No!

"Of course I wanted you. Who wouldn't? You are everything I've been told I shouldn't go near, but gods, I wanted you. I still do. You are the flame, Lydia. You drew me in, and I got burned." His hand slides up her back, closing the space between their bodies. I recognize the hungry look in his eyes.

"Fuck you, Tiernan. What kind of apology is that? I got burned, not you." She shoves him again but not as hard this time.

"You trusted me. You showed me things about you, about myself. It shook me, deep in my soul, unlocking things I never knew I wanted," he whispers in her ear, drawing her closer.

I should pull away and give them some privacy, but I can't. This has *bad idea* written all over it. She told me to stay out of this part of her life. Demanded it. Lydia is supposed to be the rational one, the one who sees through others' bullshit. How can she not see that Tiernan is a problem? He's manipulating her, preying on her desperate need to be heard.

It takes all my willpower to step away when she leans into him. She's a willing participant in this, whatever this is. If she wasn't, there's no doubt in my mind she wouldn't turn around and march out. I shouldn't be jealous. This pressure in my chest sits heavy. I shouldn't want to be in his place, but knowing and seeing are different.

I need a distraction, a comfort—someone who wants me first, who chooses me. Someone who won't ask anything of me.

My body is moving through the castle, but my mind isn't aware of its path until a door swings open, and I almost walk straight into it. Out pops none other than Lord Ezra himself.

Ezra's eyes connect with mine. He grins before leaning forward, resting a hand on the small of a lady's back who's in nothing more than a dressing gown. Kissing the woman on the cheek, he whispers something in her ear before stepping around and out into the hall with a slight nod toward me to follow him. It takes me a moment before I realize the lady in question is none other than my mother's closest friend and advisor, Lady Isobel.

I step back. My feet are lead. I can't move forward, not that I had a specific destination in mind.

"We can finish this discussion later," he says to a red-faced Isobel. Ezra strolls down the hallway, whistling as he goes. He assumes I'll follow.

"It's not what it looks like," Isobel defends. She pulls the lapels of her robe tighter.

"What did you two... discuss?"

She falls into a slight curtsy, opening the door wider to invite me in. "Not much. He asked a few questions about the princesses, Lydia, you, your father and others. Nothing else really," she rattles off a few more names. Her voice is high and a little shaky.

"Was this your first time meeting?" I ask. If Mother knows of Isobel's connection to Verralon she'd have used it by now. If my mother has her way and he's to become an ally through marriage, it would benefit everyone to learn what we can. Verralon rarely allows outsiders to their court. When they do, it's orchestrated and controlled. If Kira or Iris were to marry him, would they be loyal to him or let us behind the curtain?

"We've known each other for years, in passing. My first

husband's travels often made our paths cross. Ezra isn't perfect, but he's better than his father. That's for certain. He swings from stoic to bored to short-tempered. He possesses the attention span of a gnat. But he's loyal to those who return that loyalty and he's thinking three steps ahead at all times. Don't underestimate him."

"You seem to be singing his praises. Has this knowledge come up with my mother in conversation before?"

Her eyes narrow. "Don't threaten me, boy. I burped you as an infant. He has always been kind to me, especially after my husband's death. Verralon has a much more modern view of how women can serve as more than wives and mothers. Being respected for my mind and contributions outside of marriage might be refreshing. Something the council is lacking. Women can wield more weapons than their bodies, you know. Or maybe you don't yet? You'll learn. Or you won't." She shrugs.

My sisters would approve of a more equitable policy on women serving in the military and governing. I have a hard time imagining my father accepting a woman in his royal guard or serving on a ship out on patrol. Isobel is the sole female on the council and a rarity. Even the queen doesn't technically sit on the council, although my father listens to her advice more than anyone.

"Thank you for your candid words, Isobel, and your continued loyalty to my mother and Silvanisi. I'll leave you to dress for dinner."

When I leave the room, I catch Lydia flush with swollen lips at the end of the hallway. I storm toward her with a temper I know is unwarranted. I grab her hand and drag her to my room.

"What is your problem!" Lydia rips her hand out of my grip. I slam the door behind us. She steps back, gearing herself up for a fight. "Care to explain yourself, oh secure and mature crown prince?"

She wobbles a bit on her feet, and I kick myself for dragging her around when she's still healing. Her perfect freckled face has a few bruises and scrapes that are starting to heal, thanks to Mabel combined with her Adept blood. Her eye is no longer swollen as the bruise shifts from blue to green. Those captivating eyes are a stunning contrast to her pale skin. She gets a bit splotchy when her emotions are heightened and she's flushed red right now. She's pretty skilled at masking her emotions when it's necessary but this is the one tell she's never been able to control. Or she's unconcerned to contain it when it's just us screaming at each other.

"I saw you kissing him," I confess. Seeing her so open and willing in another man's arms unlocks something profound within me.

Her head snaps back. "Excuse you?"

"He hurt you and you were kissing him!"

"We will get back to you spying on me, but you know *nothing* about me and Tiernan. And frankly, it's none of your business. You want to protect me. I appreciate that—"

I don't let her finish. I don't want to hear about her and Tiernan. He's wrong for her. She'll see that. I pull her close and kiss her deeply, forcing her lips to part and grant my tongue access. There's no smooth build-up, just a pent-up need to experience her, invade her space, and demand a place for me in her heart.

She freezes when I deepen the kiss. My arms slide around the seductive dip of her waist. Feeling her breasts against my chest sends a wave of madness through me. What am I doing?!

As quickly as it starts, I pull back and see her wide eyes. Her mouth hangs open. I can't help myself. I pull her tight against me and lean down to kiss her again, but she puts both hands on my chest and applies the slightest pressure to push me away. My breathing is harsh and erratic. I step back. She's looking anywhere but at me. Her eyes are the size of tea saucers.

"I'm sorry. I don't know why I did that. Mother said...and then Oscar and then I saw you with him," I mutter, embarrassed to have acted so thoughtlessly on such blatant jealousy I don't fully understand. She's my oldest and best friend but not my lover. Never my lover. That's probably the one thing that's held our friendship together, and I just threw it away. Fuck! I run through my hair, not knowing anything else to say. I'm losing my mind.

Lydia's eyes soften, and she shrugs. "It doesn't take a leap of logic

to figure out why you kissed me. You were spying and saw something you don't understand. Hell, I don't understand either. Your
parents have probably been pushing the idea of us getting married.
Tobias has mentioned it more than once. You got jealous of the idea
of me with one of your guards again or maybe with anyone. We both
know you don't want to marry me. We have zero sexual chemistry
and that's not a bad thing. In fact, I think it's one of the things that
makes us unique. We'd kill each other or ruin decades of loyal friendship and trust, which I think we can both agree is a rarity. But you
also don't want anyone else to touch what you believe is yours. Tell
me I'm wrong, Ryo. Look me in the eye and tell me." She doesn't let
me answer. Her unrelenting and wholly accurate assault knocks me
down when all I want is to wallow in this self-pity.

Her hand falls on my shoulder, and I look into the eyes of my best
friend. "You don't get to pick who I love or like or fuck or marry. Is
this really where your mind is right now? One of the island's greatest
threats is coming to dinner. One of the members of your father's
council was funding the slave trade of Adepts and tried to kidnap
and imprison me. There's a rebellion raging and an imminent invasion to prepare for. Focus on the important details. Not on your
dick." She smacks me straight in the middle of my forehead with the
heel of her palm. "I need your head in the right place tonight, Ryo, or
this will all go sideways. Things are bad enough. Your emotions are
running high and you are looking for loyalty and reassurance. I
understand that desire better than most. Would it be one less thing
to worry about if we fell in love and got married? Probably, but that's
not our future. Nor do I believe it's the future you really want. We are
family."

She's right. What we share is unique and worth protecting. My
mother may not understand it and rumors may swirl about us; a
man and a woman are incapable of just friendship. But they're
wrong. I was wrong, and bless Lydia for the good sense to keep me
grounded, as she always will.

"It did feel wrong to kiss you."

"I know. I was there. Now follow me, sit down, shut up, and let me tell you the whole story."

I do as she says, following her into my sitting room. She closes the door. I collapse onto a chair, and she sits across from me. She's exasperated and has every right to be. I'd do anything for her. She's right, of course. I need to focus on what she's telling me. She walks me through every detail of her journey, from the attack on the campsite to the mercenaries, the slave collar and Asher's involvement. To her time with Tiernan in greater detail than I would have *ever* wanted. She hides nothing from me, sharing it all in brutal honesty.

I sit, not responding, absorbing everything. I don't interrupt. I don't ask questions, yet. I listen, half holding my breath and afraid to move. I hand her a glass of wine before pouring one for myself. We both need it. Possibly something stronger.

She tells me how she got the burns on her hips without divulging Tiernan's Adept status but it doesn't take a genius to figure it out. I'm furious he hurt her, especially during such intimacy, but she holds up her hand to stop my building rampage and continues. Once done, she flops back into the chair and curls up under a blanket.

"I'm so sorry you went through that. I'm sorry I didn't protect you. It won't happen again. I'd do anything to keep you safe. You know that, right? Why can't this be easy? We would be so easy," I plead, asking myself, not really asking her. How can we love each other so much in one way but not enough in another?

Lydia shakes her head. "You deserve love. I deserve love. A deep, passionate, all-consuming love. Even if it never comes our way, even if your parents push you, don't we owe it to ourselves to reach for it? To hope that it may come even from an arrangement if we open our hearts and *try*?" She knows me as well as she knows herself. She's right, and she knows it. It makes my heart crack the smallest of slivers to let go of what might have been.

"I love you, Lydia."

"I love you, too, deeply, truly, but that isn't the right path for us. That much I know. We will be each other's most trusted allies. Best friends. Appreciate that and let's both be grateful. I need you, Ryo. For what comes next, I need you. And you'll need me, too. But you'll also need a bride. One that won't smother you in your sleep. You vowed to me that I would always have your protection. The time is coming when I may have to call in that vow. Tobias is gone, Hiro is sick, Ezra is here, Asher will be exposed, the Auctus has sent for me, and the rebels are coming for our family." She ticks each obstacle on a delicate finger. Her eyes look up at the ceiling, almost doing a mental calculation. "We have a week, probably more like a few days. Don't add more onto the overwhelming pile of problems—"

"One problem at a time. Let's not borrow tomorrow's problems for today. Let's destroy Asher. I've wanted him gone for years. That one will have immediate gratification," I interrupt. The smile she returns could light up a city. Her eyes crinkle, and she squeezes in next to me and wraps her arms around my waist. She pulls me into a tight hug. I tuck her head under my chin and hold her in place, reassuring me that my actions have not done any permanent damage to our friendship.

CHAPTER 34
LYDIA

The soft hum of music pours from the doorway, channeled by the shaft of light from the candles in the dining hall. I'm running late.

It's quiet as I stand in the empty hall with a few servants bustling back and forth. Not silent, but not charged with the same tension emitting from the entrance. When I enter that room, I will hold my head high and do what needs to be done. I'll have to expose Asher, even if he's sitting a few tables away from me but it has to be done. Scary, yes. Necessary, absolutely. I swallow down the fear and push back my shoulders. I'll have to answer some uncomfortable questions. My knees shake and my palms are sweaty.

I'm not ready. My eyes dart around, hunting for an escape. I can't do this. Nope, changed my mind.

A cough comes from over my shoulder. Tobias leans against a doorframe in a sharp black dinner jacket that sets off his white hair and dark eyes. His star pendant brooch shines against the dark velvet. He gives me that knowing grin. I don't hesitate to run into his arms. The force of my impact throws him back a step. He wraps his arms around me, holding tight. Fat tears roll down my cheeks at the sheer relief of his presence. I'm not ready to be without him yet. I'm not ready.

Tobias wipes my tears away as if I'm still a little five-year-old. "You can tell me everything later. Tonight, we have a job to do. Speak your Vision and your experience. We do not speak to anything except what our eyes have witnessed. That is private or at risk of interpretation and manipulation. Seers play a dangerous game each time we open our mouths. Our words will be twisted and used but our Vision is truth no matter how it's skewed. You are the future of House Seer. *Clear mind. Clear path.* I believe in your Sight." He's not waiting for a reply. He has every confidence I'll do what I've been trained to do. He trusts me. He believes me. I'm ready to go in there and say what needs to be said, but I am not ready to be without him.

"You know," Tobias says, "this one time I had a Vision that could've saved an entire diplomatic summit... if I hadn't been too polite to share it."

I shake my head, already smiling despite myself. "Tobias."

"In my defense," he says, shifting into his usual dramatic rhythm, "I was still a novice. And the Vision involved the Master of Trade and a very unfortunate... wardrobe malfunction."

I blink. "What kind of malfunction?"

"The kind involving a loose belt, a long staircase, and an unplanned moonrise during the welcome banquet."

"Oh gods."

"Precisely." He sighs. "I saw it clear as day, much to my horror. But I figured—dignity and all. Some things a man just doesn't want predicted. And I'm not the only Visionary who's ever been doubted."

"So you didn't tell him."

"I *tried* to," he says, wounded. "I complimented his tailoring. Twice. I suggested he check his fastenings. I even spilled wine on his robe as an excuse to get him to change."

"And?"

"He said I was acting erratic—quote, 'even for a Seer'—and told me to stand three paces behind him at all times."

I stare at him. "So what happened?"

"Well," Tobias says, lacing his fingers behind his head, "he fell down the stairs. In front of fifty foreign delegates and their entourages. Took out a dessert table and Hiro on the way down. Ended up in the fountain, robe floating behind him like wings trying to fly him away."

I put my face in my hands. His story has the desired effect—I'm snorting back a laugh.

"And because everyone was too busy dealing with *that*, no one noticed the envoy from Verralon sneaking out with the trade agreements. And a case of Renatto wine. Which led to three weeks of diplomatic headaches, a brief skirmish on the Tyberon Islets, and a ruined tea harvest."

I lift my head. "You caused a trade war to spare one man's pride?"

"I *prevented* a public scandal," he insists. "Mostly. Well—I *tried* to."

I stare at him, dumbfounded.

He shrugs. "Look, I've learned my lesson. The point is—be straight and to the point. Speak it truly, speak it clearly, speak it concisely. You say your truth, and we'll deal with the rest after. And hopefully no one ends up flashing a diplomatic assembly."

"Please don't say it like that."

Tobias only grins. "Besides... that wasn't even the worst part of the vision. But that's a story for another time."

"Tobias. Is now the best time?"

"It's never a bad time to share a story worth telling," he cautions.

Brushing away the last remaining tears, I nod my head in understanding and give him a watery smile. This is all part of my training, and yet my palms sweat and chills spread over my exposed skin. That niggling doubt that creeps in the back of my mind comes forward. Am I good enough? Will they believe me? Or will they see the fear simmering behind the mask? I'm humbly aware now that I am far from ready to be a Master Seer.

I search for Asher, but he's nowhere to be seen. His usual

entourage, the ones who always seem to be at his side, are also conspicuously absent. A cold knot forms in my stomach. Something is off, and the silence left in his absence feels louder than all the noise around me.

Tobias squeezes my hand and weaves it through the crook of his elbow to escort me to our seats. Arm in arm, we are the most prominent reminder of the Auctus's influence on Silvanisi. A hush falls over the bright and boisterous room as soft music continues to play.

Standing for a Master-level Adept's entrance is a customary sign of respect within the walls of the Auctus. It doesn't go without notice that every guest from Verralon stands. I wonder if they're all Adepts or their culture holds an Adept Master in higher regard to do so beyond Merthaset.

Ezra stands with his guard at a lower table. When our eyes connect, he glares and I glare right back. He can blink first. When he shifts away, I can't hold back a smug smile at my petty victory before I survey the rest of his party.

Two women next to him are elegantly dressed and equally beautiful in wildly different ways. My eyes shift to the men in their party. I pause and almost trip.

"Lydia, are you alright?" Tobias grips my hand tighter and stops our procession.

"I'm fine," I reply, catching my breath as we continue to our seats. I can't take my eyes off the man. He's wearing gloves, but I would recognize his face anywhere. A face I've memorized. Those blue eyes. No doubt about it. He's my kidnapper. I emulate the serene expression I have seen Queen Naomi use countless times to mask her true feelings. The man meets my eyes for a moment. His brows furrow, but he glances away, shifting on his feet.

I take my seat at the end of the table, feeling the weight of the room's eyes on me. Tobias leans in and kisses my bruised cheek, the touch soft and warm, though mostly hidden beneath makeup. He pulls away and moves to his seat with a quiet grace. Once he's settled, the Adepts standing around the table take their seats, and the music swells, shifting to a livelier, more upbeat tune. The room buzzes back to life with the familiar chatter and clinking of silverware, but the ringing in my ears drowns out the noise, leaving me in a thick, pulsing silence.

But now, nothing else matters. If I am to be a Master Adept, this is my moment to claim it. The threats will always be there—those who wish to silence my voice, those who seek to use me, to control what I see, to shape the future to their whims. But in this room, I am the Master. It's time to step into that role, to stop playing at it and start acting like the power I am.

Or at the very least, wear the mask that shields my fear and swallow down the bile that threatens to rise. I need a touchstone. I need Tobias to pat my cheek or Ryo to tease me. A reminder that while everything is falling apart around me, I am still me.

Ryo tilts forward and pops his head out from the other side of the table. A raised eyebrow, asking a silent question as we have done for years. It does the trick, as though he knows what I need to get my head back to the moment and stop drifting into darkness. I give him my best *buzz off* eyes and survey the room.

I study Ezra and his group in greater detail. He's not seated next to me like he asked. His seat appears next to the king, but he's remaining at the long table with his people. Is this a snub to Hiro? Or is it a brief chat, then he'll move? Will I be moved when he does?

The kidnapping Handler studies my face while listening to something Ezra whispers in his ear. Does the man know yet what he'll do to me at some point? Has he already planned it, or will it be a spur-of-the-moment decision? Is that what they are discussing? The Handler leans back, and sings along with the music but a wariness remains.

Ezra rudely stares with those astute amber eyes, but doesn't halt his conversation. I reach for the chain around my neck, twirling my star pendant before pressing the key hidden under my bodice into my skin. His stare follows my hand. He tilts his head to the side. A curious, almost playful smirk emerges from the corner of his mouth.

He's probably just checking my cleavage. He picks up a wine glass and sends me a toast before returning to his friends. His deep laughter draws everyone's attention. He's too pleased with himself, laughing at some unknown joke at my expense.

Tobias pats my forearm, grabbing my focus. "It's time. *Clear mind. Clear path.* I'm proud of you. Are you ready?"

Nodding, I breathe in, slowly exhale and embrace years of training.

Composed, clear, concise.

Composed, clear, concise.

I make my way to the king. Ryo stands and joins me, placing a hand on the small of my back, right over the bow on the sash Colleen used to fit my dress.

"This is an uncomfortable position, Lydia, dear. Come to the front of the table, and we may speak," Hiro orders before shifting. He's clearly ill, sallow and thin, but his hazel eyes are bright even if there are bags under them.

I move around the table. Ryo stays within arm's reach but no longer touches me, respectful support but nothing more. I chuckle that he's finally decided to stop thinking with his dick, and if he listened to me more, his life would be easier. A chair is brought up and set on the other side. We need a more comfortable option here if it becomes a habit. Would a cushion be too much?

The room vibrates with heightened tension. The guests are enjoying the fine food and ample wine that's a bit more elaborate than usual, due to the royal guests, I assume. We have to put our best foot forward. But underneath the food and drink lies an undercurrent of tension. It's a taut rope, pulled to it's limit and we are all waiting for it to snap but no one wants to be the first to react.

A moment of hesitation is all I'll allow. It would be easy to put my head down, stop right now, and stay on the safe path. No, I must go forward. There's too much at stake. Asher needs to be handled permanently. None of us are safe until Asher is dealt with. The persecution of Adepts, the slave trade, the kidnappings—all of it must end. The pressure is too great, but we have to start somewhere.

I'm responsible for using my gift to help other Adepts. My oath tingles down my arm, sensing my hesitation. I rub the slight burning sensation over my mark. *Together, we stand. Together, we follow the path. Together, we thrive. Together, we survive.* This is the first time I've ever reacted to my oath mark, a gentle reminder that binding oaths should not be taken lightly and there are real and painful consequences to breaking them. Or maybe it's all in my head.

Laid bare on this side of the table, I have to set those insecurities aside. I have a job—a job I've been trained to do. I am a Master Visionary Seer...soon. Masters do not fear their gift. I am the Master of my Sight, damnit! I am rare, exceptional and formidable. Most of all, I am right.

A hush settles over the room once more as Hiro draws attention. "Lydia, I promised we would speak tonight, and I keep that promise. Tell me now what we couldn't discuss earlier. I am ready to listen." A hundred eyes settle on me.

I swallow the knot lodged in my throat, forcing it down. At least I don't have to endure a re-walk back through the Vision this time. "We ran out of time earlier. Lord Asher Montcliff is funding the slave trade—and the rebellion. He's behind an imminent attack on the castle, and we must prepare. Now. He's put a price on my head, to be brought to him alive. He's hiring mercenaries to take Adepts to the continent and masking it under his role as Master of Trade, all while sowing the seeds of rebellion."

I keep my tone steady and firm, forcing out any hint of wavering or personal emotion. The memory of my brutal failed kidnapping pushes at the edges of my mind, but I shut it out. This moment is about control. The weight of my accusation hangs in the air, and a profound silence settles over the gathering. Not a gasp, not a murmur—just the eerie quiet of disbelief. A fork clinks onto a plate. A chair creaks under someone's shifting weight. The silence stretches, thick and suffocating.

The contrast is striking, so different from the last time I spoke of my Sight. There are no wails, no cries for help, no calls to arms. Just pure, unadulterated shock.

Or perhaps there's not shock. Perhaps this is why Hiro asked me to do this here. To see unmasked reactions, witness whose eyes widen and whose dart. Who shifts and who blinks.

"And how did you discover Montcliff's involvement?" The question doesn't come from Hiro. Ezra leans forward, challenging me for an answer. His body is poised, tight, and ready to strike—none of the casual confidence I'd witnessed a moment ago.

Tobias comes to my side, flanking me between him and Ryo. Silvanisi and the Auctus, my two loyalties, are on either side of me. It's meant to be a sign of protection, but the weight presses me in from all angles, pushing, making me appear small, weak and unreliable. I am none of those things.

"I experienced a Vision that was retold in this very room weeks ago. That Vision led to my failed journey to the Cerulean Bay; we were attacked and were able to question one of the mercenaries. Surely your many spies informed you of the Vision? Or perhaps more," I insinuate. His eyebrow pops up at my disrespectful, challenging tone. His broad frame hasn't shifted. His forearms rest on the table, his back straight as a rod, and his shoulders tense.

"They did indeed, although my spies have omitted a few parts. So this lord is kidnapping the Adepts and taking them to the continent for sale. He's financing a massive rebellion. Why would he do such a thing? What is he after? You, power, wealth, or something else perhaps?"

"I can only speak to what my eyes have seen," I reply, unable to suppress my smug smirk. It's the token Auctus non-answer, and he knows it. He was clearly trained, too.

"Why is he hunting *you*? Why sell or kill all those other Adepts but want you to himself?"

"Because he wanted to kidnap her, lock her up, and force her hand. He's a violent, entitled, cruel, nasty shit of a human who has refused to take no for an answer," Ryo replies from behind me. I'd prefer to speak for myself, but I appreciate his support. Hiro flicks his eyes to Ryo and then to me. He leans back and whispers something to his guard captain. The guard leaves the hall, waving at four other guards to follow behind.

"I don't think that's the whole story, though I don't doubt it," Ezra says. "So in this Vision that took you on your harrowing journey, where you saw dark sails in the harbor with no flag or identifiable markings, did you see any people on these ships?" Ezra continues, prying for more details when he's already been informed about my Vision from his spies. "What were they wearing? What did they look like? How many ships were there? Were they fighting already? Were they fighting against you or fighting with you or fighting *for* you? Were the sails black or dark red? Or were there many different colors?" His questions come faster and faster, not giving me a chance to respond. A flush rises, heating my cheeks. Is he trying to make me look incompetent or untrustworthy?

I straighten my spine. I'm tired of being pushed around and made to feel small, made to question my gift. A niggling feeling in the back of my mind makes me clench my jaw until the muscles hurt. The timing of all of this is suspect. The motives are all too clear. "How do you know so much about these ships? I do not recall divulging any such details from my Vision. Perhaps the questions are flowing in the wrong direction."

"Lydia!" Hiro finally snaps.

Footsteps grow louder and more urgent, soldiers approaching, drawing attention away from my interrogation. Two men run to the king with matching worried creases across their foreheads. The captain takes a moment to catch his breath, pulling in gulps of air before squaring his shoulders.

"Lord Montcliff isn't in his rooms, nor does he appear in the castle. No one has seen him since this morning. His rooms appear to have been packed with haste," the guard reports, standing ready for the king's order. Hiro remains silent.

Ezra comes nearer, looming in front of my seat. Tobias and Ryo press closer, but they can't exactly shove him back without massive consequences. Ezra searches my face, but I refuse to cower under his attempt at dominance.

My head tilts, throwing his perusal right back. We look into each other's souls, neither seeming impressed with the visage. "No response? Very well, I'll ask. How do you know so much about my Vision? Are the ships perhaps yours, Lord Ezra? Are you working with someone else and wondering if they show up on time for your plans? Are you nudging our rebels to fan the flames of chaos, leaving Silvanisi vulnerable and divided? Are you using the concern over kidnapped Adepts as a distraction to meet your end?" I attempt to keep my voice calm and steady but cannot diminish my angry edge. I need to work on that, but it's too late now.

"Do you even know what that key unlocks?" Ezra whispers, barely audible over the noise in the room, but I hear him. His amber eyes hold my own, unblinking, harsh, and burning with the faintest golden glow. All the puzzle pieces fall into place at once.

No one except me appears to have heard his question. Arguments grow louder around the table. Ryo is furious that Asher has slipped through our fingers. The Verralon guards rise from their seats. Our remaining guards are not subtle with their attention solely on Verralon. The rising tension in the hall could snap at any moment. Somehow, though, I can't move. My eyes stay glued on Ezra, and his question hangs above my head.

Do you even know what it unlocks?

"Why are you here?" I whisper.

Hiro stands from his seat. Immediately, the bickering ceases. "Lydia, Ezra is here as a potential ally and a guest. I understand you are distraught from the tragedy you experienced on your journey, and I worry that may cloud your judgment and cause you to forget your manners and your position at this table."

"Hiro, Lydia is a great many things. Young, determined, direct, but no one would describe her as not having sound judgment," Tobias defends, resting a protective hand on my shoulder.

As Tobias goes to the king, whispering something in his ear, another shadow takes his place. Tiernan steps closer. Ryo doesn't quite sneer at him but gives him a thorough once-over. They both puff up and posture. Men can be such babies, but I'll tolerate any protection that I can get right now with the Verralon lord looming.

Ezra's heated gaze bounces from Ryo to Tiernan and then back to me. That infuriating smirk passes, lacking any warmth or humor. I'm becoming too familiar with that particular expression. He's compiling his puzzle pieces as I do the same. I scowl, unblinking in return. Two can play this game, and I never blink first.

CHAPTER 35
TIERNAN

I don't remember walking over and positioning myself next to Lydia. She's unleashed chaos in the hall. She seems to have a knack for it lately. As much as she shies away from being the center of attention, she can't help it. It's natural to want to witness the spectacle of her Sight. It's also hard to avoid when she's been set up to have all eyes on her.

When word got out that the Seer would be speaking tonight, anyone wanting to witness her success or her downfall flocked to the dining hall. From the moment she walked in on Tobias's arm, no soul looked at or discussed anything but the Seer, like she was the harbinger of doom wrapped in the most compelling package. Or that's just how I view her.

She's more composed and confident than when I saw her earlier. I had her right where I wanted her, where I needed her—in my arms, moaning into my mouth, begging for my touch, distracted from everything else. I can't separate my responsibilities from the pull of this woman. I need to, but it's the last thing I want.

I thoroughly enjoy watching the Verralon warlord's smug face falter as she accuses him of inciting war in front of the entire court.

She's no wilting flower. My Lydia. She also has no idea what the ramifications of her words are, or perhaps she's seen something she hasn't shared yet. I wouldn't be surprised. It wouldn't be the first time she's kept secrets.

Only the fearless, crazy, or stupid would attempt to go toe-to-toe against the strength and unpredictable rage of Verralon. She might be all three, but then again, Lydia can see three steps ahead. Can't she? She's using her Sight for more than Visions. I know it. Her eyes are wide open, observing, taking in everything, and putting the pieces together. It's enthralling to witness at her side as opposed to under the magnifying glass.

There are shadows in her Sight, though—the things she chooses to ignore, her blind spots.

Hiro studies her with Tobias still whispering in his ear, pulling his Auctus puppet strings. Something flashes across Hiro's eyes, but it passes in a moment.

The king gives her a pitying look, placating a wayward child. "Her control is frayed, understandably so. The events of the last few weeks have taken their toll." A wave of hurt washes over her face before it shifts to anger. The king doesn't believe her. Or if he does believe her, he's warning her to stop.

She seethes, practically hissing. "Forgive my outburst. I'm tired. I'm not finished, my king. I meant no disrespect. Let me finish." She growls out each individual word, a lack of sincerity dripping off each punctuation.

I can't help but smile at the blatant rudeness of her tone, all while playing silly political games. I'm not the only one; Ryo chuckles, too.

"You are finished for now. Perhaps a bit more rest is in order. Captain Whitlock, please escort Lydia back to her chambers. Lydia, my treasure, we will discuss this further in the morning. You need to rest."

I reach down to help her out of her seat, but she wretches her arm away from my grasp.

"Please, let me finish."

"You are dismissed, Lydia. Go. Before you say something you cannot take back." Hiro flicks his boney hand in my direction.

In the corner of my eye, the Verralon lord watches. He tracks how we move, studying her like he's looking for some missing piece. His eyes shift over to his men at their table. He steps back, giving Lydia a hint of a bow, barely even a head tilt. "I look forward to tomorrow morning then. Perhaps a good night's sleep will unlock something new. Sweet dreams." He grins with the same condescending smirk that's clearly a familiar tool in his arsenal to unsettle his opposition. He bestows a polite bow to the king and queen before he and his companions leave the hall together. I direct one of my men to follow.

I squeeze her elbow, reminding her that she's been dismissed and needs to leave now. With all the grace of a dancer, she falls into an elegant and exaggerated curtsy before turning and stomping out of the dining hall like a toddler. Once we're back in a quiet hall, she freezes.

"What is it?"

Pacing, she starts muttering to herself. "How did he know? His man is the Handler from my Vision. He knew about the slavers and the ship. He knew about Asher. He didn't even have the tact to look surprised," she mumbles. She's working out a puzzle in the middle of the hall.

"Perhaps you can untangle this in a more private setting," I suggest and pull her down the hall, away from prying eyes. She follows without hesitation, weaving through the dark maze of the castle, her warm hand encased in my own. Exactly where I need it to be. At least she still trusts me to some extent after everything.

BOOM. The castle walls shake. The windows rattle in their frames. Wood groans and cracks. A chandelier crashes to the stone floor where we were standing just a moment ago.

Shit. I need more time. I squeeze her hand tighter, dragging her into an empty hallway with me. "I need to get you to a safe space.

We're running out of time. Follow me," I order, but she tries to pull away from my grasp.

Another blast shutters further away but still too close. Instinctively, I wrap her under me to shield her from the dust and debris raining down on us from the ceiling. My heart pounds, thumping in my ringing eardrums. We never should have returned. I should have taken her to safety when we had the chance.

Shrieking, cries, and wails begin. We pause on the ground to catch our breath. Our wide eyes connect as another crash hits the castle, and I force her head back down, reaching my arms around and over. That third boom was too close. Screams sound from every direction. We survey the empty hallway before Lydia moves to a window, peeking over.

Outside, a swarm of rebels breach the gate. Fire erupts from the far side of the castle. It lights up the north tower, and it's spreading quickly. Distraction, attack, or beacon—what are they signaling?

"Follow me." This is the moment I need her to listen to me. This is my chance. I grab her hand before she can fight me and run off to do something crazy. She's in some sort of trance and barely registers my pull.

Mesmerized by the rebels attacking the front entrance, her eyes shift back to the fire spreading into the tower's roof. She's too calm; her eyes are almost glazed over, but I realize she's seen this event before. I've never witnessed a dream become a reality or a nightmare come to life. She's done this hundreds or thousands of times since her first childhood Vision. Her shoulders sag. She looks almost disappointed to have been correct.

"Lydia!" I shake her probably harder than I should, trying to pull her focus back onto getting her far away from here. I grab her shoulders and turn her from the window to face me. Her eyes are glassy, and her pupils are blown. "Lydia, the castle is being attacked. Snap out of it!"

I squeeze her shoulders, dragging her attention to the present. She pulls away from the haze starting to form over her eyes. Now isn't the time for Panic-Visions. My training kicks in. I grab her by the waist, throw her over my shoulder, and run down the empty corridor. I turn a corner and find her bedroom, practically throwing her onto her bed as I kick the door closed behind me.

"We need to stop them. We need to help!" Lydia shoots back up, running toward the door.

I move to block her exit. "No! Sit tight while I figure out which direction to move. I thought I'd have more time to get you out of here. Something must have moved up the timeline. Shit! Lock the door, and don't let anyone other than me inside. Don't leave this room until I return. That's an order." I look down, praying this works and she listens for once. I don't want to see her dead, but this isn't over.

"It's hysterical you think I will sit behind a locked door, twiddling my thumbs, waiting for you. I know what happens. You know I do. The north tower is on fire. The castle is being attacked. My family needs me. I won't sit quietly and let that path unfold. I have to do everything possible to shift that future." She speaks as if she has the sole power to change the future. Silvanisi's crown falling is destiny. It's inevitable. One woman can't change that. But maybe I can change her destiny and my own in the process.

Lydia moves to a dresser, pulling out leather armor and three knives of varying lengths. She drops the shoulders of her dress and lets it pool around her feet, showing no embarrassment in her nudity.

I'm momentarily made stupid. Her soft skin glows in the dim light, her bruises and bandages covering the damage of my Touch. I reach out without thinking, brushing over a bruise on her bare hip. She flinches, finally realizing that she's naked in front of me.

"I'm so sorry I hurt you. You'll never understand how sorry I am for hurting you. For all of this."

Her eyes meet mine—those impossible eyes, green and blue and fathomless—and for a single, reckless breath, I forget why I should look away. I shouldn't want her. Not after everything. Not when she's made it clear what I've become in her eyes.

But I do. Gods help me, I do.

Adepts are drawn to Adepts, and that is what I am. Though I suppress it, it's becoming a struggle each day since she unlocked that part of me I've hidden deep down for years. She's bewitched me. She's cursed me.

My hand finds her cheek before I can stop it. Her skin is warm, infuriatingly soft, and the familiarity of it burns more than any wound I've taken in battle. I want to pretend, just for a moment, that this could be simple. That it's still her and me, not... this.

She flinches but doesn't pull away, like she might be as haunted and hurt as I am, but she feels the same pull. I know it, and she cannot convince me otherwise. Her mouth crashes into mine. This isn't tender—it's bruising. Desperate. The kind of kiss that tastes like grief.

Or goodbye.

My hand slides to the back of her neck. My fingers graze over two delicate chains around her neck: one bearing the dark star of the Auctus—a symbol of what she is—and another, a longer chain weighted by a key rests low between her achingly perfect breasts. I drag a finger over each chain, each touch a battle between my need to possess her and my desire to consume her.

I hate how quickly I forget my mission. I hate that she still has this hold on me.

She's a curse I walked straight into—bare, breathless, and beautiful.

And I nearly fall.

Until her voice slices through the haze like a blade. Until her hands rest on my chest and push me back.

"Don't mistake that for forgiveness," she says, breath ragged, eyes lit with something that's not lust. "Some things are unforgivable, Tiernan." She grabs her leather armor and finishes pulling it on, tying the straps.

She doesn't look at me again. Not tempted the same way I am.

I freeze. The words strike with precision. Not a scream. Not a slap. Just truth, delivered clean and sharp.

She's not wrong. Some things are unforgivable, and I almost forgot that. Forgiveness is not an option for either of us.

"It doesn't change the fact that I'm sorry," I say. "I'm sorry for everything."

The sound of splintering wood rips us both back to reality. I shake my head at the loss of my control and step back, pulse still thundering, shame rising to meet it. My gaze lingers on her—this woman who sees through every mask I wear. I want her. I hate that I want her.

"This is our last chance, Lydia. Please, let me get you out of here. I can only do so much." I have to ask. I have to try one last time before everything spins out of control. She glares, setting her jaw. I sigh, resigned that I can't convince her to come willingly. "Lock the door. Please." I rush out before she challenges my instructions or tempts me further. I need her to stay in her room until I can evaluate the situation.

As I run through the halls, closer to the battle, I see guards fighting each other. The rebels have been hidden in plain sight for years, waiting for the right time to make their presence known.

I turn a corner and spot the Verralon group sneaking down a hall, swords drawn, ready to fight anyone who gets in their way.

"Get back to the ship, Ezra!" one of the women shouts while skewering a rebel dumb enough to approach. She's still in her gown from dinner. She slides a sword back out of him and wipes the blood off the dead insurgent's back. Barely a hair is out of place.

"This is a disaster. We can't go back to the ship until we find her. Otherwise, this was all a waste of time," Ezra commands, looking in every direction. His crew encircles him, protecting their liege. He doesn't need protection. He's furious, ready to burst with angry energy at his plan's being foiled.

"Let us do our jobs, and you do yours. Get back to the ship now.

We will find her," a man to his left yells, fending off another attacker easily. He's the only one wearing gloves. He must be the Handler Lydia mentioned.

"I'm the captain, remember?" Ezra snaps.

"If you were a better captain we wouldn't need so much reminding!" The woman smirks.

"Fine, but remember, we need her alive, unharmed, and we need not be seen taking her for this to work. Pin it on her guard," Ezra orders before splitting off with two guards in the opposite direction of the Handler and two others.

I wait a moment until I'm clear. They saw me escort Lydia out of the dinner. They can't get to her first, or everything will fall apart. We can't have come this far to end up with nothing.

CHAPTER 36
LYDIA

Sitting quietly and obediently isn't something I've ever been good at. *Keep your head down.* Not in a burning castle that's under attack by people who want to kill my family. The thought that they also want to kill me or kidnap and sell me is all the more reason not to sit and wait.

Tiernan had to know I wouldn't listen. If I do nothing to change it, I've already seen what comes next.

I need to find Ryo, protect my family, and stop this before it happens. And if I can't stop it, I need to try to shift it just enough to change the outcome. I cannot wait for others to act.

I jump out of bed, ashamed of my moment of distraction and weakness. How could I get so lost in Tiernan again? Maybe it was a moment of insanity brought on by the chaos and threats to my life. But that excuse won't hold if I examine it closely. I told Ryo to stop thinking with his dick. I'm such a hypocrite.

I shake my body like a wet dog to loosen the tight muscles. I'm still wound up and thrumming, relentless energy pumps through my veins. The tingly anticipation rushes through me, pushing me to jump over and dive into the deep end of the fight.

I pull on my leather armor and tie the straps. Ryo thought it was silly when I asked for it three birthdays ago, but he played along, always willing to humor me. I bet he's going to be thankful for it now. I'll be prepared for whatever comes next. I won't sit here and wait for my future. I won't be taken. I won't be enslaved. My country will be saved. My family will be saved. This won't be my fate.

I will change this, or I will die trying.

Through my window, I peek at the garden and mountainside looming behind it, harsh shadows cast by the glow of the full moon on a clear night. Brightened by the light of the fire raging in the north tower. I adjust my Sight to make out the shapes of more rebels emerging from the orchard beyond the garden, silently approaching the castle from the other side. They'll have us surrounded. We lose any safe means of escape if we fail to push them back.

A small group of men approaches the rebels, going on the offensive and slicing their way through the mayhem. They're creating a path to the wall, which is impressive, given that I count just three in the darkness.

Their dexterity and cooperation are entrancing while they work together in an elegant dance of blood and violence. They keep their backs together in a tight triangle, never more than a few steps away from each other. They move in harmony, each step matching the pace of the other two. If one gets too far, they quickly return to formation. They continue to move toward the wall as one unit. I've never witnessed soldiers work together so efficiently or effectively.

The path of destruction ends when they reach the wall. No more rebels appear to be coming over. The soldiers look back toward the castle. They appear to be shouting at each other, arms flailing, wildly gesticulating. One man pushes one of the others hard toward the gate and points back to the castle. The others push back. I adjust my Sight to see their faces, but they turn to leave as my eyes focus.

Why aren't they returning to help? Why would they abandon the castle when it's under attack?

Another BOOM reverberates through the stone walls, and I duck instinctively, covering my head. When I look out the window again, the three soldiers are gone.

Awe and despair conflict for supremacy in my soul. Witnessing a Vision come to life never gets less astonishing. No wonder many believe Enhanced Senses are magic and not a trait we're born with and train into perfection. I don't often get to experience my Visions or hold a front-row seat to the events. I am the messenger; not meant to bear witness to what is, only what might be.

Watching that tower burn is so recognizable at this point. I've seen this exact fire so many times now in various forms. This familiarity seeps into me. It's not comfort I feel, but perhaps a confirmation that my Sight is real. My Vision is true and accurate. I feel horrible and powerful at the same time. They can question my Sight, doubt it, challenge it, but I can't make them listen. They have to witness the truth and then, maybe, next time, they won't doubt.

They probably still will. No one likes to be told what's coming for them.

The fire will still burn. The tower will still fall. I'll be doubted but still blamed. The cycle continues. Tobias's words ring back. *Seers play a dangerous game each time we open our mouths.*

Pounding on my door pulls me back to reality. Tiernan said to lock it and not open it for anyone but him, but Iris is screaming for me from the other side. Her painful cry springs me forward. I know what's coming and what happens next. I cannot wait any longer. I have to act. I need to *try*.

I swing the heavy door open and pull Iris into my room, slamming the door shut behind me and locking us both in.

Trembling doesn't begin to describe her movements. Her eyes are wild and unblinking—darting about the room, unable to make eye contact with me. I scan her for injuries. The front of her dress is drenched in blood. The gash on her forehead shouldn't have caused so much damage, but I see no other visible wounds.

The small dagger Iris always has strapped to her thigh is in her hand, also covered in blood that must be from someone else. She's mumbling incoherently.

"Iris, it's safe in here. I can't understand you. Take a few slow breaths in and out. What's going on?" I keep my voice even and calm. Now isn't the time for distracting emotions. Now is the time for thoughtful action. When my Sight is of little use, I can still be helpful.

"They're dead," she whimpers.

A cold grip squeezes my heart. I'm too late.

"They're dead!" she wails again, louder this time, before she collapses onto the floor, her body wracked by tears. Sobbing, the bloody knife slips from her white-knuckle grasp and clatters on the stone. Her voice is scratchy and strained, probably from screaming.

"Stay in here. Do you understand me? Tiernan is on his way back and will get us to safety. I need to find Ryo and Kira. Do. Not. Move." Without yelling at her, I punch the last words.

I don't need to ask who's dead. I know. She knows I know, but she doesn't want to believe it. I warned them all, and I was still too late. I thought we had more time.

She curls up into a blood-soaked ball on the floor, hugging her legs, each sob shaking her thin frame. I grab a blanket from the back of a chair and drape it over her, kissing her forehead as I put the knife back in her hand. I don't even bother trying to move her onto the bed.

"Use this on anyone who isn't family, Colleen, or Tobias," I order, "and Tiernan!" I include him at the last minute. She wouldn't hesitate to cut him in her current state, but he may be our best chance to get through this alive.

"You trust him?" she asks, looking up through bloodshot eyes.

"I do. He's working to find us a way out of here."

If the last week has taught me anything, trust is fragile. Do I fully know anyone? Do I trust anyone completely? Ryo, the twins, too. It's a list growing shorter by the year, by the day. I grab my remaining knives and attach them to my belt, checking the position of each weapon before heading out.

The hallway casts deep shadows. A little moonlight and the glow of the fire cast a shaft of light in my path. I stick to those shadows. The hallway is deserted. I have no trouble adjusting my Sight to compensate for the darkness.

It's too quiet, but I follow the clashing and wailing farther into the castle and closer to the central hall. Footsteps come pounding toward me, and I duck behind a curtain. It's a terrible hiding spot. A toddler playing hide and seek could have picked better. Two distinctive sound patterns of boots on the floor are getting close enough that I can make out heavy breathing. One sounds like a woman. I risk a peek to see if they're friends or foes.

Kira sprints down the hall, sword in hand, away from the battle. Her other arm hangs limply at her side, and her face is bloody and bruised. She's been on the receiving end of a few direct hits to the face. Based on her bloody blade and the fact that she's alive, she gave more than she got. Amos follows close behind, running half backward, a sword in each of his hands.

"Over here!" I half whisper, half shout to them.

They both jump and spin, weapons at the ready. Kira lowers hers the moment she sees it's me, but she doesn't let go.

"Lydia, it's pitch black in here. You scared the shit out of me!" she barks but tries to keep it a whisper. She runs to hug me but flinches and groans in pain when our bodies collide.

"Get to my room. Iris is there. Tiernan went to find us an exit. He'll be back soon. Where's Ryo?" I ask, terrified I already know the answer. Amos twirls the hilts of both swords, keeping his arms loose and his back to us. A wall of defense between us and the battle. Galant and sexy as hell, but Kira can defend herself.

"He's still in the hall. Mother and Father are dead. The commander killed them himself." Kira slides down the wall and slumps onto the floor. "He's a fucking rebel leader. We heard the first explosion, and he ran up like he was going to guard Father, but instead, he leaned over and slit his throat. Then all hell broke loose. Mother screamed, and another guard stabbed her. I have no idea how Iris escaped with her life. She was next to Mother. Someone grabbed me, punched my face, and slammed my head down onto the table. Amos threw him off me, killed him, and we fought our way out. I don't know how Iris got out on her own. I thought she was dead, too." Her head hangs between her knees.

"I'm going after Ryo. Amos, get Kira to my room and stay there until we return. I'll find Ryo, and Tiernan will get us all out of here."

"Are you sure about this? Can we trust Tiernan? I will not put my or Kira's life in his hands."

"Amos, I trust you to trust me. I trust you to protect my family. We need to survive tonight. I'm asking you to help a fellow Adept. Together, we survive." My request is answered with another nod and a hand on his heart. He took the same oath I did. We are bound to aid one another.

Amos studies me for a few silent breaths. "I'll guard Kira and Iris with my life," he replies in his soft, subdued voice, kissing Kira's bloody forehead. He helps her stand on shaky legs, his hand moving protectively on her back, rubbing in small circles.

"Don't leave that room. I'll be back." We clasp our hands together, gripping each other's elbows before letting go. We take off in the dark hallway, moving in opposite directions. I need to find Ryo and unfortunately, I know exactly where I will find him. I hope I'm not too late.

I SNEAK through the darkness in silence, avoiding the notice of everyone I pass. I have to step over more than one body, but I'm the only one who can see everything in the dark anyway otherwise I'd have tripped a half-dozen times by now. I might as well be invisible.

Soldiers and rebels run and fight, some flee or clutch their wounds. Some plead for their life. Some help people escape the chaos, and some contribute to it.

I stick to the shadows.

Turning out of the hallway connecting our wing to the castle, I pause to peek around the corner. A large and rough hand grips the back of my neck tight and pulls me back into the darkness.

"Don't make a sound," the voice whispers into my ear, squeezing harder. I flinch and step back silently, following the order.

I'm forced toward a storage closet. Cormac lets go of my neck and shoves me through the door, closing it behind him. I'm trapped with the man who killed the king he had sworn to protect. A wild, slightly crazy smile passes over his face, distorting his weathered and warm features into a cruel, deranged visage.

"Nothing to say? You wouldn't shut up earlier," he asks, looming over me with disgust. He steps forward and backhands me hard across the face faster than I can brace for the impact. My body hits the hard wooden floorboards. It's nothing more than another bruise to add to the list. At least he hit the already bruised cheek. I don't have time to right myself before his boot connects with my ribs. I hold back vomit rushing up my throat.

"You rushed all our plans. You forced our hand too soon. Well, adapt and overcome, I suppose," Cormac rambles, reaching down to grab my wrists and smiling a bit when I hiss at his painful grip. He ties them together and begins unbuckling my belt. Panic seizes through me. I lean back and kick with all my weight and momentum, but he's faster and grabs my leg, twisting it until I cry out. He could break it, but he lets go and digs his knee into my stomach. I can't breathe for a moment.

"Don't worry, you little Adept abomination. I have no interest in fucking you. My nephew has that task covered." He finishes unbuckling my belt and pulls it off, leaving me with no weapons to defend myself. He tosses it to the far side of the small space.

"Why kill your king? Why? I've known you for years. Why now?" It's terrifying to know that someone so close to me and my family for most of my life could do this. Does Tiernan know of his uncle's betrayal? I need to warn him. I need to get away from Cormac and find Tiernan. He needs to know about his uncle and help me end this nightmare.

Someone slips through the door behind him. Tiernan stands beside his uncle and whispers, "This isn't what we discussed. You promised she wouldn't be harmed."

My stomach sinks. Were there warnings in the back of my mind? Yes. Did I consciously ignore them in the hopes that someone saw me? Wanted me? Perhaps. Blindsided. I'd chuckle at the irony, but the hurt, the betrayal stings too deep. I shared things, I gave things, pieces of myself, of my Sight, of my body to him. Stupid silly girl can't even see what was right in front of her this whole time. So desperate to be wanted, I ignored every warning for a warm touch.

"Plans change, my boy. Adapt. Does she have it?" Cormac asks.

Tiernan gazes down at me, a pang of regret flashing in his eyes for a moment before he shuts down all emotion. He surveys my new injuries and bound wrists then glances at the knives strewn across the floor before returning his gaze to me.

"It's on her necklace. I saw her wearing it a little while ago," he mumbles, defeated. He's not talking about the star I always have on me. He's talking about the chain tucked into my bodice. It registers then when he saw it—when I was naked, with my bare legs wrapped around him less than an hour ago. Fear, anger and scorching, crushing hurt ache in my soul, each one fighting for dominance.

"Good work, nephew. Your family would be proud. Asher will be at the rendezvous point soon to collect her. Keep her here until we have a better way to get her out. Keep your hands to yourself and your dick in your pants in the meantime, although I doubt Asher cares what condition she arrives in. Once she's served her purpose, her head will be sent with the others to the Auctus. Silvanisi will bow no longer. She'll show us the path if we have to beat it out of her. We will have all the riches needed to conquer the Aperion and turn Merthaset to rubble."

Cormac spits on me. He reaches down and grabs my ankle. I try to squirm away, but since I'm already against the wall, my options to flee are limited. Like a cornered animal, I lash out and kick him hard in the face. Enraged and ready to attack in return, he stumbles back, but Tiernan steps between us to block him.

"Let me handle this, Uncle. We have almost everything we want. If you kill her now, we won't be able to find the entrance." His voice is cold and calm as if reminding a small child to pet a dog gently and not pull on its tail. The Tiernan I know isn't even in this room.

"Proof we are on the right path." Cormac reaches down and grabs the thin chain around my throat, pulling hard until it snaps off, leaving a harsh abrasion on my neck. The key slides off and hits the floor. I make a move to reach for it, but he kicks me again and grabs it. Tiernan jumps to stop him, but he isn't quick enough when his uncle's boot makes contact. I roll over, clutching my stomach with a pathetic whimper.

Breathing hurts. I roll onto my side. Agony shoots through me with each inhale while I struggle to sit up.

"Stay here until you get the signal to move her. Don't disappoint me in this. Don't disappoint your parents' memory," Cormac says solemnly, affectionately holding Tiernan's cheek as they press their foreheads together. Cormac leans and kisses his nephew's brow tenderly—the sentiment in comical juxtaposition to the beating he gave me.

Tiernan closes the door behind Cormac, turning the lock. The click of the metal sliding into place sends a shiver of dread down my spine. He steps closer, eyeing me warily. A sense of finality washes over me.

He squats down in front of my battered body and brushes the hair hanging in front of my face. I flinch away from his outstretched hand.

"I tried to warn you. I tried to take you away, and you fought me every step of the way. Asher wants the key, and you are the map that will lead him to the treasury. I never wanted it to happen like this, end like this. I wondered if he had another Seer, but they all keep dying, and anyone getting close to answers goes mad before they, too, die a painful death. He will never give up his hunt for you. The only choice is to run and hide. If we find it ourselves, without him though, that could work. Let's run. Together. Now. This is our chance. If we find it before them, we can control it together." His eyes go soft, his voice contrite. Like he's doing me a favor, which maybe he thinks he is.

"What treasure?"

"The Auctus Treasury. The Vault of the Infinite."

I choke back a laugh. "That's a children's story. It's a fable about greed and betrayal. About keeping promises. It's not a real thing." He really has lost his mind. Wow, I am a truly horrible judge of character.

Tiernan's eyes soften. He pulls out a cloth and wipes at the blood or dirt on my face.

"Asher found something or heard something," he starts, his voice low but steady. "Hiro has a key he's always kept on his body. Then, whispers from Merthaset about a powerful Visionary. Next, Asher gets his hands on a half-witch who says the only way to find the hidden treasury is to follow the path. But no one other than a Visionary can see the damn path."

He pauses, his gaze intense. "We need Asher's money and influence to hold us over until we find the treasury. He needs the key. We want the king dead—and so does he. Asher is a temporary, convenient alliance to tide our funds over until you show us the vault."

Tiernan takes a slow breath before continuing. "With the resources of the treasury under our control, we can take down the Auctus with their own funds, eliminate them from Silvanisi, and build a better land, free of their power. Asher wants power above all else, but we want to build a new and better world, out of the shadow cast by the Auctus."

There's a brief silence before he speaks again, his voice heavy. "I was supposed to kill Ryo if Veronica failed. I was the backup, her check-in contact, and the mission leader. When Ryo asked me to protect you, Cormac saw an opportunity and took it."

Tiernan's eyes narrow, as if reliving a memory. "Cormac had danced around Asher for a few years, trying to convince him to join our cause. He's the richest man in Silvanisi after the king and prince, and has no morals. He despises but also covets Adepts' power. He approached Cormac. In exchange for funding our cause, Cormac would deliver you."

He looks at me, his expression hardening. "Cormac didn't know what it was for at first, but when he realized, he saw an opportunity to access the wealth of the Master of Trade and took it."

"So he fueled Asher's sick obsession. Lovely. That was a lovely monologue, but you are missing the most important part. There. Is. No. Lost. Treasure."

"Are you sure about that? We wanted the same thing: Adepts off our shores, the Auctus destroyed, and power restored to the true people of Silvanisi. The enemy of my enemy and so forth. Even if the treasure isn't real, the monarchy will be eliminated, and we will rebuild Silvanisi free of Adept manipulation."

"Fuck you, Tiernan. Did you forget you're an Adept?" I try to pull away but can't go far, backed into my corner, huddled on the floor.

"The Auctus is the problem. Not Adepts. If we could choose how to learn, where to live, and how to use these Senses, the Auctus wouldn't be able to use us as weapons. No longer will they hoard power for themselves. Those days are over. When we have the power and the funds, we will help other islands be free of them too," he confesses all of this while gently, almost reverently wiping blood off my cheek. "If you help us, I can keep you safe."

"You're insane. You can't keep me safe. You can't even be honest with yourself. You used me and planned to sell me to Asher to get access to his wealth then planned to backstab him to go after a myth. Don't pretend some higher moral motive that selling a person, me, isn't an integral part of this shitty plan. Are the rebels in support of slavery now, too?"

His tone, his eyes, and his touch are so tender, but his actions and his words speak of nothing but hatred and violence. Tiernan knows what Asher is capable of and what he's interested in. He knew, and he went ahead with this plan anyway.

"No, you have it all wrong. I'm a revolutionary, not a slaver. I would have never given you to Asher after everything we have shared, but... we need his funds, and he wants that key. The plan was that we'd give him the key. You lead him to the treasury. He'll keep you alive until it's found. We get the funds we need to solidify our resources. I'll then get you away and tell him that you escaped and kill him. That was my original plan, but we have the key. We don't need Asher anymore. I have you. We can find the treasury together. Yes, this could work." He starts pacing the tiny storage space. "My cause is right. Without the Auctus, you and I would be free to be together. I don't need Asher; I only need you. I need you to cooperate and play along for a bit. Keep your head down and follow along," he says, smiling softly at my shock. He's asking me to trust him. He's fucking delusional. How am I only seeing this now? How did I miss so many signs? A Seer who was blind by honeyed touches. Stupid. Stupid. Stupid.

"No." I lean back to propel myself forward, throwing all my weight against him. He's ready and prepared to stop me. His hands press firmly on my shoulders, keeping me pinned on the floor.

"I'm sorry. I never planned on caring about you. I hate myself for how much I care. It's my greatest regret. My greatest weakness. It's your fault. You tricked me into loving you, wanting you, and unlocking my Senses. You seduced me. I spent my life fighting against it, fighting the forces that brought my family's death, and you forced it out of me. You forced me to use it. To feel everything. To experience all that is to blame for every wrong in my life and the lives of so many others. We have one chance, Lydia. One. Don't fight me on this. If I don't get you away, you will lose. Asher will find you and I won't be able to keep you safe. How many times must I hold my hand out to you to have you smack it away?" Tiernan tugs my bound wrists to stand.

"Were those men who attacked us in the woods, who killed all the guards, were they with you?"

Tiernan steps back. "No. Those men who died, many were my own, many fought beside me, and I mourn their loss. He was furious that Hiro blocked his chance and diverted from Uncle Cormac's plan. Asher plays his own games and grew impatient."

"Looks like he's not the only one paying his own game." Tears sting and build before they break and slide down my cheeks. "Was any of it real?"

"Yes and no. I had an idea of who you were when this started and you were so much more. But now I see that we can be so much more. Together. So this is your choice," he says. It's not a question.

"How dare you speak of choice like you aren't making one with each word and action tonight and every day leading up to now? I'm glad we can finally have an honest conversation," I snap at him and move to strike, but he again anticipates my move, blocking me.

"This was going to happen no matter what. I don't know why I thought I could change this outcome. Hubris, perhaps, but I can't let you go. Not when we are so close to our goal. This is our fate. Yours and mine. Together we can create a new world." He pushes his forehead against mine, holding my wrists tighter.

I shove him back. I'm not getting very far, but it makes me feel better. "You may not control the cards you are dealt, but you can decide how to play them. Take some responsibility and stop blaming fate."

"What will it be, me or Asher? Those are your choices."

"Not much of a choice then. Is it?"

"Choice is an illusion for us all. Just play along when my uncle comes back, and we'll run for it together."

"I won't help you."

"Yes, you will. When the alternative is Asher? I think you will."

That mask settles back over, covering his soft gaze into a cold scowl. "Trust me. I'll get us out of here. Play along then we can go after it together. Cormac will understand when we have control of the vault."

Cormac returns, knocking to be allowed access. Tiernan unlocks the door with one hand. His uncle slips back in before locking the door again, blocking my only exit.

"The prince is gaining ground. We need to move her now. You take her through the south corridor, and I'll meet you and Asher at the rendezvous point," Cormac orders.

Tiernan nods, pulling me closer.

Cormac turns his steely gaze onto me. He has the same gray eyes. "I won't hesitate to gag you, beat you, toss you to my men, and lock you up until we have what we want. What we need. One Adept is not more important than this greater goal. You are not better than me or any of us. Know your place and maybe I'll let my nephew have you when we have what we're owed. Am I clear?"

"She's clear," Tiernan responds on my behalf. He leans down and whispers in my ear so Cormac can't overhear. "Your path has led you here, as has mine."

How did I get here? My mind races faster than I can process, unable to see the next step. I need to get out of this room to escape, and to do that, I need to think, clear my mind, focus, and remember every bit of training Tobias instilled in me.

I try to control my breathing when a damp cloth covers my face. A hand presses into the back of my head, holding it tight against the fabric. My eyesight blurs as I drift into unconsciousness. The last thing I see is Tiernan's beautiful face looking down at me. His lips press together in a thin line. Deep conflict radiates from his gray eyes. Even a shadow of pity.

Wishful thinking won't get me out of this.

RYO

Who is friend, and who is foe? The ones trying to kill me make it an easier choice. I would have preferred not to see so many soldiers fighting their brothers in arms. It makes for a confusing battle when warriors in the same uniform battle each other.

The north tower is on fire as Lydia predicted. I shift some men to try to put it out before it spreads further. I send another group of soldiers to scan the bedroom wings for anyone injured who needs assistance or to get them away from the encroaching fire. My remaining men form a line on my order to push the rebels out of the hall and into the courtyard. If we can control the gate, we can control the situation. Leaving it open is our greatest weakness right now.

I try to catch my breath and wipe the blood off my face. I have no idea how much time has passed since all hell broke loose and my parents were killed in front of me. Destruction surrounds us. I spot my father's body, hunched over the table, unable and unwilling to hold my gaze there for longer than a glance. It doesn't feel real. How will I fix this?

"Find the Adepts! Cut off their heads and ship them to the Auctus!" a rebel shouts, snapping my attention back to the present.

Lydia. I need to find Lydia. Asher put a price on her capture, so I can assume he wants her alive. The men in the rebel band don't care and are killing indiscriminately. There are no questions, only death. Would they pause if they crossed her path? Would they think of the reward more than their violent impulses?

I sprint toward the most likely place Lydia would go. Her room is tucked in the back of the castle. The halls become quiet the closer I get. Turning the corner too quickly, I slide across a bloody puddle and slam into a jagged stone wall. A crumpled and still body of a woman lies on the ground. Clutching a small bloody knife, I recognize the body.

Chills of terror wash through my veins, begging me to stop, to not go farther, but I push forward, rolling her over.

Colleen stares lifelessly back at me. Her small hand is wrapped around Lydia's knife. The poor woman who had been nothing but loving and good was taken down by such evil. My heart lurches in my stomach. Lydia will be devastated. Colleen has been a fixture in Lydia's life since Tobias brought her to Silvanisi. Hell, she's been a fixture in my life. She's the closest thing Lydia has to a caretaker, a mother. How will I tell her about this loss?

I close Colleen's eyes before placing a hand on her heart. She fixed our scraped knees, mediated our fights, remedied our hangovers, and always did her best to care for us cubs. Protective and nurturing, she was always one to give advice and tell us precisely what was on her mind. This should not have been her end. Her end should be years and years in the future, snug in a warm bed, surrounded by love. I rest my hand over hers and give her a small blessing, hoping she will find peace.

Before I can right myself, boots pound on the floor behind me. Commander Cormac runs, sword raised, bellowing a painful war cry. I barely have time to brace myself for the impact of his surprise attack, and my boots have little traction on the slippery floor. I tuck and roll away. His sword clangs against the floor, grazing my shirt. The clashing of steel against stone echoes down the hall.

"If it isn't the little prince himself," Cormac growls, rearing back to prepare for another strike. He's frazzled and worn, no longer the quick and agile force I knew him to be growing up. Cormac trained me to be a thoughtful, cautious warrior. This man before me is worn and sloppy, too. Thankfully, it gives me a chance to find my footing after being caught unprepared.

"You won't survive the day, Cormac. Was it worth it? What's the point of all of this?" I'll get nothing more than the ramblings of a delusional traitor if he's been brainwashed to hate for decades, possibly his whole life.

No one is born with hate in their hearts; it is taught through fear, misinformation, and repetition. It's reinforced by blinding, often illogical judgment, making anyone who doesn't share the same hatred an enemy.

"I already fulfilled the first part of my mission, boy. Soon, the people of Silvanisi will all join us or face the consequences of allying with monsters. This is just the beginning, and you will not stand in my way. You are a fucking joke; a whoring, drunk disgrace unfit to lead a parade much less a nation. Soon, we will have enough riches to take control and rip the Auctus down brick by brick. To rebuild a better world." Cormac holds up a bloody chain, dangling the swinging key before me. A few hours ago, that chain was around Lydia's neck. I break out in a cold sweat.

"Where is she?" I shout, rage taking over responsible thought and action.

"Your cursed whore? She's on her way to her new home by now. What Asher plans to do with her isn't my problem so long as she shows us the path first. One less Adept on my island and one more 'fuck you' to the Auctus. She'll do her job, serve her purpose, and when that's done, who cares. One less Auctus scum." He raises his sword to attack, but I block. My rage guides me now. The fighting continues below, but Cormac is slowing, showing his age and fatigue. I push the attack, knocking his sword out of his hand and kicking him to the ground. A mad smile spreads across his weathered face.

"Your time here has ended, boy. That power will go back to where it belongs. The Auctus will be forced to retreat to their pile of rocks, and this key will ensure their end. We will defeat them with their own resources."

Cormac taunts me by waving the key back and forth like a pendulum ticking in agonizing seconds of pain and doubt. Am I too late? I raise my weapon and move to strike the traitor.

The old man moves faster than I expected. He rolls away as my strike hits the ground, where he fell a moment before. He springs back up, ready to block my attack but not quite prepared enough. I press my brief advantage forward, steering him toward the staircase. It's a few more steps before I throw my whole weight toward him, shifting him to the edge.

A sharp pain slices through my bicep. I ignore it and focus on getting Cormac off balance. He moves to one side, and a foot slips. It's all I need.

Cormac tumbles backward down the stone stairs, smacking his head on the way down with a satisfying crack, landing at the bottom. His neck is turned at an unnatural angle. His eyes are wide open, but no life shines through them.

I gulp in a few deep breaths and scan the room before I leap down to ensure Cormac is dead—no loose ends. I grab the chain from his hand, still clutching the stolen key. It appears so ordinary. It was one of my father's last gifts. He wanted Lydia to have it. It must be returned to her if it's so essential and has been guarded. I can only do that if I can find her, though, before it's too late. I choose to believe she's still alive.

As I place the tip of my blade on Cormac's chest, I slowly press it down into his flesh to no reaction from the dead man.

Lydia's curly mane flashes in my peripheral as I remove my blade. Tiernan carries her over his shoulder, running away from her room. She's limp in his arms. Is she injured? I run after them, ready to help Tiernan get her to safety. He should be told of his uncle's treason and death.

He either cannot hear me shout for him, or he refuses to stop. I appreciate the desire to protect Lydia above all else in this chaos as angry as I am with the man. His aim to prioritize Lydia speaks highly of him even if I rage inside.

Then again, I killed his uncle, the treasonous assassin who killed his king and let in a rebel army. Does Tiernan know about his uncle's loyalties? Tiernan *can't* be a rebel sympathizer. He's an Adept, like Lydia. She didn't tell me so outright, but it's easy to connect her finger-sized burns with his Enhanced Touch. He's an enemy of the insurgents, too. He's with Lydia. They're together. *Right?*

I catch up to them. He's quick, even carrying her weight slung over one shoulder. Tiernan turns, clutching an unconscious Lydia, determination, and anger on his face.

"Tiernan! What happened? Is she okay? Let me help you get her back to her room."

Boots stop abruptly. He's seething with a frightening glint in his eyes as they dart around the hall. His grip on her tightens.

"Captain, where are you going?" I step toward him gingerly, my hands out peacefully. A cold fear grips my chest yet again tonight.

"You're in our way," he growls before turning to sprint away. Lydia's limp body bounces on his shoulder. Her hair dangles and swishes with each step.

Terror and impending doom slide across my skin, sink low, and settle in my gut as I watch two attacking rebels move to clear a path for him. What the hell! I chase, clutching my injured arm now sticky with blood. I slide down a narrow servant hall and take a shortcut, hoping to cut him off before he leaves the castle with her in tow. If they reach downtown Saivi it will be impossible to track them.

My weight shifts. I slide again, turning the corner to cut them off, and accidentally slam into them both. Tiernan drops Lydia's unconscious body in his fall, and she lands with a crumpled thud on the floor. That's going to leave a fresh bruise. He recovers quickly, rolls onto his feet, and unsheathes his sword in one smooth motion. He isn't showing any of the fatigue or distraction Cormac displayed. I'm already at a disadvantage in defending both Lydia and me.

"Is your plan to follow in your uncle's footsteps?" I slowly step between him and Lydia, wanting nothing more than to create distance between them.

"I plan to keep her safe, which is more than I can say for you. You've never cared. You've used her just like the rest. You wanted to control her, keep her all to yourself, wield her. But she won't be yours anymore. She's mine."

"She's not going anywhere with you. Your uncle is a traitor as are you. Turn yourself in now and I'll be merciful. Lay down your weapon. Now."

"You're the traitor. You've betrayed your people and they have no intention of being merciful. She's the key to everything I want and I'll be back for her." Tiernan shows the barest hint of a disappointed frown, like he's been dreading this moment but knew it was possible. His wide eyes cut from me to Lydia, crumpled on the floor, then back to me. "I need more time."

He manages to surprise me. Instead of attacking, he turns and runs. Lydia is regaining consciousness, holding her head in both hands. She pulls herself to sit up, groans, and scoots her butt back to lean against the wall.

"Are you okay?" I ask softly, bending down to check her face and brushing back her tangled hair. She looks like shit. A fresh bruise reddens and swells over an old one across her cheek, but she's here and she's alive.

"If one more person tries to knock me out, I will end them. Tiernan was going to take me. He's after the key. Fuck! The key. Cormac ripped it off me and took off. Fuck!" She's shaking her head in frustration. White knuckles press into her eyes. She slowly begins her breathing pattern. In for five through the nose, out for five through the mouth. Her hands shake. "I lost it, Ryo. I lost the key. Cormac. We need to find him. Your father entrusted it to me and I lost it."

"This key?" I ask, unable to hold back a hint of a smirk. The little copper key dangles, swinging like a pendulum. She gives me a pained grin and reaches out to take it. I return the smile and lean forward to put the chain over her head, kissing her gently when it's back with its owner. The clasp is broken, so I tie it in a double knot. "I'm happy you are alive, but you look like shit. I like the armor, though. Fits nicely."

"Screw you. I'm fairly certain I have a broken rib, and my brain is trying to burst from my skull. You don't look so hot yourself." She surveys me. "Your arm, Ryo!"

"I'll survive, and so will you, which is what matters. Can you make it back to your room? Or do you need me to carry you?"

"I can walk. Give me one of your knives, though, just in case. Cormac took all my weapons. How did you get the key back from the commander?" Lydia reaches out a shaking hand to help her stand. Once she's back on her feet, she's wobbly. She must have hit her head hard. She puts her weight on my good shoulder, and we hobble down the hall, checking corners and stopping for footsteps as we go.

"He's dead. The asshole attacked me. I pushed him down the stairs, and his neck snapped in the fall." She doesn't need to know all the details. She's glancing at my bloody arm and is smart enough to draw her conclusions.

"Good. You aren't going to like this, but you have to trust me. We have to stop Asher. If we can eliminate the leaders, we can stop the rebellion. Cut off the head of the snake, or in this case, the money. The fastest way to find the rendezvous point is to follow Tiernan. That's where he'll be heading if he thinks that's where Cormac is with the key. Logic would put him down by the harbor." Lydia's eyes are pleading, but her voice is steady and determined. How can she demand I leave her alone with a giant target on her back? Unlikely. She's hurt. I'm hurt. There's no hope of that idea ending well.

But I remember who she is and everything she's capable of seeing. She's calm because she's already seen what could and may still happen. She knows of one possible outcome and is trying to create an alternative.

She puts a lot of her weight on me to maintain her balance. I hold tight, feeling her sway a bit. The slice on my arm drips blood onto the floor. It's a manageable pain—a flesh wound. Or fight-or-flight has taken control, and I'll pay for this later. Probably the latter.

"Promise me you will get back to your room right away. No side trips. I'll be back soon. Please, Lydia, get to your room safely and stay with my sisters. I'll find Asher and stop this. It will all be over soon," I whisper into her hair, much more confident than I feel. I kiss her forehead again.

I can't believe I'm about to agree to leave her alone here. Will this be the moment I choose to steer fate in another direction, or will it be the decision I regret for the rest of my life?

Lydia kisses my cheek and brushes her thumb across my jaw. Tears well up in her eyes, but she blinks them back, straightening her spine. She's so fierce. I never deserved her. I'm a joke, a player, a child playing dress up on a throne I haven't earned. Cormac's words hit their mark, but it's past time to step up and be the man she believes me to be. The man I know I can be—the man I need to be to save my family and my home.

A crash shakes the castle, and debris shoots from the hall to the north tower. The fire is spreading. I need to send more men to put it out, but I have none to spare. Too many of my soldiers showed their true colors, fighting their brothers in arms. None of them will be shown mercy.

"Don't engage anyone while you are in the castle. Promise me. Get to the harbor, stop Asher. Don't stop or engage anyone in between. Trust me," she pleads.

Lydia shakes her head as we gaze out the window, watching our home burn. The whoosh and crackle of the flames drown out the ringing in my ears. We both take a second to absorb the fear and allow it to have a moment before pushing it back out. Fear isn't the problem. Fear is a healthy reaction. I acknowledge that fear, let it guide me to make intelligent choices, not act rashly, and most of all, not let fear overtake me and freeze me into inaction.

"Ryo. I love you. You know that, right?"

"Are you trying to make a move on me?" I wink. "I think it's best if we keep it platonic. Now is hardly the time."

Lydia chuckles and smacks my uninjured arm. "Your timing is impeccable. When this is over, I'm going to make you pay for that." She squeezes my hand before she takes off toward the other wing while I run after Tiernan.

I watch her go and disappear around the corner. "I can't wait."

"FALL BACK!" Tiernan shouts from down the hall. "Meet at the rendezvous and we will regroup."

Our eyes meet as his traitorous men disperse. I don't hesitate or think about what I told Lydia. My mind goes blank as rage and hatred take over. I attack. He hurt her. He had her trust, affection, attention, and maybe even her love, yet he still chose to hurt her. He chose to betray her. He cannot walk away. I need him to lead me to Asher. Only then will Lydia be truly safe.

My attack is quick, clean, and brutal despite my injured arm. Blind, uninhibited rage course through me, driving me forward with slash after slash in a brutal onslaught. I'm singularly focused on this moment. He moves to block slower than I expected for a man of his training. He recovers, though. The element of surprise is over, but with a swift kick, I'm knocked to the ground, Tiernan towers over me and spits blood onto the floor.

"I should have killed you when you were asleep in your bed. Now, I can fulfill my promises. Kill you, take Lydia, use the key, fund my army, and build a better world. She'll forgive me eventually. I will push out our enemies once and for all. I will have avenged my family. I will be the hero of Silvanisi. The only things in my way are you and Asher." Tiernan's breathing comes out labored and jagged. "I'll take care of you then deal with him."

"She trusted you and you want to use her? How are you any better than Asher?" I shout, barely able to get the words out. My arm burns with white-hot pain that reverberates through me with every impact and flex. I push myself to stand, using the wall as support.

"That's the problem, you're all too trusting. Lydia included. She'll understand when she's truly free to make her own choices. You trust the Auctus more than your people. You let them take, take, take all for a few elitists with some heightened senses. Trust will be your downfall. She'll forgive me. She'll love me again. When she sits on a throne next to me, when people like us are free to choose, she'll forgive me and see that the ends justifies the means."

His body hitches, ready to strike again. He positions and readies for his assault. He's giving me time to register his attack and prepare myself. He's confident in his victory. Possibly cocky. I hope that makes him sloppy.

Tiernan goes on the offensive, striking me again and again. Blow after blow. I'm forced to go onto my knee to block him, my injured arm unable to bear any more weight. This is my end. I know it now.

Lydia saw this. She told me, and I brushed it off. I didn't listen. I'm no better than the others who doubt her. It's a shame she didn't see the face of my attacker. A shame for both of us.

"She'll forgive me." An unhinged grin stretches across Tiernan's face as he embraces his victory and my inevitable end. He doesn't hesitate shoving his sword clean through my shoulder so forcefully it pins me to the wood dining platform, still soaked with the blood of my parents.

"You can die with them, but yours will be slow and painful. I want you to think about the choices of your forefathers. How they chose the few who could manipulate them over those who would have loved them if they hadn't bent over for masters on another island. Lydia will be mine. She and I will lead this world into a new age. She will show me the path to power," Tiernan hisses into my ear. He abandons his sword through my flesh, embedded in the floorboards, and leaves me pinned down to bleed out and die alone.

I should have not engaged.

CHAPTER 38

TIERNAN

The smoke stings my eyes while I lean over Ryo's dying body. The satisfaction is short-lived. The job isn't done.

The fire still spreads. My time and luck may have run out. I need to find Cormac, get the key, get my hands on Lydia, and then finish this phase of the plan.

The plan. It's always about *the plan*. Cormac worked tirelessly, in the shadows, for over a decade before I joined the guard. He moved his chess pieces around the table until everything fit just right, but we need funds, never-ending funds. It always comes back to money. I'm but one of his pieces. I'm one of many loyal to the Anti-Auctus cause and faithful to Silvanisi above all else.

But sometimes plans change. I'm nothing if not a survivor.

The rebels have been hiding in plain sight for years, waiting and watching until the right opportunity presented itself. We may have been rushed thanks to Lydia moving our timeline. It worked in our favor to plant the seeds of doubt. We adapt. We overcome.

Silvanisi's most fearsome and unpredictable ally decides to pay a visit just as the king is spreading his army thin to fight the rebels and block the slave trade, leaving the castle wide open and undefended.

It's almost too perfect. We couldn't have orchestrated it better ourselves. Cormac made sure that the men left at the critical points were *our* men. Lydia's Vision and her reveal of Asher as our primary funding source moved up our timeline, but honestly, it couldn't have worked out better.

We had to seize the moment. Asher's grand plans are secondary to liberating Silvanisi anyway. I couldn't care less about some alliance with the continent or setting him up as some sort of governor or whatever lofty role he thinks he's earned. My focus is on my home. On Lydia.

I don't want to do this, but I don't see another way forward. The problem is, wishes and dreams won't get us what we need. I need gold. I need *her*. And most of all, I need that key.

Killing Ryo is a pleasant bonus. He never would have let her go. He's been between her and anyone who would take her away the whole time. He doesn't want her, but he doesn't want anyone else to have her either. Selfish, entitled prick. He got what he deserved, and now the only thing standing between my future with Lydia is Asher Montcliff.

There have been a few bumps along the way. Letting myself enjoy Lydia, letting her in, and creating that nagging doubt—that's the biggest obstacle. But it's not insurmountable. It would've been easier if she'd volunteered to help me, but it's not like she has a choice now. It's for her own good.

Once word spreads that the secret to finding a long-lost hoard is a Visionary Seer, none of the dozen or so left will be safe. I'll keep her protected, right by my side. I'll love her enough to make her agree. Her body responds to me already. I'll get her mind to fall into line.

Today, I'll prove to my uncle that this change in plans is for the best. It's a smart plan, and if not, he'll understand when it's all over and the Auctus is ashes. I'll prove to him that his time and care have been worthwhile. I won't betray him, nor will I betray the memories of my brothers and parents. I'll come out of this battle the victor.

Silvanisi will return to how it should be, and the Auctus will no longer have a foothold here. Those with Enhanced Senses can choose to live as they wish. This is the only way to ensure the Auctus is stopped.

Ryo is clammy, pale, and gasping. His death is near enough now to satisfy my craving for revenge. I need to find Lydia, find the key, and get far way before the castle burns down with me still inside.

Sprinting away from the smoke thickening in the halls, I leave Ryo to meet his end alone. There's one place Lydia would have gone. She would never abandon her fake family. They don't care about her. Tobias doesn't care. Only I care. They're loyal to themselves and the dark star of the Auctus and that's it.

Cracking charred wood and the screams of those injured in battle echo. I weave through the castle hallways, sticking to side passages. The few skirmishes remaining are man-on-man, battling against one another to the death.

The rebels I pass make a path, blocking my would-be attackers from slowing me down. Nothing can stop me. I turn into the staircase and halt on my heels.

Broken at the bottom of the stairs is Uncle Cormac's twisted form. His soft gray eyes permanently gaze up at the ceiling, the bend of his neck is unnatural. I can't breathe. I survey his body, willing him to blink and sit up. I stand at attention momentarily, waiting for instructions on how to proceed, but the order will never come.

My commander, my family. He took us in, Fiona and me when we were terrified kids on the run. We made it to him alive. He promised to protect us in exchange for our loyalty to him and his cause, turning our backs on ever using our Senses unless it was for his advantage. He swore vengeance for his brother, my father's death, and revenge for our family. He protected us and shaped us into the people we are today.

Fiona's betrayal when she ran away crushed us both. She wanted to master her *gift* to help others, choosing to pursue everything we had spent our lives fighting against. Calling it a gift tastes sour in my mouth. Something in Cormac broke when she left. It was a hole I could never fill. Her abandonment was one more loss in both of our minds at the hands of the Auctus. One more person we loved that was taken from us because of them.

And now I have no one.

"I will avenge you, Uncle. I will avenge my parents. Your faith isn't misplaced. I won't fail you. I'll get the treasury for us." I hunch over his body and close his eyes. I can't take the time to grieve right now. This loss is overwhelming, but my conviction grows and solidifies. The last thing I can do for him is complete his orders and this assignment. His final request; get the key, get the Seer, and do what needs to be done to remove the Auctus permanently. For the memory of my family and revenge for all that has been taken from me.

"Put down your sword, traitor. Put your hands on your head and get on your knees," a soldier behind me orders.

In my distraction over Cormac's body, five of Ryo's men surrounded me, swords drawn in a tight circle. I recognize three of them. All of them know me. They're good men but unaware of my true mission. They'd change sides if they knew, but Cormac wanted to keep it a secret. Fewer people going after the treasury entrance would mean less competition. It's the closest guarded secret in the Aperion, and I intend to keep it that way. Although, I may be too late on that account.

"I'm your captain. You swore a pledge to protect Silvanisi. Your king is dead, and your prince is dead, too. You will do as I order. You will come with me now and take the princesses and Lady Lydia to a safe location." I keep my voice steady and deep.

"You're no captain. I saw you drive your sword through our prince. You are a traitor, and you're coming with us," another one of the men replies, positioning to attack if I don't kneel willingly. I have no intention of doing anything of the sort.

The gods smile at me. A beam falls from the ceiling, crashing on two of the men a few steps from me. Their dying screams and the plume of dust and debris are enough to distract the soldiers from closing in.

I'm knocked back, but it's all the opening I need to roll into the cloud and escape with my life. I'll figure out the next step to fulfill my duty to Cormac. I always do. I'm a survivor.

It's easier than I expect to slip out of the castle undetected. With the main gate wide open, it's no challenge to blend in with the fleeing panic of the masses. I slip my hood up and run away from the burning keep, sprinting toward the harbor and our rendezvous point on the ship Asher has at the ready for our quick escape.

The question remains: How am I going to deal with him? I despise the man. He's a violent, cruel piece of shit, but he's rich, connected abroad, and his goals temporarily align with my own. I have to play this right. I don't have a ship and I need one to get Lydia away. If I knock him unconscious, I can take the ship, and the key, and dump him on an islet to die. Or I can get him alone and simply slit his throat, commandeer the ship and his wealth all in one swift motion.

The city is in turmoil while people try to make sense of the fire at the castle. Rumors are circulating that Verralon attacked and killed the king exactly as we hinted when they arrived. Civilians are beginning to muster, ready to defend their homeland against our framed foreign invaders. Ezra and his cohorts will never leave the castle alive, an unforeseen bonus. None of the islands cooperate with the Auctus and Adepts more than Verralon.

In the darkness of the harbor, far from the flickering glow of the fire atop the hill, I spot the small vessel bobbing in the water, ready to whisk us away the moment Lydia steps onto the deck. The men are waiting for Cormac, with Lydia in tow—none of them expecting me to arrive alone. As I approach, they unsheathe their swords, eyes narrowing in the flickering torchlight. But then they recognize me, and I raise my hands in a silent gesture of peace.

"Tiernan! Is Cormac coming with the Seer? Can we prepare to

cast off? Let's get the fuck out of here." The captain claps me on the shoulder.

He's an old friend of my uncle who turned into a slaver and radical. His wife was hunted down and killed by the Auctus. He never forgave those who caused her death. He's loyal to the cause, even if I object to the slavery component. Sometimes we're forced to ally with people we would never want to associate with. We all have to make compromises in the name of change.

"The king and queen are dead, but so is Cormac," I reply. I'll find my moment to grieve my uncle, but this isn't that time. I need to box it up and open it down the road. "The prince is dead by now. The young Seer escaped during the fighting. I saw no sign of the old Seer, Tobias, anywhere. He must have fled."

"Why are you here without my prize?" Asher seethes from the shadows, emerging on the deck like a snake slithering from the grass. So the little shit won't be part of the battle but expects the rewards.

"I took a calculated risk. I'll sneak back in and take her when her guard is down. At least I chose to fight. What have you been sitting here doing?" I'll let him believe that's my plan for now until I get a hold of this ship.

"How noble. You once again forget your place, Captain. You get your funding, and I get Lydia to do with as I please. It's that simple. Control of the Seer means the location of the treasury. I cannot have one without the other," he asks, making my skin crawl. Do as he pleases with her. He's made it clear what that will encompass.

"We can get the key and another Seer. What about Tobias? He's a Visionary, too. Let's speak privately below. I have an idea," I start, but he interrupts me with a condescending hand to stop speaking. I want to break that hand and listen as the tiny bones crunch and snap. I need to get him alone, away from his mercenaries.

"The key and Lydia go together, you fucking idiot. I've tried with other Seers. Weaker Adepts haven't worked. We've tried, and they all keep dying. They picked the wrong path and led my men to madness. A strong Visionary who knows what to look for is the only way. Lydia is stronger than Tobias. I'm tired of fucking around. Both Lydia and the key are required, and I want her to pay for her years of disrespect. You will return with her and the key. You have no choice."

"You don't have the key." It's a statement, not a question. Shit. Was it on Cormac when he died? I didn't see it and assumed he passed it along to Asher. It's a setback, but I am adaptable, as always. I begin calculating a plan to get back into the castle and find the key on his body. I'm processing the best way to get back in undetected when a fist flies and connects with my jaw.

Asher looms over me. He didn't make the punch—one of his men did. He can't even defend himself against Lydia. She will destroy him, but only if she survives whatever he has planned to convince her to show him the treasury location. I should have taken her off the island when I had the chance.

The man who sucker-punched me shoves me down to the floorboards, landing another punch. Stars dance across my sight. The captain steps in front of the bodyguard.

"Asher, hear reason. We need Tiernan. He can't get her now, but that doesn't mean he won't. He can't do that if he's unconscious or dead," he pleads, reaching down to help me stand back up. He hands me a handkerchief, and I wipe some blood from my split lip.

"You have until sunrise to find her and bring her to me. If you do not deliver by sunrise tomorrow, I'll see that everyone you love pays for your failure."

I laugh in his face. "Everyone I love is already gone. There's no one left to use against me."

"Is that true? I found it useful to learn about your sister. I'm sure she'd like to stay where she is in hiding, with her lovely head still attached to her shapely body. It was interesting to discover her to be a Complex. I was quite shocked to learn you have Adept blood in your family tree. I wonder if a Complex can be tortured into Visions since they too can access Enhanced Sight to some degree. I don't think we've tried that one yet. It's an interesting angle that might be worth pursuing if I can't have Lydia. Should we go get Fiona and find out? Fiona. What a lovely name for such a lovely young woman."

I didn't even know she was alive. He must be bluffing, but how would he even know about her existence, much less her Enhanced Senses? We've kept our Adept status a deep secret. Only Uncle Cormac knew until I told Lydia.

"She resembles you a bit. The same eyes, the same arrogant jaw, the same sense of unwarranted superiority over her betters, too. She should be put in her place. Then again, maybe I'll leave her be when you deliver me what I'm after. The choice is yours. Lydia or your sister? Who will it be?"

Asher's threat burrows deep and settles in the pit of my stomach. He might be bluffing, but I can't take that risk, especially if Fiona is alive somewhere. I promised my mother that I would keep Fiona safe. I failed when she ran away. I cannot fail again. I need more time. What if there's still a way to protect my sister and keep Lydia by my side? It's not too late to have everything I want, I simply need Lydia to cooperate. To play along for a little bit longer.

"Then Lydia and I will see you at sunrise."

CHAPTER 39

RYO

If the last thing I see is Lydia's face before I die, that would be enough. To know I kept her safe. Her freckles across her nose and cheeks mix with tiny splatters of blood, standing out against the mottled bruises she already had and a few new ones emerging. She's crying, ripping the cloth off the dining table and using her knife to cut it into strips in between sobs. It always makes me sad to see her cry. She's a splotchy crier.

"It will be okay, Ryo. I'm here. Everything will be alright," she keeps repeating. "Why didn't you listen?"

I don't recognize this sensation. She stands so close I could reach out and touch her boot, but her voice is far away. The room's echos are playing a weird trick.

Men are lined up, blocking the door to the hall, protecting their prince. Bodies lie strewn across the floor, across tables. I try to sit up but scream instead.

Oh, right, the sword piercing through me is wedged into the floorboards underneath. I'm pinned down. I can hardly feel it anymore. That can't be a good sign.

Everything feels slow. Like walking through water. Am I losing my mind? Is this what happens when death is fast approaching? Is this what an out-of-body experience feels like? My sisters are both here, holding each other tightly.

"I'm going to remove the sword, Ryo, and then we must be quick. Do you understand me? You won't die today. I forbid it." Lydia's ordering me not to die. I don't feel like it's under my control at this point, but she's always been stubborn when there's something she wants. She wants me to live; therefore, in her mind, I must.

"Pulling it out could mean death," another voice says, muffled in the distance. I tilt my head and see Amos kneeling on my other side. How did I miss him? He's not a small man. He's holding my other shoulder, keeping me still until a Healer can get here and attempt the impossible.

I close my eyes. The embrace of death begins, and then the harsh sting of a slap across my face jars me back.

"Keep those eyes open," Lydia orders. I know they have to remove the sword. I'll most likely bleed out before the old crone, Mabel, can do what she needs to do. Is Mabel still alive? She would be an easy target if they were targeting Adepts.

"Lydia, I'm sorry. I should have listened. I should not have engaged. I'm not better than the rest. I'm sorry for everything. I wish for so many things. So many things I regret."

"Shut up! Stop talking like that!" she orders again through gritted teeth. Tears pour down her cheeks, creating rivers through the soot, blood, and grime.

"This may be the last thing I ever say, and I want these words to be the last thing you hear from me. Thank you for being my friend when friendship is so hard to come by. Thank you for giving me your trust when trust is so valuable. Thank you for always being on my side even when you take the other side in an argument. Thank you for keeping me humble when I needed it. Thank you for loving me unconditionally even when I made it hard."

"Seriously, you're pushing that 'unconditional' component right now," she barks between gasping tears. "Just be still while we try to fix this mess."

Tobias leans down and braces my shoulders. "This will hurt, but we need to act fast. Lydia will pull it out, and I'll stabilize you. Brandon's Enhanced Touch can't heal you, but he can minimize the pain temporarily."

Brandon comes to my other side and places a hand on my head. I cringe, a natural reaction to being touched by a Handler of his skillset, but then the pain subsides a little.

"No," I groan. "No, you need to get my sisters somewhere safe. Take them and Lydia to Merthaset. They can keep you safe. Kira is next in line to the crown." I swallow, reality sinking in that defining the line of succession is essential. "Amos, you must protect her until the crown is stable and the rebels are pushed back. Am I clear?"

"Yes, my king," Amos says, bowing his head. The air is sucked out of the room with those simple but profound words. I'm king now. The one-hour king. Has it even been an hour?

"That plan is garbage," Lydia cuts in. "I'm not doing any of that. Not a single thing. You're not in a position to make me. Tobias, find out what's taking Mabel so long. Amos, hold him still. Ryo, you won't die today. You have too many remaining ways to piss me off. *Am I clear?*"

She braces a boot on either side of my waist, standing over me. She grabs the sword's hilt and starts to pull gently. The agony of the metal sliding out almost makes me pass out. I wish I had; it would have been a far less painful way to die.

I'm twisted and shifted. Something presses into my wound. I'm lifted off the ground and placed on a hastily cleared table. I hear the clang and shatter of plates and glasses hitting the floor while I'm rolled onto my side to try to stop the bleeding from the other side.

I vomit over the side of the table. Lydia pushes into my wound on the front, trying to slow the bleeding, while someone else is behind me doing the same. Brandon's hand hasn't left my head, but he's beginning to look a little green. Dark circles shadow under his eyes.

The soldier is pouring all of his Enhanced Touch into me. He can't do this much longer before he's depleted.

Another voice joins us, barking orders. My body shifts and rolls again. Someone is uncovering and poking at my gash, and I scream, uncaring if it's a dignified way to die.

"It's a clean cut, barely missed an artery. You are a lucky one, Your Majesty." The unfamiliar voice is oddly cheerful. "He won't meet his maker today. He'll need to be sewn up, and it will take a few weeks, maybe months, of recovery but not death for our brave warrior king, the defender of Silvanisi."

I open my eyes and gaze up at the face of my Healer, Mabel. She's so old; she probably saw her hundredth birthday decades ago. She pats my cheek and sets out her instruments to begin.

"You, the quiet, brooding mountain." Mabel gestures at Amos. "You hold him down while I staunch the bleeding. Then we need to roll him over and repeat. It's going to hurt." She turns to Brandon. "Your Handler Touch needs to rest now, or you risk overextending your Sense. You did good, kid. The king is a strong lad and is going to thrash. You, little blessed Seer, hold his hand and whisper pretty distractions in his ear. You girls, go close those doors and tell the guards to stand watch outside. They don't need to see their king wail and weep at what is about to happen."

Everyone moves on her command. I wish my sisters would jump to my instructions like that. I need to learn that level of dominance from this tiny, frail old woman—my wrinkled savior.

Lydia sits in a chair by my head and brushes the hair and blood from my forehead. Her touch is so gentle, but the fury and determination behind her eyes is unmistakable.

"It all still happened. I couldn't change anything. The key, the fire, the death of your parents, you falling in a fight..." She shudders and glances over at where their bodies still lay, but her eyes quickly return to mine. "What if the rest of it still happens? What if we didn't change enough? It's all my fault."

"Your Vision isn't the problem. We didn't listen to you. We

should have done more the minute you told us, and that's our fault. We shouldn't have forced you to go to the bay in the first place. Listen to me, please. You need to get to Merthaset. You need to take that key, go with Tobias, and get the hell away from here. Asher wants a Seer. Neither of you are safe. I'll do everything I can to survive and make this place safe for you again, but it's dangerous for you to stay now."

"I can't leave. I can't do that," she whispers into my hair, another tear falling across her bruised and bloody cheek. I want to reach up and brush it away, but a sharp, burning pain surges through my shoulder. I can't hold back the scream while the Healer begins her job of stitching me back together from the inside.

Her hand on my wound is agonizing. Her Touch slides through each cut and torn muscle; it tugs, pulls, and knits. Her Touch compels the muscles back together. Each stitch is a tiny invisible needle to my skin while she sews me back with nothing but her gift.

She could rip me apart right now if she wanted to. She could end all of this if she were a sleeper assassin. But I witnessed this old lady keep my father alive for years while he battled his ailments. She's had plenty of opportunities.

She smiles down. "Oh, young king, I'm on your side. Those rebels would skewer me for nothing more than my gift. I've never been good at healing myself, so I'll have to settle for healing you."

By the time she's done pulling me back from the brink of death, I'm soaked from a mixture of blood and cold sweat. She whispers instructions on my care to Iris about the potential of an infection and how to minimize that risk. I roll onto my side, careful not to damage any of Mabel's hard work.

Kira opens the doors. She steps out to talk to a few of my men. Her boots click and reverberate through the floor when she returns. Each slight sway and bounce of the table shatters my feeble grip on consciousness.

"The castle is almost secure, but the grounds are still a battle, and the fire from the north tower is coming in our direction. We need to move somewhere easier to protect. Somewhere for Ryo to rest. Sorry, the king, I meant to say *'the king.'* That will be a strange adjustment," Kira mumbles but gives me the most perfunctory curtsy I've ever seen her execute. I'd laugh if I weren't a breath away from death.

"We need to get him out of the castle," Iris says but is cut off with a reproachful look from Kira.

"No, he's the king. He cannot abandon the castle. We need to move him to his room. It's the opposite end from the fire, and there's one hall connecting it, easier to defend." Kira's suggestion is the right move, but transporting me right now is impossible without causing more damage.

"We need a gurney," Amos suggests.

Tobias shakes his head. "They are all being used with the others who were injured."

"Could we make one?" Kira asks.

"Could we carry him?" Brandon asks.

"That would risk reopening his wounds," Mable grumbles. "And I don't have the energy to re-dress them right now. He needs to be moved but kept stable."

"Hiro's wheelchair is still in the library where he left it. That's a few doors down the hall. I'll be back, and we can wheel him." Lydia doesn't wait for confirmation, but her solution has multiple problems. My brain isn't working fast enough to point that out.

"That's toward where there's still fighting going on. It's not safe to go alone. You're a primary target for the rebels. Take two guards. Brandon goes with her. Use your Touch if anyone approaches. Hurry and don't deviate. If it looks like it won't work, abandon the plan and fall back here. No side-quests." Kira will make a fine commander one day. She considers every possible outcome but doesn't hesitate to execute a plan. There's no second-guessing in her world.

I'm so proud of my sisters. They're both so impressive in their unique ways. I'm getting weepy and nostalgic. Death is still on the horizon for me.

"What. Is. The. Status?" I groan, grinding out each word through the pain. I wonder if anyone can understand me or if it came out as jumbled nonsense.

Kira flinches but then straightens her shoulders. "The west and south wings have been recovered and cleared. The east wing and parts of the central castle remain a battleground, but that won't last long. We're pushing them back and gaining control. Everyone has been evacuated from the fire in the north tower, and a group of soldiers has been dispatched to keep the fire from spreading. I don't know their current level of success. Outside, the front courtyard and everything outside the inner wall are controlled, and we're gaining ground there, too. I've dispatched the troops clearing the west and south to push back and close the inner gate before we tackle the outer gate. Shockingly, the city guard appears under control for the time being. Some are fleeing down to the harbor. I've sent Uncle Oscar to deal with stopping any fleeing rebels trying to escape by boat. He's moving to set up a blockade."

"What of Verralon?" I mumble, weaker by the minute, but I cannot rest until I know everything.

Iris gives a fake cough. "No sign of them in the castle. Once the attack began and father... was killed... they vanished. Someone reported that he saw a few of them fighting out of the castle a while ago, heading to the gate, but there were only three. Hence, we are unsure of the whereabouts of the rest," Iris replies, suspicion in the back of her throat. She's been quiet this whole time; watching every-thing, taking it all in, and putting things together from her vantage point.

"Three Verralon men fighting their way out of the gates?" Lydia raises her eyebrows, suspicious as always.

"We can worry about Verralon later. Now, we need to get our king to safety. If the fire is spreading. We can't waste time worrying about what's happening elsewhere but here," Kira argues. She's right, one problem at a time.

Problem number one: not dying and being remembered as the one-hour king. That would be beyond embarrassing. I can already hear the pitiful ballad in my head—about a prince no one took seriously, who only survived an hour because he was too arrogant to listen to his Seer. The tune would start soft and sad, but pick up at the chorus, something the crowd could easily join in on. They'd sing it at that shitty bar Lydia likes every year on my birthday, pints raised in honor of the one-hour king. Maybe it'd even be a sea shanty. I've always liked those.

Lydia passes a glance at Iris. She agrees with my sister's suspicion about Verralon's timely absence. She bends over to kiss my sweaty, filthy brow. I must not look very kingly, but her gaze is everything I need to sustain me.

Tobias grabs her elbow and whispers something in her ear. With a sad smile, she nods her head.

"I'll be right back. Don't do anything stupid like die while I'm gone," Lydia orders and marches toward the exit, grabbing Brandon and another soldier to follow. Tobias follows, but at the door, they split off in different directions.

CHAPTER 40
LYDIA

"I have a bad feeling about this," Brandon whispers to his fellow soldier, Neil.

"That's not enough of a reason to stop," I say.

We sneak through the smoky, dark corridors, trying to remain hidden on our way to the library. It's not far. I'm unsure how we'll get a wheelchair back to the dining hall unnoticed, though.

It's quiet here now, but it hasn't been spared from the battle. A man is slumped in a corner. I don't need to check his pulse—something about the stillness of his body shows it's too late.

The smoke gets thicker, burning my nostrils. Neil leads with me close behind him, and Brandon takes up the rear. We creep through the halls, sticking to the shadows and freezing whenever we hear feet stampede nearby.

Thankfully, the castle starts to settle. That doesn't mean the rebels are removed as an immediate threat, though. Anyone could be a rebel, apparently—even Tiernan.

I let my heart address and feel that hurt before I try to push it to the side. I fail.

Was it all just an act? Did he feel nothing? Was I always nothing more than a target, a means to an end? The thought claws at me, but there's no use dwelling on it. I'll never trust his answers, even if I could get any.

He wants to use me. He's no better than Asher, or any of the other men who've tried to manipulate me. He claims he's saving me, protecting me—but it always circles back to my Sight and what it can do for him. I'm just a tool to help him achieve his goals.

For once, I thought I meant more to someone than just my gift. I was wrong. And that realization stings far deeper than the bruises and marks that cover my skin.

Tiernan wants to free Silvanisi from the Auctus, but somewhere along the way, he forgot that countless Adepts would be hurt in the process—Laymen too, from untrained Adepts having no idea how to control their gifts or working with a patchwork of training. The Auctus isn't perfect, but they serve an essential purpose. They aren't the enemy. Ryo and the crown aren't the enemy either. Greed and prejudice are—and right now, they are winning.

I need to focus on my next step. Don't get distracted. Help Ryo. Keep the key. Find Tobias. Find out what this key actually does, because I have my doubts that some ancient folktale is true. Stop Asher. Make Silvanisi safe again for Adepts. I tally the to-do list. It might be a bit ambitious, but one step at a time. Ryo needs help, and I can help him in the present. That can be step one.

Neil stops to lie down in the shadows and tries to catch his breath in the suffocating smoke.

"Go back, Neil. We're almost there. You can't die doing this. Go guard your king," I order.

Neil sighs in relief at being dismissed. He didn't want to follow me on this errand in the first place. I'll have to put him in his place when all this is over. He shifts on the ground past Brandon and me.

"Soft-ass Layman," Brandon grumbles, covering his mouth and nose with his cape. His ebony complexion blends with the shadows along with his black coat, rendering him almost invisible except for the reflective glint of his weapon. "Shall we press on? Is there any chance you can use that fancy Sight of yours? I can't see anything in this smoke."

I clear my mind and calm my blood. I let my Sight shift to filter through the smoke. It stings. We both jump as a beam comes crashing down from the hall in front of us, reinforcing our need to move quickly. I don't want to narrowly avoid kidnapping and enslavement only to die in a fire.

We reach the library without being spotted. It's a miracle, in my estimation, but I will wait to celebrate any victory. I slide the door open quietly to avoid drawing attention.

Brandon sneaks into the dark room first, sword drawn and ready for any surprise. The space is pitch black but significantly less smoke-filled. I slip behind him, letting my Sight readjust to the darkness—and scream.

"Brandon, to your right!"

Two men emerge from the darkness. Verralon men. They relieve Brandon of his sword and pin him down—not brutally, but he's not moving until they let him.

A light is lit, and a soft glow spreads from a small lamp on an ornate side table. It illuminates the beautiful space, casting warm shadows. The man in front of me grabs my arm, holding me in place in his gloved hands.

"Do you have the key, Seer?" he asks patiently, squeezing but not hurting my arm.

"I know your face," I hiss. Shock and confusion spread across the man's face, widening his eyes. "This won't be how my story ends."

"We don't have time for this," the man holding Brandon barks.

"Do you have the fucking key?" he snaps, losing his patience. He doesn't sound angry—frustrated and annoyed, but not angry.

"I will never give it to you. I'll never tell you where it is. You'll have to kill me," I reply, wrenching myself away.

He lets me go, slowly removing his hand from my arm. He steps back, holding his arms up in a peaceful display to soothe me. "That's not why we're here. I have no orders to take the key from you."

"I've seen what your orders are."

Glass shatters from beyond the closed library door, and all our gazes snap toward it. We freeze and wait. When nothing else happens, the Handler continues.

"You're wrong, but I don't have time to explain all of this. I'm sorry. I hate this part," the Verralon Handler grumbles to himself, leaning over me as he removes his gloves.

I gasp and pull away from him, trying to make a run for the door. I know what's coming, but I can't get away in time. His jagged, tattooed hand grips the back of my neck, and a warming sensation spreads through my head as I lose consciousness. The last thing I hear is the whistling of a sad tune.

Again? Seriously!

"Move her out. Get to the ship, or they'll take off without us," a man with a slight accent that's somehow oddly familiar to me whispers.

That's not why we're here. The Handler said that before he knocked me out. Then why are they here? Why did they come to Silvanisi?

I open my eyes. We're hidden between two outbuildings between the inner and outer walls.

"Ah, she's awake. Sorry about that, by the way. I feel bad for knocking you out, just so you know. Let's keep moving." The Handler stands behind me and helps me to my feet.

"I won't be going anywhere with you! Let me go!"

"You might want to keep your voice down, Seer. Rebels are on the lookout for you. Your boyfriend just snuck back in. He ordered his men to focus on getting their hands on you. Do you want them to be your rescuers?" one of the Verralon men asks, bored and condescending. They all sound so annoyed and inconvenienced, as though this is nothing more than a chore that needs to be done and not a life-or-death situation. What's wrong with them?

"We mean no harm, but you'll be coming with us. I can knock you out again, or you can come willingly. You won't be hurt, but I'd prefer not to carry you and risk dropping you on your pretty head. Given the bump on your forehead, I'm guessing that's already happened recently," the Handler says. It's not much of a reassurance of their noble intentions when I've seen what Verralon considers mercy—especially when my options are to walk out with them or be knocked out and taken.

"Nope," I reply, and bolt toward the door.

They're on me before I take my third step, and the darkness returns.

Fucking again?

THE SOUND of gentle waves awakens me. The steady rocking lulls me into false relaxation, but I shake my head to alertness. I'm on a rowboat, and Silvanisi moves farther away. A few stars peek through a smattering of clouds—or maybe smoke. The sky was clear earlier. The light from the burning castle illuminates the skyline, mingling with the glow of the moon.

The tall spire of the north tower glows like a beacon. I try to pull my eyes away while hot tears slide down my soot-covered cheeks. I've lost. I changed nothing. It didn't work. I failed. I don't know if Ryo survived, or if he and the twins got to safety. Is Brandon okay? Did Neil make it back?

"Move faster, you slow fucks! They're gaining on us!" one of the men from the library shouts. "Put your backs into it!"

"Fuck! It's slack water," another man hisses.

"Give it a minute, men. We'll be on the ebb soon if we timed this right."

"We don't have a fucking minute."

"Tell that to the tide, then."

I sit upright, but they ignore me, continuing to row and bicker as if their lives depend on it. Do our lives depend on it?

I shift my Sight to adjust to the darkness on the water. Another rowboat pushes toward us—and they're indeed moving quickly. The man at the head shouts instructions at the rowers. He turns to face our boat. Tiernan's fast approaching, a distorted visage of determination.

"There's no escape this time. I no longer have a choice. Neither do you." A familiar, deep voice reaches us, clear as a bell over the water, and sinks into my gut. "I gave you a chance."

"Shit!" I shout. "We need to move!"

"Now it's *we*, princess? Another set of arms might help." The Handler grunts through the pull and push of the oars. He nods to an empty seat farther down the boat.

Seven men row the boat. Three were from the library, two others I recognize from the dinner, and then there's my kidnapping Handler. I don't hesitate. I sit on a bench beside a man four times my size and grab an oar, mimicking the same fluid motion. A genuine, broad, approving smile reaches his eyes.

"Finley! What the hell are you doing here? What? How? Why?"

Given the situation, the bear of a man can't stop his inappropriate chuckle. It slips into my mind that he was friends with Tiernan and could also be a rebel. I freeze and jump away, rocking the boat in the process.

"Being skeptical will keep you alive, but I'm on your side, little Seer." Finley smiles, gently pulling me back down to the bench. "We all are, even if it doesn't look or feel that way. Now try to follow my arms."

We row until my muscles are screaming. The oars slice through the water silently while the boat chasing us clatters with wood on wood, the sound dragging across the water in time with our own quiet movements.

"Where are we rowing anyway? Will we row to Verralon? How are we so quiet?"

"Shhhh!" the Handler hisses. "It's like you want them to hear us. Do you have any idea how sound travels over water?"

Finley scoffs. "Ach! Ignore him. Gabriel's just salty he had to use so much Touch to knock you out. It's lambswool and leather wrapped around the oars to quiet them. And we *are* rowing to Verralon, in a manner of speaking. It's not too far now."

Oscar will establish the blockade soon, if it's not already done. I focus on getting far, far away from Tiernan. My bench companion is doing most of the work, but he keeps looking over to check on me.

"You can't run, Lydia. There's nowhere you can go that I won't find you! I'm your destiny. Come with me. I'll keep you safe. We can work together. I have a plan."

Tiernan's words aren't those of a lover or a protector. They are a manipulation I should have recognized ages ago. It was all a manipulation, and I was too blinded by a handsome face and a shred of affection to see it. Never again. I put every ounce of energy left in my body into rowing in time with the others.

"Failure isn't an option. I'll get us both through this. I promise. Come join me. Work with me and I'll let your sisters live," Tiernan taunts, his voice getting closer.

"Pull like you mean it! Tide's shifted. We are on the ebb. Stroke! Pull! Stroke! Pull!" the man in charge orders in a hushed command, barely above a whisper. He turns his attention to me. "Lydia, do they have any Adepts on their side?"

"No, they hate us. That man yelling at me is an untrained Complex, though. He can't heighten his Sight to the same level as a Seer, but he's strong—and he really, really wants to get his hands on me."

I look back and see Tiernan's expression of disgust and determination. Just a few hours ago, his lips were on mine. I assumed when I saw him in my Vision that he'd be coming to my rescue—not threatening to come after me.

"Lydia!" Tiernan bellows, his pandering tone gone, now replaced with unbridled anger.

"Lose him in the dark," a man says.

The men pull the oars out of the water in unison and get low into the boat, drifting silently into the shadow between a cliff and another, much larger, vessel. They pass around a sack, and each pulls a black mask over their face—becoming one with the darkness. Only the whites of their eyes remain visible.

Finley pulls me down next to him, squishing me into the sidewall of our rowboat, and tugs a mask over my head as well.

Silent, we glide through the water with the outgoing tide. Once we pass the mouth of the harbor, the rowers shift and begin their rhythmic pull again. Not a sound beyond the oars slicing through the water. Not a groan or grunt from exertion escapes.

The fire seems so far away now. I hope Ryo has been moved to safety. He'll be okay. He *has* to be. If he died, my binding oath would have vanished. I pull up my sleeve to check and breathe when I see it's still there, even in the darkness—the white bracelet on my skin marking his promise to me.

After a few minutes of the low, rhythmic slash and pull of the oars being the only sound in the shadows, a massive booming crash echoes across the water. Wood, glass, and stone creak, crack, and fall. The burning tower collapses, crumbling to the ground and shaking the earth. My Vision flashes before me, but I push it away and survey the blackness of the water.

We've drifted farther than I thought—well past the harbor mouth—and I make out Oscar's fleet and their established formation in the moonlight, blocking anyone else from leaving the city or any reinforcements from entering. They have the harbor under control. How did we slip past the blockade?

I can barely make out Tiernan's rowboat retreating to the harbor, surrounded by Oscar's wall. A larger boat approaches. The rebels, including Tiernan, raise their arms in surrender. I don't look away, needing to bear witness.

"How are you doing with all of this?" Finley asks, with no sarcasm to his query.

"Not great, Finley. Not. Great," I grumble.

"How's your head?"

"How would *your* head feel if you'd been knocked unconscious approximately forty times today?" I ask, only half-teasing, hoping there'll be no long-term damage. "So what's the plan? Do we row to Verralon? Won't that get cold?" I whisper.

Finley's big, warm bear arms wrap around me. He shifts to sit back on the bench, pulling me with him into his careful embrace. "You're a funny little thing," he muses, his voice a mixture of relief and exhaustion. "The plan is to keep you safe. That's always been the plan. Do you have it?"

I know exactly what he's asking for, but I hesitate. I can't trust these men, no matter how many times Finley has saved my life. Tiernan saved me too—more than once—and look where *that* got me. One of these men has knocked me out more times than I can count—probably causing permanent damage. They kidnapped me. They hurt Brandon. I don't know them, and I don't know their motives. This key has been nothing but a harbinger of danger since it first fell around my neck like a noose.

Part of me wants to rip it off right now, toss it into the inky black water, and never look back.

I purse my lips and sit silently.

"Oh, *now* she's finally quiet!" the Handler cries. Finley punches him in the shoulder, and the Handler whimpers. It looks like it hurt. Good.

"That was rude. She was working hard like the rest of us to row away. Give her some credit, asshole." Finley winks and gives me his warm smile.

"I'd never hurt her or take the key from her. It isn't mine to possess. What would I even do with it?" the Handler turns to address me. "I know you have no reason to believe or trust us, but I'm doing my best here to keep it together and get you out safely. I'll make whatever oath you want, here and now, to show you we mean you no harm. I'll ask you again, in the spirit of open cooperation. Do you have it?"

I look into the eyes of each man, waiting, pleading silently for a response. I let the moment drag as they shift in their seats. Good. Be uncomfortable. I don't owe you anything.

And yet, they helped get me away from Tiernan—which also means getting me away from Asher. I have no options. Nowhere to hide, or turn, or run to. This rowboat is my only hope.

"Yes," I answer, defeated—and everyone on the boat sighs in collective relief.

The men pick up their pace. I return to my spot next to Finley, and together, we row out into the darkness of the Aperion Sea.

EPILOGUE

EZRA

Where the hell are they? They should've been back by now. I hate sending my men into danger while I sit around and wait. It feels like something a weak or shitty leader would do. I may be a new ruler, but I'm far from unfamiliar with leadership responsibilities.

We cut our way out of the castle and snuck through Saivi's alleys like criminals. We made it aboard, and now I have to sit and wait for an ambush.

I track the Silvanisi ships shifting into position to block harbor access through my scope. It's a good thing we've kept our sailing ship hidden from view. Problematic, though, if my soldiers are on the other side of that wall of warships.

"Where the hell are they?" Maeve mutters, echoing my thoughts. She leans over the ship's edge, scanning the water's darkness below. Her long, dark braid whips across her face in the wind. Lacking Enhanced Sight, I don't know what she expects to see in the pitch-black expanse of the open sea, with only a tiny sliver of moon hidden in the clouds.

"They'll be here soon," I answer optimistically. It's out of character for me, but it's all I have to hold onto right now.

The ship bumps against something silent in the water. We don't dare light anything, relying on the moonlight to do its work. Every one of my fifty-five crew members reaches for their weapons, ready to respond. Operating a ship of this size takes more manpower than most would expect, but my crew is exceptional in more than just rigging and knots. They're trained to operate in any situation—including near-blind conditions—even the Laymen, which most of them are.

A shadow of a man swings over the railing, landing firmly on the deck. Two more follow.

"Let's get the fuck away from here," one of them grumbles before sinking to sit, exhausted.

Relief floods my body at the safe return of my second-in-command. "Bo, status report." I'll celebrate their safety when we're far from here. Gods, this little trip escalated quickly.

"Fuck off, I'm exhausted. You try rowing for over an hour straight in slack water with another boat on your tail," he barks. My remaining soldiers follow him over the railing and collapse.

"Where's Gabriel?" I ask. The final shadowy figure climbs aboard, pulling a woman over the side and gently laying her on the deck.

"Bo, the status report. I won't ask again. In my cabin, now. Gabriel, take our guest below. Men, ready to set sail. The tide's in our favor. Let's slip away while we can. Stow the ropes. Keep steady. Keep silent."

A massive paw slaps my shoulder, and I turn to see the piercing blue eyes of my cousin.

"Finley. Good to see you made it out. Nice work."

My men jump to obey. The woman, however, doesn't move at my command. She's lying on her stomach, arms and legs splayed like an exhausted starfish. Gabriel sits beside her, keeping her company but making no move to pick her up. He shrugs and gestures to the woman. I decide to deal with... whatever this situation is... later.

Bo and I head to my cabin. I close the door behind us. The process of readying the ship is a familiar and comforting sound—a steady, organized symphony of life at sea. I draw the curtains before lighting a small lamp. It would be foolish to make ourselves a beacon this close to shore.

We sit at the table that dominates the cabin—long enough to fit all my officers.

"Still waiting on an explanation of what the hell happened and who the hell that is."

"Oh, Ezra, are you ready for this? I'm not sure you're ready. We got her. It's her—the Seer. She has the key. Not the dead king. The prince is king now. He was injured but he'll survive. Probably. Maybe. The rebels were after her. That beady-eyed man—Montrose or something—has put a price on her head. Her boyfriend—you remember him, the one from dinner—tried to track her down, shouting about working with Montrose. Sounded unhinged, honestly. But who am I to judge someone else's relationship?

"She's something fierce. Guess she wisened up to her limited options and chose us. Rowed right alongside the crew. We were almost caught in the harbor, but we shook him off when the blockade started forming. They couldn't get past it, and we went dark—drifting between shadows and trapped ships. It worked! Holy shit, it worked!"

Bo grins, telling the tale like a bard by the fire in a pub. He leans back, closes his eyes, and stretches, the chair groaning beneath him.

"The Seer came with you peacefully? And she has the key?" I ask. She doesn't strike me as the type to flee a fight. I expected resistance, not cooperation.

"Well, technically, we kidnapped her. But only technically." Bo winces.

"How do you 'technically' kidnap someone? Either she came willingly or you kidnapped her," I say, pinching the bridge of my nose. My head's beginning to ache. Nothing has gone to plan since we arrived on this backwater island. But the end goal is still within reach. I'll cling to that until we have the Seer—and, more importantly, the key—back in Verralon. Hidden. Safe. Out of the wrong hands.

"Gabriel had to knock her out once or twice. Could've been three times. But once she saw her rebel boyfriend chasing us, she started rowing like her life depended on it. Which, I guess, it did. Anyway, best of luck with that diplomatic nightmare."

Bo chuckles, eyes closed, head tilted back. He might be falling asleep mid-conversation.

"I'll handle it," I grumble. His arrogant laugh follows me out the door.

"I'm sure you will," he calls after me.

Lydia lies like a starfish on the deck, all limbs limp, struggling to catch her breath. She's on her back now, staring at the stars. Gabriel sits beside her—close, but not touching.

I'm the only Enhanced Complex aboard, so I adjust my limited Sight to the darkness. I study her before she realizes she's being watched.

Everyone wants to control this Visionary Seer. I'm no different. But I've convinced myself my reasons are nobler.

"Maeve!" She stomps over at my call. "Put her with you and Rumi. Get her something to wash up and change into. Gabriel, heal her. What the hell happened between dinner and now?"

Lydia props herself up on her elbows and surveys me from head to toe. She looks unimpressed.

She swats Gabriel's hand away like a gnat. He pulls back and stays close—but not too close. Protector mode, even though he's the one who knocked her out. Repeatedly. I wonder how she feels about that.

"Your Majesty. How *convenient* all of this has turned out for you," she says, her sarcasm so thick a child could catch it. She doesn't stand. Doesn't curtsy.

"Can you stand?"

She flops back onto the deck and ignores me, eyes returning to the sky.

"Does it matter?" she replies, defeated. "I'm connecting the dots. The edges of a puzzle forming a frame before I can fill in the middle. You're the golden-eyed horse. Verralon's crest is a dark, rearing horse with a witch-blessed golden eye. I felt something the first time I saw you—a connection. A premonition. The golden eyes.

"It's starting to make sense. You're here to carry me across the water to my doom. The doom of Silvanisi. That must've been your fleet I saw. It all makes sense. Well... mostly. It's a work in progress. Do you think I'll lead you to some mysterious pot of gold at the end of a rainbow? Because it doesn't exist. You're all crazy."

She still hasn't looked at me. Only the sky. She's mumbling. Maybe she's a bit mad. I've read that sometimes, those who can see the future—truly see it—end up broken by it. The mind splinters under the weight of inevitability. I thought it was just a rumor.

But maybe that's what makes her so powerful.

Maybe it's the madness.

"Am I a hostage?" she asks, shifting to try and sit up. Gabriel immediately jumps to assist her, his hands outstretched.

"Don't fucking touch me again!" she shouts at him. A distinct, predatory growl rumbles from deep in her chest.

Gabriel stumbles back, hands raised, palms out and visible— ready to obey her command.

"Rude," I mutter. "He was trying to help you, just like he was trying to save your ass back there when your whole world collapsed. Just like he saved your ass while you were escaping your boyfriend. Say thank you, princess."

"I'm not a fucking princess!" she screams, her voice sharp enough to carry over the open water. "And he didn't save me from shit. He *took* me."

"Shut the hell up unless you *want* any ship within earshot to come looking. Is that what you want? To go back? You'd prefer that prick Montcliff? Because his endgame isn't exactly noble. He wants power. Nothing but power. And you are his ticket. That key—and you—represent unlimited power in his eyes. Same for your boyfriend. You think his goals are more honorable just because you were fucking? Right or wrong, truth or lie, it doesn't matter. It's what they believe. And the more people who believe you're the key to the vault, the greater danger you're in. You *get* that, right?"

"He's wrong. *You're* wrong. This key is nothing. It probably opens a closet. It certainly doesn't unlock unlimited power or some mythical door from a fairy tale."

"You'd be surprised how far people will go in the name of power. What they'll believe when desperation takes over. I need to see the key. Now." I'm done playing nice. She's done nothing but accuse me of every atrocity from plotting her king's death to running a slave empire of Adepts. Everything, in her mind, is Verralon's fault.

"Nope," she says, and falls back into her starfish sprawl. I can't help the eye roll. She cocks her head and studies me.

This *infuriating* woman.

"Very well, *not-a-princess* Lydia. Let me spell out how this is going to go. You're going to show me the key. Taking it from you would be counterproductive—it doesn't do me much good without your cooperation, and that's not my task. You *will* return with us to Verralon. Once there, you'll help us keep that key out of the wrong hands."

I squat beside her, leaning forward on my knees to block her view of the stars. Our eyes meet. I'm glad she's finally listening. She still hasn't blinked, and it's starting to make me uncomfortable. Ordinary people blink. These are the eyes of a supremely strong Visionary—unflinching, sharp, and ancient. Her slightly swollen left eye doesn't dull the intensity. Even in the moonlight, the whites of her eyes practically glow.

"And you have the *right* hands?" she says, voice bitter. "You'll just *use* me, then kill me, when it turns out this is all a myth? A lie? Don't you think if some long-lost, unimaginable treasure existed, it would've been found by now? It's been *centuries.* That kind of money—"

"Darling," I cut in smoothly, "just because it's a myth doesn't mean it's a lie. And who said anything about the treasure being money?"

WHAT'S NEXT?

A Hidden Path - The Senses Part Two
Coming Fall 2025

A Desperate Path - The Senses Part Three
Coming Winter 2026

A Forged Path - The Senses Part Four
Spring 2026

If you enjoyed the story, I'd be truly grateful if you left a review on Amazon, Goodreads, or wherever you like to share your thoughts. Reviews make a huge difference for indie authors like me, helping more readers discover my books.

ACKNOWLEDGMENTS

This book began as a New Year's resolution at the start of 2023! I've always loved reading fantasy and romance, and this idea had been bubbling in the back of my brain (say that three times fast). By March 2023, I had an outline and the foundation of a world. By August, I had a rough first draft that barely resembles what's on these pages now and no idea if I'd do anything with it. A thousand revisions, one total rewrite, a pause for a side-quest project you'll hear about soon, and a roadmap for the rest of the series later—here we are.

This was not a fast or easy process. It was a meandering journey, like playing chutes and ladders—one step forward, two steps back—but it was fun as hell, and I can't wait to share Lydia's journey with you, along with Ryo (who will get his own book), Tiernan, Kira, Iris, Tobias, Ezra, and some new characters.

Thank You

To my husband—without you, I'd have never have gone down this rabbit hole. I would've quit at least 195 times. Every doubt and frustration, you countered with support and encouragement. For every problem, you helped me find a solution. You celebrated every milestone with me. You encouraged me to take a private hobby and share it with others. I love you. Thank you for being better than any book boyfriend and the reason I beleive in fated mates—you are my favorite person.

To my kiddos—you may never read anything I write, but thank

you for always asking how my writing is going. I hope you see my struggles and perseverance, my determination, and my appreciation for your support. Even if all you know is that "Mommy writes grown-up books," you still cheer me on during every high-low-buffalo.

To my girls—Adelle, Bot, Jess, and Lala—thank you for listening to me talk about this idea for *years* and continuing to ask about the progress. You are the best group of friends anyone could ask for.

To my parents—thank you for encouraging reading from an early age and my first "how to write romance" book as a teen. You've always told me I could do anything I set my mind to, and that belief carried me here. (That said... you may want to skip a few chapters in this one.)

To Kelsey and Stephanie—my OG beta readers. This version is *vastly* different from the one you read back in early 2024, but your feedback was invaluable to shape it into what it is today.

To Fiona Rowan—holy shit, am I glad we found each other. Your feedback was and continues to be essential in finding plot holes, fleshing out characters, and breaking down ideas. Your comments made me laugh, shout, and push myself to think from new angles.

To Jim Adams—thank you for all the back-and-forth over tattoo designs and graphics that note each characters affiliation. Tattoos and brands are such a huge part of the story. Thank you for bringing this to life. Check out **sickofjim.com** for his fantastic portfolio.

To Keeya Marquez—thank you for working through my terrible grammar and asking thoughtful questions while editing my jumbled mess. You truly went above and beyond.

To Roxana Coumans—thank you for making sense of everything that only made sense in my head.

To Andrea Halland—thank you for catching every stray comma and misspelled name. There were a LOT. Grammar is not my forte, and your help was invaluable in polishing this book.

To Jenny Bailey from Pen Pal PR— thank you for walking this newbie through the ARC process, answering a million questions, being adaptable when plans needed to change and being quick to respond. And most of all, thank you for holding my hand.

To Lindsey Cargal—thank you for bringing Tiernan, Ryo and Lydia to life through your fantastic character art.

To My Readers

Thank you to every single person who signed up for an ARC and left a review. Your final eyes and support meant so much to this baby author.

Thank you to all my readers for taking a chance on a debut author. I hope you had fun, screamed a little, got angry, and maybe even ripped your hair out. I hope you see that everyone is flawed and that people will use mental gymnastics to convince themselves their cause is just. But more than anything, I hope you want to read book 2 and see what kind of trouble these characters get into next.

If you enjoyed the book, please consider leaving a review on Amazon or Goodreads—your reviews help other readers find debut authors like me.

Thank you from the bottom of my heart.

About the Author

Deirdre Lyons is a lifelong lover of Romance and Fantasy, hailing from the Washington, DC suburbs. Deirdre has always been a voracious reader, gravitating towards Fantasy and Romance, with an unhealthy addiction to magic, world-building, slow-burn romance, plot twists, and a touch of spice. Her glasses are constantly smudged, and her Kindle is permanently attached to her in one hand with a lukewarm, forgotten cup of coffee in the other.

Follow her at @LyonsWritesLove on Instagram, BlueSky, Threads, and TikTok.

www.ingramcontent.com/pod-product-compliance
Lightning Source LLC
Chambersburg PA
CBHW030340120726
47901CB00007B/1852